BURNT BLOOD

The Werewolf Within

RYAN HOLDEN

Prologue

Burnt Blood

'Officer Reynolds - 20th September, 3 am

"Christ, my head is killing me,"

Glancing at the clock, it was 3 am; I woke with a pounding head—the feeling of a saucepan thumping between my ears. Sitting upright in bed, everything around me was dark, making it hard to see my hand in front of my face, with my eyes taking their time to adjust. Groggily shuffling off the bed and heading to the bathroom, I thought drowning my head in cold water would ease the throbbing before taking painkillers.

Reaching my doorway, something breezed across my bare feet. I see the floor changing, barely catching a raft of dirt coating my toes. The smell of burnt wood swam in the air, making me on edge and causing my throat to shrivel. Looking up, everything was different. My eyes gradually adjusted; I could see the outlines of pillars. The burning slowly changed, bringing the sickly stench of charred meat forward, like a BBQ but with a putrid edge.

I was in a dark and scary basement—the sound of chains rattling suddenly in the distance, loud, chilling clangs against the concrete floor. It was too dark to see anything clear; my nose inhaled everything—none good. The charred meat smell got stronger, turning my stomach; I realised what was drifting around my lungs—a dead body. Only I couldn't see it. My feet shuffled forward, dragging me through the dirt; my brain became curious. A glow appears in the distance; it's my bathroom, a section at least. Holding my hand to level with the light, my fingers were a silhouette. One, two, three, four, five... And six.

The light coats around me; I see symbols on the wall, dripping in red. A deep breath told me it was blood, yet no burnt body. I headed to the sink, hoping the water might wake me up, having gone on longer than usual. My heart raced. Spinning on the tap, I watched the cold-water stream down. My hands gripped the white curved sides. The longer I looked, the more lucid I felt. But no change; an eerie breeze rushed over my back.

My eyes lingered hypnotically on the stream; I must have been lost in the moment because I hadn't noticed the colour change. I could feel cold sprays against my thumb while the draining water turned a light crimson. Panicking and looking down, I got a sharp shock that cleared my haze. My fingers looked as though they'd torn through flesh, dripping blood. There were thick clumps that dried under my nails.

The more I looked, I noticed small, frayed pieces of material, possibly clothing. Rising in a frenzy, still seeing six fingers, forgetting where I was, wanting to be rid of the blood. I kept checking for hidden cuts as the blood cleared, feeling a little crazed, desperate to wake. The familiar chill swept through, icy, causing a wave of goose skin to wrap around my body. I spun the tap off; it had gone quiet, no wind, nothing. Only to be made to jump by a loud static buzzing noise, with the light flickering, causing flashes of worrying darkness.

Still facing the taps, my eyes towards the mirror; with every flash, I saw the glass steam drifting from the corner. A cold sheet of vapour spread across, and the temperature dropped. I was scared. The hairs on my neck danced to the chill with the light still strobing. I reached up to the mirror to wipe the glass clear; feeling the moisture on my palm, I caught a shadow in the reflection as the light broke the darkness. It wasn't mine. Blinking my eyes, the shadow loomed; my hackles were waving like fiery embers. I daren't breathe; I daren't look behind. My hand squeaked across the glass, cutting rainbow-like through the fogged moisture.

'What's the matter, Georgie? Seen a ghost?'

A chilling voice whips through the air. Every hair on my body becomes a bed of sharp, piercing needles. All Stood, loud and proud. The spooky whisper was Chris; the streak in the glass cleared, and my eyes strained to take between the flickering light. It finally went out, leaving me stranded in the burnt, tinged darkness, dripping in fear, surrounded by a whistling chill and the smell of death up my nose.

'Embrace it, Georgie; let it in. Let it all back In. You must remember. It's coming whether you want it,'

He spoke again, different. Scary. Surreal from someone so quiet, my laid-back friend. This was darker, not making sense; hearing from behind had me tempted to turn and look. Only, with the lights out, it was next to impossible. My trepidation overflowed with the static buzzing around me, bouncing off the walls—the smell of blood cutting through the air.

'Become who you are meant to be. Finish what I started before bodies fall. Your reflection is nothing but a shell, a mask to fit in; take it off and set the beast free.'

The scary noises continued; I froze, my heart thumping in my ears. Terrified, I didn't know what to do. The lights flickered just as my hair softened; the sudden flashes triggered them to rise. I couldn't answer back; my eyes fixed on the glass; with each flash, I could see the shadow loom closer; I urged, running with nowhere to go. Closing my eyes tight, hoping it would all go away. Slowly squinting, a crack in my lids left me disappointed. He was still there.

'Are you listening, Georgie? You need to do what's necessary,'

Sharp, carrying a venom. Freaking me out. My neck twisted to the chill; my breathing rapidly pushed out thick, white vapour.

'I said, are you bloody listening?'

I skip off the floor, and a piercing, death scream rips through my ears; the lights fly on, blazing a brilliant white. The shadow had gone, leaving behind a decomposed Chris. A large crater where the back of his head should be. His flesh was a ghostly mottled white, eyes glazed a cloudy grey with dark dried blood streaked down his cheeks. My eyes bulged with the urge to bleed—my stomach curdled, wanting to erupt into the sink.

His head twitched and gyrated, clicking like a Rubik's cube, moving forward, forcing me back with nowhere to go. He quickly flew to my ear, screeching; the life jumped from my body; my eyes pulled wide, mouth dropped open. The screech ripped through my brain as my head spun. My legs became jelly before buckling underneath me. I hit the floor with a loud clap...

* * *

'Reality Check

"Aaarrrrrgggghhh,"

"What the bloody hell?"

Frantically feeling over my body, sweat smothered my skin. Droplets glistened on my arms as the moonlight crept through the crack in the curtains. With the bedsheets clinging, I spun my head to the clock; it was 3 am. It happened again. My memory was fresh with the decomposed image of Chris's face. My basement nightmare is warping. I could still feel the nightmarish screech ringing in my head. Feeling my chest easing, terrifyingly vivid this time, I was grateful to be awake.

The last one cut off after the red eyes, but this was next-level scary. My imagination could make up for seeing Chris and how he looked defied anything. I remembered everything: the flickering lights, the shadow, and what Chris said. He was trying to tell me something, or my head was wishing too much that I could talk to him again. To chat like old times, work on the problem and find a solution.

Instead, I had to rely on others that may not have my back. I'd already shared too much with Skip, getting him wrapped up in something he would regret later. Slumped against my pillow and headboard, I replayed some things I said; he must've left here thinking I was one sandwich short of a picnic. He wouldn't have been too far from the truth, the way things were going. Hearing whispers from my dead friend plays on my mind so much that he ends up in my dreams.

Telling me to 'become who I was meant to', and I must embrace it to finish what he'd started. There was me thinking nightmares and blackouts were my only problems. Hearing the recording of the gunshot again; was terrifying. No doubt crept into my subconscious, lingering and changing what I dwell on. I still had a pounding headache. With the sweat still pooling around my body, it had become chilly dampness; my fear subsided along with the temperature. Flicking off the covers and about to slide forward, I ached.

Like I'd fallen down a flight of stairs. Surely a nightmare couldn't make me feel that bad. Maybe the constant drinking wasn't doing me any good. Every step had shooting pains riding through my legs, making me dance across the floor on hot coals. Not that I'd ever do such a thing. The guys shown in holiday adverts make it look fun and easy; to me, torture. At least that masochistic act was controllable. Mine couldn't be seen, and there was no end in sight.

Other than the bottom of a bottle. Shuffling through the hallway, I glance at the lounge. The gun was there, the recorder, and an empty bottle of Jack. Curiously, the blood was gone.

My routine was the same as the dream's, water spinning down the plughole while my eyes adjusted to the light. Thinking of my past, returning to when I was a child, I could remember going into foster care but not much else. It was another blank space, like the ones I'd been having recently.

Who was I in the office with? I wondered what else Dalton meant about the world coming full circle. Skeletons. Why would Chris carry it on in my dream? I had to know. I didn't need or want any more surprises. I should get in touch with Charlie. A curious thing Dalton is talking about him. If anyone could shed some light on my childhood, I hoped it would be him or at least push me toward someone who might. There's so much I couldn't remember or had chosen not to. Whether he's willing is a different story.

I hunched over the same as before, leaning against the sink's rounded rim. The daze had gone. I was about to scoop a pool of water in my palms to splash my face when I got another unwanted surprise—taking a sharp drag of air, getting a taste of morning breath. I could see dried blood caked under my fingernails, and my hands looked dipped in red paint mixed with dirt. Hyperventilating, I choked, coughing so hard I felt a gush through my throat. Splattering in the sink, looking down, I see clumps of black fur, not hair, animal fur. What the hell is wrong with me?

Rinsing it all away, out of sight, out of mind, throwing my eyes around my body, looking for more blood. I caught my reflection in the mirror, looking haggard, with a sheet of stubble coming. More blood and streaks are running down my face, mouth, and body. The tears brewed, wishing the nightmare would end. I couldn't understand how it was possible, considering I'd been in bed. I had been in bed, right? Attempting to rationalise something that I couldn't. All I had to go on was a nightmare; now I'm coughing up fur and covered in blood.

I couldn't claim every drop of red fluid was animal juice. I somehow made it to bed, which I didn't remember doing. Assuming it was because of the empty bottle. I'm not sure; there wasn't anything in my flat that could cover me in blood. I couldn't have gone out, could I? Then I remembered who I had been drinking with, Skip—getting a sense of doom wash over me, the possibility that the blood could be his. Although he was a beast of a man and even sober, I was doubtful of taking him down. So, if it wasn't his, then whose was it?

Tentatively, I brought a dried patch on my arm up to my nose for a sniff, hoping I could tell the difference. I took a whiff; it was hard to tell, although it dried like humans. Freaking out inside. If Lewis, Kelcher or Harkes could see me now, they wouldn't waste a second before dragging me down to the station, assuming I'd done something wrong. Even if last time, I had needed the skipper's expertise.

I've been lucky; a mix of purposeful mistakes and a good sense of smell have bailed me out when I'm rocking. I'm dreading the moment no one is there to help. There is no bodyguard when I can't remember or come up with a good excuse. I will be screwed. I got to scrub as if my life depended on it.

Or in case of unexpected guests. Smothered in soap, I dragged my fingers through the skin, trying to peel away the bloody dirt. I soon felt near normal again, chugging back paracetamol while there was still no reasonable explanation. Unless something jumped out or Dalton called again, it would be best to keep my gob shut. I couldn't explain it, anyway. First thing in the morning, I had to call Charlie and meet and get a read on him after what Dalton said. I had to survive the night first. □

CHAPTER 1

'18th September 1.35 pm Penton Police Station, Penton, South of London'

'Watch your back. Trust no one except Andy and me; you are being framed. Chris had lied to and steered to uncover some dangerous secrets. Talk soon,'

Feeling the weight of the world on my confused shoulders. I slumped on the wooden bench, slouching my sweaty back against my flimsy metal locker, an exhausted mess. 'Did all that just happen?' I think to myself in a daze, processing several unusual comments that stood out the most. Not every day do I get made the prime suspect in a murder investigation.

None of it made sense. I was slow on the uptake or had to figure out the hidden meanings. Issues my brain was too tired for. *'Where am I in a rush to go? A moonlit walk to howl at the moon?'* Detective Dalton said in response to my impatience. Also, Sgt Morris seemed to be in on the joke. One that I wasn't finding funny. There we were, standing by my friend's dead body, and they were insinuating I was an animal or something.

I'm struggling to remember what happened between coming into work this morning until I found him, and all I have is the contents of my pockets. All that did was nark me more than I already was. I was overreacting to everything out of annoyance with myself. The slightest noise and I were jumping like a cat on a hot tin roof, making my heart skip a beat; I was on edge enough; no need to add fuel to the fire.

I hadn't realised before it was too late. I'd missed the warning signs, and now my friend is dead, murdered, to be exact, and the world is looking at me. At least, that's how it feels, anyway; I can feel myself drowning in waves of turmoil and emotions I couldn't displace. Now I'm the number one suspect, and the little voice in my head screams, 'it's a setup'.

And I wasn't the only one to figure that out as I let the message on the hastily concealed paper sink in. Detective Dalton tried to hide a note on me, theatrics and dodgy comments aside, leaving me questioning. Why? No tapes were rolling; nobody would've heard.

Then, as I'm leaving, he slithers to whisper, 'keep your head down and gob shut' in my ear. Giving his best impression of a cockney gangster that's bathed in expensive aftershave. All five feet eight of narcissism blazing a day's coffee fumes against my cheek. None of it makes sense, and I need to know the why and how if I can clear my name.

Deep in my procrastination, looking forward to a much-needed drink and toying with the contents of my pocket. I pick out the fluff when I notice my locker key—stubbily small, silver, with a flat, smooth, oval-shaped finger surface that holds a print if pressed hard enough. I reached for the other one and paused, checking that the coast was clear; the last thing I needed was curious eyes.

I was fairly out of the way, but that didn't stop me from being paranoid. Breathing in the odour of sweaty boots above my head. Row after row of lockers, like a gym changing room with lines of light pine brown benches and a row of bland grey on either side. With the key left by Chris in my shaky hand, I compared it to mine. They were the same design; each had a serial number that matched a lock.

Glancing across at first few, I suddenly had second thoughts, questioning whether now was the time to loop in Sgt Morris. I knew he'd hit the roof for concealing the evidence in the first place, and I couldn't help worrying over how deep the conspiracy goes, but I felt bad for not telling him. No, if he caught me here and now, I would have to make an excuse that Chris had slid the key into my locker at some point. After all, nobody had searched it, unlike as detective Dalton had insinuated.

Dalton bluffed, hoping I'd fall for it; his lack of conviction was telling. I hope he turns out to be on our side and not using the profile and publicity of this case to win a promotion. If the note were anything to go by, things would be fine, yet there's still a sour taste in my mouth and the thought of 'why me?' Christ, the chills.

Why did I have to be the one at that exact moment with no recollection of entering the room? Fate seems to enjoy fucking with my head. I had ten minutes to feed my morbid curiosity. If I wanted to beat the evening traffic chaos towards the A2, it had been bumper-to-bumper most nights.

I shuffled through the walkway, checking it against the other lockers, my thoughts drifting back and forth, contemplating the contents of the small grey 'Sony' Dictaphone. Could it hold Chris's last words? The post-it note on the speaker said... 'The dead still talk,' which seemed odd unless the catchy title of a horror flick.

Instead, it went with an intriguing drawn symbol of a circular winged serpent with a trident for a tail. The scrap paper that the Dictaphone rested on got my attention the most. Lots of random scribbles and comments that took a minute before they made sense. 'Pointed to by 'C' must be an informant. 'Is the supernatural real?' had me intrigued. No case files I knew of had anything like that, but it made me think of the nightmares I've been having.

The looming, blood-red eyes drift toward me as heavy metal chains smashing against the stone floor echo in the darkness—the disappearing basement stairs. I was in the third row deep; then I saw the one underneath, a little white sticky label on the corner. I'd found Chris's locker, which wasn't a match.

It stood out differently from the rest. I crouched at the sound of lactic acid popping in my sore knees. The numbers matched. I checked the coast was still clear, knowing it could all be an anti-climax, finding the locker empty. What I hoped to find were answers. My hand shook as I grated the little key along the grooves. A squealing of the grinding hinge as the door came free. My mind raced.

With the door wide, I got a little surprised. As lockers go, this one was quite neat. At least compared to mine. This one was a more thinking man's storage. A lot of random post-it notes, words that didn't make sense, a torn-out page of the A-Z with Bethnal Green circled in red ink and the letter 'C'. There was a small box of tapes; initially, I thought they were spares.

Until I saw the label, 'updates' and were at least four, maybe six weeks' worth—the weeks leading up to his death. The locker's contents had me in a daydream, staring blankly at the inked circle and 'c,' my head has gone back to the moment I found him. Two loud claps rattle between my ears. I picture the lines of brain matter trickling down, the way the blood glistened in the yellow light, littered with skull pieces, and matted brown hair, with a bullet hole dead centre of the mess.

Only the bullet was missing; it had been dug out, causing plaster dust to sprinkle across the blood. Yet, the moment I noticed the edge of another circle. Barely visible just over the top, a second shot to mask the first that had me thinking I was being 'framed.' Gagging at the thought of Chris's blown-out skull, I snap back to the locker.

I'm drawn to a printout of a newspaper clipping. It had to be the best part of being nearly thirty years old. 'A house fire in East London, one sole survivor being a young child, several dismembered bodies discovered in the basement. Believed to result from satanic worship,' My heart jumped, and flashes of my nightmare buzzed across my mind.

I could hear the loud chains clanging again, causing me to close my eyes. Seeing the darkness, watching the dust kicking in the air and, scariest of all, those haunting red eyes. Shaking my head free, I took a breath. I've never been a fan of coincidences. A clipping about a basement and I dream about one.

Why would Chris be concerned with a fire so many years ago? He'd made a spider web of taped strings to addresses in other parts of the country. Written '+1 or +2 children'. Whatever Chris was into seemed to involve missing kids. But why all the secrecy? Was it he felt he couldn't trust anyone, even me?

I could hear raised voices heading my way as the late turn began rolling in, so there needed to be more time to go through everything. There were small bundles of papers and other bits; I grabbed the tapes.

Jammed the door shut before returning to my locker; my heart raced as a few from the next shift came in. I slumped down on the bench, feeling like the day was catching up.

The brave face was gone; I didn't have the strength to keep up the pretence. I took a quiet moment to reflect as reality finally hit me hard. Looked around as most went about their business as normal. Thanks to detective Dalton, I hadn't the time to mourn or consider any emotional fallout. The surge was coming, rising like a shaken champagne bottle, and the cork was about to explode.

That's how I felt—wondering if we were safe, especially from ourselves. A mind is a fragile place, and Chris was one of the strongest I knew. My best friend was dead; I had found him murdered. All I had now been the tapes in my pocket to help. Dalton had me on edge over the higher-ups coming after me, and I had to watch my back. I needed to remember. I wanted to know why.

CHAPTER 2

'Home- evening 18th September.'

The entire journey home had me on edge. The sun had fallen away, leaving behind a sullen darkness matching my mood. Even stepping out of my car into the chilly air, I was getting dizzy by the number of twists left and right my head was doing. I was in a 16-bay carpark to the left of the flats shaped to an 'L'. I'd parked in my regular spot in bay three under a streetlight; it has the best view from my window if anyone tries to mess around with it.

I have kept myself to myself since Helen passed away five years ago. We had bought the place together. The buildings were only ten years old, and we'd figured on two to four years to stay maximum. Our first one had been our step on the property ladder with a newborn in tow.

Before looking to move somewhere with a garden, the baby can enjoy playing without the fear of wandering on the road. I always liked the idea of the quiet country villages, where everyone says hello without a death stare. Sadly, things didn't go our way—my first experience with death. Or shall I say my first two experiences with death.

There had been no warning signs in the months leading to the birth; both were healthy until the day. I'd been tied up with work when the call came into the station; Helen took a taxi. The plan was for me to meet her at the hospital. I arrived at the same time as a navy-blue Cortina estate with a white oval 'G.B.' label on the back. Helen had gone into cardiac arrest.

Helen didn't recover, and our baby died soon after. Hoisted onto a bed at the entrance to A&E. Driver didn't hang around; staff believed he'd panicked and ran but didn't get a good look at him. I got told the car belonged to an older bloke who'd passed away months before, not even registered with a taxi company. That's as far as the enquiries got; no leads to follow.

Now I rattle around the flat on my own. There was a scattering of lights in windows and the standard raised voices I'm used to hearing. The beauty of not knowing anyone meant nobody knew I was the police. Otherwise, I'd likely have regular requests for my help or hate mail. It was bad enough; I kept getting letters addressed to someone else called Mr Conrad.

I didn't need extras. I had to do a few at the beginning, stumbling for words and trying to read if the other person was expecting it. No, tonight, life seemed normal as I savoured the breeze, trying to calm my head. I gingerly walked to the white communal door. Still preoccupied with the day's ordeal—thinking of Alexandra, Chris's wife and wondering how she was coping and who would've broken the bad news.

It's not a task anyone envies, especially me; most of the time, it's given to the station newbie. You say, 'I'm afraid I have some bad news,' which puts them on the back foot straight away. Not good. In your head, it's, 'I understand what you're going through. But that's not possible unless someone has experienced loss and grief.

Everything around me appeared to be the usual. From what I could tell, it was the regular neighbours of the nine-to-five varieties; I could almost see into their kitchens as I passed. I would've had money on Dalton being told to despatch surveillance to watch me. You can imagine my surprise, not seeing anything out of the ordinary. The door opened with a squeak; inside was creepily pitch black, and I could barely make out the step in front.

The hallway light hadn't come on as usual; it was rigged to sense movement, and for whatever reason, this time, it failed. Giving it the atmosphere of a horror movie. And I was on edge; all I needed was the scary music. I'm not a fan of coincidences, and after the day so far, the little hairs on my neck and knuckles were waving in the breeze. I'm about to step forward when I felt a gush past my leg, causing me to jump.

'Cue the panicked shrieking' A bell jingled, echoing; I looked down to just about see the glowing eyes of the neighbour's cat, Lucious. A black and white menace. He scratches at my front door from time to time. Being more of a dog person, I haven't dared let him in. Yet, the menace had given me a mini heart attack—paranoia at its worst.

I shrugged it off, chalking the light up to a rare failure and the rest on my overactive imagination. A job for the morning, none less, is to contact maintenance. They'll probably tell me to sod off and wait. How bad would I feel if someone fell down the steps, breaking a leg or, worse, their neck?

I continued to stumble my way up to the first floor, allowing for a slight smile, thinking back to the cat scare; I didn't have far to go. Reaching for my keys, only carrying the essentials distracted, I stumbled to the right, nearly walking into the archway pillar. The front door had become a gloomy haze; my eyes had steadily adjusted.

God, I was looking forward to finally sitting and clearing my head with no eyes burning holes in me. My mind had become a circus with too much going on. The image of Chris haunted my thoughts. Shifting forward with the main key in my hand, darkness surrounded me in more ways than one after such an awful day. I was finally about to open and head inside...

'click.'

It jolted me back into Guvnor's office; my eyes clenched tight, grinding my teeth hard enough to pop my jaw muscles. A clunking of metal had stopped me dead, sending a chill skating across my shoulders. The nightmarish echo comes flooding back. Surreal until I felt something hard press firmly against my skull. I knew what it was; the almost flat muzzle of a gun pointed at my head. Frozen, feeling drained, an unusual lightness that has been rare until lately.

My right leg wobbled giddily, shaking uncontrollably, rife with adrenaline. I didn't know whether to fight or run. The flat, squared barrel dug into the upper curve of my skull. Whoever held it knew how to handle a firearm. There was no wobbling or wavering of a trembling hand doing something the guy didn't want to. No, I was up against intent, the confidence of what they were doing, maybe a pro.

Slowly edging out the other end of my emotional crisis. I realised I had the advantage of being in my environment. Knowing the space, I had to work in. A foot and a half, maybe two, on either side of me. The neighbour's door; was approx. Seven-eight feet behind me. If I took a larger step back, I would have the opening to the landing.

The barrel was pressed firmly with no shakes; more pressure was on the lower edge, telling me we weren't even of height. There was a closeness between us; the gap had shrunk, and the air cut off. I held my breath a moment, trying to listen for any sign of weakness. Heavy breathing was one of them; a deep inhale picked up on the gunman's aftershave, a strong, woody fragrance and a little familiar.

He tucked up close, maybe a little too close; I felt a steady gust of warmth hit the lower of my neck, intermittent, heavy breathing. Shaking my tiny hairs with each draft. Inadvertently helping with height, possibly half a foot shorter than I. Each second of the information had me growing in confidence that I survived. I still smothered confidence in fear; my leg trembling had eased a little, but the lightness was still there. With my stomach doing somersaults.

"You will forget your idea of finishing what your friend had started. All it will do is bring pain to you and everyone else."

The voice was muffled and stern; I was being warned off while following the same line as Skip's phone call. He wasn't there to kill me; intimidation sent by someone higher up.

"I have you mistaken. All I want is to go to bed and forget about the day."

I said with a huskiness of a suddenly dry throat. Trying not to show my fear, I wanted to give the impression I didn't care about finishing anything. Even if the truth was the opposite.

"Oh, come now. Do you think this is a chance meeting? Afraid not Officer Reynolds. Fate intertwined our paths many years ago, and luck has always been on your side. Heed my warning and not go digging," he said, speaking like he knew me; how could my path be intertwined with a stranger? Unless it's not? Hidden behind a mask, the muffling helps disguise their voice, making it plausible to be someone I work with.

"Did you think holding a gun to my head was the best way to try convincing me? Because it's not," I said, growing in confidence. I felt the urge to find out more.

"I couldn't give a fuck about you or what's best. Either way, the game will be fun." there was a surety about him, but I couldn't place the tone.

"Well, it's best to play alone; I'm not a fan of guns. Now you've given the message. I said, "how about you piss off," hoping he'd take the hint.

"Cocky bastard. Maybe I'll mess you up. To make sure you understand? Maybe it will be enough to force you to show what you really are and the secrets you keep," An all too familiar cockiness I hated. Reminding me of Dalton in the beginning; surely, he wasn't. 'What I really am and the Secrets I keep?' So, the message sinks in.

"Maintenance isn't good at cleaning blood or anything. So that wouldn't be a good look for the building. Anyway, I've heard you; now, can you go?"

An awkward silence dropped between us; then, I felt movement that caused my throat to shrivel along with my sense of humour. A distinctive changing of hands holding the gun. The presence shifted to my right, knocking a foot against the outside of mine. His left hand was less steady, unsure about what it was doing, rubbing up and down the back of my skull—

his first proper mistake. The heavy, intermittent breathing had shifted closer to the right side of my neck—his second mistake.

Exactly what Dalton had done before. He had opened his body up to me, putting himself in danger and off-balance. The middle of his body was vulnerable; being so close, I could gauge where to move and hit, leaving space to move to my left. Everything fell into place, but my brain played a tug of war with my body. Swaying between riding out the storm or fighting him off.

'You got this, Georgie; remember who's in charge of the situation, you,'

Chris's voice came out of the blue, sounding in my head and all around me. Enough to send another chill tearing down my spine, and my ears twitch. Was I cracking up?

'Come on, Georgina, nail him,'

This time not so much in my head, but more a whisper from my dead friend beside me. How? I had to be hearing what I wanted, with everything still raw, and now this guy with a gun shows up.

"You're so lucky to be different, possessing a gift. Instead, you've stumbled through life protected by your bodyguard. It's high time you fended for yourself. Especially if you're to survive what's coming."

'Bodyguard', that's what Dalton had called the skipper. Was this him? Muffled breathing had breezed close to my ear. Too close. He'd made his last mistake.

I dropped swiftly, swinging my forearm forward before taking all my pent-up rage from the day. Driving my elbow sharply into the ribcage. Feeling bone on bone, hearing a painful gasp for breath followed by the cracking of at least one rib. Twigs snapping under feet. The strike had rocked him, with the gun still in his weaker arm.

I swung a powerful uppercut, connecting against a covered lower jaw, sending shooting pain through my knuckles. He was wearing a balaclava that did little to hide the loud cracking of teeth before I heard two separate thuds on the floor. One is heavier than the other. I couldn't see anything; my ears focused on movement.

All the rage, hate and pain I held onto throughout the day was released on my mystery gunman. Still feeling a sickly lightness in the pit of my stomach, I could hear groaning; I was about to step forward with a boot. Frantic, scuffling across the carpeted floor, his foot pushed off against me, and he legged it to the stairs. There was no point in chasing. He crashed down half the steps before hitting the door.

I dropped to the floor in relief and disbelief, finally catching a breath, trying to understand how my world had suddenly gone from chaotic nightmares to murder and gunpoint intimidation. I'd lost my friend and was warned not to continue what Chris had started. Drained, I broke down in tears. The day and I were done with each other, and there was no one I needed to put on a brave front. Instead, I sat against the wall near my front door sobbing. My hand dropped to the floor beside me, brushing against something metal. It was the gun.

CHAPTER 3

'Home,'

    'A great man once said, 'when you're going through hell, keep going.' My hand shook, holding the glass; the gun rested next to the bottle. A Glock black, capable of holding seventeen rounds. One... Two... Three... Four... Five... Six... Seven. That's how many I had unclipped so far and stood on their end across my coffee table. Matched by a drink for each. I'm still seeing my friend's brains on the wall, a pain I was trying to wash away.

    I light her candle and let the smell of melting vanilla wax hang in the air. Glass in hand, the recorder with the collection of tapes, a locker key, the gun and bullets. Aside from the bullets, my day was laid on the table. The anchor is a picture of my Helen. I still see her, you know, drifting around the place and drinking a cup of tea; she's everywhere.

    All rolling on an echo of two thumping gunshots, ripping around in my brain. Smothered by the words in the hallway. Chris's words. What I couldn't figure out was why. Or what to do next. Procedure told me what I should've been doing, calling the city officer and my skipper, but doubt circled my mind. I stared, pouring myself another drink, a strong shot of whiskey over two cubes of ice to help numb.

    Yet, I hadn't scratched the surface of my pain. Fearing the deeper I dig, the worse my torment gets. The gunman had taken me by surprise; I was questioning who would have the guts to hold up someone they knew to be a police officer? I was clearly called 'Officer Reynolds,'.

Who could I trust? Skip, maybe, or Dalton. I slumped onto the sofa, feeling hungry; I normally go for the microwave special as I see no point in cooking for one. Still, I couldn't even bring myself to do that. Too much in front of me to go through; instead, I looked to the ceiling and heavens for answers; I knew full well that I was only putting off the inevitable.

The recordings. It had gotten too late to call Skip; besides, he probably had his own baggage to handle, judging by how he was acting at the station. No doubt he's already knee-deep in a pint or two, anyway. I substituted my glass for the recorder. The post-it note was still attached. 'The dead still talk' made me wonder what I heard. Was I delusional?

Moonlight bounced through the window and across the table, highlighting everything. Every look at the gun gave me an eerie feeling—a shudder of familiarity that I knew how to use it. Yet, to my knowledge, I hadn't ever picked one up in anger before. It had never been my thing; I'd hated what they stood for and the pain they could cause in the wrong hands.

The back of my head is a testament to the soreness of the barrel rubbing the base of my skull. My knuckles still throbbed from the uppercut to the gunman's jaw. The thought of him being somewhere nursing at least one broken rib softens the blow.

'Click,'

'It's Wednesday 18th September 1987. Everything is coming to a head, and I'm scared for my life. I'm afraid for the lives of my family and friends. What started as a straightforward uncovering of links between old arson cases and misper files has become much more. -

-It appears I've disturbed something, more like people—a dark, dangerous syndicate or group. Even on days off with my family, I am followed daily. I've had various dead animals left on my car and doorstep, the most recent being a large rat, which I have been able to keep from Rebecca. -

I stopped the tape, questioning whether I heard right. Chris was my best friend. Why didn't Chris trust me enough to ask me to help? The nightmares have been bad enough; this is a new terrifying level. What if Chris spoke to his wife about it? How would she be coping? Maybe she's in trouble, too.

My stomach churned; I glanced at the black gun glinting under candlelight on the table and then the bottle, the swirling brown ripples of 'jack Daniels' whiskey ramping up my thirst. Not knowing what to do for the best, I needed to help Chris and his family. The information on this ape alone was troubling, without going through the others. What else had Chris found out? Who was following?

Him? So many questions buzzed around my head; sipping my drink, I braced to go again.

'Click,'

'Old file notes show potential payoffs. The strange use of undertakers to incinerate remains. Kind of genius, really, when you think about it; it leaves nobody to be found. Yet to be established as its old information. I've tried making discreet enquiries about the morgue staff then and now, along with coroners to run background checks, looking for skeletons. The following started soon after; possibly contractors well trained in surveillance. I glimpsed a gun in one of their waistbands. They mean business. -

-Then came the dead animals. Today was the scariest moment yet; my brakes failed. The car had not long come back from an MOT and service. So, they shouldn't have. I've got to the point now where I'm not sure if I should continue digging; otherwise, what would be next? To think I wouldn't have even looked if it wasn't for informant 'C'; for his safety, we've registered him as a paid C.I., keeping his details private. Now, I regret it all.

'Knock knock,'

'Sorry, one sec, just on the phone...'

'Crash...'

'Hey, do you mi... Oh hey, it's only yyy... wohh! What the hell? Wait, what are you doing? Please don't. Please, doooo... cuhhhcuhhh,'

'Claaaaap,'

'*Claaaap,*'

Rocked back in my seat with the urge to be sick, I could taste the bile surging through and into my mouth. Well, wait... It wasn't so much the noise... The noise is proof of two gunshots to back up my theory, one distinctively different from the other. A slightly elevated pitch: it wasn't only that, though.

Someone had barged in that seemed familiar; Chris begged until he was choking. Chris had said, 'Oh hey, it's only yyy,' seconds before begging for his life. He recognised his killer. There was still more of the tape to play; I didn't want to, but what if there was proof that I'd done it? I must know.

'*Click,*'

'*Sssshhhhhhhhhhh,*'

'*Hey, what's going on? What the fuck, Chris. How could you? Stay where you are, don't come.*'

'*In tenebras te,*'

'*Oh, don't get worked up, my little furry buddy. Your time will come; our story has yet to be written. Your past was the intro; I'm the twist nobody sees coming. For now, enjoy the darkness,*'

'*Click,*'

That was me; I had entered the room. I'd seen the killer, and Chris was already dead. 'How could you?' I knew them too. I saw the killer and didn't stop them; feeling agitated, sad, and even a failure, my palms rested on the coffee table. I could feel sweat pooling between my skin and the wood.

I twigged on something else I'd heard as much as I didn't want to play it again, even a little. The moment after I had said, 'don't come any closer,' words were whispered. I didn't know what; I must play that bit, at least. Let alone the little speech at the end. My head is spinning. Turned the volume up fully. 'Click,'

'*In Tenebras te,*'

* * *

'The next morning, 19th September, 7 am.'

"Wwhere am I?"

A bright, Amber-gushing sky beamed into my face. I'm feeling groggy, with a jackhammer going at my brain. I thought I'd fallen asleep on the sofa again. Then my eyes cleared, looking through my car windscreen.

A rush of panic hit me; I couldn't remember leaving the flat. Or what I was doing last, glancing at the clock above my tape deck. It was Seven o'clock in the morning, yet I felt I hadn't slept, another gap to bridge like yesterday. Hangovers I'm familiar with; this wasn't that.

Although the next day's aches were similar, so was the ravaging hunger. Slowly, I was becoming aware of my surroundings, senses kicking in. With A rancid smell drifting my way every time I breathed in. Looking in the rear mirror, at first, for reassurance, I was awake, flicking my fingers, counting one, two, three, four, and five.

I was awake, but that didn't stop the symbol from coming; one, two, three and it's gone. My hand dropped out of view, and in a confused haze staring in the mirror, my heart jumped a beat when I saw a trail of dark red crust leading from my stubbled cheek to my neck.

Leaning forward as far as I could, my head pressed to the soft cream roof lining, craning my neck to get a closer look. Its blood. Dried blood. The reflection looking back showed bulging, terrified whites. My hands went in a flurry of stress, padding my body down wherever I could reach, checking if it was mine. Grabbing some wipes, I hurriedly cleaned my face. I don't know what happened, but if anyone sees it, alarm bells get raised.

Dropping into my seat, relieved that at least I wasn't bleeding. It didn't explain the smell, like yesterday, a distinctive iron twang with a twist, slightly different. A horrible aroma I'd smelt before, but I couldn't place where—a sense of Déjà vu. It came from behind me, twisting where I sat, causing springs to squeak. I could feel a warmth glaze my cheeks, finding what looked to be at least three pints of drying blood over the black leather. Maybe more.

What had I done? Maybe Dalton was right to suspect me, after all? How else could there be all that blood if I hadn't done something terrible? I didn't know what to do next. Fighting back the urge to spew my guts, I looked through the windows to see where I was, checking for passers-by. The sky had got brighter, and the day had begun for most.

Thankfully, I was home. Not in my original space, meaning I had driven somewhere, leaving a trail, perhaps even witnesses to whatever lost all that blood. It was getting too much; I could feel my stomach stirring; I stepped out to get some fresh air into my struggling brain.

The moment daylight hit my skin, flashes of an image popped into my mind, brief, but I could see myself sitting by the coffee table with a tape recorder in hand. Remembering little bits, I played a tape left by Chris, and then it went blank. That was my last moment before waking up in the car. I had a picture, the table with a gun, the whiskey, and other tapes in my head. So where did seven hours go, and whose blood had ruined my back seat?

CHAPTER 4

Nee-Naw, Nee-Naw,'

My ears jumped; I leaned against the car roof, soaking in the air, thinking about that image. When police sirens pierced the air, sparking my ears to life. The rapid breathing came back; three marked units were approaching at speed. I had nowhere to go, assuming they were for me. The facts were stacking up, making it too coincidental for them not to be for me.

Drawing closer, I saw the skipper as a passenger in one of them. At least seeing his face gave me a little hope. It didn't stop me from worrying, staring through the window at the blood, checking for anything I'd missed. It could be more incriminating. Thankfully, there's nothing else, but how would the police know to come?

'Keep your bloody hands where we can see them. Don't even think about running,'

A loud hailer boomed out, confirming they were there for me. A rabbit caught in headlights. My head went on autopilot, quickly assessing the exit options. Torn between a chance to run or give up. I still needed to call in the attack from the night before.

Putting the gun in play would only incriminate me further. I was cornered. There were three exits. Low fencing leading to Caxton fields should be to my right, but it would take a two-hundred-foot dash across the carpark.

Front left and right, approx. Three hundred feet were two pathways that led through graffiti-riddled alleyways to Pinton road.

I had less than forty-five seconds before uniformed officers surrounded me. Now or never. My heart beat like a bass drum and quicker than a marching band. Then it dawned on me that if I ran, all I'd be doing was playing into the hands of whoever wanted me to take the fall.

I wouldn't be any closer to finding my missing time or my friend's killer. Trusting the system had to be the way forward. I stepped back from my car, raising my arms in the morning breeze. My mouth was watering at the smell of cooked breakfast from the ground-floor flat to my left. Oh, that would be good about now. Instead, I surrendered to my knees amongst the rough, stone surface.

'Are you giving up, Georgie? Do you think that's human blood? Trust your senses, Georgina. Breathe it in. Soak it up, and the truth shall set you free,'

While stones were digging into my skin and the background of blazing sunshine. A bunch of uniforms were running my way. All seem in slow motion. Their noises and the sirens were a foggy muffle; a clear voice popped through my head again.

The same voice I'd heard the night before. It was Chris's voice. Why was I hearing him? I would've chalked it up to a nine-month spiral and a lack of sleep; maybe even the trauma of what I saw made me hear things.

Only, this felt different. My heart slowed, believing I could at least talk the Skip around to listening and plead my innocence. Then out popped the smug-looking, weathered face of Dalton. He slid out from the rear passenger seat and trotted slowly behind the others; time to see what side of the fence he sat on today. The sly smirk was there, and no matter how good his intention may be, seeing it made me want to break his jaw.

"Officer Reynolds. An allegation has been made that a person matches your description. Using your car with the same registration number were seen dumping a body-shaped bundle in the Thames. They described seeing a large amount of blood on your back seat."

Officer Kelcher returned to haunt me, too; he didn't get his way last time. The wind caught his Black hair with the 'Dr Strange' greying at the sides. I picture the tiny scatter of dark red near a faint sheet of stubble. I would've sworn blind the red specs I saw yesterday, nestled neatly on sprouting hair, were blood.

Only to be told it was spray paint. This time, he appeared far more confident. Dalton hung back, the sunny glow warming his wrinkled skin and tilting his head to the sky, enjoying what was unfolding or looking for the silver lining. It may have been a shadow, but there appeared to be bruising to the underside of his jaw.

"That's nonsense; I've not been near the Thames. But I've come to the car and just found blood. Somebody is setting me up," I kept calm while looking for a chink in the blue armour. Hoping my partial honesty will go some way to gaining favour. Even if I could have been.

"So, you're saying this car hasn't moved, and someone has planted blood? Do you know how ridiculous that sounds? Why are you suspected of murder twice in barely twenty-four hours?" Kelcher, with the confidence of backup, goaded me as he moved to run his hand over the bonnet, checking for heat. I hadn't thought that far; the blood had me off guard.

Dalton stepped forward, cupping his right arm around his stomach, holding his jacket closed. He was moving gingerly, making me wonder if the mystery attacker was him, but why? He's warned me. Perhaps my scrambled head was too desperate to put a name and face to the gun.

My stomach tensed up, thinking of the gun pointed at my head and getting ready for round two, this time on an even playing field without a sneak attack. My blood boiled, and I felt that hunger rip through my veins— the urge to tear someone's head off. The mystery of it all is screwing with my mind, making me question everything, including people that want to help.

"I'm in the dark as much as you are. Last night, literally. How're your ribs, by the way?"

I got my answer soon enough. Skip already had my car door open. Dalton stepped into my personal space. On the back foot, I got to my feet. Dalton's face changed; he looked confused; now the question was if he'd put on a show. My chin met his forehead; viewing eyes took a step back, one or two with open mouths, surprised that we were squaring up.

"What the hell have you been doing? I told you to keep your head down and mouth shut," Dalton whispered, causing my hackles to ruffle, yet quelling my rage. I could feel my cheeks flushing.

"What? Because you were skulking around in the dark, sneaking up and sticking a gun to my head? Is that how I'm supposed to back off?" I glared, gritting my teeth. Skip hunched over, not moving and seeming to pay attention to the back seat.

"I thought you were intelligent. Yet, you haven't figured it out. If I wanted to kill you, another body would be waiting for us. Whatever happened to you, it wasn't me. Maybe you need to think about who else would. Remember, the closer you look, the less you see. I'm trying to bloody help you," Dalton said, displaying an honesty that confused me; If it wasn't him, then what the hell was going on?

The murder. Who's pulling the strings, and what's important? "There's so much to figure out. I will not stop. It's messing with my head, but I can't."

Waiting for the penny to drop, the light bulb moment when Dalton realised I was serious, and he had to pull his finger out of his arse. My stumbling point was how they knew when to come for me and about the blood in my car. It took a few seconds, but I saw his mouth twitch and his eyes squint; my comment sunk in. He was deep in thought. I was playing chess, waiting for the next move for Dalton to catch up.

"Friend's close and your enemies closer. It's time you and your skipper had a good chat about old times. Then you will see where my allegiances lay. There's some stiff that might be hard to believe, but when it eventually comes out, it's true. Remember, secrets have been kept with good intentions."

"Secrets? Good intentions? Bloody hell, what else don't I know other than I didn't do it? Somebody other than me staged the crime scene; you saw that, right? What are your thoughts?"

Surely, photos had been taken, and he'd weighed it all up. Like, I thought there was so much more to this mess. Secrets are the theme. They've already cost a life.

"I saw many things, you being one of them. Chris was left-handed, and I knew it. I've known him a while, too, for reasons I won't go into yet, only that he's been your guardian angel, mostly. There was spray paint in the yard, which could be an excuse for him behind us. Oh, and the overlaying bullet holes. Now cut the shit; how long have you been blacking out?" Dalton threw me with the last comment, rocking me backwards, his turn to watch the penny drop, waiting for me to fill in the blanks.

"What the hell. Why didn't you say anything yesterday? How do you know? Guardian angel? This gets better," I had to know now. See what cards he was holding because he sure knew more than I thought.

"You're so fucking slow, boy...do the bloody maths and the hints we've been dropping. Think of someone in common. You should've said something," Dalton was a little narked now as if I'd added to the problems.

"How could I? It's all fucked up, and Chris's murder is the priority."

"It's like talking to a fucking brick wall. No one can help you; if you don't talk about what's happening and what's started. I'm not the all-knowing, just a pawn in the bigger picture. But you and Andy need to get your heads and acts together before shit gets worse, the cats out the bag and believe me, it's going to get worse."

"Back off, Michael. It's not human,"

Skip interrupted our awkward chat. His bulky frame shuffled back from the car. Dalton shifted his demeanour; I could tell he was about to put on a show, as he called it. He was heading our way.

"Stop protecting your boy. You got to loosen the apron strings, eventually. Besides, he can handle himself. Apart from that, how on earth do you know?" Dalton overtly winked for both of us to see this time.

"It smells different—no doubt pig's blood. I've had my share of pigs' blood and meat in my time, you know that, you tosser. It should be no surprise that I've lived many lives. So, I know the smell. The blood is a misdirection." Skip was standing between us, and Dalton was smiling. I had thought it smelt different when I first caught wind of it. Only I couldn't place it.

"You sure? Remember the taste? What about the call?"

Dalton smiled a little, no waver. As if he knew he was going to push his luck with Skip. What did he mean by remembering the taste?

"Yes, you stupid bastard. Now let's wrap up this circus. You're not making your bones today, Michael,"

Skip winked back. As Skip called it, all it took was a nod from Dalton, and the circus retreated to the safety of their cars. Kelcher left a troubling shake of his head in his wake. I may have survived; I'd been left confused by why the puppet masters had dragged me through the mud. Dalton played two roles, making it hard to see where he stood.

I had to understand how he knew what he did but gave the impression it was not his story to tell. How? Seven hours were missing, and pigs' blood was in my car. Who dumped the bundle in the Thames? Retracing my steps felt like the only way unless Skip had anything to say. He was the last man standing and looked like he was about to give me an earful.

"Taking Chris's death hard was a given, and I said to have a drink for him, but sinking in the bottle won't help. You bloody well need to get your head straight. You smell like a brewery and look like a bag of shit. We need to be smarter. Ok?" Skip's clubbed hand gripped my shoulder. Deciding what to tell him had me in two minds.

"Skip, someone attacked me last night. I knocked him on his arse and damaged his ribs. I thought it was Dalton warning me off; now I'm not so sure," I said, subconsciously looking over my shoulder as if I could feel someone watching.

"Why didn't you bloody well say anything? It wouldn't be Michael; he ended up with a GBH outside the SFC takeaway place on the High Street last night. The suspect kicked off, and Michael got his hands dirty. He took a few digs but came out on top. The tough old bastard." Skip's face was all churned up in the Autumn breeze, showing fear that I wasn't used to seeing him show.

"I get the impression this goes deep. For Christ's sake, I had a gun pointed at my fucking head to emphasise that point. Who are they, then? Did Dalton get hit in the stomach and jaw?"

The skipper's mouth dropped open, looking around my shoulders as if checking for viewing eyes.

"I had a feeling the shit would hit the fan. Chris came to me with the information he'd gained from a new '' called 'C'. A theory is that a group or family is in charge of the criminal underground, like in the old days. Only different. -

-His concerns were valid, so I allowed his investigation and kept him on a leash. Well, some things he was looking into going back to the best part of twenty-odd years. Dark, dangerous stuff I wish he hadn't found. And yes, Michael did,"

Chris had confided in someone that shouldn't have been a surprise; I didn't know many others I'd trust. If any. Skip looked worried, eyes twitching as he thought.

"Skip, Dalton told me to talk to you, said you would know what to say when I tell you... Well, I've been losing time—blackouts in my memory and not from drinks. Then there's the tape,"

I laid out my problems; hearing them aloud made me feel more vulnerable than I had felt having a gun to my head. I wasn't sure how he would react, but I needed support. If I was going to carry on with what Chris had started, I needed help.

"So, they found their way to you, then. I knew he was recording. Glad they're in your hands. Blackouts?"

He knew. Had this happened before, and I couldn't remember? Because he sure as hell seems to know. What else do I need to catch up on? I'm late for the party.

"Yeah, I have them, but I'm more concerned about how easy it was to get you a lot coming after me. Someone would need to know what I was doing." We stood in silence for a few seconds. The skipper contemplated what I'd said while mulling over his position in the middle of it all. I was thinking of ways they could keep tabs on me, feeling I was losing my mind.

"Come on, let's have a brew. Catch up time." Skip's words drifted to my ears, but I was too busy receiving daggers from Kelcher's glare. What's got the stick up his arse? Dalton had a good poker face and seemed good at playing both sides; my next step was to find out who he was working for and what the skipper knew about it.

CHAPTER 5

A sense of Déjà vu drifted in the air, with us heading upstairs. Thankfully, it was daylight this time, and I had good company. It didn't stop me from looking at the step with a sense of horror, picturing the scramble last night, the echo of pain shaking through my fist, smashing against the gunman's jaw.

The sound of a cracking bone swirled around my eardrums. All because he wanted me to heed the warning. Skip, and I stopped dead; my front door was ajar. My hackles spiked, and Skip raised his finger to his lips, shooshing me. He drew his baton, leaning into the door with his forearm. My heart jumped, hearing the squeaking hinge. I've heard it a million times before, but everything has me jumpy.

There was an eerie silence moving through the hallway. My eyes darted towards the table, looking for the moments I remembered. My first thoughts were the gun, wondering what the skipper would say or do. The cushion I sat on before it went blank still bared the butt imprint. The gun rested next to 'Jack.' Seven bullets were still at attention. My glass was empty; a momentary spark of a memory blew through my head.

It was of me holding the Glass half full. That was the last I remembered of it. The closer I got, the more I could smell it; looking like blood, human or what was in my car; hard to tell, but blood is all the same. Then came the kick in the balls. Noticed the tapes were gone—all but one. Stranded on its own next to some red-smeared markings on the table.

'Play me,'

A drawn smiley face next to it; this game was getting boring. Chris had stirred a pile of crap. They were getting personal. Dalton wanted me to back away for my good. While his ramblings about my world coming full circle, skeletons and all, had me curious. My world has always been relatively small, with no hidden surprises. At least that I remember.

"You ok, lad? You look like you've seen a ghost,"

A muffled voice slowly shook me to my senses. I almost heard the cogs grinding and was about to respond when Skip walked past the lamp. His doing that was nothing out of the ordinary, but his radio was another story. Calls were coming out; until a flurry of static interference interrupted them. At first, I looked at the stereo on low. Then Skip stepped nearer to me, and it stopped. Innocuous, but the way things had been going, the devil was in the details.

"Skip, you hear that? Near the lamp,"

"Yeah, what of it?"

"Well, why near a lamp?"

Skip paused, lifting his sweaty, rounded head in the lamp's direction and crowing eyes inwards; the hamster ran around its wheel. Sidestepping to where he'd been caused the static to come again. This time, Skip peered over and around the shade confused me. Watching my mentor go to work, to think how far we've come. When I joined, I was finding it hard to handle the death of my wife, flirting with depression and a couple of bottles of wine a night.

Skip stayed by my side and has been watching over me ever since. Acting as my work father. This was great of him, considering I'd heard he'd been through the wringer himself over the years, barely clinging to his job. Some issues began during his probation; that's where a parallel can be drawn with us. Now, he's sticking his neck out for me again. Rattling and lifting the lamp, treating it like a toy, clearly working on a theory.

"What you doing? Looking for anything in particular?"

"I'll know when I find it. But I have an idea. If true, we keep our gobs shut until it's safe,"

First off was the shade, cream with a hint of gold; Helen had chosen it as part of a set, like most furniture, to be honest. I was the one to put it together; she had better taste in interior design than I did. Now she lingers everywhere, reminders of what I'd lost.

But I wouldn't have it any other way. Next out is the light bulb. Nothing. The frustration was building on Skip's face. Shaking the lamp for all it was worth, we both heard the same thing, a slight rattle within the lamp's body. Gripping the base, it seemed a little loose.

"The screws are missing." Skip twisted and pulled at the base.

Once out in the open, the interference whales like a banshee; I was too busy reading Skip's worried expression. If it were a screw loose, it would've been kind of fitting to the situation. Yet, to have the screws missing, something was off. My hands wouldn't stay still; all they wanted to do was find out what was on the new tape. The base finally came free, and a small round object fell on a wire probably 2-3 inches long.

"You've been bugged,"

Part of me wasn't surprised, while the other part was horrified. They compromised my safety from the chaos, invaded by people wanting to know what I did. Well, the joke was on them because I knew very little. Least of all, what had happened in the missing seven hours? What I couldn't understand was why all the trouble was. I was a nobody doing my job.

"I don't get it; why the hell me?"

"That, my lad, is a question best left unanswered. This little coin-like object with wires is military-grade spy gear, so whoever owns it is not a fool or a planner, maybe both."

The alarm bells screamed. My stomach churned, and my breathing sped up in a state of worry. I wasn't about to doubt Skip's word; he knew his stuff from the marines. Being military meant I'd jumped to the next level; people above Dalton using him as a Lachie.

He never wanted to talk about it. Other than saying he'd seen and done things that have scarred him—many involved redacted files — an air of mystery that intrigued me yet haunted him. Now, I had a mystery centred around Chris's murder to solve. While trying to keep my fragile mind together.

"Can we trace the owner?"

Not knowing my arse from my elbow with these things, I found it hard enough to use our radios with dead spots and crappy signals. Skip dashed to the kitchen, grabbed tin foil from the side, and began wrapping the device in an aluminium sheet. Once done, he breathed a sigh of relief.

"Well... yes and no. These bugs are great little gadgets, but depending on the spec level, the range might not be the best. This means whoever owns it isn't far away. Maybe a mile or so if it's mobile use. Further, if it heads back to a central base. The downside of being mobile is it's a mile in any direction. The foil will block the signal while we talk."

So much for the apparent surveillance. We'd entered the sneaky bastard territory. I see why Dalton wanted to warn me; being military grade, the owners had some clout behind them. They knew when to plant the blood in the car. It's a sickly feeling, not knowing how long they may have been watching.

It would've been easy to leave with the transmitter and start searching the streets, but what would I do? What could I do? I could hardly ask them to stop. All I would get is denial. No, I had to play smart; this chess game was here for the long haul, and I had to think a few moves ahead. The problem was I didn't know how willing Skip would consider the military aspect.

"So, what do we do?" I looked around my lounge at the countless little hiding places, wondering how many more were there. Far from it, it wasn't as if I had led an exciting life. So, what were they expecting to achieve?

"We start by flagging your address as a precaution. Then we search for more. There's no point looking for 'where,'. As soon as the bugs go dead, there's no doubt the ears will cool off a while,"

Skip appeared to be on a mission, wandering around the place and listening for the interference of his radio. He had a point; whoever was listening on the other end had probably cleared off by now unless there were other listening devices. I dropped back into my usual seat, shaking with a sudden surge of anxiety. My eyes locked onto the bottle, watching the daylight ripple through the brown liquid. With a watering mouth and scratchy throat, I only wanted to drown my sorrows and numb the pain.

I felt terrible, scrambling through my brain to fill in the blanks. My hand reached out to give in to temptation. Only I ended up looking at the gun again. Wondering why? Why not take the gun back if they took the tapes and bugged me? A light bulb moment struck; what if we were in the middle of two different situations?

Reluctantly Dalton and his puppeteers, with the former playing two roles while someone in the shadows, wanted to know what I knew. I got curious about how many bullets were left and how many had a body attached. My poor little brain was struggling too much with thinking.

'Eight, Nine, Ten, Eleven,'

All the bullets stood in a line above the 'play me.' that's how many I had while picturing the rest nestled in a corpse or two somewhere. Maybe adrift in the Thames like the alleged call that witnessed me chucking a body-sized bundle over the side.

A bleak picture and one a police officer shouldn't be facing at home. Yet, I was finally pouring a drink for the skipper, too. His cup of tea was out the window. Anyone looking at me would say I looked suicidal with what I had laid out. Instead, I was playing with pieces to a huge and sadistic puzzle. The first mouthful scorched my throat, the same as always.

Most took it with anything to water down, not me. I wanted to feel the fire, deserving of feeling the raging pain on the way down, telling me I was still alive. The skipper didn't appear to have any luck finding more, so I grabbed the tape. The recorder was empty as well. They had taken everything.

CHAPTER 6

20th September 1987.'

Twenty-four hours ago, I was trying to figure out why I kept blacking out with an evolving nightmare tormenting me. That was all, though; I certainly didn't want to be in the middle of a murder investigation involving my friend of over ten years taking a bullet through the brain. Yet, I was oblivious to issues outside of my circle and never had a gun to my head.

Chris may even have known his killer—we both may have, leaving my fragile brain suspecting anyone and everyone with access to the station. For now, Dalton has to keep looking at me. What was driving him? What or who had his nuts in such a tight grip that he felt obliged to play marionette? Skip knew things about him; they played games between each other and put on shows for the rest of us, pretending to argue while carrying secrets.

I want to know them. I want to know who I can trust. I've been warned at gunpoint, with the Glock as a souvenir. The trouble is I don't listen well. I'm missing pieces of this jigsaw that I need. Skip was cradled into the armchair, not saying a word.

He was thinking hard. Visible thinkers were few in my life, so I had yet to see someone think as hard as he was. His mouth was churning from side to side, causing the cheeks to rise and dip back and forth.

A rosy red christened his face as the wrinkles set deep in his forehead. The fingers wouldn't rest, fiddling with the foil-covered bug. He wrestled with our situation, weighing the pros and cons, assuming none. I saw him form a thought, and I didn't appear to be a good one.

Then again, neither was mine. I was still fiddling with the recorder, making it as far as inserting the tape. Only, I had yet to bring myself to press play. Instead, I had chosen the bottle, and the skipper joined in. "Did you know Harkes has been disappearing lots lately" Skip said suddenly, appearing to be clutching at straws. It had been a while since I'd heard from or seen him. The question had me thinking there are concerns I'm not being told. "I know he doesn't like me, yet we've hardly spoken. Besides, I have enough issues myself. Whys that," Skip went to speak, his mouth opened, allowing the room temp air to hit the whiskey fumes. But nothing came out.

Glass in one hand, the foil in the other, he was running low on fuel for the soul, and so was I. But I knew the more we drank, the less likely we would want to deal with what was staring us in the faces. Trouble brewed in the darkness, and I didn't know what to do. No leads for finding his killer; any evidence of what Chris had uncovered was gone.

"Chris thought Harkes may have been getting up to no good. He had been acting sketchy, interested in what Chris was looking at. So, I had been running interference to keep Harkes out of the way. But the guvnor kept getting Harkes to be his errand boy. What issues are you having?"

If Chris thought Harkes may have been dodgy, then he's probably right. Chris had good instincts for that stuff. A copper's intuition that's what got him digging into cold cases. "Do you think Harkes knows what's been going on? What was Chris digging into? Also, have you ever noticed that Dalton has a strange symbol on his forearm? Looks burnt on his skin. My issues? Well... where do I start?"

The talk of Chris and Harkes digging into things brought my mind back to Dalton. He hadn't been keen on elaborating on it, so I couldn't help but wonder if there was a reason. As much as he may help in some capacity, I was taking the friends close and enemies closer to the heart. "I think Harkes may have an agenda that isn't his own. Whether he knows what Chris found is another story. As for Dalton, I can't say I've had the pleasure; perhaps it's part of his cockney charm. It's usually best to start from the beginning."

Skip took a longer gulp of his drink. I noticed his eyes kept flicking to the foil in his hand. Either he knew more about who could do such a thing. Or was concerned by how things had descended so quickly on the last day?

"Well, the symbol. It looked like a serpent in a circle with a forked tail piercing the head; it seemed so deep that it must've been painful because it wasn't an ordinary tattoo but more a branding. The beginning? Well, for the last nine months, I've been having nightmares. The same one repeatedly. Always in a basement, hearing chains rattle, coinciding with blackouts; I'm losing time. Yesterday, it happened again, the nightmare changed, and I saw red eyes coming toward me. I don't remember leaving the locker room, then I woke to find Chris," I dared to share, worried about what he said.

"Sorry, what? I saw you in a meeting room with someone but couldn't quite see who they were, so I assumed you were making statements or listening to a crime being reported. Then I saw you at Chris's crime scene. Did you say serpent in a circle? Are you sure?"

His words caused my heart to flutter; I blacked out but was awake and in a room with someone; who? What was it about? The moment I mentioned the tattoo, Skip's face turned white. The symbol made him remember something, that's for sure.

That aside, there was no hiding from the tension in the room. Skip had put me on leave to stay out of trouble. Yet, trouble is finding me. I had scratched my nail into the dried red letters on the table. If I made it disappear, I wouldn't have to obey what it says.

At least, that was my thinking. Instead, I was delaying and pushing the red crust under my nail. I looked down, seeing the flakes filling the finger edge, causing images to spark blood covering my fingers, looking clear as day. Chains are rattling over the concrete floor again. I shudder to a chill rifling over my shoulders.

"You going to bite the bullet?"

Skip broke his silence, snapping my attention back and causing a glance at the line of bullets. I noticed he'd avoided further talk on the symbol or the blackouts.

"Sorry, what" It was my turn to be surprised.

"you've been fiddling with that recorder since you put the tape in. It's worth hearing...Or not. But you won't know until you do. One problem at a time; that's the way forward. We will figure your head out as we go."

"I know. But what if it's more trouble? The proof is gone. All we've got to show for the mess is a gun and a tape left for us. The one problem at a time has become a list that's growing"

"That's not true. Chris trusted you enough to know you'd do the right thing if he had to pass the torch. He knew you would do what's right no matter the cost. Someone has found that out. You have certain people rattled. Enough for them to be warning you off. Chris may have shaken the nest, but you have them worried. If the list grows, then we must grow with it. Meet the trouble head-on; when you're going through hell, you keep going, right? Time to burn that nest down,"

Skip had always been good at the pep talks, especially on a long, weary night shift. This was different, but he had a point. The people behind the scenes had tried intimidation, theft, and spying. So, there had to be something I was missing—a puzzle. I was a threat, but I didn't know why. We didn't need me to black out again; the next time might not be pigs' blood.

'Click.' I finally took the plunge.

'Knock knock,'

'Sorry, one sec, just on the phone...'

'Crash...'

'Hey, do you mi... Oh hey, it's only yyy... wohh! What the hell? Wait, what are you doing? Please don't. Please, doooo... cuhhhcuhhh,'

'Claaaaap,'

'Claaaap,'

I clicked the tape off, feeling a bile surge mixed with whiskey romping through my throat. I'd stepped into a freezer. Hearing the gun being fired again wasn't what I'd expected to hear. It made Skip sit up, too. Clambering from his chair to my side, nearly sending the table across the room. Instead, it rocked, skittling the bullets as the whiskey swirled like an ocean wave.

I couldn't stop my hand from shaking, replaying those struggling words in my head, rehearing the gun firing. It wasn't even the original tape, so how? It almost looked like his ears twitched to what he'd heard, the way bats do, with the sun highlighting his red face.

"Was that what I thought it was?" The sound was haunting enough for the first time. Skip's face was red, stressed and bulging white eyes in shock.

"Y...y... yeah. Yes, it was,"

"Is there more?"

Skip was used to the sound of gunfire, made of sterner stuff. I jumped at the sound of fireworks. Yes, there was more. There was bound to be, right? I don't get left with an instruction like that, for there not to be more.

"Yeah, do we want to hear it? It's not like the tape is going to hear Chris rise from the dead,"

'Oh, come now, Georgie, don't be so pessimistic.'

I shuddered, wrapped up in the tape, when that whisper came again—the surreal voice of my friend—another problem for the list. Or was I going mad? How else would it make sense?

Hearing a dead person, the recent issues I've been having must impact my brain, causing me to hear stuff that isn't real. It didn't stop me from searching around with irrational hope Chris would appear alive and well. No such luck. All I got was Skip's troubled expression.

"You ok, lad? I know it's been a lot. But we must keep going. We can't let these fuckers win again."

Pep talk number two. For a big guy, he was a bit of a softie. Only a few got to see that side of him. We've had many quiet chats about his past life, as he knew of mine. Marines, he got moved around a lot. He followed in his father's footsteps. I haven't experienced a fraction of his life, and look at me, a mess.

Yet, he's still so grounded and has not gone around the bend. I know there's more he isn't saying. We'd be talking, and then his eyes glazed over as if he was reminiscing, only not fondly.

"Yeah. I have a confession to make."

"Go on,"

"Don't laugh, but I keep hearing him,"

"Who?"

"Chris. I've heard him a few times now. It feels like I'm going mad,"

The skipper didn't laugh or even smile. Not that he showed a concerned look, either. It was somewhere in between, an almost relatable expression. That's how he looked. I poured us another drink, a single shot this time. I didn't want to muddy the waters any further. A warm buzz is flowing through me. One that was in danger of being sobered by scary thoughts and sounds.

"I can't laugh, lad. Grief does strange things to the human mind. Seen friends get plagued by the dead, walking and talking about visions of corpses. Most get drugged up to the eyeballs to cope. But I think there's something deeper to it,"

"Deeper? How?"

"Trust me, ghosts exist. I see them, those I've had to kill all of them years ago. The nightmares too, more though, other things exist, that's what I believe now,"

He was serious, grabbing at his glass with fear in his voice. I got the impression he'd seen a ghost or something. Seeing him like that didn't do much for my grasp of rationality. I hadn't been one to buy into the supernatural hype.

But hearing what I had, Skip acted as if someone had walked over his grave. I wasn't keen on seeing that again with a head half missing. It got me thinking. Although they should've been thoughts for another day, I sat with a refreshed glass, hoping that Chris didn't appear.

"Well, these whispers are almost moments of encouragement, like when I got attacked last night. His voice spurred me to fight the guy off like he was watching."

"The guy you first thought was Dalton? And that's the gun left behind?" Skip pointed to the Glock, bullets scattered and cartridge adrift near the bottle.

"Yeah. I'm surprised it wasn't taken with the tapes."

"Well, it's early days yet. You might need it if the surprises keep rolling in. I doubt there's any forensics,"

He had another valid point. I was expecting him to offer some advice on how to use it. Yet, strangely, I had that feeling; I already knew. Even if I hate them. That feeling has lingered since I first took control of it.

'Click,'

'How does it feel to hear that again? I bet it was like a kick in the bollocks. Hold on to that sound. The more you dig, the less you'll like what you find. The past haunts us all, and yours is coming back, as sure as the moon lights the night sky. You mark my words.

You will soon be lost in the red. How's the hunger? An urge for blood to drip from your fingers? The closer you get to what you think is the truth, the more that part of you will grow. Until the lines get blurred. The darkness is calling, and soon you will know how it feels to lose it all.'

'Click,'

Slumping back in my chair, the glass balanced on my thigh. All I could bring myself to do was stare up at the window; the daylight slowly shifted with a gloominess casting its shade through the middle of the lounge.

The weather could read my thoughts and feelings. Gloomy, confusing, and with a sense of impending doom. The voice sounded distorted, either muffled by a cloth or modulated. I couldn't be sure, but it creeped me out—more talk of my past, knowing about the 'blood dripping from fingers' urges. How?

"That's fucking crazy. I stand by my earlier statement; you best keep that." Skip meant it too.

I could see that. After a quick finger flick to point at the gun, Skip lapsed into silence and deep thought. His eyes seemed to mist over; the recording had hit a nerve, and his mind looked elsewhere. He wasn't the only one; I couldn't understand what it implied when it spoke of the darkness other than what I saw in the basement.

"Whoever these people were. They knew me. I can't back down, not now. But I'm going to need your help," Leaning forward, trying to break that glazed expression.

"Skip?"

"Sorry... What? Ah, yes, of course. Whatever you need, lad. I said, every problem together. We must carry on for Chris. Only I'm afraid it will get blooming worse before it gets better. For all of us,"

We sat in silence again as I took on board what he'd said. Could it get any worse? How much more would I find? My glass was getting low again while the skipper swirled his around.

I chugged back the rest of my drink before clunking the glass on the table clumsily. Then it occurred to me. What if we at least played the tape for the guvnor and the suits, including Dalton? I wouldn't be seen as a pariah and would have more support if we needed it.

The flip side is the suits will probably want to seize the tape as evidence. Consider spending a few quid and getting the voice analysed. Or pass it to the wrong hands, never to see the light of day. No, I needed copies first, one for the skipper and an extra for me. I would hide it somewhere no one knew. Or with someone.

CHAPTER 7

'Officer Reynolds - 20th September, 3 am

"Christ, my head is killing me,"

Glancing at the clock, it was 3 am; I woke with a pounding head—the feeling of a saucepan thumping between my ears. Sitting upright in bed, everything around me was dark, making it hard to see my hand in front of my face, with my eyes taking their time to adjust. Groggily shuffling off the bed and heading to the bathroom, I thought drowning my head in cold water would ease the throbbing before taking painkillers.

Reaching my doorway, something breezed across my bare feet. I see the floor changing, barely catching a raft of dirt coating my toes. The smell of burnt wood swam in the air, making me on edge and causing my throat to shrivel. Looking up, everything was different. My eyes gradually adjusted; I could see the outlines of pillars. The burning slowly changed, bringing the sickly stench of charred meat forward, like a BBQ but with a putrid edge.

I was in a dark and scary basement—the sound of chains rattling suddenly in the distance, loud, chilling clangs against the concrete floor. It was too dark to see anything clear; my nose inhaled everything—none good. The charred meat smell got stronger, turning my stomach; I realised what was drifting around my lungs—a dead body.

Only I couldn't see it. My feet shuffled forward, dragging me through the dirt; my brain became curious. A glow appears in the distance; it's my bathroom, a section at least. Holding my hand to level with the light, my fingers were a silhouette. One, two, three, four, five... And six.

The light coats around me; I see symbols on the wall, dripping in red. A deep breath told me it was blood, yet no burnt body. I headed to the sink, hoping the water might wake me up, having gone on longer than usual. My heart raced. Spinning on the tap, I watched the cold-water stream down. My hands gripped the white curved sides. The longer I looked, the more lucid I felt. But no change; an eerie breeze rushed over my back.

My eyes lingered hypnotically on the stream; I must have been lost in the moment because I hadn't noticed the colour change. I could feel cold sprays against my thumb while the draining water turned a light crimson. Panicking and looking down, I got a sharp shock that cleared my haze. My fingers looked as though they'd torn through flesh, dripping blood. There were thick clumps that dried under my nails.

The more I looked, I noticed small, frayed pieces of material, possibly clothing. Rising in a frenzy, still seeing six fingers, forgetting where I was, wanting to be rid of the blood. I kept checking for hidden cuts as the blood cleared, feeling a little crazed, desperate to wake. The familiar chill swept through, icy, causing a wave of goose skin to wrap around my body. I spun the tap off; it had gone quiet, no wind, nothing. Only to be made to jump by a loud static buzzing noise, with the light flickering, causing flashes of worrying darkness.

Still facing the taps, my eyes towards the mirror; with every flash, I saw the glass steam drifting from the corner. A cold sheet of vapour spread across, and the temperature dropped. I was scared. The hairs on my neck danced to the chill with the light still strobing. I reached up to the mirror to wipe the glass clear; feeling the moisture on my palm, I caught a shadow in the reflection as the light broke the darkness.

It wasn't mine. Blinking my eyes, the shadow loomed; my hackles were waving like fiery embers. I daren't breathe; I daren't look behind. My hand squeaked across the glass, cutting rainbow-like through the fogged moisture.

'What's the matter, Georgie? Seen a ghost?'

A chilling voice whips through the air. Every hair on my body becomes a bed of sharp, piercing needles. All Stood, loud and proud. The spooky whisper was Chris; the streak in the glass cleared, and my eyes strained to take between the flickering light. It finally went out, leaving me stranded in the burnt, tinged darkness, dripping in fear, surrounded by a whistling chill and the smell of death up my nose.

'Embrace it, Georgie; let it in. Let it all back In. You must remember. It's coming whether you want it,'

He spoke again, different. Scary. Surreal from someone so quiet, my laid-back friend. This was darker, not making sense; hearing from behind had me tempted to turn and look. Only, with the lights out, it was next to impossible. My trepidation overflowed with the static buzzing around me, bouncing off the walls—the smell of blood cutting through the air.

'Become who you are meant to be. Finish what I started before bodies fall. Your reflection is nothing but a shell, a mask to fit in; take it off and set the beast free.'

The scary noises continued; I froze, my heart thumping in my ears. Terrified, I didn't know what to do. The lights flickered just as my hair softened; the sudden flashes triggered them to rise. I couldn't answer back; my eyes fixed on the glass; with each flash, I could see the shadow loom closer; I urged, running with nowhere to go. Closing my eyes tight, hoping it would all go away. Slowly squinting, a crack in my lids left me disappointed. He was still there.

'Are you listening, Georgie? You need to do what's necessary,'

Sharp, carrying a venom. Freaking me out. My neck twisted to the chill; my breathing rapidly pushed out thick, white vapour.

'I said, are you bloody listening?'

I skip off the floor, and a piercing, death scream rips through my ears; the lights fly on, blazing a brilliant white. The shadow had gone, leaving behind a decomposed Chris. A large crater where the back of his head should be. His flesh was a ghostly mottled white, eyes glazed a cloudy grey with dark dried blood streaked down his cheeks. My eyes bulged with the urge to bleed—my stomach curdled, wanting to erupt into the sink.

His head twitched and gyrated, clicking like a Rubik's cube, moving forward, forcing me back with nowhere to go. He quickly flew to my ear, screeching; the life jumped from my body; my eyes pulled wide, mouth dropped open. The screech ripped through my brain as my head spun. My legs became jelly before buckling underneath me. I hit the floor with a loud clap...

* * *

'Reality Check

"Aaarrrrrggghhh,"

"What the bloody hell?"

Frantically feeling over my body, sweat smothered my skin. Droplets glistened on my arms as the moonlight crept through the crack in the curtains. With the bedsheets clinging, I spun my head to the clock; it was 3 am. It happened again. My memory was fresh with the decomposed image of Chris's face. My basement nightmare is warping. I could still feel the nightmarish screech ringing in my head. Feeling my chest easing, terrifyingly vivid this time, I was grateful to be awake.

The last one cut off after the red eyes, but this was next-level scary. My imagination could make up for seeing Chris and how he looked defied anything. I remembered everything: the flickering lights, the shadow, and what Chris said. He was trying to tell me something, or my head was wishing too much that I could talk to him again. To chat like old times, work on the problem and find a solution.

Instead, I had to rely on others that may not have my back. I'd already shared too much with Skip, getting him wrapped up in something he would regret later. Slumped against my pillow and headboard, I replayed some things I said; he must've left here thinking I was one sandwich short of a picnic. He wouldn't have been too far from the truth, the way things were going. Hearing whispers from my dead friend plays on my mind so much that he ends up in my dreams.

Telling me to 'become who I was meant to', and I must embrace it to finish what he'd started. There was me thinking nightmares and blackouts were my only problems. Hearing the recording of the gunshot again; was terrifying. No doubt crept into my subconscious, lingering and changing what I dwell on. I still had a pounding headache. With the sweat still pooling around my body, it had become chilly dampness; my fear subsided along with the temperature. Flicking off the covers and about to slide forward, I ached.

Like I'd fallen down a flight of stairs. Surely a nightmare couldn't make me feel that bad. Maybe the constant drinking wasn't doing me any good. Every step had shooting pains riding through my legs, making me dance across the floor on hot coals. Not that I'd ever do such a thing. The guys shown in holiday adverts make it look fun and easy; to me, torture. At least that masochistic act was controllable. Mine couldn't be seen, and there was no end in sight.

Other than the bottom of a bottle. Shuffling through the hallway, I glance at the lounge. The gun was there, the recorder, and an empty bottle of Jack. Curiously, the blood was gone.

My routine was the same as the dream's, water spinning down the plughole while my eyes adjusted to the light. Thinking of my past, returning to when I was a child, I could remember going into foster care but not much else. It was another blank space, like the ones I'd been having recently.

Who was I in the office with? I wondered what else Dalton meant about the world coming full circle. Skeletons. Why would Chris carry it on in my dream? I had to know. I didn't need or want any more surprises. I should get in touch with Charlie. A curious thing Dalton is talking about him. If anyone could shed some light on my childhood, I hoped it would be him or at least push me toward someone who might. There's so much I couldn't remember or had chosen not to. Whether he's willing is a different story.

I hunched over the same as before, leaning against the sink's rounded rim. The daze had gone. I was about to scoop a pool of water in my palms to splash my face when I got another unwanted surprise—taking a sharp drag of air, getting a taste of morning breath. I could see dried blood caked under my fingernails, and my hands looked dipped in red paint mixed with dirt. Hyperventilating, I choked, coughing so hard I felt a gush through my throat. Splattering in the sink, looking down, I see clumps of black fur, not hair, animal fur. What the hell is wrong with me?

Rinsing it all away, out of sight, out of mind, throwing my eyes around my body, looking for more blood. I caught my reflection in the mirror, looking haggard, with a sheet of stubble coming. More blood and streaks are running down my face, mouth, and body. The tears brewed, wishing the nightmare would end. I couldn't understand how it was possible, considering I'd been in bed. I had been in bed, right? Attempting to rationalise something that I couldn't. All I had to go on was a nightmare; now I'm coughing up fur and covered in blood.

I couldn't claim every drop of red fluid was animal juice. I somehow made it to bed, which I didn't remember doing. Assuming it was because of the empty bottle. I'm not sure; there wasn't anything in my flat that could cover me in blood. I couldn't have gone out, could I? Then I remembered who I had been drinking with, Skip—getting a sense of doom wash over me, the possibility that the blood could be his. Although he was a beast of a man and even sober, I was doubtful of taking him down. So, if it wasn't his, then whose was it?

Tentatively, I brought a dried patch on my arm up to my nose for a sniff, hoping I could tell the difference. I took a whiff; it was hard to tell, although it dried like humans. Freaking out inside. If Lewis, Kelcher or Harkes could see me now, they wouldn't waste a second before dragging me down to the station, assuming I'd done something wrong. Even if last time, I had needed the skipper's expertise.

I've been lucky; a mix of purposeful mistakes and a good sense of smell have bailed me out when I'm rocking. I'm dreading the moment no one is there to help. There is no bodyguard when I can't remember or come up with a good excuse. I will be screwed. I got to scrub as if my life depended on it.

Or in case of unexpected guests. Smothered in soap, I dragged my fingers through the skin, trying to peel away the bloody dirt. I soon felt near normal again, chugging back paracetamol while there was still no reasonable explanation. Unless something jumped out or Dalton called again, it would be best to keep my gob shut. I couldn't explain it, anyway. First thing in the morning, I had to call Charlie and meet and get a read on him after what Dalton said. I had to survive the night first. □

CHAPTER 8

The sun shone bright, birds sang away, and I ran empty. Aside from waking up covered in blood, I tossed and turned the rest of the night, unable to shake the image of Chris and how different he was from my mind. Still felt the need to cough, but nothing came. The fur was strange, and I was not sure if I should speak of it to anyone, the blood maybe, but I will think about the rest.

Everything in the lounge seemed normal, and most of the flat—the appearance of two people finishing a bottle of whiskey over some not-so-good news. Belatedly drinking in mourning. Although I wondered which one of us cleared the dried blood message off the table, I still ached and dreaded thinking that I'd got out and got into a fight in my drunken haze. Perhaps Skip could shed some light on the matter.

'Brrrr. Brrrr. Brrrr.,'

"Hello,"

"Skip? That you?"

"Ah Georgie, you, ok?"

"Yeah. I guess so. Quick question. When did you leave?"

"Well, plenty was in the bottle; put it that way. I had to leave you licking your wounds on the sofa." I let his words sink in; all was well when he left. I finished the bottle and got into something Skip didn't know. At least the blood I woke with wasn't his, making me worry about the who or what. Did I do something fucked up, like eating Lucious? It would account for the fur but not my sanity.

"Oh, right... I woke in bed and, er..."

"And what?"

Another awkward pause, his questioning gruffness, echoed down the handset. I decided not to tell him, although the gap in my answer gave him room to overthink. I'd already given him so many issues. What would I say? 'Oh, you wouldn't believe the night I had. Another strange dream, and I woke covered in blood.' That's not a telephone conversation.

He would be duty-bound to pass that information on. To who? I wouldn't know now.

No, it was best kept a secret for the time being. No harm, no foul. As long as nobody had come to any harm. If Skip could see me now, he'd have a field day. Glancing at my hand, twisting it back and forth, irrationally checking it was still clean. I couldn't shake the lingering sensation of the crusty red flakes. There may not have been crusty blood, but the symbol became more emphatic, with a green triangle and a blue looping swirl. One, two, three, four, five, six, seven, eight and then gone. Lasting longer this time, like every other moving part of my problems, it's evolving. What does it mean?

"Erm... Sorry, I thought someone was at the door. I woke up in bed but couldn't remember getting there. Must have been more bladdered than I thought,"

That was the best I could come up with so quickly. Finding myself cranking my neck to check the front door was closed.

"Not surprised. After playing the tape. You were knocking the drinks back two to my one,"

Paranoid seemed a constant state for me lately, dragging the wired handset as far as it could around the place, seeking the windows. I was checking for anyone that stood out or a circus of blue lights. Skip chuckled down the phone, which did little to ease my stress because if I was that wasted, how did I end up looking as though I had a bloodied fight?

"Ah, ok. Panic is over. Is Rebecca being helped? I couldn't face them yet?

Panic was far from over, but my head had shifted to Chris's wife and two kids. Hoping someone decent was helping them come to terms with their loss. Poor Lizzie, she will grow up barely knowing Chris was her father. It's up to us to help her know him. The rest of us would get there, eventually. Until then, I needed to get some answers.

"Don't worry, lad, everything is in hand, as far as I'm aware. You need to get your shit together; focus on that,"

He had a point; I needed to do that, but how? So many issues at once that I couldn't trust my memory anymore. Hoping Charlie would still take my call, I finished up with Skip, made a cup of coffee, and braced myself. It had been years since we last spoke. Life does that; one thing leads to another. Paths get followed, and four or more years have passed before you know it. Even if he answered, there was no guarantee that he would want to drag up the past. They say it's best to let sleeping dogs lie. Sadly, I didn't have that luxury.

'Brrrr. Brrrr. Brrrr,'

"Hello," a tired-sounding voice answered the other end, Charlie. Riddled with nerves, I felt my throat dry by the second. Oh, how I wished I could liven my coffee up a little.

"Charlie, is that you?"

"Erm yeah, who's this?"

"It's George. I need your help," the phone went silent; my heart pounded through my ears. I couldn't imagine saying words to him after so long. or anyone.

"What the hell do you want? Nothing for so long, then out of the blue, you need help. I figured you had an army for that. What can I do that they can't?" He sounded pissed off, almost a muffle to his speech, either half-arsed to answer or half-asleep. Good question, though; he was right, too—a situation where I should've been able to rely on my colleagues. Unfortunately, bridges have been burnt or at least smouldering.

"That's the problem. I am still determining who I can trust now. Apart from that, it's too long a conversation to have over the phone."

Ready to tell him a little to pique his interest when I heard some background clicking, short of three bursts of three clicks. A type of interference, not like the bug, but an issue with the line, giving me pause. Who's saying the puppeteers hadn't tapped the phone line? Suppose they had gone as far as hiding a listening device in my lamp. Yeah, I thought I was a few sandwiches short of a picnic.

I couldn't take any chances. Chris had kicked a hornet's nest, and someone was trying to settle things down again, making problems disappear. The same way they did with the tape recordings. With an unknown voice on the last one, along with the phone call that made Skip warn me away. It was best to play safe. For the time being.

"Are you winding me up? Because if you are, I'm hanging up now. My bullshit meter only goes so high."

For as long as I remember, Charlie had always been that way. He had difficulty settling anywhere because of his issues and split personality. He could never take something at face value; he queried everything and trusted no one. Part because of being let down so much, which I could understand. There's so much of that going around as it is.

"Charlie, I know I've been a dick by not staying in touch, and I'm sorry. But you can give me all the shit you like once you've heard me. Please," I tried to appeal to his sense of getting the best of both worlds.

"Yeah, well. Not here; I'm not having your rubbish dumped on my doorstep," wise words I hadn't factored in. The way my luck had been going, anyone could make an appearance.

"Where then? Where are you living these days, anyway?"

"Not too far from where I'm going to suggest. Do you remember the first-place mother took us? A first ice cream?"

His words were a spark in the back of my mind, deep in the darkness clouding the memories of a past I couldn't remember or didn't want to. I'd fought hard to start a different life from what was expected. When he mentioned 'A first ice cream', which caused a rift in my mind, I could picture three of us sitting at a wobbly white and silver table. I didn't know what to do; I sat smiling at young Charlie with his curly black hair.

We looked a little similar back then. Next to Charlie was someone I would call mother: long, light brown hair. A heart-warming smile and emerald green eyes. On the table is a menu, the heading said 'Al's Diner,'.

That brief glimpse was enough to give me palpitations. Only I couldn't remember where sensing Charlie wasn't in the mood for me to ask pointless questions. He would no doubt give me grief for not knowing, but I wasn't infallible, the same for him, and I'm sure there are many things he's forgotten over the years.

All I needed was a little prompt; Charlie could be like getting blood from a stone at the best of times. Blood wasn't the issue for me, coming across it whether I liked it.

"Yeah, the strawberry one with a cherry on the top. Al's Diner," I showed enough to get a location and save my embarrassment, hopefully.

"Yeah, down on Bethnal Green Road. We'd gone to the children's museum, but it got a little overwhelming for me, so we went to the cafe instead. Now I live less than a mile from the place,"

"Ah yeah. About the trips down memory lane. Do you have any old photos from back then? One of my issues could involve a moment from the past."

I wasn't holding out much hope; Charlie wasn't the sentimental type, or at least he hadn't been. Then again, people change, especially in a short space of time. Chris was a prime example.

"I have one or two things. You're struggling again, aren't you?" Charlie said 'again,'. It's happened before. Why couldn't I remember? Would he bullshit me?

"What do you mean?"

"That confirms it. You seriously don't remember? That was half your problem. No, a fraction of your problem as a kid. Everyone thought I was the one with a screw loose; you were far worse, and life has turned out all Rosey for you,"

None of it rang a bell. I wished it did. Then I could understand the relevance of the recording and the meaning behind the dreams. I wouldn't say losing a wife and baby, turning out 'Rosey.'

"Well, could you give me a refresher course? Then I can explain why it's worrying me." Charlie didn't answer; I wouldn't have blamed him if he didn't want any of it. I hadn't stopped to ask how his life was, what was the latest, or anything like that. For all I knew, I could drag his family through the mud.

"Refresher? Some truths aren't that refreshing, maybe life-changing—3' O'clock. Don't be late,"

Charlie broke the silence abruptly before jamming the phone down. His tone didn't fill me with joy; I had to try. The handset stayed in my hand, listening to see if the clicks came again. Hopping, it had all been irrational paranoia. My ears strained, and for a moment, I could've sworn I'd heard a little feedback than a click. Maybe I was struggling with the reality that someone had invaded my personal space.

CHAPTER 9

'Secrets- 3' O'clock 20th September,'

My mouth watered with the smell of grease-drenched bacon swirling with scorched coffee. It was two forty-five, and I was early. I'd been going stir-crazy with paranoia, pacing around the flat. Every step to the lounge window had me staring into the car park, looking for anything new. Writing every make, model and registration number, I could see between the fear of being watched and still seeing bloodstains on my hands.

I had sweat dripping down my back and a stomach doing somersaults; none of that had eased by the time I'd reached 'Al's.' I wonder if I was making a mistake on two levels, first by dragging Charlie into the chaos and second by trying to jump into my past. Not if it had been made easier by Dalton's warning over Charlie; I was low on options. Glancing over my right shoulder, nothing stood out; other than a middle-aged male traffic warden who was going about his business checking parking meters.

With grey sideburns draped down his cap, the wind kept trying to whip away, bordering a train track of wrinkles. He looked worse for wear. The mileage on his body over the years had taken its toll, taking a mundane job to pass the time. Apart from that, I saw nothing to pause me from entering and grabbing a much-needed coffee. I felt more at ease; then I looked to my left, clocking a white Ford panel van about thirty meters away.

Rolling slowly down Bethnal Green Road. It was coming from Cambridge Heath with a poorly attempted blacked-out window. Seeing a van on the streets of London wasn't strange; plenty of builders used them. I swear I see a camera flash in the window of this one.

A glint of sunshine? I almost passed it off as that until I saw a second flash. This time I was looking straight at it; there was no second-guessing.

The van sped off to the sound of screeching tyres grating across the road soon after, leaving me feeling twitchy—part of the puppeteer's plan; to keep me on my toes. The big question is, who are the ones pulling the strings? Why wouldn't Dalton tell me? Whoever they were, something about me made them nervous; I needed to find out what that was. Just thinking about all the resources being wasted instead of looking for Chris's killer made me hurt.

Assuming they were police. The glass door opened to the right, ringing a bell to let everyone know someone else had entered—a room full of eyes glared my way. Lasting a few seconds, life in VHS paused with silence taking over. Press play, life resumes, and I'm yesterday's news. At least for these people. The glass door swung shut; habit or nerves would be a reasonable excuse to scan the room. My life has been turned upside down; I wanted to be careful.

To the left bottom corner was a group of four pensioners, doing the same routine for years—catching up on old times over tea and breakfast. The rest was a chessboard with positions scattered, filled unevenly. Some tables were by the young, others by the older, but none I recognised to be Charlie. There was a window table with my name on it. A great view of everything around me, including outside that white van or anything else.

The sun rushing through the window made the world seem peaceful. It wasn't enough to stop the back of my neck from ruffling with nerves. The logo took me on a trip down memory lane as I laid eyes on the menu parked in a stainless rack. The orange-red lettering appeared similar to back then. I Didn't want to be lingering around if Charlie reconsidered.

The diner had me exposed; not knowing what any of my new enemies looked like had my insides going through the wringer. I gawped at anyone that came within my eye-line. Needing a distraction, I grabbed a menu, flicking through it, taking nothing in; I already knew it would be coffee only for now.

"You ready to order?"

My attention got dragged from the mindless flicking by a patiently hovering waitress—an attractive young woman, no older than thirty, with shoulder-length, fiery red hair wearing matching lipstick, a beacon on her pale skin. The Uniform looked new, giving me the impression that she hadn't long been in the job unless she took pride in her appearance. Maybe it was a bit of both.

While her accent was hard to pin down, somewhere north of London, a mix of a couple of places, there was a slight tremor, a little waver that made me think she was hiding her genuine tone. Her name tag said 'Mary,'. She didn't seem like a Mary, more of a Joanne or a Jennifer. She had long pink manicured nails with smooth hands, not the kind that sees lots of washing-up or manual work. I might be way off base, and 'Mary' took the job to make ends meet.

What piqued my curiosity the most about her was wearing a pair of black, glossy high heels. Anyone with an ounce of experience from waiting tables and spending long hours on their feet knows you must wear flats. So, what gives? Christ, my head was rattled; the scenario was off. First, the van, now a waitress, didn't seem like a waitress. I couldn't rule out overthinking, but if the last twenty-four hours had taught me anything, to expect the situation to go wrong.

"A flat white, please,"

"Sorry, what?"

My suspicious mind levelled up a little; all I ordered was a strong coffee, not the one I wanted, but it would throw her off. It had to be anything but a straightforward coffee.

"You know, an espresso with steamed milk. Have you worked here long? The place hasn't seemed to age," I checked her expression. The bottom lip hung open, waiting for the words to fall out while her frown showed confusion. If trust issues didn't ravage me, I'd sympathise because chaos and I have become great friends lately.

"Ah, right, yes, of course? Sorry, it has been a crazy day so far. Worked here for a couple of years now seems popular. They must be doing something right," she stammered, forcing an excuse; only I didn't know why.

"Don't you mean 'we' must be doing something right?"

The door swung open to bells ringing through a short gust of wind. "Ah, yes. See? Tired brain got me all over the" I wasn't buying it. Mary tottered twenty feet to the Diner counter, leaning towards a sweaty, belly-bulging guy with stains on his apron that I hoped was from food. A second later, he was making a coffee.

"I see you beat me here,"

A harsh voice came my way; it was the voice of Charlie. There stood a man I hadn't seen for a while, albeit slightly more weathered than I remembered. Charlie was skinnier, a little under five foot nine, with an ageing mop of Curly black hair withdrawing to the wilderness from the sides. He'd grown a nicely crafted beard to compensate. In his right hand was a small faded blue holdall; I'd seen bigger handbags. I only asked for a few pictures; Charlie had a few albums' worth. The clock above the diner counter was already showing 3 O'clock. Time had gone quick.

"Yeah, I've been here fifteen minutes. The waitress is getting a coffee. Do you want anything?"

"Not yet. We should get this done first.

Charlie sat with a thud; his speech was laboured, seemed to carry the weight of the world and had a face like thunder, wincing a little with a hand hovering near his body. He didn't want to hang around any longer than he had to. While my attention kept getting drawn away by looking out the window and at everyone around me.

"Are you ok? Sound awful,"

"Dentist had to pull a tooth, bit into a cookie and split one of the back ones. So, what's going on, Georgie? What's got your knickers in a twist?"

Charlie slowly leaned back in his chair, letting a micro-expression of comfort escape. I wondered where else he had to be. My coffee was taking an age. Every time I looked at the counter, Mary caught my eye, acting fidgety and giving awkward glances our way. She wasn't alone; at the top, the far-left table was a white bloke dressed as a long-distance lorry driver.

Edgy, something I could relate to, causing the trouser to keep rising, and that's when I saw it. There was no guessing the guy's age because he consciously kept a baseball cap over his face, judging by the weathered hands tapping away at his cup mid -40's. Then again, he may have been used to the graft and worn. His left leg pounded a steady rhythm on the floor like a drum. The guy had an ankle holster, worn black leather. It carried a small revolver.

Now, what would make a trucker illegally carry? I'm a fine one to talk, still carrying the Glock from my attack; although Skip recommended, I keep hold of it. Assuming he was a trucker at all. Whatever his reason, it had me struggling to concentrate.

"Where to start. My best friend had his brains blown out. The scene was rigged, at first, to look like a suicide. Then the detective took the easy option and made me the target."

"What the fuck. You're kidding, right? Was it a case he's working on?" Charlie's mouth hung open in surprise. That's expected, but how did he know it was a friend I worked with?

"No. Chris pissed people off by digging into things that have drawn the wrong attention. A detective is the lead investigator for the case; he keeps warning me away, telling me my world will come full circle. Skeletons included. Says Sgt. Morris and I have things to discuss and talk about old times. He's being very cryptic, and the skipper isn't much better... Quick question, how did you know it would be a friend I work with?"

"Oh, erm... lucky guess, you work a lot, figured it would be someone there. How well do you know the detective? Someone you're close to, like a friend? Does he know much of your past?"

Charlie shuffled forward on his seat; I'd got his attention, suddenly unusual confidence. Why would Dalton know about my past? There was so much he'd said that needed to be clarified.

"Not much, mainly in passing and certain calls. So, it was better to understand my past. To see how it connects to now," Charlie went to speak just as my coffee got brought over; Mary was acting sheepish.

"C...C... Can I have the same, please?"

Stammered, strange as I'd not heard that since a kid. Mary smiled at Charlie and tottered away. One of her heels clipped an uneven tile. Another reason for wearing flats, and she would've known that. Charlie reaches into his jacket pocket, retrieving a handful of folded papers. Looking old, Charlie held them in his fist, shaking a little. I might be wrong, but he seemed to have a tremor. He'd gone from being bothered about being here to fluctuating between fear and confidence. The swings in his mannerisms and behaviour were extreme.

Charlie slid the papers across the table to rest under my chin line; they had to be twenty years old. There are ways to age paper using coffee and an oven, but these looked authentic, turning a crusty-looking brown-yellow. In my head, I was questioning whether I should open it with mounting fears over the surrounding distractions. My attention kept getting dragged back and forth until I saw Helen smiling beside Charlie. Brief warmth that I needed. If only she would stay.

"Brace yourself. The past isn't pretty,"

Charlie gave me a wide-eyed look to urge caution. That's the problem with the past; it meets the present eventually. Feeling a little giddy, I reach for the pages to pull them open. Laid flat, I can see they're drawings, not the professional sort, by the hands of a child. In the corner, written in blue crayon, was 'Charlie, age 10, George age seven'. The picture, at first glance, looked cute and basic. On a day out at the park, a family of four, 'mum, dad, Charlie and me', were the labels, page title 'home'. The closer I looked, a detail caught my eye; in the background were light grey shaded figures. My mouth dropped open.

"told you, not pretty. Truth isn't always easy, but all the juicy bits come out in the end,"

Charlie interrupted as Mary brought over his coffee. I counted at least ten of various sizes scattered across the drawn grass. Each grey figure had the word 'dead' above them. In my head, I was questioning what sort of child I had been to draw something like that. Then I saw myself, the drawing at least. My eyes were bright red, with monstrous fangs, teeth, and claws for hands—dripping blood.

"What the hell is this supposed to mean?" none of what I saw seemed true; anyone could've drawn it and said it was mine, right? But how would it explain the aged paper?

"You were a broken child and nowhere near normal. Neither of us was. At first, I thought it was funny, but then it got weird. You got weird and scary. Until...," Charlie paused, staring into his coffee, letting it hypnotise him.

"I don't remember any of that, only bits and pieces, with us having fun and you going and coming back." Charlie's words didn't seem like me, nor did the pictures. No wonder my head feels screwy, but how does any of that relate to Chris's investigation? Was it I suppressed the memories?

"Yeah, I didn't have any luck, did I? No one wanted a problem child struggling with the reality his family was dead. In the end, only one place felt like home. The same way you felt, I'm sure. We were alike, but the most damming was that neither of us had real living parents. Maybe that's why I'm so fucked in the head; I Always found it curious why you stayed; loads of families wanted you once your shit was in order. At one point, it felt like I didn't exist. Mum and dad obliging your every whim. We never found out what drove Dad to it,"

The sadness in his voice was all too telling. While he was right, I felt safe and loved there from the bits I remember. Dad was long ago; mum said it must be his time, not waking from his sleep. Another tragic tale in our lives. The scary part is, what happened before all of that? When life wasn't good.

"Until?" Charlie's eyes darted to my face, and I could feel others burning into my skull.

CHAPTER 10

'Al's Diner, 20th September.'

The sound of stainless steel grinding against cream porcelain was rattling my ears. All I could do was sit in silence, waiting, not wanting to flick pages anymore until I knew more. Charlie had me hanging off his words, 'weird and scary, until'. That's how the drawing looked, but I couldn't imagine myself like that. I'd stomached half my coffee before letting it get cold. If only that burning feeling in my head would do the same.

The guy in the cap would flick the peak every couple of minutes to throw a glance my way. It was three-thirty. He'd been nursing the same cup since I'd arrived. I wasn't doing much better, yet I needed help to get the ankle holster off my mind among the many things going on. Here we were, sitting across from each other, acting like strangers taking a walk down memory lane to a time we were more than that. We were brothers. Family should look out for one another, and I'd done anything but that. I understood the hostile vibes Charlie had been giving off. He was pissed, and I couldn't blame him.

Would he back me up if the shit hit the fan? It may depend on where he stands with everything. Not that I wanted it to come to that, but the more I looked, the more I didn't like the demeanour of 'Mary' and 'Trucker Guy.' His leg was still pounding to a decent rhythm while Mary kept herself clear from serving anyone else. A couple of years working here, my arse. Schoolboy error. I made eye contact with her, prompting a wry smile before awkwardly clopping her way over.

Catching her heel on the same raised tile, she had yet to learn from the first time. I had to keep my eye on the ball and not her curves; my mind needed to be clear to get Charlie talking again. With her being attractive, there was every chance she could make me forget any notion I had of her being up to no good, with the crisp uniform hugging her busty figure while she batted her hazel eyes at me.

Mary sauntered back to the table, this time paying more attention to the drawings than us. If I'm not mistaken, I got distracted by her perfume, Estée Lauder, quite like Helen's. I check back. Charlie and Helen are there again, sitting next to him. Mary's fragrance had stirred my memories.

"Same again, please," Catching Mary off guard.

"Sorry, what?" Mary looked startled, almost as if she had forgotten why she had come over.

"You were about to ask if we wanted anything else. But I beat you to it," I was being polite, while 'Mary's' bug-eyed stare came across as creepily intrusive.

"Ah yes, two coffees, right?" Mary had forgotten already. It wasn't as if I'd seen her serve anyone else.

"Yes, that will do," Charlie piped up gruffly, grimacing in her direction, irritated by her awkward but straightforward mistake. Mary had a surprised look and hurried away. Leaving us in silence, I was looking at Charlie's twitching left eye, wrestling with what was to escape his mouth next, appearing stressed. Hopefully, the coffee was better without the foam.

"Come on then, out with it," Charlie threw a blank expression in the air.

"You must remember; I joined the family when no one knew what was happening with you. At least no one would listen. The things you said you could see and speak to scared us. Topped off by red eyes, and you are covered in blood. You were dripping in it,"

Charlie spoke softly and quietly; his words were a slap to the face and a bolt back to my nightmares, the one I woke from to find the body with the red eyes. Not the one with Chris. Those eyes drifting in the darkness still make me shudder. I sat, trying to form a response, thinking that more dots would be connected from my childhood to my dreams. Now I needed to know if there was another connection to Chris's murder.

Anxiously, I scratch fingernails across the wooden table, causing Charlie to shuffle back in his chair, looking frightened. Why would he be afraid of me? He was waiting for me to fly off the handle and lose my temper.

"What the hell do you mean? Covered in blood? Red eyes?"

I look at my fingers on the table, staring; I see flickers of the crusty, dried blood streaks—Embedded flakes crammed under the tips of my nails. Clear as the beard on Charlie's face. My grip on reality was loose, slipping by the day. The blood came and went; my heart roared away, and Charlie's words circled in my head. The thought of what he'd said happening to me as a child didn't ring true.

Red eyes like the drawing. Maybe our imaginations had run away from us. Then why would I dream of them? Deep down, I was mortified by the idea of me scaring the family when I was young. The way Charlie describes things, I was a screwed-up child, and now I'm slipping again. How does that explain hearing Chris?

"you tell me you don't remember? I shouldn't be surprised. They took you to many specialists until a guy who seemed quite trippy helped you,"

Charlie glanced at the counter, then the window, before looking back at the counter. He suddenly carried a worried look on his bearded face. It was his eyes, though, quivering as they moved, pushing his wrinkles to gather in the middle of his forehead. I know I slip easily between moods, but it could be bipolar acting up for Charlie. What I didn't need to be doing was worrying about how he was going to behave next; hard enough watching Trucker guy Mary and the van. Was there more to him, though?

"That's my point, Charlie; I don't remember shit. Not beyond maybe 8 or 9. But I've been plagued by bad dreams and blackouts for the last nine months. They seemed to worsen; I blacked out and woke to find Chris's body. It's not the first time I've ended somewhere I don't remember, and Skip said he saw me having a meeting with someone earlier in the day, yet I don't know. I had been changing, drinking my coffee, and then it went blank.-

-My flat had a military-grade snooping device planted. And they assaulted me at gunpoint to make me walk away from finding justice."

I looked long at Charlie's face, waiting for the gravity of the situation to hit home. When his left-hand reaches for the bag he brought with him. More of an involuntary reaction caused by a subconscious thought or memory. I thought it was because we were talking about the past. I had only asked for information and pictures, yet he's bought something else.

"So that's the mess I'm in now?"

"Yeah. For that, I'm sorry, but I have no one else to turn to."

"No. It's not you. Look, sorry if I came across as rude. When you called for help, I was already expecting you. A few weeks ago, an odd bloke with long black hair, quite scary, approached me and turned up my front door. He was elusive, knew a lot about me and put me at ease. Handed me a package and said you will need help soon, and I was to give the contents of this bag to you,"

So, it wasn't that I had pissed him off. He was expecting me. But how? Who was the odd bloke? My mind raced with those questions before I looked at the bag again. Is that the package?

"A few weeks ago? An odd bloke? Shit, has someone else been watching me? Perhaps he planted the bug and not the police."

How could anyone know what was happening to me weeks ago? My troubles were only my dreams and blackouts, mostly.

. Unless, like what Skip saw, I'm not so much sleeping but a different persona? I could be great friends with him, for all I know—finding it hard to take my gaze seriously from the bag or any of it. Mary clapped her pins to the floor as she finally returned with our coffees. I darted my head in time to see her pause by the trucker's table. He whispered something to her ear as she leaned sideways, keeping her tray flat.

"He looked familiar, but I couldn't place him. The guy wouldn't give a name; he said he was an old friend. Not hanging around for a lengthy chat. Mr Tall and scary handed me the goods and told me to expect to hear from you."

"How would whoever they were, know I would need you? How would he know your address? And why the hell did you take it? Remember, mother told us not to take things from strangers?"

The strain was getting to me, making me jumpy. Mary placed her tray on the table before dragging the coffees to us. Wrapping my hands around the hot cup, looking deep at the swirling light brown, I wished for it to be stronger, wanting to add another brown liquid to the mix. Where would it stop? My tastebuds would enjoy the swim and end up drinking until I felt numb.

"As you said, someone is listening. There's no telling how long that bug has been live or why, but it must have been going on longer than you realise. Could there be a different plan at play here? A person or persons expecting your moves and thinking a few ahead. Highly intelligent and highly motivated. Maybe even know you better than you know yourself."

Charlie had a point while resting both hands around his cup. He gave a reassuring smile. I didn't know how long that bug had been there; Skip found it by chance. Was I the only one? Was Chris monitored too? On the recording, he talked of professionals following him; it wouldn't be farfetched to say his home has eyes and ears watching and listening. To my knowledge, I hadn't spoken of Charlie or his home. In fairness, until earlier, I wasn't sure where he lived.

We were surrounded by awkward silence again, allowing me to overthink. Splitting my attention, I needed to know what Mary and the Trucker guy were doing, with an eye looking out the window now and then for the white van. Flashes included not ruling out the chance the old Ford transit had been harmless. I poised the cup near my lips and was about to take a sip when I slid my hand forward, hitting the pile of papers by accident.

They were on the back burner; call it delaying the inevitable since seeing the first few. I didn't want to see any more tragic glimpses of my past. There was little about the last couple of days I had wanted. No point in putting it off; I flicked the pile open. The shock of what I drew so young would never get old. Red eyes glared up from the old surface. They may be in crayon, but it didn't make them any less haunting.

Ironic, I was thankful as the next page opened, looking much the same, except for several more drawn figures marked as dead. Thankfully too soon, I could see the how next to the scruffy words 'Dead'. Each one showed a different manner of death: 'stabbed', 'shot', and 'run over, to name a few. Christ, I was a disturbed child, quickly becoming a disturbed adult. Charlie's face changed, seeing what I was sifting through again.

He looked in pain, a grimace out of sympathy for me, perhaps. No matter how much I tried, my brain refused to believe that these drawings were nothing more than an overactive imagination. Yet Charlie is adamant otherwise.

"We need to Irish these up a little." Charlie reached into his pocket and retrieved a silver hip flask. Music to my ears. My tastebuds were going through withdrawal, needing a fix.

"You have perfect timing," giving a quick smile of appreciation before carrying on with the musings of a devil child.

In each one I went through, I noticed a common theme: blood. People are lying dead on the floor in pools of crayon blood—memory lane took a drastic turn. Not for the better. I could see a picture the size of a child, yet more of a monster with claws and teeth. It was standing outside a house. The Orange and red crayons had gone to town. Drawing a raging fire or as close as any child could resemble a picture. Speech bubbles come from the windows, saying, 'help me,'. What had I done?

Bile surged through my mouth; sadly, no triggers—no spark of repressed memory in the darkness. Mary and Trucker-guy seemed more intrigued; both became more obvious in their stares. I saw the trucker's face, partly shadowed, but I saw enough. A thick greying moustache was underlining the trucker guys' flatter noses. With motorway lines dragged around his skin, he had to be in his late forties. Flannel-wearing and gun-wielding, looking dodgier than a Sunday market VHS tape.

Charlie tipped a shot in my cup and went to pour one in his when I heard an 'oi, not in here,' coming from the big guy behind the counter—causing Charlie's hand to shake as it retreated. My attention moved sharply to the bag. The last page was open; at first, glance, confused. At least what was inside had to be of value or importance in Charlie's head. Telling me, he's had a good enough look—making me intrigued.

The page had divided; one side shaded in all black crayons, with the drawing of a small boy in the middle, half-beast-like and half-human. The other half of the page was normal, the view of a happy family. Outside of a house. In the black were a load of red eyes. The boy looked torn between two sides. All I could think of as I raised my whiskey-freshened coffee was that the drawing showed a tug-of-war between good and evil. Charlie's face looked uncomfortable.

"Do you know what any of this means?" Feeling the steam drift from the cup to my lip.

"Not really; you wouldn't talk through that time. You drew a lot. But I saw how you looked; so unrecognisable it was scary," Charlie lowered his voice a little, checking around him.

"A lot? What happened to it all?" I was curious based on being given only a handful of drawings. Strange, too; it may be because I've grown up, but the idea of me drawing made my head hurt.

"They... well. Mum burnt them. Said it would be best not to have reminders afterwards,"

"After what?"

"Well, being young at the time was hard for me to understand. But from what I've heard, there was trouble initially. I overheard mum on the phone a few times, talking about the past and how a fiancé wasn't what she thought and had to make sure they kept you safe. You were lucky to have that."

Charlie spoke with sadness in his voice, eyebrows narrowing like a 'V'. Recently, I saw everything as black and white, maybe even too predictable. Now, I'm struggling to know what the truth is. The unnerving constant since the nightmares started has been red eyes. I need to find how it all connects. Breathing a deep sigh of stress and worry, I was about to take another sip of my coffee when Mary and the trucker guy moved in unison.

I stopped short, watching the pair resume their positions—odd behaviour. I didn't take a sip, resting the cup back on the table; my hackles were rising, feeling a ripple down my spine.

I caught the reflection of a white van; it seemed the same as earlier, rolling past before stopping around four car lengths to the left. The sun was still beaming through, making the glass look almost mirror-like. It may be panic over nothing, I thought. Yet, with the unnerving hairs bristling on my neck, it was time to trust my gut.

CHAPTER 11

20th September 1987, 4 O'clock.'

Now, I've heard some horrors from my childhood. Nothing had helped me; the situation had worsened. I wanted to know more. To do that. I needed to see what was in the bag. The one delivered to Charlie out of the blue. I couldn't help but feel his story was a little suspect; what stranger turns up randomly bearing gifts, predicting I would need help? I needed the comfort; if full-blown whiskey wasn't on the menu, I had to make do with what was on offer.

Thank heavens for small mercies, clutching the cup, savouring its warmth before taking a large mouthful of coffee. I enjoyed the droplets a little too much until I got the aftertaste of something else. At first, I put it down to the shit coffee, but the bitterness was left behind for a second. Charlie sipped his coffee like a lady sipped wine. Tentatively enjoyed every drop on the way down, minus the alcohol.

If the vacant expression on his tired face told me anything, his mind had drifted elsewhere. Doing so made me jealous that I couldn't afford the same luxury. My mind would go in one direction, bouncing from one problem to the next, without stopping to appreciate in between or take on how anyone was feeling, caught up in the mess of Chris and me. So wrapped up, I didn't ask after Charlie's life and what he'd been doing. Or take the time to understand the consequences. Nearing 4 o'clock, there was only so long a place like AL's would allow us to hold a table for coffee. Weak stuff at that.

"So, what have you been up to since we met last?" Charlie's attention snapped back.

"If it's all the same, now's not the time for a catch-up. We don't need to add more drama to the" Charlie looked sad, dipping his eyes low and taking another sip.

"What do you mean by more drama?"

"You and I both know why you aren't in touch. At first, I put it down to you, holding a grudge because I didn't make the funeral. Then I thought it was because of your job, not wanting to associate with a problem like mine. I wanted to come and nearly called a few times. I've had issues and memories of my own to navigate,"

Charlie's voice filled with emotion; the funeral of Helen hadn't come to mind in a while. Let alone for me to hold a grudge. Charlie was way off the mark until I put a face to the guy who killed Chris and the ones fucking with my head. No, life had gotten away from me. Burying myself in the job as a way of coping, I didn't give thought to much else. Time ticks on quickly, and this year is no different.

"Honestly, Charlie. It's not that. I had to hide in what I do—my way of coping, even more in the last nine months. Forget about me for a minute; what's going on?"

"We can chat about that later; I feel a little uneasy. We've got eyes on us." Charlie's narrowed whites darted towards the counter to show.

My hand slid to the back of my waistband; the feel of cold metal grazed my fingers. The gun was still in place. I wasn't used to carrying one, but needs must. If Charlie was picking up on it, there had to be something about 'Mary' and the trucker guy causing alarm bells. Further vindication to trust my gut.

"Yeah, it feels off. The trucker has a gun strapped to his left ankle. Waitress Mary possesses all the grace of a stilt walker on ice. She's wearing heels. Everyone knows-"

"-you don't wear heels if on your feet all day in a place like this. Yeah, I remember mum giving the do's and don'ts to a waitress before," Charlie interrupted with a slight smile, a rare one so far.

We were on the same wavelength and guard. We weren't far from the door, but I was looking for a backup option if our fears came true. Perhaps Mary heads over and aims to be a distraction for unknown reasons. Maybe even flirts a little. She shows a little skin to catch my eye; lord knows it's been a while since Helen. Mary would stand in front of us, dressed in her figure-hugging uniform, slowly leaning forward, smiling and dripping some cleavage. Who wouldn't find Mary attractive?

All the while, the trucker guy has summoned the enthusiasm to hoist himself from his warm seat. The trucker would clamber to another, slightly colder seat nearby, offering containment; he would have unclipped his gun from its holster. Or have that ankle resting on the opposite thigh for easy access. The cap flicks up, allowing us a full view of the trucker guy's face. I would be obliged to soak in as much detail as I could.

My short-term memory is intact and good with faces. So, I would remember the face I would seek once we'd escaped and regrouped. Trucker-guy would do that to show he held no fear and wanted to intimidate us. Did either of them know what I did for a living? His stance would be broad, hanging a long thick leg half into the walkway. Meaning he could trip us without moving if he wanted to. That walkway leads to the left side of the counter, where I could see two doors.

One was a toilet, ruling that one out. Leaving the other as an unknown. I hadn't seen anyone come or go. So, we would take a risk trying that way. The other option would be to evade Mary's advances. Darting to the right, where the walkway was longer, covered with a two-tone brown beaded fly screen. My bets were on a door leading to the yard. The van was still parked where it had rolled to a stop.

The mistake they made was parking as far down as they had; there was space for us to exit right and then double back around to my car. We had the unknown of who or how many were waiting inside it. All conjecture, but the way my luck had been so far. It was bound to happen. We could dwell on the 'why's.' later. Charlie and I were chugging back our coffees, acting none the wiser, and I got to enjoy the tinge of whiskey for the road ahead.

Charlie had his hand on the bag, looking weighed down by being around it, piquing my curiosity but mindful of the eyes on us. With a heavy sigh, Charlie caught me looking and pulled the bag onto his lap. A part of him was eager, taking a deep breath before exhaling, and he was bound to be nervous. Having eyes on us didn't help; the zip slowly slid open to the sound of grinding crocodile teeth.

'*Oooh, presents, this is exciting, Georgie,*'

Chris whispered again; I twitched, not wanting to be obvious; it's how I imagined a ghost would talk, a haunting, whispered echo with a little fade to the words. As strange as it was, and I might go mad, I wasn't scared. Not like his dream of him.

"Right, what I'm about to show you is foreign to me, so there's no point with a million and one questions. All I can say is that it's weird, heavy, and intriguing." Both hands had disappeared into the bag's darkness, leaving me on the edge of my seat. Literally.

I was full of excitement and apprehension, thinking that staring at a nearby table's plate of food would quell that moment. Full English fry-up. My tastebuds ran wild, causing the saliva to pool around my gums. I was hungry, but we didn't have time for that.

My first glimpse was of a lid; it looked old, a dark grey, metallic, mixed with something else. Even that part made Charlie right; it looked weird and very ornate, decorated with a mixture of raised, embossed symbols around the edge.

A few I could understand, the others I wasn't sure. There was a moon next to a dog and a person. The dead centre was a blood-red half-moon shape jewel in a circular blackish band. With the lowering sun beaming through, it caught the gem's surface, producing a mesmerising glow that had me momentarily drawn in. Everything was quiet, and I could see a misty, dark red. My eyes widened until I glimpsed a shadowed shape. It was a beast.

"Georgie... Georgie... Are you ok?"

"Huh. Sorry, what?"

Charlie broke through my trance; the mist faded away. I was waiting to see the box hoisted fully clear of the bag. Taking it in its entirety, I'd not seen anything like it. Antiques are one thing; this was something else altogether. Shimmering in the rays, it stood more like menacing, clawed paws on four feet. More raised symbols decorated the sides, yet not a handle insight. Charlie looked weary of it, pushing his upper body back deep into the green plastic clutches of his seat.

"You were in a daze; your eyes looked as though they had a slight glow. Couldn't have, right?"

"Maybe a trick of the light?"

"Seemed more than that could be stress, I guess,"

"Maybe. I have to say; the stone was bloody hypnotising,"

"Well, it's spooky. As for this, it doesn't open; I've tried,"

That would explain the lack of a handle, but how to explain being drawn in by it. Maybe Charlie saw the light bouncing off the gem and across my face. Or he'd given too much stock to childhood drawings. Time has a way of distorting what we know. Each year that passes, our brains alter versions of what it remembers. That's what I was hoping anyway, and the drawings themselves were nothing more than imagination.

The box, though, there had to be a way to open it. It would defeat the object of being a box. I wanted to touch it, to examine what it could be or hold, but I was afraid. Charlie seemed to get edgier, shuffling the box back into his bag. I felt sick. At first, I thought it may have been the after-effects of the strange glow. An uncomfortable surge was moving through my stomach.

"I don't feel so good." my head became hazy, and my eyelids were heavy.

"Hey, what's wrong?" Charlie's voice echoed as the zip streaked closed.

All my senses were fogged; the feeling of a nasty head cold and a hangover rolled into one. Only my vision became blurry. My heart was King Kong beating his chest; I skidded a hand across the table, attempting to find leverage and move up. Instead, I scattered the crusty papers. Panic had taken hold; I had lost control and didn't like it. I'd been drugged, accounting for the strange aftertaste still lingering. Helpless, I was relying on Charlie to stick with the cause and help. Hopefully, he'd be able to ward off the advances of Mary, the trucker guy or anyone else that fancied coming our way.

"We got to go, Georgie. Focus on my voice, ok? Keep calm; surely, they won't make a scene with other customers,"

Charlie had gone full circle, sounding assured under the circumstances and exactly what I needed; my heart struggled to stay at a steady rhythm. We had to rely on the risk of collateral damage being too great for them. At least six patrons had been chowing down, and I wondered if the owner was in on it, maybe coerced. My hand brushed Charlie's sleeve, grabbing a tight hold. My other scruffily grabbed for the papers, stuffing them in my pocket.

I didn't have long; the heaviness was real, and my legs turned jelly. It didn't help that I couldn't make out my hand if it were in front of my face. Attempting to stand, I yanked Charlie into the table, clumsily sending a cup skidding off the smooth surface. I heard the porcelain shatter on the tiled floor. Usually, I'd be embarrassed, but the situation is different. Dribbles of sweat trickled from my forehead; My blood boiled, and my pulse quickened, throbbing through my temple.

What drugs was I given? Charlie dragged me from the table, sensing the closed space; I could barely make out the shadows heading in our direction, stifling the air in front of us. Out of nowhere, my feeling of vulnerability had become rage, brewing in time with my blood; unsteady and on the verge of collapse, I clung to Charlie. A fire scorched through my veins, causing every fibre, muscle and tendon in my body to thunder, screaming for help.

The hand gripping Charlie's sleeve pulsated before hearing a loud snapping of tree branches, torturing sounds vibrating in my ears. Only the noise was in my bones, leaving me in agony, experiencing pain I'd never felt. The kind that brought tears to my eyes, feeling my fingers being pulled apart. Each click reminded me of Chris in my nightmare, the Rubik's cube. If I weren't so dizzy, I would've been freaking out. Searing heat fizzing from the fingertips, tearing movement from under my nail, shredding through Charlie's sleeve.

This experience wasn't a hallucination, dream or blackout. All too terrifyingly real.

I heard an 'ouch' but thought nothing of it, fighting to stay lucid enough to hold on and escape. The hate I had hidden deep within was roaring to the surface, needing a target, wanting to know Chris's killer. Imagining the killer standing in front of me, I wanted to tear the head off their shoulders to feel the skin shred apart in my hands as my fingers drove through the flesh.

The metallic taste of blood swilled around in my mouth, the same as in my dreams; I liked it. Striving to escape, I struggled to stay close to Charlie and awake while battling against myself. Charlie dragged me across the floor; the rage inside wanted to stay and fight. The rational part of my brain wanted out fast; its willpower was fading. I could hear a second heartbeat pounding as loud as mine. Charlie was scared, and that helped beat back my rage a little. The bell boomed, and the door crashed into the wall, hammering into concrete.

We flew through to the open as a wall of overwhelming smog, and cooked food punched me in the face, nearly knocking me on my arse. Every sense had dialled up to one hundred. I was hearing, smelling and feeling a million different things at once. My brain kept repeating, 'what the fuck is happening to me?' There was a loud, bone-chilling screech of metal; I heard a van door grind open. My feet were struggling while my hand continued to stretch painfully.

"Keys. Quick, where are your keys?"

"Pocket, side pocket,"

"We need to hurry; they've hung back a little but not much," every word was foggy, muffled in slow motion.

"I...I... I'm the one. I'm the one,"

"Yes, you've been drugged by the looks of it. It's all so fucking weird,"

The last word trailed from Charlie's mouth; his tone had changed, and I could hear a slight smile in his voice. The pitch changed; a softer tone encased in a calm hum. Perhaps one of relief that we'd got out, curious even in my current state.

Losing my battle, I could barely string my words together, about to drop at any moment. Footsteps were beating the pavement in our direction. At least four sets I could make out. Landing heavily on firm seats, I recognised the smell of leather anywhere; it was my car. The door slammed shut with a loud steel thud. I couldn't move; the fight and rage had gone, eyelids pinned closed as my head flopped to one side. There was a screeching of tyres before my body got flung around. We were on the move, and I crashed out.

CHAPTER 12

'Safety- 20th September 1987 6 O'clock,'

"What is going on? Charlie. Who are these people after him?"

"No idea; at first, I thought it was all to do with the death of Chris. Now, it's more like the past has finally come calling," Skip.

"What do we do? His world will implode, all of ours will, and you have known a hell of a lot longer," Charlie said.

"We do what I've always done; look out for him. When someone finds out, most of their life has been a lie. That's going to hurt. He will be angry and could lash out," Skip said.

"Not as much as knowing the truth; that could hurt you all. Especially the dark, dirty, and secretive parts; I know there's more you haven't shared. Do you know if there are others?" Charlie.

"Honestly. I don't know; I've wondered since that... well, the day my eyes were ripped open—all the old scary stories about what goes bump in the night and myths. To think it may all be true. He needs steering; he turns thirty soon. As for telling you more, put it this way, there is such a thing as over-sharing," Skip said.

'Clank... clank... clank. Ssssp,'

"Woah! W...w... where am I? What's happening?" My heavy eyes creaked open, waking to a spoon battering a cup and raised voices.

My heavy eyelids matched a heavy, dizzy head. Everything seemed foreign to me for a few seconds, thrown by the dim surroundings. A slight yellow glow hovered over a small table to the left of my head. I was on an unfamiliar sofa. Comfy but unfamiliar all the same. Had I been captured? One of my first thoughts until I felt the luxury of the cushion under my hand was that kidnap wouldn't be this comfortable.

I'm taking in the sights, trying to see where I am, along neatly decorated walls. Split by a white dado rail, the bottom half had been wallpapered with lime green stripes, and the top was plain cream. Everything had a place; almost obsessive-compulsive how the coasters, newspaper and remote controls were neat on the glass coffee table. Only one person I knew to be that obsessive—Skip. The voices I'd heard were familiar. My head beat like a drum and was still drenched in a misty haze, making it hard to trust my senses.

Tiny flashing images kept appearing in the back of my mind, trying to remember what happened and how I ended up on this rather plush brown leather three-seater. Finding, I could bounce back to sleep, flopping my sore head against the armrest. All I'd do was delay the inevitable and my search for answers. My right hand was aching like I'd been punching a wall. Looking down, one was distinctively fatter than the other. Knuckles turned a shade of blueberry, and I couldn't remember how.

Bending and straightening, I flexed my fingers to get the circulation going, albeit painfully. In doing so, I noticed the dried blood crammed under the nail's edge of my middle finger. Some of it had sneaked its way up the grooves on either side. A little panicked, I compared hands, fingers and arms, frantically patting over the rest of my body. I last remembered being at a table in 'Al's diner. I had... I...I... erm. Crap, what was I doing?

Getting angry with myself, straining my brain, I scraped at the dark red crust, barely flicking a fragment, when a spark went off in my head. Getting a scary glimpse of Charlie and me, I staggered forward, grabbing onto Charlie's arm. I felt a quick burst of pain. I see my pulsating bloody hand growing into a dark claw. The image fades the moment I stop picking, leaving behind a racing heart and me breathless. What the hell is going on with me? I lie down, staring at the brilliant white ceiling, asking myself that question repeatedly and wondering if normality was a thing of the past.

After A few seconds of calm, I finally remembered what I was doing at the table. I had been looking over a pile of old drawings. Horrifying ones. I struggled with them the most because I couldn't remember drawing them as a kid. Or into anything like that. My eyes flick around the room, looking for my coat; I'd stuffed the papers in a pocket in the heat of the moment.

"Ah, she's awake. About time Georgina," Skip's voice breaks the reminiscing. He was standing in plain clothes, made up of blue jeans and a smart polo T-shirt. Smothering a cup in his hand, he smiled briefly, pumping up his rose-red cheeks.

"How did I get here?" Wondering how Charlie would know where Skip lived.

"I brought us here. Nice car, but the gears are sticky," Charlie stepped from behind the skipper, looking calm under the circumstances.

"Yeah, but how did you know? I didn't even know where Skip lived." The pair of them squirmed. I could feel the tension levels rising.

"We all have our secrets, Georgie, granted some more than others. Apart from that, a lot can happen with the years ticking by,"

Charlie attempted to diffuse my curiosity by turning it back on me. All that prompted was for me to dig more. It's in my nature. Besides, he'd apologised for not coming to Helen's funeral. So, it wasn't all on me. However, I happily admitted my part in the prolonged absence.

"Yeah, you were going to fill me in on what's been happening with you. I noticed your left hand has a tremor. So, are you two drinking buddies now or something?" Pulling my aching body upright on the sofa.

"Nothing like that. I knew your foster mother from years ago. Said I would monitor you; then Charlie came along, and trouble followed him too. So, I promised to watch you both. I've kept my word, Georgie. But Charlie called for help, so here was as safe a place as any," Skip sounded unconvincing. Focussing on his usual micro-expressions, I looked for the little telltale signs, like the ones he gives away playing poker. The twitching eye, the constant gulping. This time it was the waver in his voice, the fade in the words as he spoke. Skip was holding back on me.

"So, what aren't you telling me? You know more than you're letting on, don't you?" I called them out, feeling unusually abrupt, fed up with being in the dark, wondering what else I didn't know about myself—that and feeling hungover as shit. Even without a drink, I might add.

Charlie kept shuffling. Slipping his hands in and out of his pockets, jingling change. Not knowing what to do with himself. While Skip seemed to wrestle with a thought. Chewing on the inside of his cheek. What did Charlie know? Skip was about to speak. Pausing with his mouth hung open, catching flies, watching Charlie. Must've had an idea to interrupt his process.

Skip trudges over to a mahogany side cabinet and reaches down to a set of doors. One side flips open to reveal a shelf of bottles; the other is full of files. Skip takes a dusty-looking whiskey bottle in one hand and slides free an old brown folder with the other. Usually, I'd be gagging to crack open the bottle, but I still had a strange bitter taste in my mouth and was curious why he was bringing out a folder. Judging by the age, it would have been a good ten years or more. That style hasn't been around for a while. Tiny beads of sweat were scattered around his shiny forehead. Made me wonder how bad its contents were.

"What you got there?" Watching the skipper gaze at the folder cover, daydreaming.

"Let's just say we need to decide what's the better of two evils." Skip dropped the folder on the table with a clap, causing dust to graze the air. Skip's words were ominous. Would I prefer the evil of being back at the diner or here in the skipper's flat? Because what I was expecting to come next didn't feel good. That sums up how life has been going.

"Well, I've always preferred my evils to come in 40 proof. Nothing good was coming from the other evil. I'm getting sick of the surprising kind." Skip had dusted off one of his prized collections.

"We're going to need it. If you think life is crazy now, what comes next will fry your brain." I didn't see what option I had other than to nod and smile. The fear was growing little by little inside. Sensing whatever was coming next, the skipper had been sitting on for some time. But why wait until now to break open something collecting dust?

"It's fried enough as it is. What's a little char grilling between friends?" Trying to put on a front. I didn't know which way was up. The diner was still raw, and seeing those drawings in my mind was a constant as I waited for the other shoe to drop. The first is a plimsol-like old whiskey, the other a steel toe cap boot as a brown folder with a curious label on the front.

'Case File: Arson 1962. OIC Pc Morris,' Charlie reluctantly joined us on the sofa, bringing three glasses and seizing the initiative of pouring some Dutch courage.

"What's this then?" Charlie looked confused, letting me know he wasn't in on the latest development.

"This haunts me. When you've been around the block as often as I have, there's a chance of picking up a haunting or two. Only this one was beginning what changed my life." Skip's face reddened; he looked in great emotional pain.

What I needed help to understand was how it involved me. And from 1962. Why else would Skip bring it up if it didn't? My mind pinged back to when he said he had known our mother for many years. How did their paths cross? Were they more than friends at one time? Had she been in trouble?

Questions I wanted to ask, but there were better times. Skip grabbed his drink sharply, flushing it down his throat like water, gasping with fire raging in its wake. His demons must be bad. Charlie merely sipped, as he did with the coffee. While his eyes darted around us before searching the ceiling, looking for guidance; if he found any, perhaps he could sling some of my way.

"Well, I know a thing or two about hauntings and nightmares,"

Sliding my gaze to my hands again, recalling the eyes in the darkness. Most of all, the night before, the dream, and waking with blood under my nails. Hallucinating the same at the diner makes me question what is real. My hand still hurt, so there had to be something in it; flexing my fingers, catching a strange expression from the Skip. It gave me cause to be frightened, not that I wanted to show it. If the skipper or Charlie knew anything, I needed to know. Good or bad. Judging by their current behaviour, it was going to be all bad.

"It was a wet and windy night shift. On 17th February 1962, I was a year and a bit into my probation working from Bow. HT borough. Having spent five years in the Marines, I was used to being told what to do. -

-As a newbie, I expected to get all the grunt work. That's the way it was and still is. I needed the experience of shitty, gut-wrenching calls. It builds an officer's character or makes them shit themselves and quit. I was doing well; until I got sent to Canton House. -

-a lovely four-bedroom cottage on the edges of Victoria Park. An arson in progress, the fifth in two weeks. The others had been in family homes with no survivors. Although neighbours had mentioned kids, being taken. It was horrifying,"

The tears rained down; Skip paused, catching a much-needed breath. I'd not seen him this emotionally before. Yet, he looked like he had been bottling it up, waiting to explode. He's always been the tough marine, yet he'd been holding back. My fears rose; what did his secrets hold in store for me?

Conversely, Charlie looked pissed off, even if he was fighting not to show it. How could this story affect him unless it triggers an incident or part of his life? We don't know. A cavern had formed in his frown line, eyes looking down.

CHAPTER 13

Officer Andrew Morris - Nightmare Feb 1962,'

Hotel Tango panda unit receiving,'

"Go ahead,"

'Call for a fire in progress at Canton House, top of Parnell Road bordering Victoria Park. The garden backs onto the canal. You're the closest unit available.'

"Is anyone believed to be inside?"

'I'm afraid it's too soon to tell. We have limited information, and the caller is anonymous; someone is trying a callback. The call itself appears to originate from a payphone. You need to assess the scene; potentially, it could be a hoax,'

"Received; there's been a few real ones lately, so it could be the same. Please keep me updated."

It wasn't the type of call I fancied, hoping it would be a hoax, but there was a feeling that the recent pattern would continue. I've been bugging the suits for weeks, trying to point out the obvious. Only to be shot down and told to stay in my lane as it's knout to do with me. Be seen and not heard. That I'm a lad that's wet behind the ears. Sadly, that's not in my blooming nature. Besides, it's easier to ask for forgiveness than for permission.

It would only lead to a jungle of red tape and delays. So, yeah, I would be the good soldier and head to the flipping call, but my mind was already expecting the worst. Weaving my way towards, heading through, beginning Pendal Road, my fear rang true. It didn't stop the heart from machine-gunning. The smell of smoke, mainly burning wood and furniture, drifted through the car's vents.

The call was genuine, and there had been no update. Light traffic, pedestrians and the road. So, anything obvious, anything bad, would stand out. A mist of deceptive soaking drizzle hung in the air as an eeriness crept through the darkness. I rolled slowly up a stone gravelled driveway, smooth wet pebbles grinding against one another, causing the tires to squelch, skidding to a stop. A few fire trucks had cut across a grass verge to the left, leaving churned grassy tyre tracks in their wake.

The sight of water fairies laying siege to a brilliant white-coloured house took a few seconds to sink in. Set amongst a mini forest, it seemed strange for anyone to target a place so out of the way. It was set back from the streets and backed onto a canal and the park, with even less chance there would be much foot traffic to make a show. They were fighting bravely, attempting to save the lovely family home from ravaging by the raging yellow embers that seemed hell-bent on ripping through a ground-floor room to the left.

Sliding into the nighttime air, I got whipped by a chilling breeze, and the stench of burning crawled up my nose. I couldn't see any passers-by, curious onlookers or even a nearby payphone. So how the hell was the call made? The night fell silent, apart from the crackling pops of charred wood battered by powerful water jets—no other sirens. I took a step back; call it fear or patience. The flames seemed to become far more aggressive, but it had me backing away until the smell changed.

The kind that makes me fear the worse, full of dread with a sickly sweet taste washing around my mouth. A smell I recognised and one I never wanted to come across again. I can still see my mate 'Chinni's' face melting and me frozen, not knowing what to do. Even if I had been kidding myself that it wouldn't happen again, the unmistakable, horrifying smell of scorching flesh has smothered the air. My thoughts pictured someone burning alive; perhaps, If I went in from the right, through a window, or maybe a side door, I could give them a chance.

I was anonymous to the water boys; they were too focused on saving the house and anyone in it. I took a deep breath, chewing on the smoky air, before edging my way forward on a separate path. I trudged through the fallen leaves, forming a layer over the rubble, making my footing easier to manage, scuffing up a slight slope. The closer I got to the house, the further I was from the crackling, allowing the eerie to follow in my footsteps. Hearing the faint humming of nightly nasties, I scanned the building side, taking in the countryesque wall climbing red and green vines.

'Hotel Tango, panda unit. We have an update for you when you're ready.'

My radio blares out, making me shudder. What could they have to update? I was on scene and yet to know anything other than the horrid smell.

"Go ahead," Taking another deep breath of smoke.

'A neighbouring cottage further along the canal bank looked out of their garden after hearing a loud pop. They spotted at least one suspect, maybe two, leaving over the fence. Shadows boarded a canal boat. May have been carrying a dark bundle, but it was hard to see.'

Was that even possible? I wondered. With the daunting darkness and the suspect not wanting to be seen, they wouldn't use lights. Yet, no one would expect the canal system, and the police don't usually deal with anything like that. The route could take someone to at least Burnley. Able to hop on and off along the way without being noticed.

"Did they sound sure?"

'As sure as anyone could be in the dark,'

"Any idea of names for who lives?"

"We have the family name of Conrad, listed since 55. But are also registered foster carers with children of their own. Unfortunately, there's no information on how many children are under their care." It wasn't making any sense. Who would target a place so set out of the way? Foster parents, of all people. It didn't fit.

The information I'd gathered on the spate of Arson was that there were children involved, and the homes were close to water. Not sure if they were foster placements too, but if they were. The suspect could have a grudge against the system. So many fall through the cracks. There's bound to be a wronged child with hatred in their veins. Angela and I considered adopting after enough attempts to start a football team. As we were considering our options, lady luck came a-knocking.

Three years on, little Rosalind is doing great. Unfortunately for me, she takes after the mother in the bossy department. The radio dropped out once more. I shuffled further along the stony path. Every scuff and crack had my hairy back on the end. Angela swore blindly once that I was a bear or a yeti in my previous life, only I got attached to its fur. I'm not too keen on summer, and the whole vest-wearing makes for grim viewing, part man, part silverback trying to catch a tan.

The stiff breeze had my mane flapping and my throat desperate for a cuppa to wash away the sandpaper. In the distance, a separate low fence shielded the murky waters. As suggested, it wouldn't take an Olympic athlete to skip that. I should check to see how plausible the update was. The pathway heading towards the fence line was tricky to navigate in the dark, making it hard for anyone to escape quickly.

I crouched in the drizzle, skimming the oozing rainwater off my face and clearing my eyes. My footing slipped sideways, stubbing into what I thought was a step—dam near tripping over. Thanking my lucky stars, I was alone, sparing the windups. Whatever I'd hit wasn't quite a step, the thickness of brick but solid wood. My eyes slowly adjusted, ears twerking bat-like, listening to the water fairies going toe to toe with a ferocious beast and sounding proud of their efforts so far.

I was standing at the foot of an old-fashioned basement entrance with double wooden doors; I had only ever seen it in movies or on farmhouses. There was no padlock on this one, giving me a way in if I dared. Common sense was telling me to back the fuck off and wait. Bravado told me to stop pussyfooting around and get down there. Lives could be at stake.

Even if in the deep recesses of my limited intelligence, I knew they were already gone.

The charred flesh stench was too pungent for them not to be. A matter of how many, and pray to God no kids. That cut deep and longer; I don't enjoy taking work home with me. But something like that would be what I see when I look at my baby girl. I hovered my hairy knuckles over the door to feel for heat; it seemed ok. The devil on my shoulder tried to nudge me forward. While the angel was too busy downing a pint to care. Still crouching, I paused, thinking no good would come of it. Then came a moment that caused ice to grate across my panicked skin. My heart leapt into my mouth.

'*Hhhhheeeelllllllpppp,*'

A faint, bone-chilling whisper croaked through the cracks in the doors. They sounded young, struggling. Barely any reverb in the throat; they had to be slipping away. I gripped the edge of the door, splinters slicing deep in my haste. The first one crashed open, letting loose a gust of pent-up dust, followed by death's overwhelming, stomach-emptying smell. There was no turning back; I was all in. The second door.

Followed suit. Cupping my mouth as I found the first step. I nearly stacked it but stumbled my way carefully down a few.

The croaked whisper came again, a static shock to my system. It was always possible, but it felt unexpected. A dim flickering glow pierced through the darkness and the stench of death. At first, I thought the fire had spread far quicker than I imagined until the tired eyes focused. The flickering glow of a candle flame, the lower I got, the more of them I saw scattered. Each flapping of light whipped shadows across the decaying walls. The smell was so strong yet not fresh. No, I was inhaling wave after wave of decomposing flesh.

'*Hhhhheeeelllllppp,*'

The voice came from the shadows to the right; my feet slipped into loose debris and a glass bottle, causing me to jump. The far wall straight ahead was flaking white, the flame dancing away. Within its glow, what I can only describe as freaky, dripping red paint drawn in a circle. A picture of a snake/serpent looped, head crossing a forked tail at the top. Halfway down, it had dragon wings. Why would someone draw such a thing? A cult? It wouldn't be the first time. Moth to a flame, I was sucked in. Shuffling closer, the flicker seemed bigger and the shadows less. It stopped me dead in my tracks. Wishing the bloody angel had done its job and persuaded me not to go.

The light lashed downwards, casting over a horrific view. Kneeled to the floor was the body of a man, decaying black flesh; any remaining blood seeped and pooled. I say remaining because the head was missing, frayed, rigid neck flesh and necrosis set in. My eyes dart downwards, seeking the head; my stomach was fighting to keep its contents. A metallic aroma blended with the stench, another familiar smell. Blood.

The edge of my boots stopped mere inches away from a crimson pool. I look up to compare. The picture wasn't in paint; it was also blood. An unknown suspect slaughtered this person and used their blood. The darkness made it hard to see other wounds; a chopped head was enough. The body looked to have surrendered. I turned to look elsewhere, forehead clapping against a light cord. My hand clutched, clearing my lungs and slowing my frightened yet racing mind—the cord pings with a loud click, and the bulb spasms to life. I wished I'd kept it off.

Questioning my sense or grip on reality would be an understatement. I had forced my way into a basement of horrors. Blood sprayed throughout, enveloping the thick dust and grime in its path. At least four adult-sized bodies were scattered, all beheaded in kneeling positions. The bodies were much more than decomposed; they burnt—more likely to mask the wounds, but not because of the house fire. The suspect placed the bodies exactly where they wanted them; looking down, etched onto the uneven floor, was a circle.

Including two triangles, one upright, the other flipped. Devil worship or some relatable satanic nonsense. Crikey, the number of weirdos in the world hoisting boards, saying, 'the devil is coming-the, the end is near,'. It beggars belief how dedicated they are; this was different. The situation frightened me. Sweat dripped from my face; I frantically spun from side to side.

I lost my sense of knowing what to do. The more I looked, the more I saw horrifying symbols on the walls that I didn't know. Being a betting man, I would say religious—taking me back to the earlier thoughts of devil worship. Jars upon jars stacked on shelves containing liquid, and... well... They were harvested organs and preserved.

'*Hhhhheeeeellllp,*'

'Der-dum, der-dum, der-dum, der-dum,'

My heart was thumping two to the dozen through my ears. The whisper cut across my horror, reminding me why I'd stepped downstairs. Only I got hit with the urge to walk away. To skip through the dirt and break away as quickly as I could. What if the voice was a trap? I was lured to my death by the actual killer. Who'd hung around knowing the attention would come? It's a twisted thought but was not inconceivable.

Suppose the blooming angel had put down its pint long enough to slap the devil senseless? I would've stayed out. The voice could be a survivor in need of saving. My ears home in, following the beacon. Splash after splash of dried blood ripped across the floor. The further I shuffled, the more the blood looked like rounded prints, bouncing a ball in the paint—a glance at the bodies. Where were the heads? I could hear the clunking of chains. No more candlelight, relying on my senses to guide me.

A shuffle across the dirty floor made me pause. My eyes focus on the silhouette of a tiny figure—the size of a child — matching the spooky whisper for help. I took a small step forward, wary of what may lurk in the darkness. A slight haze of red pierced the blackness, eye-shaped. My feet stuck to the floor; I felt a draft whistling past my neck, sending a wave of goose pimples rippling over my body. I was well out of my comfort zone; the bodies were one thing, but an animal with red glowing eyes that's another. I daren't speak; life experience hadn't prepared me for anything like this.

I should stop and radio dispatch with an update. What would I say? How could I explain? The fire was a crime scene; what I'd found in the basement was a murder investigation. They needed to know about the bodies. A niggling feeling deep inside was urging me to wait. To find out more. To understand what the red glow and the whisper belonged to, even if it was nothing good. Fighting off the chill of fear, I shuffled forward some more. My foot scuffs, rattling debris across the floor. It was a spare old candlestick holder. The kind that belonged on a mantlepiece. Thankfully, the candle was still intact.

What happened twenty-five years ago.

CHAPTER 14

'Morris 17th February 1962.'

The light is dimly flickering, my path easier to navigate. I'd always been quite clumsy; some would say two left feet. I carried my body awkwardly, making stealth attempts even more troubling. My mother would say I was like a bull in a China shop,' if a China shop worked out of a dingy basement, in a house that was on fire and had a scary voice calling for help. I would agree because I couldn't turn, step, or stand up fully without bumping or bashing into a pillar or fragile-sounding rack.

  The further through I got, I could hear banging upstairs. Footsteps were my first thoughts, the water fairies winning their battle. Whatever the case, I didn't have long to grasp the situation, spraying my little light forward, creeping carefully towards the red in the darkness. The daunting glow would come and go, in tune with blinking eyes yet longer gaps.

  '*Hhhheeeellllppp,*'

  A young whisper with gravel to it. I'd got within a few feet, letting the flame dance, only to get the fright of my life. A body, same as the others, all burnt and crusty. A char-grilled shell crouched over. The chains I'd heard earlier clamped onto the wrists of the body dug in deep. Hanging limply from a thick brown splintered pillar eroded over years of bearing the weight of a home and its family. No matter what they were. It was small, the size of a child, older than my Rosalind, but not by much. Maybe five or six years. I could feel my earlier beef stew working its way up. My mouth took on the bitter early warning saliva, and I fought hard to stop the wrenching. Yet, all I wanted to do was spray my guts everywhere. My head was dwelling on Rosalind. I was staring at someone else's dead child.

Bending for a closer look...

'*Hhhhheeellllppp,*'

The whisper rocks me on my heels. The head turns, the sound of solid burnt flesh crunching in my ears, and that red haze returns and beams straight in my face. Dam near blinded me. What the hell was I looking at? How was it still able to move? Rational thinking fell by the wayside. My body was on autopilot, using instinct to help regardless.

'*Hhhheeeelllppp,*'

The whisper was coming from the burnt, child-sized shape. Emotions I shouldn't have crept in. Pain and sadness for someone or something I didn't know, only that I pictured my Rosalind in their place. Looking over their body, I could see the severity of the burns; no one could survive. The burning would resonate deep within; blood and flesh would boil, bursting through scorched cracks in the skin.

How could this one muster the strength to call for help, not once, but many times? Why were the eyes red? Too many questions for my little pea brain to handle. Why did they still have their head, unlike the rest? Searching for anything to remove the chains, whatever ounce of life the child was clinging to wouldn't last long. From experience, I'd witnessed casualties with far less damage, last mere minutes. There was no telling how long ago this massacre happened or if it related to the fire upstairs. Hanging on a rusty nail embedded into the wall were a pair of bolt cutters, looking as though they'd snap in two rather than cut anything.

"It's ok; I will get you help." Shaking, I attempted to sound optimistic, albeit in dire circumstances. What else could I say? Hang on in there; all be alright? I couldn't. Too much had happened already; lies didn't need to make it worse.

The chains hit the floor with a heavy clunk. The body tumbled sideways, looking fused by the roasted flesh. I froze, clutching the cutters, the rust biting my skin as I held them tight. I could feel it, and I didn't mind. The slight stinging kept me lucid. Realising I didn't know what to do next. My brain had checked out, eyes swivelling left to right, taking in the horrors, having overcome one hurdle, the next trickier. The haunting of death was in the air, the smell of decomposing flesh carried by the wind rushing through the open doors.

The gloom smothered me, so thick and spooky I half expected one of the other bodies to stir, headless. I wouldn't rule anything out if it was possible for the small one. Besides, I've seen zombie films coming back to eat brains. They wouldn't get much from me, but it wouldn't be for the lack of trying. I needed something to cover 'red eyes' to carry them safely.

Viewing the blood-dripped circle on the wall as if it were the first time again. Slightly fresh eyes, it seemed familiar somehow, but I couldn't think why. Underneath was an old carpenter's workbench, used for many things other than cutting wood. My candle flickered toward its surface, casting shimmers across several small puddles of blood. The vice spun tight, gripping a bony appendage. Crusty, rotting away with the stem of a wrist poking out past the metal jaws.

I spun on the spot to check if the other dead were missing anything other than their heads. If I were to guess, it came from someone older, maybe forties. It wasn't from them, which had me wondering what the 'Conrad Family' was into. There was no escaping that sickly feeling. My only reprieve would be to get the small body to safety and let the plonkers in flashy suits handle the rest. I'm sure they would be equally stumped as I was. How they would explain away the religious-like circle on the floor with the surrounding dead was anyone's guess. Nobody was putting the pieces together after I stumbled upon a minor incident in a larger picture.

I may well be a gobby probationer. I had enough common sense to see through the bullshit when someone was trying to make things appear different from what they were. A fire started at a point in the house, not near the dead. While they seem to have been in the basement longer than a day, there's the survivor; how? The house had me spooked, and I didn't want to hang around any longer. Sifting through some boxes, I found an old dust sheet. Dirt in the wounds was the least of the problems.

'*Hhhheeeelllllpppp me,*'

A shiver rushed down my spine; the whisper came again. I clutched the sheet in one hand and the cutters in the other. Not wanting to let go. Not knowing what to expect next, the cutters could be handy should the need arise. Only this time, it sounded close, too close. My throat became a gravel driveway. The wind was whistling through; I thought the words carried. That was my fear of talking; deep down, I knew it wasn't possible. Nor would it be possible for the body to move closer; it shouldn't be moving at all.

Yet, what should and shouldn't be possible seemed out of the window. Was it even human? The voice had to be, but the red eyes weren't normal. I went to shuffle forward, hands full, and the candle left in place of the sheet, meaning I couldn't see too far in front. A deadweight crunches onto my leg. I thought a dog bite at first was the only rational explanation. Barely keeping upright, I drop the cutters in the dust.

My trouser leg rips. I can feel it tugging, and the flesh of my calf tears through, sending searing pain through my body. Panicking, I'm caught in two minds, freezing up with tears dripping from my eyes. Should I reach for the cutters or stretch behind for the candle? The footsteps upstairs creaked louder. But so did my speeding heart. In the background were the faint echoes of more sirens. I'd turned my radio down, so I wasn't up to date with any calls or if someone had been trying to raise me.

Though I wondered if the water fairies found anything else. With the candle in hand and burning pain in my calf, I shone it downwards, getting the shock of my life for the second time in one night. A char-grilled black arm is hanging from my lower leg. I could see the brutality of their burns so much clearer. Head to toe, like crispy bacon. Bright, bubbling pink fluid seeped through cracks in some areas, while in others, there were craters down to the bone. The pain in my leg was worsening, burning, and I could see why.

Fingers, well, more like claws. They were buried deep and holding on, blood spurted free. All hair and clothing were gone, incinerated by fire, and all I could see was another dead body in waiting. Morbid as it sounds, that's what I thought. They didn't stand a chance. Then I felt the same about the chances of moving. The head spookily spins, cracking the burnt flesh further, twisting up my neck; Ruby-red eyes glared my way. So deep, so consuming, I was swimming in two pools of dark red. Creepily soothing. They were so intensely hypnotic that I could almost sense the pain seeping through; they wanted to reveal everything they'd endured—their innermost, darkest secrets. I willed to listen.

'*Save me,*'

Chills, yet I had to try. When I noticed the other hand, the sheet was about to be draped over its body. Claws, a bear? Or a dog? These were dripping with blood and not their own. That's the nearest I could compare after initially thinking I'd been bitten by one. Torn between common sense and the notion that this child could be a terrifying beast, I didn't know what to do. Police officers aren't equipped mentally or physically to handle such farfetched scenarios. But that's what I was thinking of, and fear. That the world as I knew it was far scarier. Although a nightmare for another day.

I spread the sheet while struggling with the pain. Its hand withdrew and flopped to the floor, leaving behind blood trickles, pressing and tucking the sheet around the body, breathing in the putrid stench oozing from its wounds, gagging, longing to taste the freedom outside. The hard skin beneath my touch felt brittle; I worried about causing further damage if that was possible. Fully covered, I hoisted the body up to my chest. Take another look at the sadistic basement of horrors. The red glow drifted away as the eyelids closed. The body was light, and I could still grip the candle.

I stepped forward through the jungle of death; my leg ached slightly. While I could not shake the distinct feeling of being watched. And not by any of those making noise upstairs. It made me on edge, even more so than the horrors. Praying in my mind that who or whatever I was holding would survive. My palms pressed firmly against the fragile frame, allowing me to feel a beating heart. It was faint, but they were hanging in there.

The closer I got to the steps, the stronger the breeze felt—a welcomed rush of damp air, only for a sudden, sharp gust to whoosh through, rocking me back in my heels. It whipped around the death chamber with precision and ferocity. Killing each flame that dared be in its path, including the one in my hand.

The whistling was louder, haunting—almost a howl, stranded in darkness. I could barely catch a shard of moonlight as its low glimmer broke through the entrance. Not enough to guide my way. So, scuff after scuff, I slid through the dirt, kicking up dust, hoping my toes would stub the bottom step at some point. That was my only option unless I wanted to wait and see if anyone popped down to help.

'Don't do it... Unless it's death you seek,'

My body went numb; I couldn't move. To be so close to freedom and get stopped dead by a deep, stomach-churning growl of a voice. The air around turned arctic. Each word rumbled through the air like thunder. My ears twitched, pinpointing where it started, and life slowly came back into my limbs. I shouldn't look, but my frightened curiosity was getting better.

There's a saying I like, 'know thy enemy,' and I needed to put a face to the fear I was feeling. My shaking hands gripped the fragile shell; my terrified head slid to the right.

"Wwhhoo are you? I'm not here for trouble, but they need my help," Struggling to summon the courage of my conviction, words trickled out of my mouth as lifeless as the body I was holding. Taking over my leg and not stopping there. I felt that burning in my calf, steadily moving upwards. The sweat rained down, feeling my body temp suddenly skyrocket. My stomach churned and knotted.

"Don't worry about me; I doubt you'll be alive long enough to be of consequence. You people live your lives, so two dimensional ever stopped to think the world may not belong to you? Trouble? And yet, trouble seems to have found you."

"Then who does it belong to? Who am I holding?"

"Are you that naïve? Who created the campfire stories? It's always been there, that fear of what goes bump...in the night,"

"Stories are fictional thoughts to amuse those interested. So, what are you trying to say?" Feeling as though my backside had fallen out.

"That life as you know it will change, and the boy is nothing more than a glimpse,"

"I don't want any part of that. No trouble. I only wanted to help this... a boy, you say?"

"A boy. The beginning. An experiment. Many things that, by the looks of it, he's nearly dead." Every word was terrifyingly grating, rumbling through the air. My soul was fighting to check out. While the blood surging through my veins boiled. I should make a dart for it, but with the pain consuming, I wouldn't have made it far.

"Maybe if I leave now, we can still save the boy. And trouble can forget I was ever here? I'm a nobody. I can safely be oblivious to my two-dimensional world and not say anything." Thinking it was so farfetched, who would believe me anyway? Fully turned to where I'd picked the body up, I was back, staring into the black abyss. Only to have my throat shredded to pieces by dryness. Coming from the furthest point in the room was another pair of darker, blood-curdling red eyes. They had to be at least seven feet in the air. I was damn near the verge of pissing myself—a deathly red in the darkness.

CHAPTER 15

'17th February 1962.'

The wailing of sirens ground to a stop, and creaking floors above cause dust to fall through the slither of moonlight as it thrust forward down the stairs. The wind continued to whistle, keeping the hairs on my arms honest and to attention. At first, adrenaline played tricks on my body, but that soon changed, moving my leg. That surge of searing pain continued to spread; the source had been left numb. Realising it had become dead weight.

No feeling, just a means to keep me upright, barely happening. I couldn't take my stare away from those damming red eyes. Not quite feeling hypnotised, but an intriguing lure about them. Fear can make a person do strange things, and the human body reacts. If I was going to be killed, I might as well be facing forward instead of taking a cheap shot to the back, hobbling my way up.

The distance between us deceived me; if I guessed, it was at least fifteen, maybe twenty feet of darkness. The red eyes swayed side to side, tilting headlights. I was thinking about what to do next. It had been so sure about me not being alive long enough to be of consequence. I had landed in a trap, baited with the dead and one almost joining them. My heart raced with loud thumps through my eardrums. Could red eyes hear it, too? A no-win situation and I had to inhale the nauseating stench of charred flesh while waiting to see if I would knock on heaven's door.

"How does it feel?" the terrifying voice broke the silence.

"Cuh, Cuh. How does what feel?" figuring it somehow knew of my wound.

"Don't play dumb. Do you think I can't smell it? That I can't smell you? You are simply dripping with intoxication," That was the problem; I didn't know what to think.

"I'm not. But I can't say what you could do because I don't know who or what you are," Shaking, stating the obvious. While hoping to be given a hint.

"The toxins are coursing through your veins; his claws penetrated and tore deep enough to muddy your bloodstream. So young and has no control. You will beg for mercy," making me look at my leg even though I couldn't see it, poisoned by the thing I was carrying. The thing referred to as 'he and boy.'

My eyes quickly shifted upwards, about to ask if there was anything I could do, not wanting to die. A few tears rolled free at the thought of losing control of my fate; looking ahead, the red eyes vanished. Twisting my body left and right. Feeling on the edge of paralysing fear. I had to try; maybe it left me alone. Letting the toxins do the job, drifting through my body. I was burning from the inside to out, in agony. I'd experienced a gunshot before, and that didn't compare.

Jabbing my good leg forward, scuffing across the hard floor, I attempted to drag my other leg along for the ride. I felt a rush of air zip past my cheek, about to pivot toward the steps. It wasn't the whistling wind I'd been used to; no, sharp, sudden and with spooky precision. It served as a reminder that I hadn't been left alone.

Frantic gasps for breath, straining my eyes to see anything that could help or give me hope. It happened again, this time on the other cheek. I was being toyed with like a cat caught by a mouse and wanted a little fun before tearing its prey to shreds. I'd become prey. Was that the fate of the headless foursome? Then again, it wouldn't explain what's in my arms.

Then nothing. An eerie silence bounced around in the darkness. Other than the persistent pounding of my heart. I slid my palm carefully through the sheeted back of the boy in my arms, barely feeling a heartbeat and out of rhythm. More worrying was the heat steadily rising. Barely clinging to life, the body felt different. The fragile, burnt carcass underneath felt a little thicker, becoming heavier and scaring me even more.

'*Ssssssssmmmmmmmm,*'

"My, my, my. Your fear is intoxicating. So vibrant and overpowering that I can almost taste it. In fact, why don't I do just that? Save you from... well, from you," Out of nowhere, I feel the scorching warmth of breath ruffle my hackles like a hurricane—bouncing up close behind—bringing the sickening stench of blood. I was trapped, scared shitless by an intimidating presence I couldn't see. Each word tore strips of flesh off my neck. I could feel it drifting closer—heavy, gravelled breathing.

"Do you feel it yet? The burning? The searing pains. Every fibre in your body is pulling apart while your blood boils to the point of melting your brain, and you die,"

"What? Why? It's just a scratch," Mind games to get me guessing or begging for help.

"A scratch? Oh no, their claws sunk in. They wanted more power. To feed off fear dripping in the darkness. That's why I'm here,"

"Who are they? Who are you?" Allowing my fear to drip.

"The door got opened. Now there's no closing it. Instead, a mistake happens, and the only way to fix it is to burn everything down,"

The voice was terrifying, and I did not know what it could be. Yet, putting my fear of being ripped to shreds aside for a moment. I felt sorry for it, even if I didn't know how much to believe. Struggling with the pain spreading and boiling, I almost felt my veins throbbing. Was this it? Was I nearing the end?

"If this is it, and I'm dying too. Can you give me a proper answer? What am I holding?"

"To the world, he's a child. Underneath? Well, that belongs in your nightmares,"

My hands shook; what had I done? Why didn't I leave it be? Too wrapped up in my need to help and do good. I should've realised something wasn't right with the other bodies.

"I... I... I need to go... I need to go to the hospital."

As my breathing became shallow, I felt like my body was getting weaker. The fiery breath drifted closer, singing the peach fuzz on the tips of my lobes. Another gush of air swished past my neck; I could sense a presence gliding in front of my face. I couldn't see a thing but felt it was a hand or, as it said a claw. With the sound of fingers rubbing together, I held as still as possible, trying not to breathe.

"Or I could end you now? Save all the pain. I could rip your throat out in a second. Or I will leave you to it? See if you survive the night," it growled by my ear.

I was a terrified, shaking mess. Tensing up, I closed my eyes, praying it would be over quickly. I could hear a flurry of raised voices—Sounding near the basement entrance. Clenching the body in one arm close to my chest, I slipped the other hand down to my side, feeling for my radio.

With the voices sounding so close, I figured on turning up the p. r, hoping it would draw attention to my way, scaring off whatever was behind me. If I could get help, then what would I say? The child turns out to be evil; what do I do? I had to do something; I was holding a living thing. My forefinger skimmed the stubby black dial at the top of my radio, sending a loud echo of screeching voices into the gloomy basement of death.

The wind whipped past. Along with the fire and brimstone breath, the presence disappeared. The flaming red eyes had gone. That had been caressing my skin with the subtlety of a sledgehammer. Feeling on the verge of turning blue, I finally let go of my lungs, releasing the moments of panic oxygen I'd stored in anticipation.

Relief, confusion and fear were battering me. I could barely keep upright, with the pain becoming all too much. My life is cradled in someone else's hands. That's the best I could assume, hands. To acknowledge anything else would shatter my sense of reality. Although those haunting eyes were doing a fine enough job as it was. That, and the carcass, felt heavier by the minute.

'*Who's down there?*' I hear a voice hollering down the steps; great timing, too.

"Officer Morris, quick, I need help; there's a horror house down here. I have one survivor," I called back, struggling to breathe and get my words out. Toxins were running a mock, and I was scared.

I stumbled backwards onto the steps, almost dropping the body, clinging to the sheet with my fingertips. Perhaps having my throat ripped out would've been mercy, saving me from the pain rampaging. 'If I survived the night,' those words flickered in the deep reaches of my mind as I felt my life ebbing away. The hard corners of the wooden steps dug into my back; I was dead weight, draped halfway up. Looking up at the worn-down beams, I used my last moments to savour the details. Everything suddenly became different, not enough to stop me from noticing the symbols carved across the main support.

Latin. 'Porta Ad Inferos,' Doorway to hell. Old red eyes did mention, in between scaring me shitless, that the people that lived here opened a doorway. A doorway to what or where? So much for everything being black and white.

I could barely keep my lids from flapping shut; a flurry of hands grappled at my arm, pulling me from the sheet. I clung on in every sense. Help separated us, and I got hit by a sudden rush of fear. The sheet slid open as it got dragged away, revealing a perfectly normal-looking child. No death-bringing burns or red eyes. No sign of anything wrong.

Other than some dirt brushed across bare skin. My body skipped across the steps to be hoisted into a waiting hospital bed. I slumped back, eyes flickering, capturing the blood oozing from my leg and then to the sheeted child dumped on another bed. The rain had eased, leaving a sobering chill in the air. Not enough to keep me lucid. Did I see right? He had healed; my eyes shut with that last thought while my body felt on fire.□

What happened twenty-five years ago.

CHAPTER 16

'17th February 1962,'

Bright lights beamed all around; this was the moment of my exit, seeing foggy silhouettes of figures stepping closer. Were they coming to guide me? A jumbled mess, believing I hadn't survived the night. Regret, sadness, and anger were all paying a visit because, deep down, I didn't deserve to go out the way I had. Surviving gunfire and a stabbing in a past life, only to come up short in the next, making it a fraction through probation.

"Officer Morris. Officer Morris. You're finally with us," I hear, breaking through my brain.

The white light got brighter, beaming directly into my eye. Good job; I didn't need them anymore, as I was damn near blind.

"Officer Morris, can you hear me?"

"Erm... yeah. So, is it up or down?" In a state of confusion.

"Pardon? up or down?"

"Yes. Fluffy clouds or hellfire?"

"What? Where do you think you are?"

"I'm dead, right? About to meet my maker or the bastard below?" Trying to read the puzzled tone of the responding voice.

"Right, well, any plans for that have been put on hold, thankfully. It was touch and go but a course of our strongest antibiotics. Fifteen stitches, and you are sleeping through, helping you live to fight another."

The foggy silhouette subsided, and I stared at an older gentleman dressed in a white doctor's coat. He sounded posh or at least had an expensive education. No doubt a 'geek' or 'bookworm'. Endless hours of study. Rather than partying. And fair play to the doc because it's got him in front of me, lashing my face with a torch. Very wiry. He was no bigger than five feet eight yet looked taller owing to a skinny frame with his coat draped off like a hanger.

He was parading a balding dome, making the light brighter as it bounced off the shiny, smooth runway to his forehead. The saving grace was the rough thoroughfare wrapped around the skirting above his ears, something to hold the arms of his thin-framed spectacles in place. They made him look sophisticated, even if he peered his brown eyeballs over the top.

"Crap. The boy? There was a boy; where is he?"

My head finally cleared, allowing the panic to come flooding back. The Doctor flicked off his torch and stopped upright before stepping closer to the side of my bed. He scribbled on his clipboard, making sure he avoided eye contact—wanting to avoid the question. An intoxicating waft of blood drifted through the air, causing my mouth to swim with drool, a lust like no other. I wanted to taste it.

No, I needed to placate an incredible thirst aided by an insatiable hunger. But why? What brought this overpowering sensation? Perhaps the side effect of the strong antibiotics. I could go around in circles, guessing, but the lure drove me crazy.

"The boy is hanging on by a thread. He's flatlined twice in the night. Not to mention the convulsions he's endured. And has a resting body temperature that's off the charts. In medical terms, he should be dead at least two times over,"

The Doctor perched himself on the side of my bed. He gave me a long stare this time, waiting for my response. Perhaps he thought I could shed some light on the situation.

How could I? When it hadn't sunken in yet? It didn't stop me from smiling, relief that the boy and I had survived. The odds on me alone were knout all, with those haunting red eyes still drifting in the blooming darkness of my mind. It toyed with me. The notion of 'doorway to hell.' It would've been farfetched not so long ago.

Now, I'm nursing a deep claw wound and a ferocious hunger that is getting greater by the minute. What was wrong with me? Why was I feeling like this? I could taste the sweetness of blood in my mouth, dragging my tongue heavily across the underside of my teeth—an unusual sharpness.

My eyes narrowed, becoming fixated on the Doctor's jugular; every breath, swallow, or word caused the clean-shaven skin to tremble slightly. The overhead fluorescent lighting painted a teasing pale complexion of the carotid artery. A vibrant, juicy artery full of blood made it hard to resist, pouncing forward and ripping it open with my bare hands.

I was scared for myself and the Doctor. Feel a savage lust for inflicting pain at levels I've not known before. Even in the Marines, I always had a sense of compassion and control, but this was different. I was experiencing a raw, unadulterated need to shred through flesh.

"Is he being watched?"

"What? By police? No. But Social services should make an appearance by night-time. For what it's worth. At this rate, it could be a trip to the" The Doctor displayed a deep 'I don't give a fuck,' look.

That was a look I wish I could relate to. That's not me. Instead, I picture my daughter Rosalind. That once char-grilled child may still have parents somewhere, depending on his circumstances, ending up in care. I kept my mind on that, pushing the lust back into its box for the time being. His words caused some panic, though, if no one was watching. Those people may come for him. Not that I'm sure anyone would know he survived.

"Doc... Has anyone else been by? Paying interest in him?" Hoping he gave the all-clear.

"Not as far as I'm aware. But I've had a busy day so far. I'll get a nurse to check on him soon. Why? What's wrong?" The doc allowed an ounce of concern.

"Thank you. The boy is the sole survivor of a suspicious house fire; I'm worried about his safety if the suspects had set it on purpose. Someone may come for him,"

Ensuring I stopped short of talking about the dead bodies. Doing so made me wonder how the investigation was getting on—surprised that I could see no other officers loitering nearby. Whatever the circumstances, there should be a guard on either of us for continuity until I blooming woke.

"Anyway, how are you feeling? All your recent tests have been fine, quite remarkable considering how you looked through the night. So, we should clear you to leave in a few hours. All being well,"

"Yeah, I'm ok, be back cartwheeling before I know it. Could murder a cuppa, though. Help knock the rust off,"

I didn't dare speak the truth. The doc's face would be a picture if I told him how I felt. My urge to rip his throat out and taste his blood instead of tea. That and every sense has been ramping up quicker than the church passing the collection box around. Throughout our chit-chat, my ears kept pricking up to the noise in the background.

The faint whispers in the hallway. Or older lady ten beds to my left, whose heart is beating out of rhythm and loudly. To me, at least. I needed to get home and lay in a quiet, dark room until everything settled. I knew what was happening, and I didn't like it. I was losing control and felt it best if I was somewhere less busy. So, I was going to lie my arse off.

"Ok. You need to be on antibiotics for the next seven days. The wound wasn't pretty. I would say that I haven't seen anything like it as bites go; teeth marks don't match anything I've seen. We took samples, and a closer look showed micro-organisms thriving within the fluid forming around the cuts. Judging by the damage to the muscle, you could have a slight, permanent limp."

His words had me lost; biology was never my strong point, but if the child was anything to go by. Perhaps it meant I healed quicker like the boy did—a thought best kept in my head. Instead, I stared blankly and looked dumb, which wasn't far from my usual demeanour. My mum used to say I wasn't blessed with much other than being able to look stupid. Which was ok as long as I wasn't.

"Sorry, Doc, small words and short sentences for me, please."

"Right. The wound got infected. But instead of making you sick and causing the possibility of gangrene. Your body heat and the surrounding ooze began healing the wound, repairing soft tissue far quicker than usual."

The pain at the time was excruciating, yet the Doctor claimed I was being healed. And that warning rang in my ears. Why did it feel like I was dying?

"Why was I out cold?"

"I don't know. Your temperature spiked to double the safe levels for an adult too. I hate to say it, but what's happening with you and the child? Is a little out of my league. I've sent your swabs, bloodwork and a tissue sample to one of the top labs in the country to analyse. I figure you would want answers,"

The Doctor was coming across as keener than a hooker in Soho. His curiosity may have improved, but to get his mits on samples to send off, he was worried or another sneaky bastard. Suspicious of everyone, trusting no one and hating the world, that's me, hopefully, over nothing.

"That's fine, doc. Shouldn't I sign a release or at least get a brew? All seriousness, don't you need consent?" I was bluffing my way around a subject I knew knout about; it sounded plausible; what if my blood suddenly became the one-stop shop for all of life's ills? They'd want me dissected like a lab rat.

"That's unnecessary; it's routine. We must rule out anything serious. Got to be careful about spreading infectious diseases. Then we will contact you back in for a follow-up on the stitches; by that time, the results should be back,"

I kept his words hanging in the air, replaying them repeatedly. While my ears home in on his frantic heartbeat and accelerated breathing. Telltale signs of worry, and to me, worrying signs the doc didn't have my best interest. I pushed the right buttons, and my scary level of hearing was picking up on either the sneaky, or he was bat-shit scared. If this were a sign of things to come. I wouldn't be disappointed.

"Anything, in particular, you guys testing for? A dose of the plague was last week" I tried easing the tension; all I could hear was the bellowing of saliva before he went to speak. His eyes glanced left and right as two other white coats walked past. He leant forward, a coffee drinker, stifling my air. He was about to share a secret.

"Well, we must test and cross-reference with any known animals with healing antibodies. A wolf, maybe?" The doc had my full attention like I had his.

What happened twenty-five years ago.

CHAPTER 17

Sgt Morris 17th February 1962,'

It was good if that was a stab in the dark, for a guess. A claw-like hand buried into my flesh, and from the doctor, who said it was out of his league. A wolf made my wound, and I couldn't wait to hear his thoughts on the boy. There was no waver in his voice, no stutter or rapid breathing. He was confident in what he was suggesting. Which told me he knew more than he was letting on. I don't like slimy gits like that.

"Your guess is as good as mine; a tonne was going on. I have two left feet and am clumsier than a toddler on ice. I thought I'd stumbled into a rake or pitchfork. Only, within minutes I was sick as a dog," trying not to elaborate too much. Hoping my vagueness would quell the Doc's trip down the animal lane. The more we spoke about it, my mind drifted back to the moment. Having my fear seep from my pores. I never wanted to feel that vulnerable again—fear paralysis.

"Oh. Is that a politically correct answer? Toeing the party line. I see. Well, you and I both know what it is. Don't we?" There it was; the sneaky Doc dropped the act; I knew he'd show up, eventually. The corners of his mouth crept into a smile. His eyes shone like a kid in a sweet shop. Too excited at the thought, putting me on edge and shuffling backwards in my bed.

"That's all I remember. Come to think of it, have any of my friends been by? Looking for updates?" bugged that nobody else was here. Wherever here was, I knew I was in the hospital, but not which one.

"One or two. They asked me to call your station when you re-joined the land of the living,"

Doctor slippery was now interrogating my leg. He had peeled back the thickly packed dressing, exposing the air to the stitches; a slight tingle ran through my leg. His hand dropped from blocking my view; his mouth hung open in disbelief. Peering down, I saw it too; my leg had healed, leaving remnants of dried blood and scraps from the suture stitches resting on the skin, serving a little purpose.

His face moved to within inches in case his eyes were betraying him. A little too close for my liking. Only, I had the feeling that soon enough, I would be the one being crossed.

"Hey, Doc, what's the verdict? Am I losing it?" I was waiting for the bullshit to flow; he's probably thinking he's gonna win a Nobel prize or Pulitzer, whatever the blooming term is.

"Lucky for you, no. But I'm afraid you've become a medical anomaly that I wouldn't feel comfortable releasing you back into the public just yet. For your safety and the safety of others,"

Grinning like a Cheshire cat. My hackles perked up, dancing in the sterile air. My blood boiled like a teapot I wished I was using, sweat running down my cheek. The hospital ward was now a sauna—my eyes shifted from smugness to staring at the pulsating veins in my arm, becoming engorged, watching the muscles twitch and expand. The rage was back, bringing the pain I felt in the basement.

'Click, click, click,'

The sound from my hand resting on the bed grew; each bone was excruciatingly moving, breaking and changing. Broken bones were plenty as a nipper into all sorts of crap. This was worse. Blood spat from the edges of my nails. Dark black claws slowly and painfully edged from under my nails. I quickly hid it under my bedsheet and fought hard to control what was happening. My urge to kill him roared sky-high. He had to move before I lost my fight and the Doc, his life.

"Whatever you say, doc," Shocking myself with a slight growling edge. He didn't flinch. Instead, he minced his way over to a nearby reception desk. A good thirty to forty feet to my right. He was making a phone call while checking in my direction. He had to be talking about me, fuelling my rage.

'*Derdum derdum derdum derdum derdum derdum,*'

My heart beat rapidly, trying to focus. To see if I could control the situation and my fate, fighting hard to slow the beats down and quiet the brewing fire. My ears twerked to the doctor and who he was calling. Hoping it was nothing more than updating the station.

"He's awake. There's been a development. Both survived, and patient B is exhibiting signs as well now. It would be wise if you sent containment. Maybe sooner rather than later. Don't know who's calling the shots," the faint echo of the doc whispering into the handset.

"Finally, some good news. Our sources led us to believe it had failed. Has anything else gone on? A strange visitor came by? Or is anything out of the ordinary happening?"

"What besides him healing completely and the claws growing from his hand? No, nothing strange about that at all," The Doc had his sarcastic hat on. More alarming for me, he had bloody seen. The conversation I heard did little to help keep the anger at bay.

"To make an omelette, doctor, one must break a few eggs. If they have survived, what we trapped in the house has too. Meaning it may seek the cleansing of creations against its will. I will have Two local detectives head your way shortly. Don't worry, they're on the payroll; keep watch and be careful,"

The voice on the end of the phone knew about everything, including what sounded to be 'old red eyes.'

Detectives on the bloody payroll; could it get any worse? Having corrupt coppers after me will make it flipping hard to trust. I'd plugged the genie back in the bottle for the time being, but it was only a matter of time. Whether I could control it was another story. Who were these people on the other end of the phone? They had to have some clout behind them to line the pockets of those willing to turn a blind eye or join their cause.

Whatever that may be. My leg healed, so there was no reason to stay. In my mind, at least. I kept watching for a moment until the doctor disappeared out of sight. Flopping off the bedding to see I was butt naked under the hospital gown. I had no clothes or shoes; I checked the side cupboard, but nothing. Where were my kit belt and PPE?

Slowly shuffling past my curtain, my feet braving the cold sky-blue linoleum floor. I didn't want to draw attention to myself, trying to tread carefully and quietly. Under the bed next door, was a pair of brown slip-on sandals. They looked a little small, but the heel was open-ended. I barely broke stride, slipping past, jamming my fat-size tens in each one quickly before moving on. No one was paying attention in an otherwise busy ward. I'd made it to the hallway when I noticed a lurker-. He stood out from the rest, leaning against the wall with no particular purpose. At least six foot three, maybe four, dressed all in black with long, dark, wavy hair, looking a little menacing.

The hallway was long, with a million doors left and right. All too confusing, making me need a floor map or a sign to point me in the right direction; I couldn't leave the boy. Halfway down, there was a large floor listing with arrows. The sign above said 'Welcome to Royal London Hospital,'.

At least I knew where I was. Second-floor 'Children's ward.' All for self-preservation, but the kid was just that, a kid. He had to be there unless, by bizarre circumstances, he'd been quarantined off, which wouldn't be a stretch considering the worries over infections. My blue-white floral gown would stand out without eye contact with anyone as I walked by. I didn't need to get dragged into a conversation; that would only hold me up.

Giving time for the doctor to return to my bed and notice I was gone. No doubt landing, him in hot water with his secret employers. Not that I cared for the bald git. He made his bed; he could lie in it. The drama would follow, security guards on alert, and my walk would become a sandal-attempted run. I'd got as far as a sky-blue-painted corridor branched off with a set of brown double doors and a staircase that would take me to the floor I needed. I wasn't going to chance the lifts; that would only have me trapped.

Being careful not to stand out, I couldn't shake a strange feeling I was being followed. Slowing down as I neared a vending machine, using the glass to look behind me. Sure enough, the tall bloke in black. Even his reflection looked intimidating. My hackles were up but seemed unusual. Yet, I lingered, getting a sense of familiarity I didn't understand.

Had I come across him on a call or in passing somewhere else? I was about to walk on when I caught a glimpse—a quick flash of light. Red. At first, I thought it came from the machine, but I took a quick double-take and caught it in time. A death ran down my back; the eyes haunted me. That's how it felt, something I never wanted to see again in those horrifying red eyes. It was brief, but they belonged to the tall stranger. It was too dark to know how he looked in the basement; now, I have him to worry about.

Self-conscious, I continued, coming across an expensive-looking machine standing outside a room—the type used for monitoring the body's vitals. The room gave a patient more privacy, especially with a bigger family. Draped over the side was a white coat with a name tag attached. A doctor's coat. With a quick flick, I pinched the coat and slipped it on. Seeing a chance to blend and lose my follower or anyone else that came my way.

'Doctor Preston' was the name on the badge, making me wonder if it was a man or a woman. Either way, it would have to do. I ducked behind a magazine stand near the hospital shop, looking between the racks; my follower strode into view. He stood imposingly, appearing to be sniffing the air. Not a quick sniff, a deep lung-filling inhale. I pity the smells he'll pick up as a guy with a colostomy bag is wheeled past. He had to be on the trail of my scent, which terrified me.

My body was soaked in turmoil and sweat. I could feel the blood brewing, yet I was scared shitless. How close that thing came last time. The presence in front of my bloody face with the threat to rip out my throat. That reminds me, boy, do I need a cuppa. My hand clung to the wiry rack, steadying myself with the pain.

The claws grew, one by one, shredding through fingertip skin, causing spurts of blood. I needed to move on before anyone else saw a few doors down was a 'store room', and it wasn't closed. Perhaps I could hide in there; he might give up and go, but it is highly unlikely. Or he may go looking for the boy. I couldn't let that happen, but I needed to be more conspicuous to get around.

The coat aside, I stood out like a sore thumb; I needed out of the gown first. Sure enough, inside were pile upon pile of different colour scrubs. I grabbed a set of blue ones, just like Baldy had been wearing. Within seconds, I was changed and felt far more secure in my deception and nakedness. I slipped out, drifting amongst the herd, going left and right, overwhelmed by the orgy of smells—no sign of the tall bloke anywhere. I continued to the staircase.

Edging through the door, I slumped against the wall to catch a breather—more relief than exhaustion. Wondering how red eyes had found me. Was he going to finish the job? I had two parties interested and didn't know who I could trust. After hearing that phone call, I wondered who else was on their payroll.

What happened twenty-five years ago.

CHAPTER 18

The claws had carefully retreated, leaving a stinging throb in their place. In contrast, the stomach-churning cranking of bone and twisting muscle pain had gradually subsided. If only I knew how to control what was happening to me, 'It' would take over. I could feel something inside me growing by the minute, a beast trying to take over—a force or freak of nature. Whatever 'It' was.

I was fighting against animalistic rage. We all have a little of that in us, but this is different; another consciousness or side of me wants out. I only have to smell a dribble of blood, and my mouth floods, and it scared me senseless, reaching levels I never knew possible. How much longer could I keep it at bay? I couldn't say.

The scary feeling I didn't have long before everything that makes me what I am gets consumed and taken over. The rational side of my brain becomes a passenger. For now, I'm in the driving seat, nervously trudging my way through the stairwell; every voice, bang or step echoed, spiking my hackles on end. The doc was right about one thing; I had muscle damage, causing me to limp, even though I try not to.

Persistent, nerve-jangling echoes. What if my follower could be whomever he wanted? A farfetched thought drifted into my mind, and so did the attempt to explain how a child left a smouldering, char-grilled shell that was now fully healed. Or my leg, fifteen stitches completely disappeared. How was I even going to explain that to the reprobates at work? They'd be curious about the battle wounds on the front line. Although not as hard to explain as the mental scarring, haunted by images of last night.

They won't go away, seeing those horrifying eyes again. Hoping it was all my imagination, but it was all too terrifyingly real; I couldn't escape them. Even in the window, turning to walk the next flight, I spot a reflection that makes me jump. Frightened, stranded with no clothes or backup, followed by something unexplainable. I glance over my shoulder, but nothing's there. How had it come to this? I found it hard to understand why no officers posted to keep watch.

I've done guard duty for far less—usually a drunken disorderly or an average pub brawl. Yet the survivor of the horror house gets nothing. I was stunned when that sheet flopped to reveal the boy's healed body. The duty officer has protocols to follow and should at least be concerned about the child. Was the entire station paid off? I'm up the creek without a paddle if that's the case. Leaving me with no official avenues to go down, and I wouldn't put my family at risk.

Alone and vulnerable. I had no choice but to protect the kid, approaching the landing for the children's ward, my stomach in knots, dreading the thought of red eyes lying in wait. A chill ruffled across my shoulders.

Hesitating, I hovered my hand near the door, ears twitching, focussing on the other side, filtering through the background noise. Checking for danger, a sense of relief washed over me. I heard nothing other than the sad beeping of machines. Whipping up my collar, I tucked in my chin to hide my face, stepping forward and about to push through when it dawned on me that I was a doctor. A fake one, but a doctor nonetheless. So why don't I try playing the part?

Pretend to be unfamiliar with the building and still finding my way around if I get stopped. Edging through, I spotted a stethoscope hanging from a silver metal trolley. Without skipping a beat, it was soon hanging around my neck. And my deception felt more natural. Looking ahead, I could see four rooms left and right; each had a whiteboard nailed to the wall with writing that I assumed would be the patient's name. Clearing my throat, I grabbed the sides of my coat and stood straighter, attempting to project an air of confidence.

Making me wonder how many had come beforehand. I never knew what the kid was called other than the family meant to reside, 'Conrad'. Were the bodies theirs? Brutal by anyone's standards. To lose their heads and still get burnt was sadistic, even if they were into some weird shit, chaining up a child. The scene confused me. Burnt bodies in a circle, the charred child in chains, all roasted long before the house was on fire. By who? The suspect over the fence? Or the caller from a payphone nowhere near the home.

I was missing information, a key point I couldn't see. As coverups go, it was lousy; why originate the fire on the far-left side with bodies in the basement? I was thinking back to the call. Another fire to go with the spate we'd reported recently. Why would despatch only send me? A single crewed probationer, while knowing an arson pattern was forming. I have life experience but knout on the job.

It didn't add up. Perhaps the whole getting sick and dragged death's door didn't help. But there was a puzzle piece awry. No one is covering the kid and or me. Then there's the call. It was taking the shape of a setup; to what end? The doctor's excitement over my blood and healing was an unexpected bonus.

Had they expected me to do a brief, non-suspicious report and let it get brushed under the carpet with the rest? After all, being a probby, mistakes were to be expected. Right? Or worse? Could they be trying to put a spin on it all? A former marine turned police officer suffering from PTSD goes to a routine call and has a panic attack. The sight of the fire sends the inexperienced officer into an apocalyptic spiral. Killing four family members and leaving fifth fighting for their lives, strapped to machines, helping them breathe.

Even considering such a thing felt beyond the realm of possibility, yet to go back twenty-four hours, the same for growing claws from under my fingernails. Both are chillingly farfetched, yet now I have the dried blood crust on my hands to prove it. The sterile path was eerily calm, a little too so. Was I walking into a trap? If I were Baldy locks, this would have been one first places I checked. So why so quiet? Maybe it's the stench of TCP, people not wanting to be around it, because it sure was singeing my nose hairs.

Reminding me of growing up, my mother was obsessed with hygiene, especially in the kitchen. Each room I passed toyed with my emotions, taking me to the edge of tearing up. Seeing the kids dressed as marionette puppets with tubes and wires hanging out of them was heartbreaking. It made me think of my Rosalind and home. This caused panic to surface again. What if the voice on the phone sent suits to my family after I disappeared? I hadn't yet spoken to anyone, so they may not know I was in the hospital.

The closer I got to the end, the smell changed dramatically, becoming overpoweringly strong. My nostrils flared. The drool swirled around in my mouth, trying to seep through the cracks in my lips. Pain crept back in with every step. A loud clicking bounced around the walls; my hands were taken to the edge of exploding; I had the urge to scream at the top of my lungs, releasing the pressure of a boiling kettle.

The dark black-grey claws slithered painfully forward; blood streamed to the floor. My body was on fire; my fears came true, and I had no control. That smell was intoxicating—the sweet, iron aroma of blood swirled through the air. Someone was dead.

Looking through the glaze of a hazy red mist with my heart thumping ferociously in my chest, I could hear the fiery essence coursing through my veins. I was consumed and feeling ravenous again; the smell had set it off. It hadn't taken much to spark my lust. I wanted to have crimson juices drape over the claws. To feel them shred through flesh as the rage boiled over. These thoughts and feelings conflicted with the rational side.

Especially the police officer part of me, sickened by them but flipping, enduring them. My bones were crunched, moving, and breaking at once. A pulsating beacon. The lure was coming from the last room on the right. Stopping in the doorway, letting the drool rain-free, I could see what had stirred the beast. Flowing towards and across the floor was a large pool of blood. Swimming in the middle was a headless body dressed in a white coat. A doctor.

I look up, and everything suddenly stops. All the pain, the hunger and the rage had disappeared. Quicker than pressing pause on a tape or turning off a light switch. The claws were still out, and my muscles throbbed. But the rest had gone—Allowing my fear to surface with good cause. Standing in front of the window with the low early evening sun shining through, the horrifying silhouette of my nightmares.

The menace from last night—blazing his blood-curdling eyes my way; a chill rippled down my spine. He was holding a decapitated head, parading a trophy. Frayed skin flapped in the air conditioning's breeze, and streams of red juices flowed down.

I recognised the face, the shiny dome of doctor Baldy's locks. The devil in disguise had eliminated a problem but created another. How was I going to explain this? I couldn't; with the blood edging towards my toes, my mind went blank, unable to think of what to do next.

Soon enough, someone would either look for the doc or carry out a routine check on the boy. Yet, the thing that stood before me didn't seem to care. All I knew, being around those red eyes had caused the pain I was going through to slowly ebb, feeling the claws retreating to the sound of curdling jelly.

What happened twenty-five years ago.

CHAPTER 19

My blood cooled, leaving me at a loss to understand how? The blazing stare disappeared, leaving behind a menacing pitch black. That aside, he looked normal, tall and intimidating, but normal.

"Who are you?" Summoning the courage and a voice with the rage easing to break the silence.

"I see you survived the night," he growled; every word made me shudder. Until recently, not much could scare me. He and all of this did.

"Barely. But now, I don't know how to explain it. I feel broken, with an overwhelming urge to kill." Feeling the adrenaline coursing through my veins instead of the fiery rage. My heart was still full throttle.

"You have been lucky; very few humans can handle it. You should embrace it. Surely there are people you would love to cut loose on, ripping to shreds? Or are you the meek and mild type? If that's the case, don't panic. Soon enough, changing will be as normal as putting on that ridiculous white coat."

The venom in his words had my legs trembling; yeah, some people blooming pissed me off. But I'd do knout about it, same for most, I expect. If we all got on, the world would be a boring place. As for changing, that comment had my head spinning.

"Changing? What the heck. You got to be kidding. To what? Are my family at risk?"

"Why spoil the surprise? Your family? They became collateral damage when you got hauled out carrying that boy." displayed a stare that chilled me to the bone. His deep black eyes narrowed at the corners, focussed while bordered by a black-grey beard; his mouth formed a half-smile. Confident intent exuding power.

That terrifying confidence caused the sweat to pool around my brow; my feet shuffled backwards. I was in a moment of regretted changing my mind. I had to leave and get home to my family, meaning I had to abandon the unconscious boy to the menacing beast. He could've killed him already, yet he hadn't. He made a blood river across the floor, dangling the head in the air, showing off. Was I that obvious, or could he sense where I was? Did he stop my pain?

"What do you mean? I haven't spoken to them yet, or anyone."

"That's why I despatched the doctor for you. No, your family will be leveraged. They can't get hold of the boy."

His words rocked me—the dangling of my family on a hook. The thought of my loved ones dragged into the mess made me feel sick. How could I be expected to put an unknown child above my family?

"I...I... I can't; I can't do that. I saved him already. That should be enough. My family need me," Feeling caught in a no-win situation.

"So what? You're going to up and leave? You know I could've killed you, right? I still might. Will you leave the kid at the mercy of those sick bastards? What's stopping me from tearing your throat out right now?"

He flew into a rage. Lunging to lean across the bed, his face moved to within inches of mine. All I could smell was death. Every breath he made filled the air with searing heat and the sickeningly rancid smell of death. It took everything I had to stop from shitting myself there and then.

He could end me at any moment. If I hadn't realised that before, I sure did now. I was a pawn—a means to an end for him to get revenge on those who wronged me. Staring him in those dark black eyes, being that close, told me as much, not to mention the blood-red blaze.

"You're right; Nothing is stopping you, yet I'm still here. Perhaps you need me."

"Maybe your squirming amuses me. The lack of intelligence is surprising, considering your uniform symbolises hope and strength. All I saw last night was weakness and fear. Intoxicating fear of something you didn't understand. -

-And still don't. In the same way, 'they' don't know what they've done. Some are already different, yet want more. Everything you people class has nightmares to justify what you all do and to feel better about it. I ask you, who is the real evil?" He slid his body backwards, his temper easing. He had a point about what we would call and describe scary beasts. The same goes for what I've seen in combat. Who is the real evil? I couldn't answer. Not honestly.

"It's not every day I see something like that. I was expecting a house fire. The rest, I have no answer. Are you going to kill more?" Slowly I was freaking out.

"Who knows? Maybe I will like the chaos and watch you destroy yourselves. I'm here now and not going back. The boy needs to be safe now. He's made it this far," he let loose with a scary, gravel-laden chuckle.

"So, what does that mean? What now?"

"You watch over him. He's only a fledgling right now, but there will come a time and a need greater than now that you will have to be by his side. There's something different about him."

"What do you mean?" Wondering if it could get any worse.

"You'll see. Do you think I was the first attempt at power? A first attempt at reshaping your world?" He looked at the boy, who seemed to breathe heavily and rapidly; his body glistened with sweat.

"Wouldn't it be easier to kill him?" I couldn't believe I was saying it, the words trickling out of my mouth, and I couldn't take them back. But if what he had said was true. Then it may end up being safer for everyone.

"Typical human answer. No. Deep down, that fragile wreck is a child who knows no different and will be confused. Would you kill your child? No. So he's no different,"

"So.. but...I... I am still trying to figure out what to do. Or who to trust, and now, this... this... thing is brewing inside me. I'm scared."

I knew how crazy I sounded. It felt like there were two of us vying for the same body. Anyone would be the same, going through what I was.

"It's not a bloody baby... You need to understand fear is an illusion of the unknown and the inevitable, designed to create excuses for the weak. But you're not weak. Otherwise, your body can't handle the change. So don't let fear control destiny; that thing inside is you, a version of you anyway. Watch over that boy. Or else,"

The smile disappeared, and the eyes suddenly burnt bright red. All I could do was nod and agree. I had no control over my body, leaving my mind a stranded passenger letting his menacing words sink in. Fear was my companion, and no escaping it. The pale bald head clutched in claws had my eyes glued. I hadn't noticed until then. But he had long, thick brown-red claws, different from what I've been producing. They were buried in the skull, using it as a bowling ball. Yet the only thing he would strike was fear deep into the far reaches of my soul.

The head gets tossed through the air with a quick, cartilage-crunching flick. Causing blood to spurt down the coat front. My natural reaction was to catch. Clutching the still warm and completely disgusting head, fighting the urge to be sick, before my hands flung it onto the bedside table.

Looking up, I expected the red eyes, but nothing. The boy seemed so peaceful and helpless. While inside, he is something else; if I were to believe what I heard, so was I. These were unimaginable thoughts, yet they were dancing around in my head. The days of going to a straightforward burglary or robbery could be a distant memory if what he said is true. The idea goes against my upbringing.

Since red eyes had done his vanishing act, leaving me in trouble. My options were limited: stay, get caught and pretend I found the mess. That wouldn't work; they would look for the obvious target, especially if it's someone 'on the payroll'.

Or I could grab a wheelchair from the hallway and take the kid on a little ride. Maybe no one would bat an eyelid, thinking it's a genuine doctor pushing a patient. I was leaning towards this option being the safest, looking at his innocent face as I heard sirens squealing from outside the windows.

The sun was disappearing, making it easier to drift into the darkness once outside. Only where would I take him? I didn't want him around my family. Then the brain cells sprung into life, doing a little happy dance around the emptiness of my mind. There was one place that might help, an old flame that's still a friend.

She would throw me a bone. I've never spoken about her to anyone at work. Life before my wife, so any connections there. An emergency foster carer, from time to time, didn't like the politics and red tape of it all, so she got out unless there was a desperate need. Miss Hannah McCormack. I was desperate.

CHAPTER 20

'Officer Morris 1962,'

The alarms sounded off, and it wouldn't be long before guards were rampaging to the main hospital entrance to be on alert. What the staff had told them to look for was anyone's guess. A chainsaw-wielding maniac covered in blood or a samurai warrior fresh from slicing a head off. While all it took was a set of razor-sharp claws attached to a six-foot-two beast in a skin suit.

Facedown shoulders in. I got to stare at my toes, poking out the end of brown sandals and a wheel on either side rolling forward as we made our way from the lift. Turning right towards the sign 'Emergency exit'. I still had remnants of the doctor's blood smeared across the toe tips—a dark reminder of what we were attempting to escape.

My hackles were waving at visitors, shuffling past and taking our space in the lift. That feeling of being followed was back. Sneaking a park out the corner of my eye, I couldn't see anything—a looming shadow, causing a dull tension headache to pound away at the back of my skull.

With a quick spin, I bashed the safety bar with my back. Pulling the kid and the chair through, looking for anything behind. The mayhem had started; two guards hurried towards the main doors while a smaller single door on each side remained vacant. They wouldn't want to cause too much of a scene, not a huge hospital full of patients and visitors.

Neither looked up for it; one was short, a bit of a fat bastard, and three chins competing for the same resting spot on his chest. He probably had the stamina of a sixty-a-day smoker. While the other was a little leaner, once upon a time, had lofty aspirations to become a plod. He probably failed; knout discipline. Already busy charming the pants off an attractive lass sitting, reading a newspaper.

They had my scrubs brimming with confidence, spinning forward, getting whipped by the night's breeze, a mix of takeaway food and pollution, with the lure of a spicy curry getting my nose twitching. It's London, for sure. I faced a long stone slope to my right and three large metal dustbins to the left. It was the makings of an eerily quiet loading dock: several daily visits, likely for clean linen and scrubs. Not to mention disposing of medical waste.

I stood gathering my thoughts a moment; the loud rumblings of the hospital's air vents spinning drowned them out, with a few clunks thrown in for good measure. Like flies on shit, I'm drawn to waft from a smouldering cigarette butt squashed in a green ashtray bin bolted to the wall. Even a quick drag, a cigarette in one hand and a double whiskey on the rocks in the other. Oh, how could I do with one now?

Wash away the taste of that blooming blood that keeps swirling around in my mouth. Knout around, but here not so long ago, raising the old blood pressure slightly and for my eyes to dart around, checking. My hackles limped to attention. There was only so far I could get away with wheeling a patient wrapped in a flowery gown and white bed sheet down the road in a white coat and scrubs, one sprayed with another doctor's blood, no less. I'm up the shit creek; no uniform, warrant card, or money. I needed to get to Leyland Avenue in St Albans; anything short of a miracle was what I needed.

I was about to set the wheelchair in motion when a 'D plate' blue and white ford transit came screeching in backwards. Of the noise of it, the fan belt needed attention. The motor wasn't old; the company had to run it into the ground. The name on the side was 'first-class medical,'. A delivery, Knout, was on the dock. Maybe some seedy entertainment for the doctors and nurses?

How else would they unwind the hours they do? Slowly, I edged us forward. Envious that the kid could stay asleep. It's hard enough to keep this thing inside Flippin quiet. What version of the little rug rat would wake, anyway? Pain and full of fear were his state in the basement last night. Waking in a wheelchair would shock anyone; I remember going on a stag doo that ended up that way. The chair was also chained somewhere on the M25; Lymington Spar rings a bell. Imagine the sprog.

I could feel it, though—the thing inside of me. It's fighting to be heard and free—a parasite that wants to feed on human flesh; right now, it's feeding on my soul. That's all I could think of it as. If it's even a fraction of what that boy could be, then it scares the shit out of me. I didn't want to become a rampaging murderer. Old red eyes have no problem with it; what's a ripped throat between friends?

I couldn't let that happen, but in the last few minutes, there was a shift within—a stirring. Gripping the wheelchair handle, I see my hand pulsing and shaking. Now wasn't a good time. Night has set in, street lights one by one flicking on with the biggest of them all in the sky, full and bright. It was a full moon.

I watched the driver exit the van, a young bloke with a clipboard dressed in a grey uniform—the shirt and trousers of a delivery driver. We were waiting to see what he let loose from the back of the van, weighing my options. I could talk our way into getting a lift, explain I'm a copper with no I.D. and wearing a dead man's blood.

Or wait and see where he goes; perhaps the van gets unattended, and we can hide in the back. I would have to lose the wheelchair and bundle the boy in, but it could work. The side barrier of the ramp was high; we crept forward more, and I ducked down. With every moment I waited, my stomach was churning, my heart racing with the pain flowing through again.

Bit by bit, it felt torturous, bringing tears to my eyes. Looking through the gap in the barrier side, I watched the delivery bloke hoist one blue sack after the other onto the ledge. Then the droplets caught my eye. Drips of blood trickled, and the claws slid free, quicker and fuller this time, but no less painful.

The sound of breaking bones tunnelled through my ears. How was I able to do this? It shouldn't be possible. Yet it was happening; each claw stretched at least three inches with the tips looking razor sharp, leaving me no doubt about how red eyes cut through the doctor's throat. Each pulse from the claws through my hand rippled down my arm.

The skin fluctuated back and forth from normal to darker, more muscular—at least three times the size. I couldn't stop hyperventilating, sweat dripping down my back. Clenching my eyes closed and cranking the pressure of my sockets, I slowed my breathing, trying to halt the change while fearing being heard. Escaping was hard enough without stopping me from dashing down to that innocent worker going about his business, tearing his jugular out with my bare hands.

Clutching his throat, letting blood dripping to the cold concrete floor, I watched his lifeless body drop. That's the urge I was fighting to stop, tethered by thoughts that never in my wildest dreams would've come to pass until now. The delivery driver dumped his fourth amongst the dust, approaching for a fifth.

Without knowing how many bags were being delivered. I had no idea how long I had to decide—setting the wheelchair rolling, hearing the squelching of rubber rumbling down. I'd reached three-quarters of the way when I heard a loud bang from one metal van door.

Both were open; I assumed the driver did it for a reason, making access to get past and walk up the side to the front. Putting me in the delivery bloke's eye line, I stopped at the slope's brow. My ears were twitching, cutting through the noise of spinning fans.

Three separate heartbeats were thumping away—all at varying speeds and distances. Mine was pounding to the rhythm of torrential rain bearing down on a metal bin lid. The kid's barely a blip on the horizon, no spikes—going at a steady forty per minute. In the distance was the other, elevated at an even hundred. Typical for someone getting their hands dirty; surreal, I could hear them. If there was an upside to this chaos, it knows what it would take to quell the beast.

I'd got carried away with myself, too focused that I didn't hear the footsteps. Out of the blue, like a fox breaking into the henhouse. Still hidden, I couldn't see anything; they were heavy. They were in tandem for a few seconds with the lighter, more scuffed movement—another steady heartbeat. Then nothing. No beating and no steps. You could hear a pin drop, worryingly so. I held still, being cautious if this mess had taught me anything.

Expect the unexpected. Easier said than done with the darkness creeping in. Shoving the wheelchair forward, I stepped slowly, attempting stealth. The chair suddenly gives a short piercing squeak, making me jump before darting my head left and right, panicking. I expected the footsteps to come, but nothing.

Gathering speed, we moved closer to the van, stifling my breathing, fearing it was too loud. Then I heard, with a sense of blooming trepidation, a low drip. 'Tap, tap, tap,' followed by the distinctive smell. The bulking arm lasted longer before fading again. The nearer I got, the worse my reaction.

Loud cracking of bone; my body was being pulled in two. Absolute agony, and I've been shot and stabbed; this was a cricket bat to the spine. I battened down my teeth so hard to stop my screams that I could feel pressure mounting in my jaw; several grew longer. At first, I thought saliva was seeping through the cracks of my lips; when the wetness splashed on my toe, I saw it was blood.

My body was changing taller and painfully widening. Both hands had become huge and menacing, with all claws pointing, sharp and ready. My brain checked out, and I was at a loss for what was happening other than torture. All because I could smell blood.

I was in danger of losing control, moving to the van's rear, but no one. The bags were still in the loading area. Even in the bloodlust haze, I controlled myself enough to look around. Allowing the scent that wasn't my own to guide me, I noticed a large rainbow spray over the closed door. Red streaks dripped down the white panelling, another trail of droplets starting two-three feet away from the van and heading towards those large metal bins.

I knew the poor old van driver was dead. My ears twerked for footsteps, feeling the raging bloodlust while it scared the other part of me senseless. Maybe Old Red eyes were still around. Was there no end to his depravity? Praying I wasn't next after all. On the back foot, with limited options, I was trying to summon the composure for what to do next.

I quickly wheeled to the driver's door, looking through the window, keys still in the ignition. The night's temperature was dropping, and the boy was barely dressed. Sensing an opportunity, I lifted the lifeless child from the chair. I laid him across the passenger seats., letting a musky dust spring up. We couldn't hang around, and stealing a van wouldn't be my usual way of doing things, but needs must. Focussing on the chance to escape, I could push the beast back into the box again. The claws subsided, and arms returned to normal. While the pain and breaking of bones trailed off.

There was no time to check the bins and see if he was still alive, with no heartbeat; I didn't hold out much hope. Why kill a random stranger? Nothing made sense. I could hear the laughter coming from the stairwell. Two people. With a final frantic search around, the van doors slammed shut, and I was in the driver's seat with the engine ticking over.

Ticking would be an exaggeration, more a spluttering and struggles of a diesel-sapping tractor. I would only hope it wasn't as slow. The boy remained asleep surprisingly; I watched his little chest rise and fall, and his heartbeat remained steady. So peaceful, hoping that would be his life ahead.

We chugged forward, letting the squeal of a failing fan belt ring through the air. About to turn left onto Stepney Way when I gave a cursory look in the cracked offside mirror to see if the laughing twosome had come outside yet. Fearing they'd see the blood and me driving away. Only to see the mysterious, looming presence of the menace with red eyes.

Long black coats, jeans and matching shirts only buttoned three-quarters of the way. I should've been surprised, and maybe a tiny part was. He was true to his word., watching and deciding to take another life to help us escape. Why?

What happened twenty-five years ago.

CHAPTER 21

'Officer Reynolds 1987,'

Was that the truth? Or a work of fiction? I had no words. My mouth stayed shut, letting my brain attempt to digest what I'd heard—picturing the image of long, dirty claws slithering from the skipper's fingers. I thought he could wind me up, but the pain etched on his face was all too real. It defied everything I knew, and to think a boy had caused it.

One that shouldn't have been able to survive being burnt. Who was he? Where is he? And what's the relevance to me? I still had the feeling he was holding back.

"Was that the truth?" Taking a much-needed mouthful of whiskey. I can see why he dusted it off.

"Every word, lad, every blooming word," skip breathed heavily as he spoke without moving his eyes from looking down.

Charlie looked agitated. He slid further away on the sofa, fidgeting. Still, his eyes were crumpled together. Charlie had a problem. I don't know what it was, but the story bothered him too. I watched his fingers drag up and down his legs before standing up. Wincing again and heading to the holdall on the side. Charlie was hurting; maybe that's what he'd been holding back. I'd forgotten all about the antique-looking box; what could be so important about it, and who was the person who brought it to him?

"So, what happened? Were the claws real? Or are you trying to wind me up with that bit?"

"The pain? Has it started yet?" Skip finally removed his eyes from the hand and glass to stare directly at me.

His wrinkles gathered, displaying a troubled look on his face. Even if he'd avoided my question, there was more to that story. A picture paints a thousand words, and I was looking at the opening scenes of a terrible movie—especially producing claws. In the back of my mind, there was an element of denial. A voice tells me it was all bullshit because that would make me feel better. Safer.

The more I thought about it, the more I saw a parallel and an unusual feeling deep within. It was creeping up on me. The night has moved in rather quickly, with the moonlight shining through. Charlie pulled the box out of the bag and carefully let it rest on the table.

"Do you remember any of the Diner incidents?" Charlie reluctantly sat back down while keeping his distance.

"You, ok? Seem in a bit of pain. Erm, a little. Why?"

Reaching for the bottle. I was getting the feeling the rest of the story was coming. And I wouldn't like the 'what happened. "To answer your question, George, I'm having bowel trouble, being probed for cancer. I didn't want to bother you because it might be nothing. So, forget that. Have you seen them yet?" Charlie piped up, arms folded, finger pressed firmly on his lip.

'Oh, for Christ's sake, Georgina. Were you ever good at connecting the dots?'

With Charlie's confession swirling in my eardrums, I heard a Chris again; this time, it made me freeze. The story, the pictures, and being drugged all had me on edge and feeling jumpy. My hand gripped the bottle mid-tilt as the hackles shot up. Every time I hear him, I drift into that nightmare. How different Chris was. It's harder than it looks, trying not to seem mad, no matter how near the edge I am, slowly looking around without making it obvious.

'Oh, so it's like that, is it?'

This time it was close; I could feel a chill hovering near my right shoulder. I had to be cracking up, or Chris was haunting me. Penance for not saving him. Yet every time he spoke, it was to do with what was happening.

"You're not real. You're dead... sorry I couldn't help you, but that's the end," I tried to whisper.

"What's that, lad?" The skipper had heard, leaving me in a tight spot, feeling my face turning red.

"Erm... I said. This mess can't be real. With Chris dead, will we ever see the end of it? You know, this nightmare," Trying my best not to sound like a total fruitcake. That was the best I could do.

"Happened again? "Skip took me by surprise.

"What?" My eyes darted to Charlie, sitting, cupping his face in his hands. As if I didn't want to speak in front of Charlie.

"Come on, Georgie. We're all friends here, you told me already. May as well come out with it. So, you heard him again?"

Skip called me out, although I was still on the fence about the 'we're all friends here' part. Edging back in my seat, still feeling that chill, it was more of an irritating stroking motion up and down my neck. Looking blankly ahead for a few seconds of silence, I had an out-of-body experience. My brain had removed itself from the surreal situation. Was this all happening?

"Yes, I keep hearing him at weird times," I felt defeatist by saying it aloud.

"There you go, lad, wasn't it too hard now, was it? Knout wrong with sharing the load, ya daft sod. Have you seen them yet?"

Skip meant well and, to a degree, had a point, even if he was irritating me with the impatient tapping on the table. His intentions were good, but I understand there's more on his mind. Charlie's little revelation bothered me; it's not the thing to blurt out unless Skip knew already. The pair were now opposite sides to me; I was about to be interrogated. Not that I had much more I could say, other than the crap I've seen freaks me out.

"We have some proper catching up to do. What do you mean? See what yet?"

'He's talking about me, stupid. He's right; I would likely lose control of my stomach. Christ, wouldn't that make you shit your pants? The ghost of your dead friend pops up as you're,' Chris's voice drifted around me, bringing that chill again.

"Only my nightmare recently. That was fucking scary." I shifted my eyes to the box. The intrigue was back, but it would only be a distraction from what else the skipper had in that folder.

"It's going to get worse before you get a grip on it," Skip reached for the bottle with a heavy sigh.

"Get the grip of what? Seriously, someone tells me what the hell is going on because I'm getting bloody tired of being told I'm something else and all these cryptic questions. I'm freaking out... While dealing with the idea linking to Chris's death," I banged my hand on the table, causing the others to jump and blow my top. I'd boiled over quickly. The idea of things getting worse tipped me over.

The pair looked at each other before Charlie looked at the box and then at the skipper. Who flipped open the folder, sliding out a few old newspaper cut-outs and nodded 'no' to Charlie. There was another secret between them they didn't want to share just yet; I didn't like not knowing.

"Look at these."

Skip slid the papers over to me. One was a picture of a house with a news article underneath. It seemed like Chris had been in his locker. Perhaps from a different newspaper. The headline reads, 'Arson kills a family of four'. Late last night, a fire tore through a family home in Bow, East London. A family of four, with no way out, sought refuge in the basement. Sadly, there were no survivors.

"What's this about?" Feeling a little confused. It was sad and all, but I didn't understand.

"That's the watered-down version. Chris had found what wasn't made public. The original mentions a child survivor, but it got redacted, a cover-up instigated by the police, local authority and some very well-connected people around that part of London. -

-A family of sorts that are into many things, none of it good, and they seem to control what goes on. They still" Skip had his glass raised inches from his chin.

"How do you know all of this?" Still needing some clarification. Had I missed something?

"Well, that story I told you. That was the" Skip looked at me with raised eyebrows, waiting for me to cotton on.

"Woahh, wait a minute. So that was the fire where you saved the young boy. But you said it was a horror basement with devil worship and heads cut off. So, what gives?"

I slowly put the pieces together; I could be forgiven for being a little behind in connecting the dots. There's been a lot going on. First, Dalton and his games make purposeful mistakes, alluding to more going on. Then skip tells a covered-up horror story. Until Chris found out, and now he's dead. Oh, to be oblivious again.

"Yep. That was the best way forward, according to the big bosses back then. But Chris found a string of Arson occurring again. The deeper he looked, he found a pattern all over the country. Suspicious crime scenes have been going on for decades. Each case marked suspects unknown with no forensics."

Skip pulled the paper forward for me to see. If only we still had the tapes he'd made. They would've given us a better insight into what he found and something to take to the SMT. For now, the information we have is hearsay and nostalgia, especially as the skipper's story didn't fit the narrative.

"What's this?"

"The past,"

"Who's?"

"Read it and see,"

The lack of straight answers was overwhelming. Instead, I was drip-fed information that required brain power I didn't have the strength to muster. Yet, their expression told me it was all bad.

'Search continues for missing toddler snatched from his home in Surrey. A young boy's kidnapping occurred early on Friday, 17th April 1959. He was aged two years. The family home in Denby way was broken into while the household was asleep. It's unknown what the main intention was, only that it appears the boy was all that was missing. The family are distraught and unable to comment,'

"Sorry, Skip, this is tragic, but how is it relevant? What does it mean?" The weirdness of our situation continued.

"That's you, George. The boy taken from that house is you,"

Charlie dropped a gut-reaching bombshell on my lap. My eyes were stuck reading the same clipping repeatedly, hoping it would disappear or the reality would sink in. They looked so serious for any of it to be untrue. Yet, I thought of being snatched from my parents all those years ago. And I didn't remember anything. Not that I imagined a two-year-old would, but I don't recall anything before foster care. And now my world has been turned upside down even more.

"How do you know?" I barely croaked words out as the shock settled.

"After I left the hospital, the boy was taken to somewhere I trusted. Somewhere safe where no one knew, the boy could grow up none the wiser. Only, as I explained, the boy was different."

Yeah, it wasn't me struggling to connect the dots anymore. The skipper was feeding me scraps. My head was in a daze, and all I wanted to do was head home. Sleep and forget the drama for a few hours before returning to what matters—Finding a murderer.

"Look, I applaud your goodwill and dedication to the cause. But for Christ's sake, enough with the boy already. How the hell does that fit in with me snatched from my parents? And thanks for shattering my world,"

I fired off, tired of the dance. At least Dalton was a bit more forthcoming, albeit not near the whole story. At least it was at me. And that's saying something. Feeling my face burning red, I looked back at the house that had been torched, trying to find a connection.

It must've been a minute of silence; my eyes fixed deeply on the black-and-white picture. A wide lens had captured the crowd; all seemed to be sucked in by the destruction and the ambulance crew, except one. A tall-looking bloke with long black hair and eyes matched the printing ink. No white, pure black. He was looking straight at the camera. Even in the picture, he looked scary—much like the skipper described.

"What you looking at, Georgie?" Charlie broke the silence, and I slid the paper to face him.

"Who's he? The only one not bothered by the circus." Charlie leaned forward but arched his shoulder away from me. It was almost offensive, coming across as scared of me.

"Shit. That's who brought me the box. The guy looked as he does in the picture. How?" Charlie came across as surprised but different; we grew up together. He's a few years older, so as kids, our interests weren't far apart, as I remember, and most of the time, we got along well as foster brothers. Then we grew up. I also knew he wasn't as shocked as he made out.

I looked at the rest of the crowd for any others that stood out, just in case, when I heard a pattering of nails on wood. It was coming from Skip. I turned to see what's got him all impatient when yet again, I was left open-mouthed. The moonlight beamed through, capturing the surface of the coffee table, the box, and the skipper's hand. I could hear a sound akin to trudging through thick mud sloshing beneath my feet.

A large brown-black claw tapped the table as the others slowly slid from the fingertips, glimmering under the light. Everything I'd heard was true, and I was at a loss for words. My mentor, friend and close ally in this mess now had claws rapping against the table.

"What the bloody hell? You weren't bullshitting me."

I couldn't take my eyes off them. I should be petrified, and a part of me was. But it also intrigued me. Compounded by the truth, opening my eyes to the possibility of so much more, and I wasn't going mad.

"No, Georgie, I wasn't. It's finally coming back, and I can do knout about it. Don't be scared, lad; I wouldn't hurt ya. We've come too far, you and,"

"Finally coming back?"

"The scary-ass bloke in that picture helped. He made that part of me, the Flippin thing within... Well, let's just say he helped keep it quiet. But only for a while; it and I would be needed to help. What I've learnt, though, is two peas in a pod, lad. It's me, but"

I couldn't get my brain around the fact he had to carry that secret all these years. But at peace and being needed to help had me stumped.

"Be needed to with what?"

"With what's coming. I wasn't the only one." Skip's eyes darted to Charlie, who looked at the floor, not wanting to say anything.

"The boy? Where is he? What happens with keeping quiet?"

"The information is all there, lad; you open that rattled bonce of yours. Think deeper than a tight git with short arms and deep pockets; feel for those memories, and it will be clear as mud. I mean clearer than it is now as for the other. The echo of my blooming past will return to haunt me by the time of the blood moon in October. The boy? He's a little conflicted now and in need of," Charlie looked up in time, cracking a slight smile. It must have been an inside joke because I didn't get it.

"I got to ask something. Was that the case that cost you?" I remembered the talk of problems early in his career that cost him a lot. I had to know.

He glared in my direction, making me shift awkwardly in my seat. The claws were out still, and fury had scorched across his face. I'd hit a nerve, not intentionally, and suddenly found myself scared. Feeling a chill run down my back, and it wasn't from the ghost of Chris, who had fucked off, I might add. No, this was unadulterated fear. Skip threw the rest of his glass down his neck, screeching a painful gasp.

"It cost me everything, lad. The world I had changed when I entered that basement, only I didn't know it. A warning was sent, and I got lucky that I kept my life. Every Goddam day I wake and pray for the chance to make those bastards pay. When I understand it all,"

"Do you know who?"

"All I have is the memory of some words written in blood. They were on the blooming wall behind you," I looked; I don't know why. But I half expected to see it.

"What did it say?"

"The devil's circle. Someone has been looking into it quietly; all they have so far is that it's a group made up of large criminal families that control London, maybe further,"

As the last part passed his mouth, I could picture it vividly, imagining the horror of finding streaks of blood and wondering who it was and how he must've felt. The weight of losing someone never goes. I see Helen walking around the room with me always. The hospital and that car have different circumstances, but I carry it all the same.

The longer I stared, the more I was lost in the moment. So much so that I failed to notice the loud thumping that had crept up out of nowhere. I heard the loud beating of a heart, which wasn't my own.

My ears homed in, causing mine to skip a beat in panic. But once I noticed, I began hearing all of ours thumping at different rates and rocking me off my train of thought. What the hell was happening? Just like Skip described in his story. Wait, no. It can't be. No, I can't...

CHAPTER 22

The voice of safety rattles from behind the green door at 73 Leyland Avenue, St Albans. It was 10 pm. I was getting ready to knock on the door of someone from my past. The Boy felt heavier, barely a sack of spuds earlier. He was burning up; I couldn't stop looking over my shoulder, carrying the same fear of being watched.

The vivid image of 'red eyes' haunts my every move in the rear-view mirror. I was rife with nerves, anticipating the reaction I was about to get. Expecting help, knowing Hannah had every right to slam the door in my face, she was the only person no one else knew.

"Andrew? What in god's name? Why are you dressed like a flipping doctor? Change of career again? I mean, what the hell, after all this time? You suddenly decide to darken my door,"

Hannah looked the same. I was twenty, and she was eighteen. I'd decided that my blooming life needed direction. Fearing I would amount to knout. I saw some of this world. The lure of visiting different countries at her Majesty's expense was too good to miss. I signed up for the marines; Hannah thought it was too dangerous and didn't want to follow me around like a little lost sheep, only to one day see me in a body bag, and we broke up.

My current wife, Angela, and I met on one of my stints of leave, and the rest, as they say, is history. Hannah, dressed for bed, hurriedly threw on a white gown to cover her silky sky-blue pyjamas. The best part of Five years later, and there she stood—five-foot-four inches of agitation.

Flame red hair dangled below the shoulders of a small frame. Her bright green eyes beamed through the brown-framed glasses she hastily adjusted on her pale, tired face. Hard to tell what was pissing her off the most. The time of night I'd turned up or come at all. The doctor dress-up part would take some explaining.

"I need your help, Hannah,"

"With what?" Hannah edged forward, curious about what I was holding.

"Well, it's not to play doctors and nurses... It's with this... With him. Just a child," I was going to elaborate more, but it wasn't a doorstep conversation.

"What the hell! Yours? What have you done?" Hannah expressed the typical look of worry. As if I'd snatched the child from the mother or something. No, that happened to the sprog long ago.

"It's not like that. The Boy's in danger, and there's knout else safer than the only person I trust right now. As you're not on the scumbag's radar, I hope not." Her face softened, becoming more sympathetic toward the child. Her eyes widened as her hallway light gleamed off the whites.

"Why? What's going on? Why is the Boy shaking and sweating so much?"

"Can we come in? We needed to get inside as soon as possible. We're too exposed. And it's not a conversation I want to have out here in case of prying eyes,"

Taking a quick, panicked look over my shoulder into the dark purple night sky. Knout but silence. Peace in a well-to-do street littered with houses and parked cars illuminated by the yellow glow of street lamps. So calm, I hear the wind whistling past in tandem with my heartbeat as my eyes catch a look at the full moon. My temple was pulsing, and it took everything I had to stop the claws from sliding forward as the loud bone cracking started.

"Hannah, who's there?" A man's voice booms out from inside the house; that was a surprise I hadn't expected. Not that I thought Hannah would remain single. Only, in my flipping haste, I hadn't factored in other complications.

"I... Erm... One-minute dear,"

"That's my bloody fiancé. And you'll be introduced as an old-school friend needing the help you mentioned. Ok? Nothing else needs to be said," Hannah whispered, leaning forward, glaring her eyes to make sure I understood.

"Fiancé? I'm so sorry for disturbing you. There's nowhere I'm sure I can trust now. I will do and say whatever you want; unfortunately, there's no time to waste,"

I checked back to the Boy; my ears honed in on his heart. It had gone from barely beating to more of a runaway train thundering down the tracks. We ushered in, clopping on dark wooden flooring throughout the hallway. To the left was a doorway that appeared to be a sitting room. A staircase to the right and ahead was a set of white double doors, slightly ajar with light creeping out. It was the kitchen and where I'd heard the voice come.

"Mathew, we have company. Bring the brandy. We're going to need it," Hannah called out; it was music to my ears. A much-needed drink to straighten my head.

"Thank you, Hannah. You're literally a lifesaver,"

"Well, I'm not sure I like the sound of that. Oh, you're lucky to catch Mathew. A short while ago, he had to rush out, a locksmith by trade, and he had an emergency call out."

Hannah smiles slightly, guiding us through the first door to the sitting room. I laid the Boy down, still covered. I heard his heart slow a little, steadying. He's sweating buckets; at least I didn't fear his chest exploding. Mine was quite the opposite. I was entering foreign territory, bringing my problems too, a stranger's home for all intents and purposes.

A million thoughts rampaging through my mind. The biggest one I had was what I would do if the claws came out; worse, I couldn't control that part of me. The blood lust slowly crept back. I sat near the Boy, keeping a respectful distance from Hannah, while I heard heavy footsteps coming from the kitchen.

Stood in the doorway, looking less than pleased but playing host as requested, was a white bloke in black pyjamas and a dressing gown, a year or two older than me. Stocky with black curly hair and a goatee. He was carrying a tray with three glasses and an unopen bottle of brandy. The room was tense, more than having a night disturbed. An unusual look on his face, dark and menacing. I've seen a few in my life. The ones that put on a show, but underneath, there's evil. More so since I've been on the job, domestic violence perpetrators.

"So, who's this then?"

He had an old-school East London accent mixed with an Irish twang. The closer he was, the more it made easier to size him up. He was a little under six feet tall, weighing one hundred and eighty-two pounds. Give or take, by the looks of it, predominantly right-handed. My curiosity peaked further as he bent to place the tray on the table. His pyjama sleeve had edged back, revealing a strange, five-pointed star in a circle.

I've never been a fan of coincidences, and I sure as hell weren't changing that opinion soon. It was the same symbol I'd seen in the blooming basement of horrors, with the dead bodies stuck around it. My eyes fixated on the symbol, hearing only muffled voices until a hand shook my arm. Waking up, it was Hannah. She had a confused look on her face.

"Andrew, you, ok?"

"Yeah, sorry, I'm exhausted. It's been quite the day. Quite the twenty-four hours,"

"Your eyes, they looked black. Completely black,"

"Probably the drugs I'm prescribed. The docs had me high as a kite," Knout idea what Hannah meant, but I had to come up with something.

"Maybe, but it was bloody freaky. Mathew, this is Andrew, an old friend who needs our help. Andrew, this is Mathew, my fiancé," Hannah went about introductions while the symbol played on my mind.

"Pleasure. But what the hell is going on, and why do we have a twitchy kid on our sofa?"

Mathew spoke with authority, trying to be serious. Still, I noticed a creepy, sly smile. Then, a little further up on the cheek, two red specks. It could be from shaving, but it was blood all the same. Although the Boy was twitching, it was much less than he had been so far, which had me thinking there could be another twist in the young lad's frightening escape. The sum of those two things gave me a feeling of unease. I had become side-tracked.

"This Boy is a victim of a terrible fire, costing him his family. It seems the suspect wants to leave no stone unturned to get rid of him. He needs somewhere safe and off the record until I know who can be trusted."

I wasn't going to tell them the truth, not with the wrinkle that is Mathew in the mix. Every turn I make leads to somewhere or someone that puts doubts in my head. When were we going to get a lucky break? Hannah looked at Mathew with pleading green eyes, passing him a drink she'd poured.

I didn't have him as a stupid bloke; he's bound to have figured out by now that, once upon a time, there was something between us. I was more intrigued by what Mathew did for a living. The real job that caused red specs on his cheek, and not the fixing of locks.

"Well, if Han says it's ok and vouches for you, then it's all good," Mathew took his drink; the sly smile was there still, and my hackles had bounced to attention, making me question if I was doing the right thing. But what choice did I have?

"Appreciated. Truly. More than you know. Can I use your phone to call home? I haven't been able to let my wife know I'm ok since my shift the other day." No sooner had I mentioned my wife than Mathew seemed to perk up a little. Perhaps he felt a little threatened in his own home. The smile was bigger.

"Mi casa es Su casa,"

Mathew had made himself bigger, stood with an open stance and seemed more at ease. Even Hannah looked concerned. I chugged back my brandy, getting a much-needed warmth, numbing my senses for a few seconds. Not enough that I don't notice the Boy stirring a little. His eyes flickered open and shut; he could wake up any moment. What version of him would wake up worried me.

CHAPTER 23

'Behind Closed Doors,'

'Brrrr, Brrrr, Brrrr, Brrrr - Click,'

"Hello. Angela? You there?"

"Tut Tut Tut. Mr Morris. Did you think it would be that simple? Well, you know what they say, Eye for an Eye. Tooth for a Tooth. Kid for a Kid,"

A deep east London voice grated down the phone, taking the wind out of my sails. I'd figured on someone going to my house, but only to check if I'd returned. Not hang around, waiting for my call. Had they hurt my family? Tears were building with my worries.

I looked into the room; Hannah and her husband were quite relaxed with little worry aside from what I brought to their home. The boy was now tossing and turning, improving by the minute. Anyone else would see a helpless kid. Yet, I faced an impossible choice: my helpless family or the helpless boy. The thing inside was waking; my muscles pulled tight. What if I let it come? See what happens, go home and fight to save their lives.

"Please don't hurt my family,"

"We haven't yet. What can I say? The night is young,"

"Please leave them alone; I will do what you ask."

"We don't need you for anything. We have what we want; you can keep the reject; they'll be dead soon. The question is, can you make it home before your family joins them? Before they're skinned alive?" my legs turned to jelly with my heart pounded through my ears.

"H...H... How do I know you haven't already?" I croaked my words out.

"Come here, bitch. 'Aaarrrrrgggghhh heeelllppp, let me go' See, she's still breathing for now. Let's see how much longer. TikTok,"

Angela let loose a high-pitched throaty scream and squealed like a banshee down the phone, jarring my bones; I was helpless and quite far away, and thought filled me with doom.

"Who are you? Why are you doing all of this?"

"We are the last people you ever wanted to cross paths with, and soon you will know,"

'Click,'

The phone line went dead; my hand drifted the receiver back to the mount before facing the room. Hannah read my expression; my look of worry became hers. I brought the boy to her to be safe and out of reach. I didn't think about the risk to my family.

"What is it, Andy?" Hannah interrupted, topping up our glasses.

"S...s... someone's at my house. They have my family,"

"Who are they? Andrew. Are we supposed to take you at your word?" Matthew threw his two penneth worth into the mix while keeping that slimy smile on show. I don't know what it is about him, but he was oozing nothing good, and that one comment was in my moment of pain. It made me want to rip his throat out. What did Hannah see in him?

"Matty, for Christ's sake, behave. I trust Andy, and if he says there's something wrong, there's something wrong."

Hannah had a fire in her tone. I knew that well. It hasn't mellowed any since I felt her wrath. Only, in doing so, 'Matty's' face changed. If looks could kill, there'd be a massacre in the sitting room. It was fleeting but long enough for me to see Mathew drop the act. I've always thought, 'never know what goes on behind closed doors,'.

That is a statement so true, from what I saw. Their domestic bliss was the least of my worries; I had to get home. All because of what was lying on the sofa. His twitching had stopped, and the temperature looked to have eased. He was turning a corner. I was staring at a kid who, on the face, seemed so innocent. Now, the lives of my family were in balance.

"I know knout of who they are, only since the house fire, weird things have been happening and getting unwanted attention from people I'd least expect. Doctor's make phone calls to people who have detectives on their payroll. All are suddenly wanting the boy. Now my family is in trouble."

Hearing my words out loud, you'd think I was making the shit up. Did I make the right choice by bringing the kid here? Or had we gone from one hellish situation to another?

"Leave him here; I'll drive you to yours. It sounds like you might need the backup, anyway. Hopefully, stop anyone from dying," Matthew offered to help, catching me off guard. Why did he assume someone would die?

"Why would you do that? Just now, you thought I might make shit up. So, why? Don't get me wrong, I appreciate it. But why?"

I had to know; I had to push and see if there was a motive or a sudden self-righteous need to do good. Not that I would believe anything that came out of Mathew's mouth; hidden agendas of late had poisoned my mind; too much had gone on in a short time. And none of it has been good.

"I wouldn't hear the end if I didn't try to help. The boy is fine here until we know otherwise,"

I looked at Hannah, who nodded in agreement as she moved to cover the boy with a cute, multi-coloured knitted blanket. The kind my nan used to make, more crochet than the boring woolly jumper. It seems like a neat floral pattern and another string to Hannah's bow. I glanced at him next, noticing a wave of gooseflesh ripple, probably prompting Hannah's care. That's when I clocked his eyes. Flickers. The lids were letterbox flaps, open-shut -open-shut.

Now, I don't know if he was dreaming or any life was going on there. But when those lids flipped open, I saw a blackness that made me shit myself—a spooky midnight black with a dim moonlight glow around the edge. At first, I thought it was a nice change from the glowing red. Then I worried about Hannah and how it would affect her if the kid woke up and went psycho.

"Andy. It's fine. I haven't forgotten how to foster, you know. Besides, it could be a trial run. After all, that's what you'll need if your friends are few. Gives me an excuse to cut down my hours at 'Bryant and May' people keep getting sick,"

Hannah smiled, not fake or with any hidden malice. It was her same old genuine ways. I've kept tabs on her from afar. She'd started her application to foster years ago, and I knew of her on-off fostering through social workers I've met through the job. Only, it's never seemed the right time to carve open old wounds. Until now, desperate times call for desperate measures.

"I haven't thought that far ahead yet. Until now, it's been about safety. The boy will be traumatised and, more than likely, hard work. So, how long have you two been together and engaged? And what the hell are Bryant and May?" The subtle approach might work under the guise of security for the kid. There was more to Mathew than met the eye. And I wanted to know what.

"A little over a year now. A matchstick company in bow," Hannah gave an awkward look to Mathew, who smiled back as he withdrew the glass from his lips.

"What engaged?"

"Both. A whirlwind that I didn't want to stop. And when you know, you know. Eh, sweetheart," Hannah pouted a loving smile towards Mathew, who looked a little awkward with it all.

"Er... yeah... Absolutely. When the old pitchfork chooses its prey, there's no stopping it. You could say fate had set us on the same path. What would be the chances that we both go into 'the classic book emporium' for a copy of 'to kill a mockingbird,' coincidence eh,"

Mathew gave a grin from the corner of his mouth. What would be the chances, indeed? Some would say fate; I would say a carefully concocted plan. I didn't have Mathew pegged as the classic book type. Whereas Hannah wouldn't go anywhere without one. Perhaps his intentions were genuine; having liked her, he did anything he could to find a common interest—a way to get her talking.

That's what I was hoping, and not that she would be unlucky in love for a second time. Because I loved her back then, my life would knout without direction. Time will tell what Mathew's game is; for now, I needed his help and fast.

"Well, in that case, if the offer's there, then, please. We must go now,"

I fed Mathew's ego through gritted teeth, checking on the kid; his eyes continued to flick open. The black was still there, reminding me of the five-pointed star tattoo on Mathew. Could he be one of those fanatics?

CHAPTER 24

"We'll take my car. They may have noticed that van you came in."
With his cockney bravado, Mathew was gearing up to go, wearing a white
polo t-shirt, blue jeans and a black leather waist-length jacket. I was mid-
draining the dregs of my drink when he piped up, walking back into the
sitting room.

What should be an innocuous comment to Hannah's ears, but mine
got rocked. My mind raced. How did he know I drove a van? It wasn't even
mine. So how could he possibly know how I arrived? If I wasn't on edge
before, I sure as hell was now. I stood silent for a moment, digesting what
he'd said and deciding how to react.

I could blow my sodding lid and throw around accusations, which
would get me nowhere. Hannah would stick up for Mathew as I'd expected,
and Mathew would say he heard the squealing noise coming down the road,
so he looked out the window to see me pull up.

Or I could play along; his car meant he would want to drive. Judging
by the appearance, I guessed he took care of it. And wouldn't want a Mr
Nobody, who once dated his current wife, to get his hands on what is
precious to him. The car. I would have a slight advantage; although he could
crash us, he likely wouldn't. I had him down as an Audi Quattro man or a
Sierra Cosworth, something sporty with a bit of oomph.

I was a bit like Alice in Wonderland, falling down a hole and ending
up in a strange new world where everyone hated me. Only now, I had a

dinner party with the mysterious mad hatter to save my family. Did I have a plan? Did I Eck? Other than turning up and hoping, bullshit baffles brains. To do that, I kept quiet, pretending I didn't hear his comment. At least not in a way that mattered.

No, I intended to go with the flow and what he suggested—praying that I had been overthinking the situation. Something that seems to happen far too often now. What I hadn't realised was how lousy my poker face was. I must've shown my hand as soon as he spoke because no sooner had I turned to check on the boy, and Hannah was alright with it all still. My face met a look of surprise from Hannah.

Hannah was bright, on the ball, not one to let the world go by, and she didn't miss a trick, especially when her fiancé knew what I'd travelled in. It took a second for her to regain composure; I watched as she heavily cleared her throat. It was now that the gravity of my situation hit home, not least for Hannah. No words were uttered.

A look was good enough. Hannah got up, disappearing out of the room momentarily, leaving the two of us in limbo with the fear of what we could face washed over me. I couldn't help but look Mathew up and down, trying to see what else I could glean from him other than right-handed... As that thought crossed my mind, Mathew changed stance, grabbing a pen and pad with his left hand before writing a note.

Even as he took a few steps, it was left-foot dominance. Was he ambidextrous? That couldn't be ruled out, but it was as if he'd switched the right side off as soon as Hannah left the room. What's his game? Because I've not known someone to turn like that.

They say the devil is in the details; if I weren't looking, it wouldn't have been noticed, much like the tattoo. Glancing towards the doorway, he came within breathing distance as the alcohol fumes singe my nostril's hairs. The paper gets shoved in my hand.

'Keep Your mouth shut,'

That's what it read; Mathew stepped away in time for Hannah to walk back in, reverting to right-side dominance. Stunned, I quickly whipped the paper into my doctor's coat pocket before Hannah saw. She seemed a little on edge with a twitching smile. Then I noticed her right sleeve; she kept it pinched down to her palm, unlike the other.

"Right, when you get there, see what you see, then call the police for help. There's got to be some of your friends happy to help. More importantly, be safe,"

Hannah brushed past me rather clumsily as she went to hug Mathew. As she reached her arms around his neck, I noticed the sleeve was no longer pinched. My pocket felt heavier. I looked over my shoulder to check on the boy, only to see Hannah with an expression of worry, mouthing, 'be careful,'.

I spun to walk away, feeling the pocket swing and hit my leg. It was hard, metal; I didn't reach for it. Instead, I continued as normal, full of dread with the note in the other pocket. The situation had an air of doom about it; who was this person who was so willing to help but delivered a warning to keep my mouth shut. We said our goodbyes and stepped out into the chilly night air.

A beep echoed in the dark street, followed by a flash of amber lights cutting through a slight fallen mist; I'd called it right, Audi. A black sporty number with a long springy radio antenna. Surely, there was no way I was getting my hands on the steering wheel. So, assuming that would be the case, I head for the passenger door, only to hear.

'Not so fast,'

A metal jingle rattles the air, and I look up just in time with the keys coming within inches of my face. I only understood if he wanted control over the situation. With me behind the wheel, my hands would be occupied. We swapped sides; the interior had a well-maintained freshness about it. Jet black squeaky leather seats to go with the black interior.

The engine started with a powerful 3.2-litre rumble that shook my hackles to attention. I need clarification on why I would be trusted. Not that I'm a bad driver, just that... well, it's not normal.

"Right. Now man to blooming man. What the hell is going on? Why am I driving, and why do I have to keep my mouth shut? What are you hiding?"

If something was going to happen, it might as well be now—no point delaying the inevitable. I feel for the added weight in my pocket to see what Hannah had slipped me. Straight away, I realised it was a small revolver. The spin barrel type differs from what I used in service. But a straightforward 'click, point, shoot,'. What Hannah was doing with such a thing was beyond me. I was.

Grateful; it takes a lot to go against someone you love. So, for Hannah to see a problem and try to help says a lot.

"Because it would be easier," Surprised. What did Mathew mean?

"Bullshit. Now tell me what you're up to. Your act isn't that convincing."

My words carried fire with them, yet Mathew didn't flinch. Instead, his goatee curved to form that slimy smile—typical overconfidence, and that's dangerous. He reclined his chair a few clicks and stretched his legs forward, sliding a hand into his jacket pocket.

"I don't know the way, do I? Be quicker if you drive. Anyway, I need to keep an eye on you. As for keeping your mouth closed, that was for the best. For the sake of dear old Hannah," Matthew was confusing me by the second.

"What, your fiancé? Why her sake?"

"You wouldn't want her getting hurt as well, would you?" Not the talk you'd expect. That one sentence had me frozen, mouth open, as I clutched the seatbelt.

"Sorry, what?"

"It was the van. My comment about you being seen in it. Considering you never told me what you drove,"

"It had me thinking, yes," Trapped in a confined space with Mathew had me on edge. My hand hovered near the pocket. Was that even his name?

"That won't do you any good; I'd have a bullet in your skull before you could blink," The Irish tone of his voice came to the fore, thicker. His comment rattled my bones; my hand darted away.

"Who are you? Are you going to kill me?" I summoned the courage to ask. He slowly turned his head to face me, the smile still there but broader. There was a cockiness I didn't like. He had to be connected to those who the doctor called, but how? An expectation I would turn to Hannah; how would those people even know she had been in my life? I'd kept her from everyone.

"This is bigger than you know; information is power, and we know everything. The lengths we go to would surprise you,"

"What? Like getting engaged?"

"Exactly. Hannah is lovely and all, but her on-off job is more important. The access she has." He mocked with a menacing laugh; Hannah was being used because of her access to foster children, even if she was semi-out of it. I'd walked a child into their arms.

"Kids? How long had you been setting her up? How did you find out about me?"

"Months, background checks are thorough, connections in places you wouldn't believe. The dossiers my employers have on people of interest are unbelievable. I don't know how they knew you would come here; I got called to say you were on your way but had some business to take care of."

"So, what's going to happen now? Did you know there were people at my house?"

"We are going to your house; we will keep calm and normal. Then I will make your death look like a suicide. Once you've killed your family, that is?" I didn't know what to say; I suddenly felt empty. A place meant to be safe has turned out to be anything but. My family was in trouble.

"Why? Why all this effort? Is my family dead already?"

"Highly likely. This effort is to make sure everything is as it should be. And that's quiet,"

I only had to think of my family and their position. How scared they were. It made my blood boil, feeling that terrifying thing within again, fighting to get to the fore. I had to think of something. He planned to kill me at home, so I had some time. Would I be able to get to him before a shot got fired? I tried to focus on the road; I kept looking out of the corner of my eye.

Watching him recline back in his chair, hand in his pocket, watching me. The look on his smug face sent a shiver down my spine. I thought of my claws, a picture of them tearing through his throat flesh. That's what I wanted to do. I had to play it smart and be careful. He wants the boy with them and for his people or employers. No doubt, use him or his blood being as he'd survived.

"Why the sad face? At least the boy is in good hands, right? So that's a win, an even bigger one when I let the family know the kid lives. They'll reward me for sure," He smiled, getting under my skin. It took everything I had not to crash the car. He didn't have his belt on and would go through the window.

"So, who are these people you work with?" I could see the cogs turning; he was deciding how much he should tell me. After all, if he were going to kill me, it wouldn't matter what I knew, would it? His heart was steady; Mathew was too calm.

"Yeah, I'm not doing that. I'm not risking it. The people I work for always know. They have ways of sniffing out betrayal. I'm not going to spill my guts for you. All I'll say is family, and there's more than one."

More than one? My heart was pounding, but it wasn't only fear of him. We were heading into the unknown, and I didn't know if Angela and Rosalind would still be alive when we arrived. All I could do was pray.

"Oh, come now, lad, you have the upper hand here. It's a fair way to go in silence, so you may as well talk a little. What can I do? Only one what?"

"Have you not figured anything out yet? People in places you wouldn't imagine were a clue. Think how the yanks do it."

I didn't look, focusing ahead, following the snake-like flow of red lights. How could I figure anything out? Every turn, there's been a problem or a dead body? What do the yanks do? Other than the right to legally carry a gun.

"Come on, I'm tired. It's late, and I'm no good at guessing. No one will know unless your car has a bug? If that's the case, then they don't trust you. Your bosses have no faith in your ability to get the job done."

I didn't mean to poke that way. Still, without thinking, I tried getting under Mathew's skin, playing him off against his employers and seeing how brave he was.

"Piss off. The family knows they can trust me. Shit,"

He cocked up, pressing a finger from his free hand to his mouth to be quiet. He said family, which made me think. Yanks and family gave me the idea of a mafia-type situation. Then I thought better of it; that stuff doesn't happen here. Mathew had been bugged, though.

CHAPTER 25

'Broken Home,'

We were outside my home, twenty-five Dilston Grove Bermondsey. The lamp lights were on, and a shadow was beaming against the left sidewall—at least one adult-size. That's all I could see from where I was. Quiet, everyone keeps themselves to themselves, and no one knows what I do. I've taken pride in keeping my work-life separate until now. I didn't want problems turning up at my front door.

My porch light was still on, making it easier to see no one was waiting outside. Everything felt calm, a little too so. My heart wouldn't rest; my ears could tell that. They also told me that Mathew, next to me, was as cool as a cucumber.

He was close to my back. Near my right shoulder, with the gun in his left hand. Digging into my back. Looking around as we headed to the door, nothing stood out. No typical bad guy vehicle. It's normally a black four-door of some sort, enough power to stand a chance of getting away. Black, dark blue or white is the go-to colour of choice. Or a crusty old van is attempting to blend in as a works vehicle. Whatever that would be for these people.

There was none of that. Next door had a beige Ford Escort. A couple of doors down had a green racing MG. So, nothing is out of the ordinary. That worried me. Was it all a ploy, a setup to see how I would react and what I'd do? My brain was reaching to explain why the world outside my house seemed so normal.

While his heavy footsteps continued a couple of steps back, I could still feel the metal of the muzzle brushing my spine as we neared the point; I had to do something. Try catching Mathew off guard. The way the last forty-eight hours have unfolded set the bar for the guard level that should be up.

To say I didn't see this coming would be an understatement; perhaps I should've. I was too focussed on what might be behind me without thinking about what may be in front. I never imagined Hannah would let herself be fooled by someone like Mathew.

The eerie night singing of a nearby Robin or nightingale buzzed in the background; A sobering breeze whipped past my face as my foot touched down on the raised doorstep. Alexandra nagged the same blooming doorstep to re-lay a little over three weeks ago. Uneven, she said, someone will trip, she said. Only a quick job, she said. It took bloody ages. Now it's nice, even as Light cracked towards me, streaking across the grey stone slabs.

The door was ajar. I froze on the spot. My stomach twisted into knots, showing that the shit had hit the fan. Last week I went to a domestic call; I found the front door open, just like this. I see the lady of the house on the floor. Too badly beaten to move after her husband stormed out, leaving the door open. So yeah, nothing good in situations like this.

"You sure you want to do it?" The words drifted over my shoulder, causing a slight shudder in the silence.

"Why? You're going to kill me anyway, so I may as well see,"

"I don't give a toss either way,"

"Well, I want to know first; I have to,"

"It's your funeral,"

Trusting myself or my senses was no easy task, with emotions blurring and blending; I had to give them a go. Mostly, I felt fear; while on the verge of going in, I felt it even more, knowing what was to come. I closed my eyes, ears straining to hear my thundering heart. Slowly, I heard more. My brain jumped to the worst-case scenario, making tears trickle down my cold cheeks. There was nothing inside: no frantic heartbeats, heaving breathing or squealing pleas. It took my breath away.

I breathed in deeply, inhaling the cold smog in the air, the damp grass across the road, cut earlier in the day. Then further. Bringing a smell; I've had to come across far too much in the last day or so. Not the kind I wanted in my home or ever expected. I had picked up on the overwhelming and intoxicating stench of blood—lots of it.

The tears became rainfall. The door swung open with a nerve-wrangling creak. It's always been there and ignored. But now, in a terrifying moment, the creak sounded spookily loud. Behind it was a wall of stench far more potent than I first inhaled. I was fearful then, even more so now. No one came. No bad guys rushing to greet us. Just silence and fear...

No sooner was the door fully open than my fears were compounded. I couldn't move from the spot. I didn't want to. My stomach knots had become a bubbling mess. Not of the rage, I'd been experiencing. I was too heartbroken for that. In a fleeting second, my world had blown apart. I didn't know why. Yes, I'd saved a boy. That's more than expected.

But to face nothing other than pure horror and savagery wasn't called for. The lounge diner was a crime scene, and strung up from the ceiling light was the blood-covered, skinless body of a woman—my wife. There was no one else it could be. I could see the fleshy white, pink, and red textures dripping with stomach-emptying fluids. Those bastards had mutilated her, going beyond a straight kill. They shredded and peeled her body like she was a spud.

My world was changing before my eyes, yet I couldn't shake a strange feeling. The blood was driving me nuts and fuelling the thing inside. Little by little, the rage crept in. I didn't have the strength to hold it back. Not now. Edging forward, the smell grew stronger. There wasn't much of the lounge that hadn't splattered with blood.

Then it finally dawned on me. Where was my daughter, Rosalind? Wiping the tears from my cheeks, I became frantic, hoping she hadn't met the same fate. In the lounge, I saw something else, a message painted and dripping red across the back wall above the plush purple sofa.

'The Devil's Circle,'

"Don't forget this," I hear a click, the gun pressed against my head. The metal grooves rubbed side to side over the thin skull flesh and hurt, not compared to what was to come.

"You don't have to do this. Isn't all of this enough? Isn't my family enough?" I could barely speak between gasping sobs. Everything good in my life was gone.

"It has to happen,"

"Please, I'm begging you,"

"Too late."

I had no strength for a fight. I closed my eyes tight, tears rolling down my cheeks, closing off to the world, expecting, waiting for the end. A few seconds passed, nothing other than silence until I felt the pressure ease off, sliding limply and suddenly down my skull. I heard a heavy thud on the floor and a smaller one. My eyes were still closed, straining eye sockets. Slowly I turned, cracking the eyelids open.

An overwhelming sense of relief hit me, and sadness rolled into one. Mathew was dead on the bloody floor, throat ripped through by the only thing I could think of, 'old red eyes'. No one else was around. The gun had fallen two feet away. I still had that empty feeling; my eyes drifted, letting the horror sink in. My wife was dead, but... Wait, where's Rosalind?

I could only see one body. I ran through the house, calling her name, but I heard nothing. No cries for help came back. My ears were in full flow, with no other heartbeat. The only saving grace was there was no other dead body either—a glimmer of hope in the darkness. I still had something to cling to. I flipped the note, bracing myself.

'We trade you—boy for your daughter. He will die soon enough, anyway. Don't come looking. Don't interfere. Or more will die, and it will all come back to you. We will watch,' I didn't get it; they mentioned trade, alluding to me living, yet Mathew said he'd been told to kill me. 'The family knows they can trust me, is what he said, yet the note makes me think it's not the people he thought. Is there more than one family—all on the same devastating path?

I peeled my eyes away from the note. As positive as the news was that Rosalind was alive, I've been around long enough to know these situations never end well for the one taken. Yes, there was hope; she was alive, at least. But for how long? My house was a bloodbath, and I would look guilty. I had to get help, praying I would see my daughter again.

CHAPTER 26

Charlie clunked his three quarts full glass down heavily, drawing my attention to the papers with a spray of whiskey landing on the crowd. The paper soaked it up sponge-like, making a trail for another glimpse of the mysterious long-haired bloke—a haunting from Skip's past. My hand shook, trying to understand, feeling I wasn't connecting with what I'd been told. Daydreaming, lost in a haze, wondering what the hell is going on.

Who was I? they had turned my world upside down; I remembered very little of my childhood as it was, but now it seems I know even less. To hear that there could be a terrifyingly valid reason; rocked me. Going back nine months, I would've dismissed it all. Pass it off as nonsense. That's the past. My nightmares have been telling me a preview of a story.

Thanks to Skip, that story begins at the start of his career. The bone-jarring sound of heavy iron chains rattled in the darkness, crashing loudly onto concrete. I'd thought of them as the ghosts of Christmas past. Now they're the ghostly sounds of my past.

The tale was too detailed not to be true, backed by the newspapers, and Skip had had plenty of time to be sure. We've worked together a few years now, and he's helped me get over Helen's death. He did that, knowing what he did. Why hadn't he told me sooner? Were they playing me for a fool? Did Skip want me on the borough to watch over me for other reasons? That had to be why he didn't seem so surprised when I told him what I'd been experiencing.

I wanted more proof, but I wasn't going to get it from these two; I'd settle for another point of view, with one person in mind who'd been cryptically warning me. He could end up being a crucial piece on the board. Whether, right now, he'll give the right answers or even straight ones remained to be seen.

That aside, I was bothered by something else. Dalton told me to worry about Charlie. I had that in mind when I summoned him, but the curve ball I got when it turned out he knew more than me already. It has me questioning who to believe.

The former turns up bearing gifts in the form of an old box with no lock or handle, only Latin lettering. Was Charlie given it? Or a lie? Until I could be sure of everything, there was no way I was attempting to open it yet. My head spun with a harsh reality circling my brain; deep down, Skip must hate me.

"Did you find her?" I snapped into Skipper's reminiscing, breaking out of procrastination.

"No, lad, I tried. Over the years, there had been clues and whispers. But until now, she's still in the wind."

"Skip, you mentioned Hannah; I realise mother's name; did you tell her about Mathew?" Charlie's eyes dart to Skip, who begins fidgeting with his empty glass and looking toward the bottle. I'd slapped a nerve. What else didn't I know? It had to be more about Mathew.

"He's dead, lad; as I told you, his true colours came out, and he met with an unfortunate ending. One of a few along the" Sweat dribbled down Skip's forehead, Charlie's too. All Skip had done was state the obvious and avoid my question.

How would Charlie know any of that old stuff? He was a few years older than me, coming later to the home, and Mathew wasn't around. So how would he know of his existence? Something didn't add up. Too many secrets, something my dear old foster brother was equally guilty of. The more the day has worn on, the more I've heard; I've watched his behaviour; he's been acting off.

'Brrrr, Brrrr, Brrrr, Brrrr,'

The house phone interrupts; at a good time, Skip jumps up, seeming grateful for the distraction. It was also my chance to make my excuses and visit that 'keep your friends close and enemies closer,'

"Hello,"

"Yeah, it's me. What happened?"

"Flippin' heck, not again. Ok, I will be in as soon as I've had a coffee to shake off the cobwebs." That's all I heard before Skip put the phone down. His hand was back to normal, a little shaky; other than that, he was ok, brushing it down his face. He was being called back in; the look on his face told me it wasn't good. Charlie remained emotionless, wide-eyed, glaring at the bottle.

"Everything ok?" I already knew what the answer would be.

"There's a body, a bad one,"

"Isn't that CID territory?"

"Normally? Yes. But this affects us; It's being dragged from the Thames. Throat has been torn through,"

"How does that affect us?"

"That anonymous call seeing your car dumping a body-shaped bag," I'd almost forgotten that, blurred by the other issues. But the blood was passed off as an animal.

"Yeah, but the blood in my car wasn't human?"

"No. But until the coroner can give an accurate time of death. All roads lead to you,"

"Yeah, and I'm sure that would be convenient for everyone?" My mouth ran away without thinking, making Skip's jaw drop open, turning to face me.

"What the hell is that supposed to mean? Do we want this? Is any of it? Oh...you think we're setting you up? Listen to yourself, you bloody idiot. Fucking ridiculous," Skip flipped, face turning red; I'd pissed him off. If he was acting, it was a bloody good performance.

"You know what, Skip? Right now, I'm not bloody sure of anything. I haven't had a decent sleep in months. Fucked up dreams. I black out and wake with blood under my nails. You drop this bombshell. I was drugged, and somebody shot Chris in case I've missed anything. Now Another body has turned up in the Thames. And I'm being made to look guilty," I fired back, feeling a frightened, freaked-out mess.

"Hey... Calm down, ok. We're all on the same side. Yes, I'm pissed and carry tons of baggage, but that's not on you. A kid can't be blamed for the crap he can't control. You didn't ask for any of it. Since then, I've tried to keep you safe from afar; you might not like how my motives sounded, but I thought that keeping a distance and guiding you with little prompts until I could bring you close would save the trouble. The past was going to come out, eventually; we have more to contend with than most,"

"Yeah, but how did you know I would join the police? What made you so sure? All the talk of what's inside waiting to come out, what is it? Why do I black out? Could I be killing and not remembering? Like the body, they've just found?"

It couldn't be me, could it? Even if I felt sure that was the case, the memory was blank and waking up in the car didn't help. The evidence road was being engineered towards me. I needed some space, a chance to clear my head but be safe with no more trouble.

"That was where your mum came in; we figured a structure and extended family would be good for you. A friend in training school owed me a favour. Hence you came to this borough. The other crap, well... I had them, too; I often woke up at bus stops. Sometimes naked, bruised, broken all over and never recalling how I got there. -

-I figured it was that side of me taking over. We're two things... I mean entities in one, each fighting for control. One is a potential killing machine. The amount of research I've done over the years. I keep coming back to the conclusion. We're shapeshifters,"

Skip knew more. Dropping one bomb after another. Answers were needed and pushed him hard; a part of me wishes I hadn't. Never would I have imagined what he told me.

"Are you sure? I mean, is that what this is? We need to know more; I don't want to be a danger to anyone,"

"We won't let that happen; that's why we've been keeping you close, to be safe until we can handle what comes," Skip's red face was easing and was making sense.

"What do you mean 'we've', both of you? This doesn't seem right, though, having to hide and be secretive; we need to be out there looking for the actual killer and then focus on the other stuff. It feels like no one else is trying."

I was the easy target for whoever was in charge, and I still couldn't put my finger on the connection with Chris. What element of his case stirred the pot?

"Yeah, Charlie has been keen to help. He knew about you from a young age, and your mother told me to watch him too. Now it's all taking shape. I know it's not you, and that's what I will say when I go in. Until then, you need to keep your head down. Even more so with what you know now,"

"What I know is a lot of things from the past; newspaper clippings about a boy. Oh, I should be dead already. I will keep my head down. In my way,"

I understood what the skipper wanted. Still, I thought it pointless to attempt being housebound after it backfired last time... I had to find a way to draw no more attention—Especially with the fallout from the 'Thames body' to come. Even if Charlie has been helping, I can't help thinking he has a problem with me or what Skip spoke of; Charlie looked uncomfortable and edgy.

"With each day passing, you will experience strange things and need to be careful; I've got to play nice while trying to keep my shit together. So, I expect you to do the same."

My mind flashes back to the image of a claw sliding from his finger under the moonlight. To think he must keep a lid on that; how it was even possible defied my imagination. Then I got to thinking, putting together some dots.

CHAPTER 27

'Friends close, enemies closer: 9 pm Railway Tavern,'

The ambience of cheesy pop music, sweaty, stale beer and peanuts made a pleasant change from the unfortunate usual. Those stories were playing over and over in my head. I had to persuade Charlie from being my chaperone. He insisted on coming, wanting to watch over me, considering he's been at arm's length until I called. I found it strange.

I'd been blaming myself for dragging him back into my life, but by the sounds of it, he's been on the periphery for longer than I'd realised. The secrets they're keeping felt the least of it—the worried expression when I mention Mathew; what else weren't they saying? What else had Charlie been up to? Christ, I could do with a drink, something to strip the lining of my throat and numb my senses.

Skip introduced me to the devils on the shelf, acquiring a taste for such toxicity. These little things make it harder for me to believe my silly notion of his hatred towards me. I pushed a little too far earlier. The case and the chaos around it have screwed with my brain. I hope the next little venture sheds some light. Why didn't I die back then? I had to find out what my frenemy knew.

Right on cue, a draft of overpowering cheap aftershave rushes through. I hear the squeal of the pub door hinge. I don't think I will ever get used to things like my heightened senses; they are going crazy right now. The footsteps were heavy and uneven, with the right foot leading the way. I counted six strides from the door to the corner of the first table, where a blissfully happy couple was enjoying a bottle of red wine.

Ten steps past the friendly giggles, sidestepping the last-minute shuffling of a chair backwards by an oblivious, slightly drunk bloke in a suit. Who had been more concerned about telling the time on his watch through squinted eyes? Another eight, and I had the diminutive figure looming by an empty seat to my right. The aftershave did very little to disguise the overcoat of cigarette smoke. Marlborough, at least 20 already today.

"I wondered how long it would take you before you called," the Cockney prince said.

"Well, I never imagined I would. So that's a point to you."

"Oh, I never had a doubt. Just wondering why it took you so long to figure things out," Dalton headed to the bar, leaving that comment hanging. Were we on the same page? I felt pressure to get answers while trying to play nice. Skip didn't give much away when asked what side Dalton's allegiances lay on. I had to say something to get him to open up.

So much so that my head was hurting, daydreaming, watching the ice melt in my drink. Sticky elbows were a short distraction as I waited for Dalton to return. He clopped back, carrying two pints now; I didn't have him down as a heavy drinker, so I assumed one was mine. That one act of generosity had me on the back foot. I was all set for a game of verbal insult tennis.

"There you go. Get that down your neck; I have a feeling this conversation is going to need it."

"Cheers. Why did you agree to meet?" He was staring at me, silent apart from the frothy sips of his pint. I was waiting for a reply. While Dalton was slipping down some humility with that pint, I may have to eat some humble pie myself if I wanted to get anything from him. No, scratch that; if I was going to get the answers I wanted.

"Because you and I have more in common than you think. Judging by your face and that call, you have some worries and need straight answers."

"You hinted at many confusing things. None of which has caught Chris's killer. And you keep dancing to someone else's merry tune. Stop me when you think I shouldn't be worried."

"Fair point. But it's not what you think. There's a target on your back now. I've tried warning you. Screwing everything up, so you get free. I had to follow up on the call; I'm getting pressure from above. How else was I going to get you thinking? Make you realise there's a bigger picture. Now, that body has surfaced from the Thames." He knew already I figured it would filter to him, eventually. But being off, I counted on him not being OIC. Skip had his reasons for going.

"I heard. I promise. It wasn't me. At least, I don't think it was,"

"Memory blanks? I knew someone else that had them. You're right, though; I know you didn't. But someone is trying to make it seem that way. I believe someone is setting you up."

"Let me guess, Skip? Do you have anyone in mind that might want to do that?" I took a large gulp of beer. Much needed. My heart raced, feeling knots in my stomach.

"One or two. Maybe even a blast from the past. I can't prove it, though. Not yet, anyway. And yes, Andy, my friendship with your Skipper goes back a while. I know everything. That's why I have this."

Dalton slid his arm forward. Pulling back his sleeve narrowly, avoiding sticky alcohol rings on the table. Revealing that serpent ring on his skin. It was the symbol I saw on the post-it note Chris had left. Frayed dark edges burnt deeper; it was branding—the kind of cattle.

"Let me guess, Lewis and Kelcher, maybe even Harkes? What the hell is that? Why would you do such a thing? It looks bloody painful,"

"How did you guess? I can add more to that list. Andy was right. You have what it takes to be an outstanding detective, maybe even a necessary evil for the darkness to come. So, if this bullshit drags on for a while, I thought this would cheer you up. Mutilating myself, I did a bloody painful thing to help your Skipper. Absolute agony that nearly made a grown man cry, that's for sure. -

-Cost Andy a rare bottle of single malt, but I saw it as my way of helping him and the many others who have lost children up and down the country. I was part of a central London misper unit. Our paths crossed after the massacre at Skipper's house. -

-The name on the wall was the first clue. So, I used street-level contacts, greased a few unsavoury palms and had the bosses create a deep cover backstopped with enough of a past not to cause issues. It was a long operation, but eventually, we nicked the right scumbags and got our 'in" Dalton slid across what appeared to be a warrant card. Opening the thick black leather, it was my detective's credentials. Dalton displayed a kindness I never expected for what it's worth now. It's official, 'Detective Reynolds'. Helen was gleaming with pride, a big wide smile fixed in my direction.

"Wow, thanks for this; I don't know what to say. It's appreciated,"

"Don't thank me yet; you will be under my guidance if we get through this. Figured it is best that way, knowing what we know."

Did I ever imagine I'd be working under Dalton when he burst in on me at Chris's body? Never in a million years. Would've got better odds on picking the winner at the national. He's greatly changed my estimations; it could be an interesting partnership. I couldn't help smiling back at Helen; if only we could crack open a bottle of Champagne together.

"That's a big 'If' at the moment. So that was true; the house and his wife. Skip mentioned 'the devil's circle.' is that who you mean? I take it; you've finished the deep cover assignment,"

"Well, no. Once you're in... Well...you're in until you end up in a body bag. So, it's still going. I can go months without contact, but when it happens, I must report to the DI and fire it up the ladder. These people are so bad that I fear for my life daily—a highly connected and well-organised family, The Whitlock's; it took two years to earn the trust for their name.-

- They're into a million ways of shady shit and control various parts of London, looking to expand further north. We're talking about drug trafficking, people trafficking, murder, and kidnapping. Child kidnaps to order. And so much more. To make it worse, according to rumours in the minion grapevine, the family is uniquely different, the same way you and the Skipper are. Not the people to be messed with."

He knew so much and seemed to take an enormous risk. If these people are so dangerous, he must watch his back; maybe that is another reason he's glad of our impending coalition. There's no telling if anyone knows his secrets. What if Lewis and Kelcher were on the 'Whitlock's' payroll? Maybe Harkes too? In this day and age of financial struggle, anyone is fair game to be turned except me, Skip and Dalton.

"I thought those organisations were only in America or movies?"

"Ha, we should be so lucky. You see. Over here, the bad guys aren't content with the usual gangland shit or being a crime lord. They must go a step further in the evolution pool." Taking the plunge to meet Dalton was worth it; it worried me, and I got hit by the realisation we were only pawns in a bigger game. Yet, without him, I'd still be circling the dark.

"What have they had you do? If it's anything like how I think it is. They got you doing something shady. You know, to prove yourself," There's a grey area, a guideline an undercover must follow and could push towards if the case was a high priority. Yet, like with any job, there are hushed stories hidden in the 'old sweat' archives. How far has Dalton strayed past that line?

"Nothing too serious. Don't worry me, old mucka; I'm a good boy, as you'll see; I might come across as a heartless bastard, but I'm not. For this level, there are contingency plans upon contingency plans when the hardcore shit gets asked of me. Fake outs, using unclaimed bodies from the morgue to stage a scene. Trust me; you need a strong constitution for this shit,"

"Can't you fake your death to get out?"

"Sadly, it's not that simple. The family or lower rungs of their ladder see me as a cop gone bad. I die; they'll send someone to check I'm genuinely gone," Dalton dropped his head in his hands, sounding defeatist, letting out a heavy sigh. I hadn't seen him like this before. So far, he'd been confident. But now his guard was down.

"There has to be a way; it can't all be on you; what's skip said to do?"

"Short of dying for real. We only have a few options other than causing noticeable problems. So they lie low and leave me alone for a while, again," It's hard to believe the sacrifices Dalton and Skip have made over the years. I'd been focused on my issues since the revelations started contemplating anyone else. Instead, I only saw a picture of where the world had turned against me.

"Speaking of dying, what exactly do you know or figured out about this mess and the links with Chris's death?"

"Well, for starters, you should be dead; as a child, they chained you up in a basement and burnt you to death, amongst other things. You miraculously healed, thanks to the creepy stuff the Whitlocks or whoever is into. It's all real. And a demon is involved; I tried to call bullshit all of them years ago. I saw a few things that ripped my eyes open to the endless possibilities we aren't alone in the world... In the beginning, I thought Chris stumbled upon that information, made the links, and someone wanted to shut him up. I learnt he had an informant. I'm not privy to,"

Dalton mentions a demon. The red eyes in my nightmare. Skipper described the same in his story and that bloke in the newspaper.

"That's what I'm struggling with; Skip got hurt and lost his family over this and me. He got changed because of it. Now what?"

"We're not sure, other than it's coming full circle. Only, I have a theory, and you will not like it."

"Oh, tell,"

"When Skipper's wife got killed and his daughter taken, there was a mess with a guy called Mathew. Now your Skipper said Mathew was about to shoot him in the back of his head to clean up. But mysteriously, had his throat ripped out. That was the story we stuck with, what I didn't tell the

Skipper. He disappeared two hours after the coroner removed Mathew Causton's body."

"What the hell do you mean, disappeared?"

"We found the coroner dead at their office, and Mathew was,"

"Why didn't you tell Skip?"

"He had enough to deal with, and by the time he was ready, Mathew still hadn't turned up, so I saw no point,"

"Right, so where are you going with this?"

"What if Mathew has come back? He knew quite a lot back then, into quite a lot, but I have no idea who Mathew aligned with. Skip mentioned they ordered Mathew to kill him while knowing some suspects had Skipper's wife. We thought they were all part of the same people now; the more I think about it, I'm not so sure."

The situation kept getting weirder; how could Mathew have survived? Skip told me Mathew's throat had been ripped out. So how had he disappeared two hours later?

"He should be dead; then again, so should I. What now?"

"Now, lie low while this body in the Thames business gets sorted. Let the Skipper find out more, and then we can debrief and devise where to go. We don't want more bodies to turn up; it will only get harder to deflect. Take a trip to Scotland and visit your foster mother; if you need more convincing about what we've said, Hannah will tell you. It could be a good way to stay off the radar. Oh, did you speak to Charlie?"

"Yeah, you could say that. We had a little catch-up; I feel Charlie is keeping something from me."

"Well, I would add him to the suspect pool if I were you. Trust your gut because mine tells me he's a little off. Does he still live in Bethnal Green?"

"While we're at it, why don't we start a 'dead pool' too? Guess who will die next? So, whys is that? I took a long sip of my beer, looking at most customers, drunkenly oblivious. Dalton gave good advice, but I couldn't wait around for the answers to come to me.

CHAPTER 28

Midnight-Dockside Lambeth Bridge 21st September 1987.'

The Albert Embankment was a chaotic carnival of flashing blue lights brightening the night, riding on the crest of eeriness. London Bridge was closed. Blue-white cordon tape flapped in the mild breeze, carrying the stench of polluted, salty water and doom.

LAS had abandoned their wheels halfway up the pavement of the Embankment, blocking off a space to prevent would-be voyeurs. Officers, the coroner, and medical responders huddled together in a clearing having a 'mother's meeting'.

A passer-by or, if the pattern has continued, an anonymous caller probably felt obliged to ring 999, and everybody came as a precaution. LFB was still by the water, packing up. I don't envy them at this time of night, having to go there with little visibility. I could see staff hastily erecting temporary shelter; little spits of rain had fallen.

They hastily stretched blue plastic sheeting across the pavement. Under the streetlight's glow, I saw a body-shaped bundle wrapped in bin liners. I hung back, using the shadows as cover near the bankside wall, close enough to see but far enough to stay out of sight.

I couldn't resist looking over the thick stone wall and imagining how the body dump happened. On low tide. It would take two people lifting three and a half to four feet high before getting enough leverage to throw out. Hitide with choppy waters would be easier, needing only one person to hoist over and drop, allowing the current to drag away from the edge.

The anonymous call to the police mentioned one person; I hoped the view didn't trigger a memory of me hurling a large wrapped corpse into the slimy green cesspit.

There was an eeriness about the murky surface, with a sheet of fog steadily moving in. I sure as hell didn't want to go out that way. I'd prised the location of the body from Dalton; I know he told me to keep my head down. I couldn't; yes, I intended that trip to Scotland for some answers, but there was an unshakeable feeling I had to come to see.

Dalton had to head off elsewhere, trying to tap more information on the newest name to the suspect list, Mathew. I could go around in circles wondering how he'd survived. Especially towards me; I was a child when he died. What would Mathew's motive be? Who was he affiliated with? If it wasn't the people at Skips?

According to the story, neither party was on the same page. I thought about how the throat was ripped out. Skip described his leg injury. What if Mathew's jugular didn't get ripped through? Bleeding to the verge of death. But became something else.

Another unexpected twist. If so, Mathew would want revenge, maybe even connect with old friends. Chris pissed on the wrong person's shoe to warrant being silenced and the cover-up. The dots weren't connecting between his death and me. How could I rule it out after everything I've seen?

That brings me to The Whitlock's. Until then, I hadn't heard of them. That's the point. Make sure the shit doesn't come back to their doorstep. Dalton says he hasn't done anything bad for them; would he admit it if he had? He'd played both sides so long that it might be hard for him to tell the difference. He seemed ok in the pub, but I'm finding it hard to be sure of anyone at the minute.

Taking a deep breath and closing my eyes, I focussed on my hearing. The way I could hear heartbeats trying again. The mass of voices travelling on the sound waves drifts through the endless wind. I heard laughter coming from people driven numb by these everyday occurrences. Others are discussing their weekend plans. It was the huddle nearest to the bloated, wrapped bundle I drifted to next. The sound of bubbles and oozing fluids cascading onto the plastic sheeting. A blade slices through the tight liner. Then...

'Oh my God, oh my God. Ewwww. Urggghhhhh,'

Gasps for air; the decomposing, rotten flesh sets free a stench that has viewing eyes gagging for their lives.

'Holy shit, that's officer Lewis. Look, there's his name badge,'

Rocked on my heels, not for the first time lately, I catch the echo of their words pinging away in the distance, leaving me feeling my luck was about to turn from bad to worse. The suspect pool had been reduced by one, and I was back to the drawing board. It just got even worse—A heavy-footed clop exited a car.

The ground was shifting beneath my feet. It would be best to put the pedal to the metal and breeze over Westminster Bridge as far as possible from me and the scene. I could tell those feet anywhere, bulldozing his way forward. It was the skipper.

'What the hell are you doing here?'

My ears pricked up at his whisper, and the immediate thought was, 'what the.'

'I can smell you, Georgie lad, and there's no mistaking your heart going two to the dozen.' He was right; my heart was racing. I wasn't sure if it was for Lewis's dead body or if the skipper knew I was there. Feeling a little stupid, I whispered back. If anyone had seen me, they would've thought I was mad.

"How? I mean, that's bloody freaky,"

'One of the few upsides of this weird crap. My senses get ramped up, worse the closer we get to the moon. As I'm sure you're finding out,'

He had a good point; they were upsides, strange, but all good. Now I was in a genuine dilemma: leave or stay. He knew I was around; I had to see his reaction when he saw who the body was. A test of sorts, listening for his telltale signs he was lying or unsurprised by the name.

"Skip, where's Charlie now?"

'I don't know; why?'

"A scary hunch,"

'Well, I must see this. Hang back out of the way, ok?' I did as the skipper told me to, scanning the crowd for conversations. It was surreal having a conversation so far apart from hearing whispers. That was until...

"Holy shit, Lewis," Skip saw the name tag; judging by the smell drifting my way, it would be hard to see who the body was.

'Georgie, it's a name-tagged uniform on a body. I can't tell who, 'He whispers.

"How long do you think?"

'Hard to say. Anywhere from two days to two weeks, depending on where it was beforehand. Which doesn't track. Lewis was there when they found you at Chris's body. Then you're flat.'

Water degradation would normally make it impossible, but after only two days, not so much. The body might have been stored elsewhere if the crowd noises were anything to go by. I only hoped contact DNA might be trapped if the body wrapping was tight enough.

"Dental? Can you see if they're intact? Also, at the scene of Chris's body, Lewis wore collar number seven eighty. I could've sworn that number belonged to someone else."

My collar number doubts resurfaced; someone walking around posing as Lewis. I heard a heavy sigh of reluctance to move forward until shoes scuffed across the pavement, followed by the overt gagging and churning of the skipper's stomach. Yes, I could hear that much; if I weren't focussing on prying eyes and Skip's reaction, I would gag too.

'Without touching. The face is blooming distorted, parts sunken with lips like a prune. All I can see is a ninety-year-old's mouth. No teeth. Wait, seven eighty, you say? That was Martin Tanner, a thirty-year-old who retired a few months ago. Shit, I can see some numbers. Wait, these say five twenty,'

One of my worst fears came true. The body was the real Lewis; I remember the numbers assigned to the name. Then who the fuck is the guy in Lewis's uniform, and where is he? How the hell was he so calm when they found me?

"The throat, can you see?"

'Ripped through, not fully but deep enough to make them bleed out.'

"By what?"

'Meant to be claws, but...'

"But what?"

Skip suddenly stopped whispering; other footsteps approached. He didn't sound sure about the wound inflicted by claws. But why make it seem that way? I heard another voice, a familiar one. It was the guvnor, he interrupted Skip, getting him to move away from the body. The situation didn't sound good—none of it. I considered leaving for real this time when my ears caught something that stood out.

'So, where's your boy?' Ins. Mitchell

'Who? I have no children, none that aren't missing, anyway. You told me to leave that alone, remember?' Skip.

'You know what I mean. George. Where is he? No one was at his home,' Insp. Mitchell.

'Come now, Sargent, harbouring a murderer. Is that the policing standards these days?'

A voice I didn't recognise, a London accent mixed with something else. I couldn't tell if it was even this country, but it was worrying. Oozed confidence, yet felt a little sinister.

'And who the bloody hell are you?'

Skip got knocked on the back foot; his heart roared to a ferocious tempo. His apprehension increased my fear and the urge to run. They'd been to my flat, already deciding I was guilty.

'*Andrew, this is Warren Whitlock, sent by the mayor's office under a new professional standards initiative to audit the handling of priority crimes, with murder and the response to young person cases. In particular, the Murder of Chris*'

'*And now, officer Lewis, it appears someone has a hard-on for killing police these days. I don't know where he is. He didn't kill Lewis or Chris, it doesn't add up, and the throat looks like an animal attack.*'

I slumped further into the darkness, near a half-naked tree and my car. I was shocked at the steps they were taking. Remembering what Dalton told me about a crime family from Enfield. The Whitlock's. So that's how nothing sticks; they know people like the mayor.

'*An animal attack? Any you have in mind?*' the voice of Warren Whitlock sounded confident, a little too so. I thought he was testing Skip; see what he knows or back him into a corner.

'*Well, I'm no expert. You're best getting a vet. But if I were a betting man, and I'm not, by the way. Not anymore. It's a claw mark, the size of a bear,*'

'*A bear. Not in London. It looks like the coroner has a job and a half,*' Ins. Mitchell.

Skip was dumbing it down, knowing if he said what it looked like, some might think he was mental. By some, at least. Others would mull over the possibility, wondering if such a thing could exist. Perhaps the rationale was an escape from London Zoo.

There was a moment of silence other than footsteps. All three of them stepped away, breathing varying sighs of what should be stress, for Skip at least, only for two to stop short. One heartbeat was calmer, the other still racing. That was Skip.

'*One moment Sargent,*'

'*If it's all the same, I don't have time for interviews or reviews. We have murders to handle.*'

'Cut the bull, Sargent. This isn't a game you will win,'

'Sorry, what?'

'I said you should bring him in.'

I cupped my mouth in surprise, even though I shouldn't have been. Not really. Not if the name meant what Dalton says it does. Warren Whitlock had let slip he knew what was going on, at least as good as. My only question is, did the skipper hear and play dumb or had Whitlock taken by surprise and not register.

I skulked to my car, not wanting to be seen, trying to gauge the audacity of a man like Warren Whitlock. For someone whose family is synonymous with a 'million ways of shady,' He sounded like he would linger awhile. A bullshit p.r. stunt that doesn't make sense.

Why would anyone want it highlighted unless the Whitlocks knew what's been happening lately and wanted to be closer to the action? Meaning someone close to us is feeding them information. For the mayor, money talks when you have a political campaign to run.

Feeling safer in my car, I stared up and out the window at the full white glow in the sky. Feeling hypnotised, my gaze lingered. That was until a sudden wave of pain rode through my stomach. Knotting up, cramping, but thousand times more painful, I struggled to breathe as sweat dripped down my face. Then I saw it—hand clutching the wheel. Blood spurts forward; a claw slithers out of my index finger. Then one after the other, they all followed until I had a hand full of thick, grey, terrifying claws.

The same way Skip described it. And how I saw it at his house. I could feel the anxiety brewing; I didn't want to see them; I didn't need it happening. What if someone spots my car, and I'm writhing around in pain with a claw for a hand? It would be game over for me.

I closed my eyes tight, hearing the loud beating of my heart through my eardrums. Taking a deep breath, I fought hard to slow it down, feeling the knots ease with every deep breath I took. The beats slowed too. Finally, I slumped into the arching of my seat, exhausted over an event so small.

Fearing the worst, I cracked one eye open to look at my hand. The claws were gone.

With a loud exhale, I couldn't stop a smile of relief from spreading across my face. A glance into the mirror at my reflection; this wasn't a dream or nightmare. The change was real; this was my life now. All but ready to slowly drive away without drawing attention. From the corner of my eye, I saw an object on the passenger seat.

Not sure how I missed it in the first place, but it caused a slight panic. I was staring at the box left with Charlie at the house. How the hell was it here? Had he been here too?

CHAPTER 29

My fingers traced across every ornate groove and bump of the lid; so old, a dark grey, made of a material like metal and another unknown substance that resembled bone. The mixture of symbols around the edge-raised embossing gave the impression that they served a purpose; I'm yet to find out what that is.

Hooked, like in the diner, I was looking at the moon, sun, and a dog shape that I'm sure was a wolf, but the person and other symbols I still didn't understand. It was vaguely resembling Latin. The blood-red half-moon shape jewel in a circular blackish band sucked me in. With the moon skimming its surface, it glistened, producing a mesmerising glow that locked my gaze at the diner.

This time around, no shadowed beast, but the pull was undeniable. Unique yet strangely familiar, giving me a sense of belonging, resting on its four clawed paws. The decorated symbols on the sides were more similar—a few could pass as English.

Fiddling, some parts felt loose. They did more; I could push them down. Row by row, I worked my way through, five lines down on all four sides. Grabbing the notepad from my pocket, I jotted down each symbol letter I could press down. Time wasn't on my side, hearing my name in the distance and not out of fondness.

Oh, I was regretting my curiosity now. Being out in the open had me vulnerable and on edge. Glancing around, making sure no one was nearby—

no one was watching. The blue light carnival is still in full swing. I could no longer hear Skip's voice or Warren Whitlock; I heard something else.

They were circulating my description and details as a person of interest. Then came the registration number. Dropping my pen, I'd pushed my luck far enough. I was too close not to catch a wandering eye if anyone looked this way. Nine. That's how many I have found so far. One looked like a reversed 'E', a crooked 'T and A.' keeping my lights off; I rolled backwards with the minimum of revs, trying not to alert.

Ever so slowly across the damp road. Gravel crackling beneath rubber, I wheeled forward, lights off still and nervously looking in my rearview, watching the crowd fade into the distance and further down the embankment. So much is going through my mind; where could I go? If they've been to my flat, someone will watch for real this time. Skip's house would be one of the first places they'd look.

My options were limited. Scotland was looking increasingly likely to be my way forward. All I had was the clothes on my back, spares in the boot, my wallet and a freaky box.

'So, what's the next move, Georgina?'

A Velcro chill cuts across my shoulders as a haunting whisper breeze behind me. A tentative glance in the mirror causes a shudder. That's all I needed driving from a dead body in the night's black. It was Chris; he looked like shit, the same as my nightmare.

Decaying flesh oozing blood from his eye sockets. Chris's jaw swung loose the way it had at the crime scene. This time, he was less menacing and more death-warmed up. Ironic as it was, he was... Well... Dead. I shook my head, not wanting to embrace the elephant in the car. Thinking of the logical next move was where my mind should've been. Instead, I had the insane urge to respond.

"What do you want? You're not real, a figment of my imagination. Right?" I hoped I wasn't going crazy, but he would disappear.

'Even if I was a figment, would that make me any less real? I need you, Georgina; I need you to help me find peace.'

It was my turn to be left, with my jaw hanging open. How could I help someone no one else could see, let alone find peace? I couldn't even handle what was going on with me. Every time I attempt to get on track, something else happens, like a dead body.

"How do you know that? How do I do that? I've been trying; all I find is more trouble,"

'Denial. That's what you're in, denying seeing me so you don't feel insane. It's not like you didn't see the dead as a kid or draw them?'

How did he know that happened? I've only just been hit with the revelations. Is Helen a ghost or a memory?

"It's not like there's an instruction guide for this; everything I'm hearing feels new to me, so how did you know?"

'It's not like there's a manual for being dead, either, is there? Yet here we are. Time to polish them claws and get with the program. Watching that drama at Skip's house unfold is quite tragic, really. That brother of yours is shifty as fuck.'

That's both unsettling and reassuring to think the ghost of my friend was watching the whole time yet questions Charlie too.

"How... How do I help?"

'Follow what I was working on, a house fire in Bow, a rescued child that healed. Gets fostered, and something bad happened, but I can't remember. It goes black to the sound of gunfire. There's a face, a glimpse, and then it blurs. But...I...I... think I knew them. I remember feeling that I wasn't scared until... nothing.'

With every piece of information crammed into my brain, it's a box filling up, gradually reaching the point of bulging at the seams and creaking under the strain of trying to stay together. Pressure building until it's fit to burst. That's how it felt. The more I've heard, the more I've seen. I don't know how much more I can take, the ghost of my dead friend telling me he was making connections to the child. It cost him his life, I cost him it, and the person who killed him was familiar.

"Ok, say for a minute I buy into this 'find you peace' bullshit, and I can see ghosts. Is there anything at all you remember? You say blurred; maybe if you tried?"

I couldn't believe I was attempting to talk to my dead friend, a ghost. Wait a minute—the drawings. Charlie gave me pictures I had made as a child. Each of the grey figures. Showing the word 'dead' above them. Seeing myself with bright red eyes, monstrous fangs, and claws for hands was all adding up. No wonder I don't remember; seeing that shit must've fucked me up as a kid. Have I been seeing Helen's ghost all this time?

'No, but there's another article mentioning the Surrey incident. A fire occurred a week after the family had their child taken.' Why hadn't the skipper mentioned that as part of his story? He spoke about the boy, me, being snatched but not on fire. My plans were about to change. Regardless if someone is watching, I must risk heading to Skip's place for that folder. Home is another story.

* * *

On autopilot, Chris haunted me in the rearview, and his words reminded me of the missing tapes. Who has them? Who was the voice on the edited one after they shot Chris? The smart money had been on Dalton, but he has shown me a side to him I didn't expect and information that blew my theory a world apart. Should I tell the skipper about Mathew being alive?

Dalton thinks he may have come back. Perhaps he's the killer, but how would Chris know him? If the Whitlock's were such a prominent criminal family, why would one of them stroll down to a murder crime scene? With the guvnor, no less. Was Mitchell on the take as well? Another Whitlock lackey. There must be something in it; he's not a stupid bloke and wouldn't make rank without some ounce of intelligence.

He would've checked credentials unless the mayor vouched. What was Warren Whitlock hoping to gain? Sizing Skip up? Being so far away from the scene left me at a disadvantage because I didn't get a view of what he looked like, only his scent, a very woody yet sweet with a hint of death. And not because he was near Lewis's body; this was more the warming of dead skin. I went to a sudden death once; I've been to a few with a similar couple.

One had been dead for weeks. Taking a tumble, landing next to the radiator with the heating on high. An older white guy's body was liquified and turned black when a smell was reported. Then there's Mrs Silas, seventy-four; she'd been dead a few hours. Her heating was on, she was still in bed, all snug, and they had kept her body relatively warm. That's the smell I was picking up on, an ominous emptiness with dying cells kept warm.

Looking in the mirror again, Chris was gone, leaving me with the notion it may not have happened, still denying the possibility. That I could see and talk to the dead, trapped, left in a limbo of having unfinished business is what I thought after Chris wanted to find peace. In his place, a single, off-white headlamp is weaving its way through the traffic behind me with a purpose. A street light allows me to glimpse the bike chassis colour, dark red.

The rider was all black, calling me paranoid, but it seemed to want to catch up. I had to be sure, accelerating before faking a sharp left onto Parry Street; I wanted to see if it would follow under the flyover. It did, dropping off a little. Perhaps two cars back, sitting behind a ford Granada. Coming through the other side, I narrowly hung a sweeping right onto south Lambeth Road, avoiding a yellow VW camper parked awkwardly on the left. I hoped the acceleration at the last minute would throw them off. It didn't.

Sweat dripped down my back, and the light followed my driving line. Rolling down the window, I listened for the engine, wanting to know how much power it had and how quickly it could go. My money was on a 125CC and a top speed of seventy. A loud, high-pitched screech with a slight growl towards the end. It got worse as we passed a built-up area.

CHAPTER 30

With a panicked dryness papering my throat, my eyes pinged back and forth in the mirror, ensuring they stayed in my sight.

The plan was to make a fast loop without jumping lights. Double back to waterloo bridge, shoot over and head towards the A10, where I'd have the chance to put my foot down a little—reaching the A201, a quick mirror check, it was suddenly gone. It couldn't have been my imagination; the behaviour was too suspect.

Maybe the rider realised they'd been made and backed off. Either way, it was bloody strange and worrying. But I could breathe a sigh of relief. The chaos was getting to me. On edge for the next twenty minutes; my head was on the swivel right until I neared the skipper's home. One turning short of Dilson Road.

The street nearby was dead; keeping the window open, I dropped my lights again, creeping forward. Looking at every car, I passed. Not a van in sight, but plenty of vehicles; most I could picture belonging to a neighbour. Turning into Dilson, it was much the same dark black night sky. Faulty street lights here and there.

Eerie, but nothing stood out. Two doors down, that's how close I was—paused, feeling how easy it had suddenly become. If that was possible, the outside world had got quieter—no nightingales or insects, no footsteps or rumbles of passing cars. I ditched my car in the shadows by a service road leading to some garages.

Like Kelcher and co came steaming to my back when I found Chris, with no thought or foresight, tempted to rush through the front door; this wasn't the time. I needed to think and scan my surroundings better. Think how a burglar would—looking for alternative entry and escape routes. Even if I took the lazy front door with no issues, I once needed a good Plan B— failure to prepare and prepare to fail, as they say.

The service road sloped over rough brown concrete to a row of dilapidated garages. The doors went White, Blue, White, and blue alternating.

A little to the left was a muddy alleyway with tufts of grass bearing up to the left and right. That was the path I needed in an emergency. It ran behind the gardens, so if the shit hits the fan. I can escape via the garden door and skip the fence without breaking my neck.

That was the plan in my head, at least until I stepped out of the comfort of my car. A damp, smog-riddled breeze rushed past my face from right to left. Ominous until I caught the metallic aftertaste. The hackles rippled to attention in the wind like the rasping spray from a deck of cards. It was blood.

With the changing direction of the gust, I couldn't pinpoint where it was coming from, but being so close to Skip's home had me fearing the worst. The stomach-twisting knots were coming, and I couldn't stop them.

Muscles pulled, pinged and twisted; I felt bone-jarring pain roaring through me. It felt worse than before. A glance at my hand, the ghostly grey claws slid scarily forward, and blood gushed, but that wasn't what I smelt. My body was changing, skin darkening, looking harder, feeling bigger, a more rigid shell. I shifted, and it terrified me.

Rushed thoughts blazed through my head; my eyes were drawn upwards to the glaring full moon. My body was on fire, trying to handle all my emotions at once; Fear, panic, anger and power rumbled into one; I struggled to control my feelings. That smell triggered the other part of me. I don't know how; I don't know why. But I feared being caught. Panicking over where that blood was coming from, I hoped it wasn't the skipper's home. Not again.

Yet, the anger surprised me, an uncontrollable rage that had my blood boiling, heart pounding, and lust for inflicting nerve-shredding pain. Hand in hand, with a sense of power I've not felt before, not that I could remember. There wasn't time to dwell on what was happening to me.

I quickly shifted focus to getting in his house and out again—fighting against my body and the thing wanting me to embrace it. Stumbling heavily across the uneven pavement, I hear a squeal and a hiss from an angry cat far in the distance. My hearing had dialled up another level. If only I had control, it would be one less problem to focus on.

Closing my eyes, I reach for something to help centre the brewing storm, searching the darkness of my memories. The image of my wife drifts forward. She's smiling; it was warm when we'd been out for a picnic at the park. Helen got a little sunburnt, even complaining she was cute. I had a rare day off enjoying some quality time, simpler with no stress, shape-shifting, or dead bodies. It's her smiling face I wanted to see, to feel her smooth skin beneath the roughness of my clawless fingertips.

She breaks through, smiling. My heartbeat slowed like a regular sinus rhythm; Helen was my anchor. I had to hold on to her. The claws stayed out, feeling more natural. I daren't catch my reflection in a car window; I wasn't ready for that. Tapping into highly heightened senses. Smelling other things, I wished I couldn't.

Following the blood, moving forward confidently, how long that would last was anyone's guess, but I had a hold of it. I was fifty feet from the front gate when I heard it.

"How does it feel?" A throaty rumble pierced the air in my direction.

I didn't want to answer. Because that would be me acknowledging that my night was about to take a further turn for the worse. It had rocked me on my heels even with feeling stronger from the slight shift. There's another heartbeat, steady. Confident. Followed by the sound of friction, fingers or nails rubbing together. Wait, maybe even claws.

I clung to her image; she soothed me, slowing everything down in the darkness. At first, perhaps subconsciously, I was coming to terms with the crazy.

That red haze was back, like the diner—a bloodied glow. Everything showed as either black or red. My heart was going two to the dozen. Stood in the doorway of Skip's house was a blackened bodily shape, not as tall as the skipper or me. At most, a medium build. But what concerned me were the long-pointed fingers that made me look at my hand. They were claws. A reddened fluid dripping from the tips had to be the blood I smelt.

"Wh... who are you?"

"Let's not waste time playing games; I know why you're here. How could they know what I wanted when I wasn't sure besides a folder and the chance to regroup for a minute? So, I ask again, how does it feel?"

"No games. Too tired for all that bollocks. How does what feel? You're going to have to be more specific. I feel a lot of things right now. And one of those is pissed." I'm slowly edging forward.

"How does it feel to realise all you are is one big, dirty secret? That's all alone, and nobody is looking out for you anymore. The pain is about to come full circle. Ironic that you darken a doorstep like before." There wasn't one ounce of waver in the voice as it beat a path to my ears. I could feel a few tiny hairs on my ears dancing with fear.

'You're not alone, buddy,' Chris appeared out of nowhere, loitering nearby, my invisible cheerleader.

"Secrets have a way of breaking out, eventually. Dirty is the only perspective. As for being alone, that's a feeling I've lived with; it's nothing new, nor's the pain, so why don't you either fuck off or tell

Me what you want. Besides, how do you know I'm alone," I holler back, attempting bravery to mask how I feel.

'Because I want to watch you all suffer. I will watch you all burn. The golden boy with his bodyguard. Everyone's favourite problem child who can see dead people. Let you feel what it's like, and lose those you love." 'talk of seeing dead people, a bodyguard and losing those you love' grabbed my attention. Whoever this knew me, or at least about me. Maybe even more than I did.

"Why would you want to waste time doing that? I'm a nobody. A footnote in another crappy day,"

"Ha ha ha, don't play the fool now. You and I both know otherwise. Do you ever think about the past? Think about the pain. Remember the smells, the screams? The sweaty twitches on a sofa? Maybe even the chains?" The voice didn't sound familiar, but it could be modulated again. The only part he said I could relate to was the chains; as haunting as they are, the past and I weren't familiar as much as I've tried.

"I have no idea what the hell you're on about. Who are you, and why are you at my friend's house?"

"Friend? Shadow? Bodyguard? Or the reluctant surrogate father who should've died? Because of you, I have none of that."

I stood fifteen feet from the gate in a state of confused rage, softened by not understanding who or what he was talking about. With the blood still circulating, I had to know I had to make a move in case Skip was inside, bleeding out. Not that he should be home yet, but the blood worried me. Sensing his movement, I edge to my left. His feet scuffed across the rough grass. I felt he wasn't there for a standoff; he was about to escape.

I dart for the gate, catching my foot on the uneven floor. Grabbing hold, I nearly ripped it off, not realising my surreal strength in this heightened state. The silhouetted figure darts over a three-foot hedge and makes its way over the neighbour's side gate, leaving a strange attempt at a growl in his wake. I didn't follow, too concerned about what may have happened inside.

The front door was ajar; I couldn't hear anyone or anything inside. The coast was eerily clear. Yet the smell of blood wasn't. Stronger now, different though. Carefully treading through the short hallway, I peered around the door frame; the lounge was almost how I remembered it last. Almost. With one horrifying exception, a large pig carcass flayed across the coffee table with blood dripping down—a glance up to the same wall from Skip's wife's death. There was a different message; in more blood.

'Eye for an Eye, Tooth for a Tooth. Is the big bad wolf ready for the truth?' Breathing a sigh of relief that it wasn't human. Whoever that was, is enjoying playing games. All I seek is the truth and an end to the chaos.

CHAPTER 31

Reynolds, 25 Dilson Road,'

Staring at the flayed pig, whose organs spewed across the carpeted floor, my stomach churned. I don't know how butchers do it, day in and day out. I much rather see the cooked version. Feeling the claws retreat and my heart ease, I was more like myself. The mess on the table could easily have been Skip I'm staring at or Charlie.

Whereas the latter seems to be a mystery. It didn't sound as though Skip knew either—working around the room, picturing where each of us sat last—replaying right until Skip had his face in his hands before the phone rang.

The strange interactions between Skip and Charlie made me believe something else was missing from the story. A truth that thing was referring to, maybe? The pig aside, there was nothing else on the table. I knew where the box was, and I still needed to digest how that got into my car. It must've been Charlie; I don't know how, but why do that?

The folder was missing; Skip had left it on the table when he left, and I'd gone shortly after. I thought about the side cabinet where he retrieved the old whiskey and the folder. It's rude of me to contemplate sifting through someone else's stuff, but I didn't see any other way. Aware Skip may come home at any moment, I went to the cabinet doors, glancing at the doorway out of paranoia.

With the cupboard open, there was plenty to drink, and it sure looked appealing, but no folder, leaving me frustrated at the lack of answers. I didn't want to get caught, so I had to get a move on. There was no choice; I had to invade his privacy quickly. If he came home, everything would be fair game; I would say I found the house insecure, which I did.

'What's the matter, Georgina?' I jump in surprise at Chris again. I might get used to it, but while I'm creeping around in Skip's home looking at the 'bloodied message' and worried about him coming home, it feels like I'm treading on razor blades. It wouldn't be so bad if he appeared in front; I would still jump at first, but at least it would be less frightening. Like watching a horror movie, the tv is in front of me, and I know something will happen; when it does, I still jump, but it's ok.

"What the hell now?"

'I could ask you the same. I leave you alone for a minute, and porky has paid a visit,' Chris's comment caused a slight smile to creep on my face—a much-needed moment. But that's Chris; he had a sense of humour that could find the funny in anything.

"Yeah, that's the least of it. A message on the wall,"

'Are you ready? For the truth? Whatever that may be,'

"I'm not ready for any of it, but I need to know. The same that I need to know who killed you and Lewis."

'Oh, he's gone too?'

"Yeah, a body in the Thames,"

'It sounds like body bingo at the minute; I'm curious whose number is next. How sure are you it's him?'

"I'm not. But it has Lewis's actual collar number; the Lewis that caught me at your crime scene was wearing the numbers of a retiree. Still wondering which one is the real deal,

'Beats me. I'm dead, remember. But trust your gut... I'm relying on you,'

If I were to trust my gut, I would tear the house apart, looking for clues to link the stories, the past, and me. Now that the folder's gone or at least hidden somewhere else safe. He may have more if he has one folder from all those years ago. It's a game. I like to call it 'show and tell' when a friend is greedy but too tight to chip in for the beers.

They ask if you have any alcohol; you do but don't want to share the good stuff, so you get the obvious cheap stuff, making sure your friend sees it. Now, what Skip did was show a little of something to tell me what I needed to hear—producing from his obvious place without revealing 'Aladdin's cave. It's sneaky bastard stuff but effective.

Being a nosey shit, I poked, prodded and rummaged through anything I could. The lounge was a bust until I saw a blood smear on the glossy white door frame. Moving closer, it looked like an arrow pointing to the stairs, with another streak on the wall directing up. So, I followed. The creaking of each step prickled the hairs on my neck. The feeling of a haunted house reaching the top of the floral-patterned carpet, I faced four rooms; one was a bathroom, and two were open bedrooms.

Yet the fourth was closed, with a 'bloodied smiley-face.' painted on the door. Curiosity killed the cat. But I'm no cat. The silver handle was cold to touch; a part of me had second thoughts about invading Skip's privacy. If the stories were true, they had done once before it, to horrifying effect. He was a friend and mentor; this was wrong. But the need outweighs the bad.

I was at the point of no return; the door squealed open, needing a dose of WD40. The inside air was stale and dusty, cooped up, waiting to be released. Fully open, I saw a child's 'my little pony' bed to the right—a pink and white wardrobe to the left corner and a chequered pink carpet. I was in his missing kid's room. He'd hoped all this time, not wanting to change a thing in case they found her. I got distracted by overwhelming sadness, sensing the emotions trapped within the four walls, the relatable pain, all feeding my own.

What I nearly had; even though he never made it, for a short while, I had a son. Dragging my eyes away, looking around before I moved to the wall behind the door. My heart skipped a beat—a brown wooden desk, folders and an entire wall looked more like a spider web. My head was bouncing right to the left, with pictures, lists and places linked by strings, with two larger photos in the middle.

What the hell had Skip been doing? In his daughter's room, of all places. One picture showed a young, dark-haired girl. It had to be her, no older than three, with a cute chubby smile that melts a heart. The other was a boy about five. It sucked me in; I could feel my eyes narrowing to focus on the detail. He seemed familiar. The more I stared, the little sparks went off in my mind. Flashes of the boy in a house.

Brief and strange. There's an A4-sized diary on the desk, faded beige—old as the missing folder- had a piece of paper edged out at the top. Flipping the cover straight away, I noticed that the paper belonged to a newspaper clipping. It's a copy of the one Skip showed me earlier—the house in Surrey and the boy aged two taken in the early hours of Friday, 29th April 1959. The family home in Denby way. The number twenty-five was written in a black pen at the top and circled. That had to be the house number; Skip found out where I needed to go; why didn't he tell me

The first page had an extensive list of names, ages and places—all in the skipper's handwriting. Page after page after flipping page. Skip had created a record of missing children up and down the country. Was he keeping tabs on Dalton? I could tell it anywhere; he has a unique way of looping the tail on the 'G's and Y's.' there had to be hundreds, all in black and white, while they searched for his daughter. Skip had been holding out the hope that could drive a person made or make them do something irrational.

I slapped the cover shut, feeling dirty. A grubby unwashed one that wouldn't scrub away easily. I'd seen enough. Although I took the clipping, the wall was overwhelming and had taken years to put together. Another curious thing about Skip's web of mystery, pinned across the bottom, is a long grid of moons and years; the cycle until the new moon, followed by a blood moon. The next one is in.

September, three days after my birthday. Scribbled on a scrap piece of paper above it, 'calming the shift, ancient Egyptian talisman from the god

Anubis,' Skip seemed to have his fingers in many pies. But I had to wonder how much of it was for his self-interest. And what else would he do to get what he wanted? Anubis was a God with a head of a wolf. I remember from school; what's the link to the shift?

I was engrossed, my eyes gazing at the two pictures in the middle until I heard a banging of the front door and a bellowing 'hello. Who the bloody hell is in my home?' It was Skip. I hadn't closed the door behind me. It hadn't crossed my mind to do. The lure of the blood and the wonder of what the hell had happened outside. Who was that person? A sudden realisation hit me. Skip was enduring everything I was, and no doubt could hear me. I didn't want to be caught in his kid's bedroom.

That wouldn't be right. My head spun, looking for a way out and feeling trapped, just like beginning all of this, finding Chris. I clap my eyes at the window. Only one would open but appear wide enough for me to squeeze through. It had to be a twenty-foot drop. What else could I do? There was a creaking of steps, heavier, scarier; my legs shook. He would surely hear a heartbeat or catch my scent. It was now or never.

The window was stiff; the metal frame ground together with a slight squeak that caused me to cringe and look over my shoulder. Hearing the creaking step boards echo through my ears. I pulled myself up on the ledge and leaned sideways out the window, hand resting on the wet stone. The wind whipped across my face, giving me second thoughts. Contemplating, edging back inside. Skip's heavy steps were at the top.

My heart sped up. I feared being caught on the ledge. My hands throbbed. The claws were coming again; the moon was beaming down on me through the black sky. Feeling the familiar adrenaline spike, I hung my legs over the side. I see a spurt of blood. I couldn't let that be left behind. The ledge felt deep, at least eight inches, enough to slide across, with my back hugging the glass as tightly as possible, pulling the window closed.

I took a deep breath and jumped, expecting to land in a painful, crumpled heap on the garden slabs, maybe crack or twist an ankle. I didn't.

Instead, I was on my feet, bended knees and feeling strong. I wouldn't have thought I would feel so good from that high, but it felt like a three-foot wall. It was about five feet. I stuck to the escape route I had thought of earlier, easing through the back fence.

I'd landed on the flat muddy pathway, about to run to the car, when my mind pressed pause. Hanging back a moment, I could hear scuffles from the creatures of the night. A stray cat or a fox darting in and out of gardens.

All I saw were glowing yellow eyes; something inside me clicked; a primal instinct was causing the red haze to come again. It was brief but caused the creature to fuck off. I can only assume my eyes glowed back, my way of telling it to piss off. Still, it was automatic, with my consciousness feeling like only a passenger.

With number one million on the surreal moment's list sinking in, I hugged the fence, listening, letting the chill graze my face to cool me. The electric noises from insects beat their way to my ears. All until the squeaking of metal on metal. Skip was at the window, and I stayed ducked below the fence line, peering up when I could.

He looked pissed, a red-faced beacon in the night. But he didn't examine the window, too focused on what he'd come home to find in the lounge. Clutching my chest, I slumped into the mud, breathing in relief. Every breath out was a white cloud carrying my fear. I sat, taking stock of how it had come to this. 'Is the big bad wolf ready for the truth?'

CHAPTER 32

'Layby A3- 7 AM 21st September 1987,'

The sun bounced through the window; a cluster of rays darted between the front chairs, caringly warming my midriff. My neck felt sore, bordering on locked at an awkward angle. Every move sent shooting pain behind my ear.

The rolled-up jacket did little to weather my movement through the night. Restless, with a lot of information weighing heavily, how much life had changed this year.

A chill had muscled in overnight, almost arctic. I was lucky to have spare blankets in the boot. I appreciated having our old navy blue, green and red tartan woolly picnic blanket as a cover. It started at my lower chest before being dragged three-quarters over my face.

To wake to that little warmth coming through was nice. My body ached head to toe, the price of having nowhere to go. Hotels would've been the second or third places on the list to check within a hundred-mile radius. Sleeping in my car wasn't on my to-do list but a necessary evil. Especially so soon after passing out from being drugged in the diner.

That's my life now, unable to risk going home. The run-in at Skip's place was a sobering warning to expect the unexpected. Instead, I drove until I could drive no more, playing over the pig massacre and blood message on the wall. It felt direct, and they knew me.

Never in my wildest imagination did I expect to find a misper board upstairs. It made me wonder how many years he'd been at it, how many lies he's told, and how many secrets he's kept. Finally, I pulled into a Layby on the A3 and bunkered down for some needed rest.

If the map was right, I was only twenty minutes away. Still not far that I couldn't turn around. What was I hoping to find? A kidnapped child from over twenty-five years ago? How does anyone comprehend a bombshell like that? If there had been a fire, there wouldn't be much left, but maybe someone knew where they moved. The fear of the unknown was real, eating me up inside.

The strange grey box was staring me down, and I'd put off trying to figure out any other letters or symbols. There was another a niggle in the back of my mind, adding to the many already circling there. Wouldn't he have gone there if the Skipper had known the address all this time? Wouldn't he have told me at the end of that story? I know he's holding back from me, and it's more than the secret board in his kid's bedroom or the list of missing kids.

It was a little after seven o'clock in the morning, and I didn't know what to do for the best. The people I trust could be counted on one hand. With the list of truths, I've been getting even shorter. Charlie's behaviour had been odd, keeping in contact with Skip behind my back. I knew little about Warren Whitlock and his family to include them on my suspect list. Now the talk of a resurrected Mathew.

Since we parted ways, I wasn't the closest foster brother, but I didn't get why they were in touch. Was he another pawn in Skip's crusade to find his daughter, or was there something I was missing? He's the only person left with the box, and it ended up in my car. Lewis was there until the body was on the Thames. I need to find out who was wearing the uniform at Chris's crime scene, and Harkes is always missing carrying a chip on his shoulder. Those were the feasible ones.

Who were the voice on the tape and the looming shadow outside Skip's house? Alluding to things from the past. How did they all connect? And where's the mystery bloke who gave Charlie the box in the first place?

The chess board is taking shape with pieces positioned for 'checkmate.' Who was I playing against?

A puppet master that's pulled me out into the open, painting a target on my back. Evidence moulded to fit a narrative that forced me on the run. Stood outside, stretching, overlooking the relatively empty road, so used to either being drugged, followed or attacked with a gun. Hoping to get someone's attention, I don't like being used. I had to take back some control. And there is a talisman out there that can help control what's going on with me. I need to find it.

This dead calm unnerved me. Opening my door to get in, wary for a moment, hearing cars coming down the motorway. A check over my shoulder, watching them breeze by, I could relax again. Even if only a little. About to head off, my brain felt messy and needed a distraction. I figured about playing some music to ease the tension—a little genesis to lighten the mood.

'Click,'

I press play, waiting for 'throwing it all away.' Where I left off last, nothing happened straight away; my finger poised to press eject; It might have got tangled, as sometimes happens.

This is officer Chris Wells; another week has passed since my deep dive into the corruption suspicions I raised with Sgt Morris. My update is in two parts. The first is broader, scratching the surface of issues. That goes alarmingly deeper than I first expected and further afield. So many crimes have been allowed to go on unresolved with no oversight. Missing person reports are at an all-time high with branches of priority crimes and arson. Arson, intending to endanger life and murder, is not far behind. -

-it seems often, it gets swept under the carpet. A particular case caught my eye, cross-linked from out of the borough—Burglary, the kidnapping of a young boy. Reports claim the family was unassuming. But in doing some digging, the names of the family given for the reports were already dead. A family that had been presumed dead in a car crash up in Yorkshire. Although the car exploded, search teams could find no body parts. Police believed it would've been next to impossible to be any. -

-A bizarre set of circumstances ends up with the kidnapping. I'm awaiting a call from Constabulary officer Jenkins in Surrey to discuss this further. My update has increased Sgt Morris's interest, keen to know what I find regularly. Now for the second part of my update that involves the Skipper himself. I noticed another pattern of events.

One arson twenty-five years ago, when the Skipper, a PC, attended, someone had redacted his case papers. Still, soon after, there was a suspicious crime scene at Skipper's home; They blocked most of it out. -

-A murder took place, and the suspects took a child. The deceased adult male disappeared from the coroner's office, Mathew Causton. The incident was written off as a sadistic body snatcher. I did a deep dive into Mathew Causton. Before that night, Police wanted him in connection with two murders in the south of Wales and several kidnaps around Dumfries, Kilmarnock and Livingston in Scotland.-

-It's more recently that's alarming; his passport flagged at Luton airport. As far as I'm aware, dead men don't do planes. That adds to the many strange connections I've been finding. To think the prompt came from the unlikeliest sources. I'm at a loss for how he knew. My hunch to have him on the C.I. payroll is paying off; for now, there is a niggle. I'm unsure of His motive.

A tear ran down my cheek; my friend was onto it. He knew something wasn't right. Sgt Morris eagerly awaited, indeed. The name Mathew has popped up again, a dangerous man that Mother luckily escaped. How was he alive? Who the bloody hell put it in my car, though? It had to be Charlie. What was he trying to gain?

Did Charlie want to open my eyes without telling me himself? Because it's made me want to go there even more. It was a mess—all of it. Tapes found, tapes go missing—mystery voice of the gunman, whom Chris may have known. Now a Deadman walks.

* * *

'25 Denby way, Chobham, Surrey, 8 am,'

The street was quiet, expected for eight o'clock in the morning. I was twenty-seven minutes away but decided on stopping nearby, a slow drive around the village of Chobham, on the river Mole, just north of Woking and surrounded by heathland. That's where the house was, in a small, quiet village on Denby way. It had the feel of 'well to do. They are slightly better off than others. Not a lick of rubbish in sight; even the payphone was spotless. It makes a change from the usual 'call girl postcards'.

The type of houses to stand the test of time was built in the late 1930s -40s. With their unique stamp on the place, some were named with one obvious similarity. The hedges. All neatly crafted and shaped. The kind that people spend their Sunday hours grooming to keep up with the neighbours. That's what I saw when my eyes went door to door, alternating between glossy black, red or blue. All except number twenty-five, standing out like a sore thumb and not for its splendour. Not how I pictured it from the tape.

Where a once-thriving front garden stood, there was now six feet tall by at least that wide, silver metal fence panel coated with black dirt showers. They ran the perimeter of the corner property, cutting off from the pavement and short grass verge. The property had died; nobody wanted it to contaminate the rest of the street.

They had all but disowned it. Only the kid was taken, according to the stories and the tape. But I saw nothing more than a shell—time had left a carcass dressed in burnt white paint, taking hope and happiness. The roof had a carving of bust red tiles; some were stained black. The rest is open, with burnt matchstick beams hanging in the air. Shiny black flakes looked purple when they caught the sun.

There wasn't a window that survived being blown out with scorch marks raking across the walls. I stood outside, soaking it in. The wind carried that old burnt wood smell, damp and full of nothing good. The family was gone, although to Chris, not for the first time. The front door had some flimsy-looking wood padlocked across to deter intruders. Looking around, I couldn't see any of the locals even trying. It won't take much to bust open if that's what I would do.

All I needed was a local calling the constabulary on me if the Jenkins from the tape turned up. My hands gripped the metal fencing, feeling loose enough to manoeuvre a leg from the concrete stabiliser; the screeching rattle sounded loud. I'd made a gap about two feet wide towards the bottom—a quick look for passers-by and curtain switches, making sure nobody heard or saw. I took a deep breath, crouched, and began shimmying my way.

'*Taking your time Georgina,*'

'Fuck off, Chris,'

I stood amongst the black, charred debris of wood, glass and the remains of a broken home, my broken home. I could picture the red-amber flames raging against the windows, heating until the house couldn't hold it in any longer. Chris appeared at an inappropriate time. I should be grateful he's the only one I can see so far, judging by the drawings I made as a kid. There was a couple of inches gap between the door and the frame.

The padlock looked tough—a thick, silver yale one with a spinning cover over the keyhole. In a few yanks, it wouldn't budge. All I was doing was making noise, risking being caught. So, I did what any mentally confused bloke on the run with a beast inside him does.

I took a deep breath, gripped the door and tried to concentrate on that part of me and the power it brings, remembering how it felt jumping from Skipper's window. Nothing happened. I closed my eyes and tapped into the pain that's dug its hooks in my life of late, even the revelations of pain gone by—the moment I found Chris—getting attacked at gunpoint. The nightmares and the terrifying stories about my childhood. My heart thumped, and my pulse quickened, pounding through my ears.

I felt it. One by one, a claw slid forward. I felt stronger. Everything heightened to the point I heard voices but couldn't see anyone nearby. My eyes opened, and I yanked on the door again with a swift move. It came flying open. The lock ripped off the frame with its bracket still attached. One, two, three, four, five, six, seven, eight, nine, ten, eleven, twelve seconds, and it went again. I'm looking at the silver shackle in my hand, claws wrapping the looped catch when I see the symbol appear on my wrist again. If only I knew what it meant.

I'd released a torrent of built-up, burnt particles. Everything inside is decimated, as expected. My first step gave a loud creak, jarring my hackles. The claws stayed out, and the red haze came. Not fully, but it came—a blood-red glow around the edge of my vision. The hallway was large. A doorway to the left and a staircase ahead that swings round to the right and above a door.

That was the remains of a kitchen, but next to it was an opening, no door but darkness. Spooky, possibly a basement. Not my first choice to visit. I still have that last nightmare in mind. The walls were mostly black, but any white patches had pictures. Hard to tell what they were from where I was, but they made it seem like a home.

What happened here? Why burn it down?

I continued forward, wondering what I was hoping to find. Anything to give me hope and some resemblance of the truth. Stood less than two feet from the staircase side, I noticed indents in the wood, covered in black dust, but they were there. I brushed my hand over, cutting through the filth. I felt them on my palm—all different shapes, running my hands up and down the length of the steps stringer. There were lots of them in the box in my car.

'Ancient Latin Georgie,'

My neck twisted. That much I had understood for myself. Chris popped up out of nowhere again to state the obvious.

'See the truth through different eyes.'

'That's what it says, Georgie,'

"How the hell do you know that?" Taking the word of a ghost, was he even that? I thought ghosts could only haunt one place. Then again, what do I know?

CHAPTER 33

Denby Way, Surrey 8.30 am,'

Dwelling on the symbols, what normal family carves a message on the staircase? Then again, life isn't normal. I could feel the house breathe, and it sounded fragile, the wind whistling through, causing it to yawn. I decided on upstairs first, carefully keeping my footing to the edges with the most support.

Every timber squeal made me feel I could crash through while imagining I was walking the steps in my nightmare. It was damp, smelly and burnt, but there were still some. Without the carpet, I would have.

My hand brushed across the smoked walls as I walked, fingertips feeling the thick, gritty dirt and torching left to rot for years. There was so much sadness and fear trapped within its frailty. I could sense it. I could feel it. In the first picture, up close, was a dark frame. The colour before, I couldn't tell. The heat had broken the glass, and flames had bubbled the photo paper.

Black blisters had destroyed the faces, but there were four shapes, two adults and two children—one younger than the other. Going by the sizes, a difference of only two years. It made me think back; I couldn't remember being in any family photos while in foster even as an adult. I hated my picture.

But those loving captured moments as a child with parents, I don't have any. I'd planned to change all that when our baby was born. I wanted to be the father that I couldn't remember having.

A few spaced a couple of feet apart as I climbed the steps. I am still trying to figure out what I was hoping to achieve; my goals would've been different if the house had survived and I'd found someone living here. I was trying to save a wasted journey, hoping to unlock some deeply entrenched memory as a toddler. Based on a morbid story, one that I had yet to decide if I believed or not. I mean, what does a child remember, anyway?

The place wreaked of burnt matchsticks. A million of them all lit at once. Reaching the landing, it was worse than the downstairs. So much worse. I couldn't even figure out where the point of origin would be other than it was somewhere upstairs. To start, there didn't make sense for a quick hit-and-run. No, this had the makings of a coverup, ensuring the fire reached the right places to burn everything in its path. There was another smell coming through, though—an accelerant—petrol or similar.

Someone walked over to my grave. A chill grated down my back, soaking in the devastation with every step I took. Something bad happened here, for sure. Long after, they kidnapped the boy. But why? The pictures show another child; maybe those people returned and left no witnesses. There were four rooms, one to my right, one halfway down the hallway, one opposite and another at the end. I was drawn to the one halfway down, a pull to see. It was a child's room, not fitting the older of the two.

It had been fire damaged, but the door had been closed enough to keep most of the fire out until it was extinguished. A lot was intact and neat looking. A shrine that the family didn't want to disturb, hoping one day they would get the child back, the same way Skip had hoped for his little girl. I say 'they' and 'the child' out of a subconscious reaction that will continue until I get definitive proof.

Moving on, looking at the room had emotions stirring, yet, as I went to walk forward, I noticed more carved symbols around the frame. Remembering the one downstairs, I look over my shoulder, expecting to see Chris. Let him translate. He wasn't there, nor was Helen. But the words popped into my head.

'See-through different eyes,'

It was making me think, the red glow—a deep breath, the same as I did at the front door. My heart sped up; my stomach knotted. Then it came— the blood-red haze. At first, a veil was over my eyes, but I knew I needed to be different, to stop fighting and embrace it. That would be the only way to use it to my advantage. I needed to know more. The glow became a much lighter red, almost normal, yet different. I saw things differently.

The symbols glowed a bright berry red mixed with green, and so did the wooden frames. The threshold seemed different, too, made from other materials. I ran my hand over the edge; it felt solid; the closer my head drifted, I picked up a scent from the wood, not the burnt coating—a rotten berry-like tinge, almost stale fruit. I've not known wood to smell that way, let alone glow.

I was about to check the other frames when I saw the floor, dressed as a crime scene, where someone tried their best to hide the blood. The fire may have torched the carpet, concealing what would've been there. Five large splatter pools and several slashing arterial sprays arching across the walls seemed to be throat height. I saw beyond that, causing a dry throat moment, counting the large splashes and then the sprays.

The makings of a slaughter; my only question was, who's? I didn't want to go any further after seeing the trail of splashes hit the stairs. So, I turned back and followed down, stopping short of the ground floor with my toes pointing to a stream splash near the bottom step. My head scanned, taking in the hallway as if it were the first time again. Picturing it without the burnt damage, how it would've looked.

There were more sprays, lots of them, over wooden floors. Something bad happened. I was now sure of it. Stepping down, bewildered and horrified, I caught sight of the symbols again. Slap bang. Next to it was a large handprint, dragged downwards sluggishly; someone had struggled, wounded or fatal. Looking down from the sliding mark, I notice a section of the skirting board that's different from the rest of the frames upstairs. I crouched for a better look, tapping away; I noticed the panel was loose. Levering it open, a draw slid out.

'Scccrrrttt,'

A scuffing noise makes me jump; I've become a nervous wreck since the trouble started; I look around with my fingers poised, floating inches from pulling the wood fully out. Nothing there; my other eyes were still in control, and I had kept my claws ready.

I took a deep sniff to see if I could pick up the scent of anyone or anything else; everything I was doing felt like trial and error. Who did I have to explain things to? A Sgt with his version of the past. Or my nightmares, blackouts and weird shit that's happening to me. Then there's 'keep your friends close and your enemies closer' at the forefront of my mind. I'd floated adrift. Close to nobody and seemingly the enemy of everybody. To make matters worse, death seems to be wherever I go. Like now, the doomed feeling I had broken into at least one person's final resting place.

The draw pulled fully out, only a small space but enough to conceal a neatly wrapped bundle. The material was brown; to the touch, it felt silky, maybe even velvet with some age. A black leather cord tied it together. It was slightly bigger than the palm of my hand and weighed a little more than a bag of sugar. Moving to stand up, I felt something else move inside; two items wrapped.

There was also the basement. Wary of being caught and tempted to open it. I wanted to see if it was the one from my nightmare. I only know a few places with those sorts of things. Always saw it as American or posh places that turn it into a wine cellar. Ooh, wine, that would be good about now, that or whiskey. I hadn't eaten for a while and needed to fill a void.

Moving on to the dark doorway, an object in one hand, I fumble for the bannister with the other; my foot searches for the next step, catching the edge before tripping down. There's a rounded wooden pole that I grip and steady myself. With no lights or power, I was flying blind until the bottom. I could use my lighter.

I don't smoke, but it's a habit, burning away stray or frayed threads on my uniform. Carefully step by step, until I reached the bottom. Twenty-seven. That's how many steps I had to navigate. Twenty-seven precarious steps feel as sturdy as a twig. Out came the lighter, a silver flip-top that can be temperamental. Can't we all?

On the fifth attempt, it finally lit, throwing a warm amber glow around the darkness. The space was huge. With the light in the air, I couldn't see where my feet were going. So I shuffled forward, scuffing through the dirt, kicking dust into the air and taking myself to the sneezing point. Mostly, it seemed like a typical, dirty basement.

That was until I flicked it to the far-right corner: chains, thick heavy chains—sets of four up and four across. They were different heights but seemed to be arm and ankle height. I wasn't in the basement from my nightmare, but there was something equally spooky about it.

The wall had another chart on a larger scale. Moon cycles, and drawn next to it was a table, counting the days until the next full moon. As I moved closer, I connected some seriously scary dots—chains, moon cycles and claw marks. There were hundreds of claw marks on the floor, the wall, and even a nearby pillar.

There was nothing else of note, but what I saw was enough to have me asking serious questions about the family that lived here and maybe even myself. The stories would have me believe my life started here. The more I connect the dots, the moon charts, and what's been happening to me. Had me thinking of the box, the emblem of the wolf?

Mix that with people. A family like the ones that lived here, and you get werewolves. Could that be what I am? What is the skipper?—my hand shook, causing the flame to flicker. The earlier confidence in embracing the vision and senses had drained away. Thinking back to the fleeting lusts for blood made it worse. Was I a monster? What about the thing outside Skip's house the other night or what the skipper met all those years ago?

It was time to leave. At least get out of the basement. Every whistle of wind or creak had me flashing back to my nightmares while fearing the house would collapse. I put my foot on the first step, getting made to pause and hearing a noise. Unlike the yawning of a tortured family home, footsteps weren't mine. My ears twitched; I wanted to listen past the wind, pushing past my pressure on the step, causing it to creak.

I ignored the scurrying of a mouse ten feet behind me. I was focussing on upstairs. The noise came again; to me, it was a loud, slow, thumping echo—one after the other, two sets. I heard the footsteps of two people moving in unison, but neither spoke. My first thoughts, a nosey neighbour had seen me after all and called the local constabulary.

I couldn't hear any radios. My hand reached for the rear of my waistband. The gun was still there; my problems had consumed me, so it felt as normal as carrying a wallet. Forgetting it was even there. I slid the package into my pocket. I slid the gun free with the other.

Quietly, dragging the slide back until I heard a double click—safety off—all within seconds and the smoothness of a veteran gunman. A skill I don't remember learning. Maybe I have more like that. Skills I never knew I had. Something useful, like being to strip and rebuild my car engine without a moment's thought.

Now that would be useful, saving me a fortune with the mechanics. Maybe even in other languages, English can be a struggle as it is. Same for Dalton and Skip when they get carried away. For now, it's a gun. I drop onto my knees to feel the way up. Footsteps or tripping would draw attention. My left hand was flat, feeling the rough dirt as I went, while my right was balanced on the butt of the gun. I'd made three-quarters of the way before stopping to listen again.

The footsteps were heading upstairs. One set, at least. One foot is heavier than the other through limp, dominance or extra weight. Too heavy to be a holster. Maybe a metal rod. They had made it to the top. I wanted to move but was wary of the other. I stretched myself flat up the steps, so my head was near the top.

The hallway seemed clear, and feet were moving upstairs. If I was quick enough, I could reach the front door, pulling myself clumsily from the dust. I darted forward while the coast seemed clear.

'Click,'

My heart jumps to an echo stopping me dead. A hammer booms, dropping back—the gun chambers. My throat is a desert. I had my gun-holding hand low to the front, fresh air whipping through, carrying newly cut grass. With the sun beaming through the doorway, they wouldn't have seen it. Yet.

CHAPTER 34

Denby way 21st September 1987, 9 am,'

Facing the open doorway to the outside. Breathing in the closeness of freedom, I could hear the sweat pebbles drop—a deep swallow of nerves before moving two steps forward across the gritty black hallway. I was sensing the space between us. A gap of nine to ten feet separated us—three and a half large strides, four at most. Five to seven casuals, taunting with all the time in the world strides depending on leg length.

Death wasn't on the agenda, not if I had my way. They would've fired straight away. They would've been a coward without the emotional baggage of having to look me in the eye while a nine-millimetre piece of brass spirals through the air. No, these wanted something. I wonder if they'd come looking for anything and I'd found myself in the wrong place at the wrong time. Or they'd followed me, which was part of the game.

I had been careful; I'm sure of it. Mindful of any vehicle that wanted to remain exactly two cars behind me. I watched for any that repeated the same moves as me for long periods. Like the motorbike last night. I still need to find out who that was, whether they were part of a collective tail, interchangeable with others if made. These could be part of that. Were they after what I'd found? It could be valuable. I could feel its weight in my pocket, which was stone-like or similar to my hand. My blood boiled; adrenaline surged through my body. Flight or fight, flight or fight. That's what I had to decide.

With my mystery attacker's gun pressed within my fist, chambered and ready to go. I could turn point and have a standoff. I've never fired a gun in anger in my life. But like before, there was a strange sensation I knew how. I knew I had my firing arm to the front and expected two to three pounds of recoil. Not enough to throw my arm, but enough to let me know I'd fired.

Or I may get beaten to the punch. My turning causes a reactionary warning shot. I was playing devil's advocate in my head; what if I slid the gun into my waistband? Introduce myself as a new detective given the unenviable task of investigating a cold Arson case. Ironic really. One of two things could happen at that point. They may come at me based on an irrational hatred toward the police.

Or they could shit the bed and run. It was a 'He'; I could hear the deep, gravelled, husky breathing before another swallow. A smoker too. This was the part I hated about having heightened senses—my sense of smell. Benson & Hedges was his brand of choice while using 'Ralph Lauren' aftershave to mask it. He was making me think this one liked money and nice things on someone's payroll to help him afford those nice things.

The footsteps upstairs were scraping through the charred carpet, heading our way. The uneven walk was more pronounced on the flat surface. I leant towards an injury, old or new; I couldn't tell.

"Well, well, well. Look at what we have here. I'm afraid no" The voice came from upstairs—a Yorkshire accent. Or somewhere near there. Not London. I didn't respond, and I didn't put the gun away. My hackles were doing the macarena. The uneven stepping came as he made his way down the steps. Hand sliding reluctantly down the burnt bannister. He was in charge. The other guy could've spoken already, but he hadn't. No, this man I had to convince to leave me be.

"It's been a long time coming. So, what's your interest here? Nostalgia? Family memories? Or you are looking to see if there's anything worth it." They didn't know who I was but had me pegged as either a scrounger or one of the family returning. He'd reached the bottom; that heavier leg stumbled, nearly giving way. That was his weakness.

"I'm a nobody, me. I was passing and wondered what had happened here. But don't you think it's rude not to introduce yourselves? Didn't your mother teach you any manners?" deciding against the police angle, I wanted to see their reaction. To see how quick-tempered they were.

"You're right; that was rude. Let's say some people have a vested interest and ask us to keep a lookout. Now, what's in your pocket? What did you find?" They had been watching, making me wonder what made it so important. And why wait until I found it to make a move?

"In my pocket? You don't want that thing. I will tell you now; the cold wasn't pretty. So, other than that," I knew they weren't going to buy it. But I had to give myself some thinking space. He was moving closer, ten feet away. And five feet from his partner.

"Oh, but you do, and you know it. So, what's your actual interest here? I ask again, what did you find?"

"Told you, just passing. Found? Does blood count?" my mouth had a mind of its own.

"Blood? What blood? Oh... wait," Something twigged in his mind; both took cautionary footsteps wide. My blood comment rattled them for reasons I didn't know.

"Yeah, lots of it,"

"S...so how did you see that? I couldn't see anything," stumbling on his words, sounding a little freaked out.

"Hard not to; bloody stinks too,"

"Huh, erm... How? You're one of them, aren't you?"

"Y... yeah...one of those bloody dog things," the panic was genuine.

"What the hell. A fucking dog? Really? I've heard it all,"

"If not a dog, you're not far from the bloody truth. Where's the rest of your family?"

"Ok, I give up. This is the old family home, but I haven't been here in years; I'm looking for any sign of where they may have gone or what became of them."

"Shit, you're the kid meant to have died; your friend has caused some problems digging into business that doesn't concern him. Not no more, thanks to our little birdy. But I sense you have no idea what's going on, do you?"

Why do scum bags enjoy being cryptic? Couldn't he say, 'we have snitched on the payroll embedded within the police?' He made me think about who the little birdy may be. Lewis is dead, with somebody walking around in his uniform. Kelcher? Or Harkes?

"Who are they? Oh, and who's Mathew?"

"Can't tell you, now, can I? Don't want them ending up in the river, do we? Mathew? I... I don't know who that is."

Did he know Something I didn't? River? Lewis? A bigger picture was fast becoming apparent; it involved me or had to do with me. He stumbled at Mathew; he knew something, but how much?

"Well, if we're done with this little back and forth. Shouldn't you be leaving? After all, if I understood you, this is the family home. That makes you trespassers and not me, so if you'd be so kind as to piss me off. Fuck you very much, and don't let the door hit you on the way out." Whether it was my family, I needed more. I wasn't going to that 'more' with them around.

"Wow, a sense of humour. Ok, Mathew died years ago, but your paths are fookin intertwined. That's all you're getting. Now hand over what's in your pocket," the guy with the gun pointed at me finally spoke. He has a scouse accent. It seems this group is quite diverse with its scumbag pool. Yorkshire was still unsettled, nervously rocking on his leather heels. They wanted what was in my pocket and didn't seem to care what had happened to me. Yet. While realising I was the kid that should've died, I added a wrinkle to their plans.

Scouse held firm, although I could hear a rattle from a shaky hand. The outside was clear; no walkers or gossip merchants having a chin wag on the street. I contemplated walking forward. Step out into the sunshine, let the breeze hit my face, and smile because they wouldn't want to risk exposure.

That's what I was figuring from our conversation. Slipping the gun into my waistband, I took a step forward. Yorkshire and Scouse shuffled in unison while lacking the courage of their conviction. Yorkshire's nerves had rubbed off. My pulse sped up, my instincts reacting to their movement. My hands stayed in front; I watched the blood spurt. One by one, the claws came—quicker this time. The familiar haze came, too, feeling far more natural this time.

Euphorically strong, an empowering rush through my veins. Changes were happening, new things—my teeth grew, causing jaw muscles to bulge. They felt strange, like when kids dress up for Halloween with fake teeth; that's how they felt, fake. Another terrifying experience. Maybe being called a dog was an apt description; I now had fangs.

'The shift', as written on Skip's Misper board. I didn't have full control; I could feel my body responding to danger, and my move might backfire; I had a stomach full of fear, even if the knotting pain was less. Their heartbeats raced; fear had become their friend too. I could smell it seeping from their pores.

Behind the bravado and gangster persona, they were scared people, but people were all the same. They'd seen someone enter a derelict house under their observation, not expecting anything other than normal. The mood has changed.

I would happily turn back time before any of this had happened, armed with hindsight and trying to change the future. I didn't want any of it. To be seen as a monster, to feel like one. While having doubts about whether I've killed. Reading the tension, I shifted back, hoping to ease the mind of the trigger finger Scouser.

His breathing was rapid, bouncing from side to side. A child who needs the bathroom because they're about to piss their pants. I should know. I was one once. Scouse was getting fidgety, having gone in so high with pointing a gun. There wasn't much room for him to go other than de-escalate with the risk of looking a fool. So, what does any idiot with a gun and a point to prove do in this situation? He gets irritated by my lack of compliance or willingness to jump to their beat.

Now, he has it in his head, 'why don't I just shoot him? End it now,'. But Yorkshire seemed a little more seasoned. Perhaps that explains his uneven walk. He may swim with fear, but he wasn't ready to make knee-jerk reactions that no one could come back from.

I hadn't heard any chambering of a gun in his direction. Or even the sliding of a blade from the material of his jacket or trousers. Some like to get up close with a knife and their victims. Make their presence felt. Look them deep in the eye to read their fear, watching the life drain away from their victim as they're set free.

"Why would I hand it over? Why do you want it so bad? It's not like you knew it was here," they could've been watching for months and not known.

"None of your goddam business. Now hand it over, and you walk,"

"I walk? Oh, can I? Geeze, are you guys for real? Let me guess; you work for Warren Whitlock, his bitches," trying not to be too sarcastic, but I couldn't help it.

"Who? No idea who that is; maybe one of the other families,"

"I can't keep up with all this inbred gangster nonsense,"

"I wouldn't go running your mouth so freely. You have no idea what these people are capable of. What they are. If you think you're Mr golden balls. I'm afraid you'd be barking up the wrong tree," I heard a little chuckle in his throat. The idiot found himself funny. What family could it be? And what did he mean by 'what they are?' I certainly didn't think I was special.

"Barking? Should you be saying that right now? What are they?" Drifting my claw protruding hand to the side so they could see and get a sense that I wasn't fucking around either. I hear a unified gulp from the pair, not knowing what to do next; I hoped the show would be enough.

"So... It's true... You're one. The Apple didn't fall far from the tree," I could hear the fright in his voice.

"I'm one, what? I don't know what this is. That's why I'm here— looking for answers. So, what are they?"

"So much more than you would ever want to know. I can honestly say this bloody game keeps changing. Now we are treading aimlessly in a strange world of demons and... well, let's put it all together as other nightmarish shit. -

-Lines have been blurred for decades; people don't know their arses from their elbows. What you need to understand... Soon as they know you live, you might wish you'd died back then,"

His words momentarily blew my mind. People talk about police work and the public being better off not knowing what goes on. It turns out that even we were in the dark about what goes bump in the night. To think I was struggling, believing I was a freak, or going mad. Yet, I hear there's more right under our noses. Did the skipper know? Did he figure it out through that funky web of mystery? More to the point, the kids that have been going missing. Is that because they're different?

'What you doing, Georgina? End them already. They're going to kill you,' Chris said.

'Georgie, it's not your time. Quick, move,' Helen.

I didn't move. I didn't dare to look. Listening to my ghostly followers.

"So, is that what you'll do? Go tell them about me?"

Yorkshire's heart remained steady, and he kept his distance. I got the impression he didn't care if he survived to indulge himself some more. Scouser. That was a different story. His heart was beating so fast that I thought it would explode. He was muttering to himself, ever so quietly, not to be heard by his henchman friend. He didn't understand either. Seeing my claws scared him, 'unnatural and an abomination,' is what I heard him say. He could have a point. It's only been recent that I've had to play with the hand I'm dealt. The good and the bad.

I slid my right foot back, pivoting on the ball of my foot, turning slowly to face them to meet the surprise guests. Mindful of the scouser's trigger finger, I moved carefully and calmly, not wanting to freak him out. I was about to glimpse Scouse as he was the nearest, barely noticing the edge of his curly black hair. His heart screamed for mercy. His lungs gasped, sucking in enough air to break the point. Two small beads of sweat rolled through his forehead wrinkles. Free-falling past his outstretched hand holding a Glock 14, plummeting to the ground, heavy metal pans crashing on concrete, ringing my ears.

'Clap... clap,'

That haunting thunder-clapping fills the hallway and my mind. The same way it did when all of this started. A loud whoosh. 9 mm brass flies. I feel... It Searing... pain, red hot poker cuts through my flesh, gliding effortlessly through butter. First shot, my stomach caught the low rib bone, rocking on my heels, and my body buckled in a semi-foetal position. The second shot burrows into my chest, throwing me into a broken heap on the floor. The world is a painful echo, bouncing my heartbeat in the darkness, gradually slowing. The smell of blood pollutes the air and my throat. My lungs are squeezing, wringing every ounce of oxygen. The lids are heavy. Ever so sleepy...

CHAPTER 35

A shaky hand at a torched home in Surrey. Riddled with fear of something they found hard to understand. Instinct and self-preservation tell the body to 'Fire.' Not once, but twice, to make sure. Leaving me flat-out painting the floor red until...

The light slowly creeps through the darkness, and my sense of smell quickly rocks me back to reality. Inhaling that blood and charcoal dust as it's pulled from the floor. It had crimson rain puddles across the black surface. At least three pints, maybe four. Cracking my eyelids open, I was awake from the darkness again; this time, I remembered those thunderclaps that rang my bell.

One... Two... Three... Four... Five. That's how many fingers I saw—a little bloody, tips painted red from me laying on the floor bleeding out.

The aftermath of the pain lingered in my body's way of telling me it had happened. How did I survive? A sense of surreal, 'am I here?' The blood loss told me it should've been fatal. Still flat on the floor, I feel where the blood had soaked through my clothes; there are two bullet holes. Patting away, there's nothing—ripping open my top; I expect gaping holes in my body. Instead, I find two round, slightly grey scorch marks on bare skin coating the beginning bruises. Upper chest and abdomen. There were a few streams of dried blood, but that's all.

Moving my top, I heard a rattle. Only slight but confusing. I shake my top open fully, and two crumpled bullets fall to the floor, causing a gasp to escape my mouth. It shouldn't be possible; I should be dead for all intents and purposes. The marks on my skin, my body ejected the bullets. Yet, I could still feel the heat that trailed in their wake. Cupping the shells in my bloody hand. The symbol is already on my wrist. One, two, three... I reach twenty.

Remembering everything that led up to that moment, slowly sitting upright, I'm facing the wall and front doorway. Listening to Yorkshire's and Scouse's heartbeats, I hear dead silence. A rush of panic I feel for my pocket. To my surprise, it's still there. Why? What the hell stopped them from taking it? Dragging myself to my feet, I turn to face the hallway. My jaw drops open; it's a bloodbath. Next to impossible to tell who was what. There were body parts scattered everywhere, with sprays of blood standing out against anything with some lightness.

The sprays were in slashing motions, as I'd seen upstairs. Heads bloodied and skittled across the debris. I'd be foolish to guess who was who. Only one gun was on the floor, the one that shot me. I'm not sure if that was a miracle or a curse. Curious and confused, I sought their limbs to check the branding. Hard to imagine it being any different. My head tried to justify them by ending up dismembered because they were bad guys.

Two forearms. Both right hands. Not the branding, but the weird symbols that Skip described on Mathew. Followers of his? That would explain their confusion over families; Mathew was alive. I looked at their legs and pockets, seeking I. D's or anything to give me hope and point in the right direction of the bastards responsible for the 'bigger picture'.

Their pockets are empty, except for obsidian coins or tokens; hard to tell. Its edging was gold, the appearance of a railway track. On one side, there's a symbol, that same serpent, for the scumbags, while on the other is a phone number, '0100 666 6311 and 6227.'

It must be their safe number or how they get help, but why the fancy coin? I was drawn more to the idea of the train station and turnstiles.

With the track lines on the edge, a phone box would keep it. Unless they had them rigged, too. Certain ones they know are different. There're hundreds of stations in London; it would be a shot in the dark. One that's best done when I have a backup and a cleared name, a clue for a later time. It was weird enough moving around dismembered body parts.

I was amongst a mini massacre. By who? I should've been dead and was out for the count. So, it couldn't be me. Who? The hits keep coming. My pocket swings against my leg, reminding me of its contents. Time to see what all the fuss was about, retrieving the silly brown bundle. I took a deep breath and began untying the cord, rigid from its confinement. The material flopped over my palm, spraying dust in the air while revealing something strange.

Well, two things. A pendant was the first thing that came to mind. The material was wood tied on a leather cord instead of silver or gold. It smelled like the door frames upstairs without the burnt part. Flipping the case open, I see a photo, a smaller version of one on the wall upstairs—a family of four. On the back is an inscription it reads 'family never dies. Was this family mine? Everything pointed that way, and it scared me, realising I knew nothing. Feeling myself tearing up, I shuffled the pendant into my pocket; the other object the pendant came with confused me. An odd-shaped stone, rough to the touch and solid. Then it was, in the centre, carved the same symbol I'd seen on my wrist. The triangle with a looping swirl arching the tail to the right.

Throughout the grey-blue stone were grooves leading to a gem. I stared, the sun bounced off the surface, and I was in another moment of haze. Hypnotised by a blood-red sparkle, I was in the prism, and everything turned red. I could see shapes of people, a man, a woman and two children; I was watching a flash memory—an imprint of a moment on the stone. In happier times, the adults were smiling until they weren't, all happening in slow motion.

The front door smashes open; a group of four, masked in dark clothing, burst through. The man and woman dash for the kids; the masked suspects beat them with bats, knocking them to the floor before grabbing the smallest child. The other was left behind, looking down at the adults. I snap out of my haze. Stumbling into the breeze away from the house, armed with more mess than when I went in. Breathing deeply and inhaling the cleaner air reminded me how far from home I was in so many ways.

It wasn't a quiet break-in; the suspects raided the home looking for me. If I wasn't confused before, I sure as hell was now. I'd edged through the fence gap, looking all around, mindful that I should call in the bodies anonymously as soon as far away. The street was quiet; the only other thing to stand out was a black saloon sixty to seventy feet away to my left; it looked empty.

Did it belong to Scouse and Yorkshire? I shook my head, trying to unload that I'd died. Albeit temporarily, chucking a smile of relief into the air at the thought that I was still alive and kicking two 9mm shells later.

While finally accepting my situation. I was different; these people that lived here once were my parents and are missing. Maybe even dead, and those that drove them away could be the same ones responsible for the murders of Chris and Lewis. Maybe more by now. Makes me question how many lives have been taken by these people that we've yet to find. All the while, no one knew or acknowledged their existence.

The stone shuffled around in my hand; I couldn't help the nervous fidgeting strolling to my car. Head on the swivel, feeling sure someone should've seen or heard something; the gunshots echoed loud enough to draw attention. So, why didn't anyone come? I didn't like the eeriness of this little village. In this type, everybody knows another's business on first-name terms, yet nobody reacts to gunshots.

The house across the road has low pristine hedges and wide bay windows with the perfect view of the remnants I've just left. Not even a curtain twitch. Stepping all around my car to see if it had been tampered with. Or if there were any more surprises on the passenger seat.

'What the fuck is happening?'

The gem flashed; I panicked, moving to the driver's door, and the flashing stopped. Moving my arm in different directions caused the flashing again. Confusing, flipping it in my hand and was about to put it with the pendant—yet another inscription.

'Family finds Family,'

I kept asking myself, sitting in the driving seat again. Was I destined to find this? Had it been left for me to see where I belonged? Picking at the frayed burn holes from the bullets, how on earth did I survive, and who butchered those guys? Tapping my pockets, forgetting which had my keys, I hear a jingle, but my hand taps something else, plastic. Instantly filling me with doom, dropping my head against the seat. I knew what it was, another bloody tape.

Sliding the tape free, it's different from the rest; this one was black with a white label saying 'time to play and another smiley face. The rest had been an opaque grey. Ejecting the other, I had them both in my hands to compare. The writing looked a little different; Chris makes an 'e' look like a 'c' with a dash through the middle.

On the latest tape, it's a normal lowercase 'e.' It had to be someone else; how could the tape get in my pocket? I slowly wheeled away. Heading anywhere but where I was, in case anyone else or the police came, multitasking isn't foreign to me; I can listen and drive.

'Click,'

'Is it George, Georgie or dear old Georgina? How have you liked the run-around so far? The preview of what you've all been too naïve to know what's in the dark. All it took was a nudge in the right direction. Now, you know a little about what goes 'bump in the night. Only a little, because we haven't met yet. You don't know me... the real me; you don't even know yourself. But I know you all too well. Now, I need you to listen; hopefully, I will have your undivided attention by this end. After all, 'why grandma, what big ears you

have. All the better to hear you with my dear,' We are going to play a little game called 'the three little pigs. I'm sure you've heard the fable probably a couple of times before bed, your first task. If you want to save the first piggy and learn some truths, go to the Straw Sheds, Wood Oaks farm in Watford. Instructions will await, along with the means to save them and your first truth-

*   -Right now, you're saying, 'no fucking way, how can I know it's true? I assure you you have one hour to get to the first task, fail to do so, and they die, call the police, and die. Trust me, I will know, and the truth will be made public; you won't want that. Understand that I'm already a few moves ahead. Oh, and no, I'm not associated with the families. If you're still on the fence about this and let them die, it will all... come back to you. TikTok.'*

This game has taken a turn, claiming to be a few moves ahead. What the hell? The rug has been whipped from underneath me, blindsided. Whoever was on that tape knew me; they knew my nickname.

CHAPTER 36

'12 pm 21st September 1987.'

All on its lonesome, in front of a five-by-five feet, light brown fence, a bright red phone box is set back six to eight feet behind a perfectly trimmed grass verge. Tidy, and still not a calling card in sight. My heart beat two to the dozen, and my car's engine cried out for help and rest. I had drained every ounce of power from it, taking it to the limit between the speed cameras.

I'd made it with ten minutes to spare and stopped at the bottom of Denham Way, the last bit of road, before heading onto a rough, muddy path. I saw the phone by chance, with the task of saving three people, more than likely close to me or that I know of, playing in my head. It was worth calling a couple quickly to see if they answered and rule them out.

First up was Skip's home; it had a droning disconnected tone of death, worrying me. I tried several times, all with the same result, praying to God he wouldn't be one of the victims. Not that I wished Ill on anybody else. Who'd be brave or strong enough to take on the big man? Next up, Charlie, the slippery sod might be up to no good, but I had to try; I didn't have long. I got the same result. My head was spinning, with the bass drum pounding between my ears, too preoccupied to see the bastard had thought of everything.

Written on the blue phone directory in what could be blood was, 'TikTok, no police and no help,' finished with another annoying smiley face. I had six minutes and forty-five seconds left; there was no point in trying more.

My brain was already compiling a list, and there was no checking it twice. Sgt Andy Morris, Charlie Masters, DC Michael Dalton, that's who my money was on. Mother was too far away to be troubled, and these were the ones in my life now. Especially with Chris being dead. I couldn't shake the feeling the body pile would be bigger by the end of the day—only a question of who would be on it.

Sparing a few seconds of calm, taking a deep breath, I hoovered up the smell of the groomed grass and a mouth-watering cooked breakfast. They were simple things, but they reminded me that life could be normal, and so could people. I jumped in my car. Asking for a little more from her, wary of traps and any other farfetched crap that could be in place along my route to delay me.

The main entrance had white-beamed fencing running right and left. My first obstacle was a cattle grid vibrating beneath the wheels, not that I could see any cattle around. I drove slowly through the dirt, an overgrown walnut tree perched picturesquely fifteen to twenty feet in on the right-hand side. It was almost defying physics, the way the branches reach out, looping above the path and acting as a shelter. Forming a large palm cradling the sky.

Beyond that are harvested runways of golden straw fields on either side of the firm dirt road. It looks damp from the previous day's rain but solid enough to spray the undercarriage through my journey. I could hear the rattling of metal.

The view in the distance was wholesome; somewhere, I could live happily without the mayhem. There were three large sheds or storage hangers made of light brown wood and silver metal sheeting for the roofs. To their right was a large White House, an ideal family home, but hard to tell if anyone was in or lived there.

No cars were in sight, only an array of yellow and green large farming equipment. I had no idea what any of them did, only that they were big and probably expensive. Farmers work hard, proper long hours, getting up at dawn and slaving away through the day, all to keep this country's agricultural industry ticking over. So where were they? The farm looks maintained, and yet no one is in sight.

I drew closer to another weird situation, hoping it was all a false alarm. One minute to spare. Only to be haunted by that dripping crimson-red smiley face; it was blood. The puppeteer painted it across a plyboard, leaning against the furthest, weathered shed to the left. I knew where I had to be. Stepping into the open, feeling giddy, my legs trembled, consumed by the unknown. Too late for Chris; now, someone else's fate was in my hands.

A small grey tape player hung from a rusty screw next to the annoying face; a sharp dryness hit the back of my throat; I'm not ashamed to admit I was scared. These things have only brought bad news. The fear didn't stop me from noticing the puppeteer had used human blood, copious amounts, hoping it would stir my senses. He was right; the drool pooled around my gums, confusing what I wanted to do.

'Click,'

'Nice of you to join us, Georgie; now the first game is quite simple. Behind the door is someone you know, maybe even someone close to you, who knows. Even I forgot in the excitement of it all. Even for someone in your condition, the blood lust is gripping your balls; it's drifting up your nose, pissing on those little taste buds. Can you feel it? The buzz, the Adrenaline causing the hairs to spike?'

'The downside for you, buddy, is that you won't be able to tell; I've covered the head and hands. That way, there'll be no preference over life. Not like the way you've been brought up, your life over anything else. This one will be out of reach, caged like an animal. Do you know what that feels like, a caged animal trying to escape on the verge of turning rabid?

When you open that door, a timer starts. A large air dryer will switch on, blowing hot air like the big bad wolf. Only this will inflate a balloon attached to a guillotine rope. Once it reaches breaking point, 'bang' the balloon explodes, releasing the sharpened blade down on the unwilling participant's neck, like cutting cheese.'

'Don't worry; that tired-looking face will have time to save them. If you do, the pair of you walk on to the next, armed with the truth. It's time for you to give back, starting with the pint bottle resting on a pressure plate in a box; once the bottle is full, the pressure will release in a draw. Get in that cage in time and tie off that chunky blade before it drops; you save your friend.' To do that, you must play the game.

'It takes eight to ten minutes to draw a pint of blood; feeling generous, you have eight minutes and forty-five seconds to be the hero. Now, know the saying 'looking for a needle in a haystack? You will look for the missing needle piece in a straw stack. You must be fast. I will watch,'

'Click,'

I had no time to waste; after a quick look around, there was no one I could see. The door swings open to my right; stepping in, sure enough, there's a large black cage, got to be ten feet by ten feet square, with a green digital countdown timer beside it. That alone takes some planning, making me think this has been in the works for some time. Left and right, there are stacks of straw, a brown wooden ramp walkway branching up from the left, running the length to the other end of a barn, and a platform with railings. I could smell the scent of panic oozing from the captees' pores.

Inside the cage, someone was strapped to the guillotine; as implied, they had black covers over the head and hands. Boards screened the sides of the cage and either side of the victim, so I couldn't see anything other than large, painted smiley faces dripping.

The guillotine looked improvised, wooden, with an angled blade at least two feet long. A funnelled hose is taped and fed to a balloon, and a heavy-duty air dryer slowly inflates. I watch as the balloon lifts, raising the blade and releasing a safety block. The terrifying game was underway; flight or fight; what I wanted to do and what I had to do were completely different paths, and I had to act quickly.

Directly in from of me was a Perspex box. They had drilled it into the table and bolted it to the floor. A milk bottle stood in the middle with a clear rubber tube running through a small hole to the outside. True to their word, part of a needle is missing the pin. The haystack was close to the right; I hated needles and giving blood so much that I fainted a few times.

A phobia only a few trusted people knew, and one of those is dead. Quickly I dive in, clammy hands first looking for a needle in a straw stack. I soon clip a packet, four inches by two inches. Head spinning, I rush the packet to the syringe, ripping the pin free.

I could feel myself turning jelly-legged, sweat plastered across my forehead, skin feeling a shade of Casper. The timer rumbles through my ears as the needle presses against the flesh, puncturing a vein. I stare in disbelief and lust, watching the blood flow, only broken by the sound of kicking feet from the guillotine.

The red fountain poured into the bottle; I had to look elsewhere to fight off the sickness. Eyes pinballing around, I remember the message saying, 'I will be watching.' It makes me wonder how, perhaps in closed-circuit television, there was nothing obvious.

That's the point of a perfect bluff. Either way, the person trapped looked real and needed help; what truth we would get is another story. The timer was down to six minutes and thirty seconds, and the bottle was a little under a quarter full. I had to remain calm; otherwise, the veins would collapse, the blood would stop, and I would be screwed. All I could do was watch, wonder, and think while taking smooth, slow, deep breaths. The wind outside whistled, weaving in and out of the timber slats, causing woody ripples along the way.

How had the puppeteer pulled this off, let alone what was to come? The farm could be abandoned or, worse, the owners held hostage. Farfetched thinking, but if the last few days have taught me anything. Expect the unexpected.

My right leg shook; my throat was drying, approaching the halfway mark. The timer had four minutes and fifteen seconds, and I was barely halfway through the bottle. The flow needed to improve. Otherwise, I won't have time to unlock and tie off the blade. I will be light-headed and leggy, making coordinating harder and wasting valuable seconds.

'Keep going, Georgie; you can do it. Get that blood pumping. Think what makes that blood boil,'

Chris's came at the perfect time; I was flagging rapidly. He gave me a kick up the arse when I needed it. I close my eyes; search the darkness, waiting for Helen, her smile to guide me through the turmoil. The salty-sweet stench of adrenaline seeped from my pores, sucking the t-shirt to my skin.

Blood slowly bubbled, stomach began to painfully knot. It was happening; I pumped my hand like a first. With every flex, I watched as a sharp claw slid free one by one, making painful blood crescents in my swollen palm.

My eyes lingered, watching the detail and curvature of each one, thinking of the damage they could cause, how primal they looked. Blood dripping down; the more they've come, the more I like it. My arm swelled; blood fired into the bottle.

The rage and lust were getting strong, too. My eyes catch flailing, covered hands, getting hit by a desire to smash my way through the cage and tear them apart. I had to regain control; time ticked away. Mentally, I was pissing in a hurricane, balancing on a tightrope. A fine line between depravity and control; playing someone else's game with limited moves—three from being checkmated.

With two minutes and ten seconds to go, my vision blurred a little; I was becoming light-headed, nearing three-quarters full. The queasiness rumbled through my stomach as breathing laboured. Looking at the blood drips and the clock chipping away had me swimming in genuine fear; I didn't know if I could make it. Everything about the table seemed solid. In a panic, I yanked and bashed at the draw; it wasn't budging. Drenched, I searched nearby for anything to bust open the grey, heavy-duty, narrow compartment.

'Tut tut tut, did mummy not tell you to play by the rules? That's going to cost you.'

The puppeteer's voice bellows around me; I look upwards to see dirty speakers hooked above the door. The timer lost twenty seconds; it was borderline as it was. Now, the struggles had worsened, proving he was indeed watching. Pumping my fist out of frustration, trying to speed up. The blood flowed quicker; I was down to one minute, with a fraction to go.

'Drip drip drip, TIK TIK TIK TIK,'

It was going to be close; I couldn't stop the panting, heart thundering, foggy loud beats through my ears. I felt I was going to faint, knees knocking together; I'd lost the feeling in my leg—a numb heaviness.

'Drip drip drip tik tik tik.'

Thirty seconds, the last drop hits the red pool in the bottle, and the draw flies open. I ripped the needle out; blood spurts in the air, and my mouth waters. My free hand clumsily grabs at the little silver key. Everything is heavy; I stumble sideways left, kicking across the straw-scattered floor. I could barely keep myself upright, knuckles pressing against the dusty concrete.

My eyes were still blurred; I threw myself towards to cage, lashing the gate. The metal grinding echoed in my drums by jamming the key into the padlock. Thirteen seconds left, my heart is about to explode; clammy and unsteady, I have to pull the gate backwards, and I nearly fall, swinging back on my heels worse than a drunk.

Eight...seven...six...five...four...three...two...one...

Bang...☐

CHAPTER 37

'12 08 P.m. Oakwood Farm,'

'Little pig, little pig, let me in, or I will huff, and I will puff and blow your house down. That's how it goes., right? I have to say, well done, Georgie,'

Rough twine from the rope bit into my hands with strands piercing, causing blood dribbles down my arm. Sweating, dripping. I struggled, but I'd made it in time as the balloon popped, echoing through the shed and rattling the tin roof. Slumped to the floor, swimming in the dirt, my clawed hand gripped the rope. Gasping for air, I had saliva spraying forward; the clamminess was still there, but so was a sense of relief until the speaker boomed.

A victory lap was on hold; the puppeteer saw to that. I was weak but able enough to tie it off, pulling as tight as possible, making sure it was secure, weary of what would happen if I didn't. Being a pint of blood down, I wasn't feeling too good. Dragging myself upright, I dusted off, looking at the flailing arms.

I was waiting for the other shoe to drop, the puppeteer was having too much fun for my liking, and so far, I've evaded 'check.' I kicked the clamp free to remove the top half of the guillotine brace, allowing the victim to push themselves upright slowly but remaining quiet.

I force one of the side panels loose, flipping the panel around, and I see a picture. It's black and white, a photograph of a young child, a girl. The same one is on Skip's missing person board. It could be a copy, but clearly taunting. One after the other, I hear the covers shake free from the victim's hands, landing on the floor.

'So, Georgie, are you ready for some home truths?'

The puppeteer booms out again; he must be close; how else was the game working? Every word was jarring, knowing he could be about to drop the other shoe. The victim stood up, not tall enough to be Skip, while the build was more Dalton but hard to tell in a navy-blue boiler suit.

'First, on your friend's back, there is a two-digit number that will serve you well going forward. Second, when the suit comes off, there will be a gift bag for you containing your first truths. Do hurry. Oh, I hope he likes the picture. It won't be what you're thinking,'

The figure stepped toward me; my head darted to the side to read the number. It was '17.' Leaving me confused, with no idea what it could mean. With hands-free, the victim began stripping; it was Dalton, wearing the same suit as the night before; he must've been grabbed, leaving the pub. With the covers coming down, there was a black cotton bag hung around his neck; I yanked the hood free to reveal a red, bruised and cut face of Dalton, gagged. His hands were shaking as he pulled it away, and drool spun loose with it; Dalton was a wreck.

"Thank fuck you came; I owe you one," Dalton was busy trying to look normal again with the bag, the last to come off. If I were a betting man, this hasn't happened to him before, which makes two of us with two to go.

"What's a bit of blood and sweat between friends?"

"Is that what we are now?"

"Beats the alternative. Besides this situation, we will have to work together to get through the day. So, what do you know about this?" Showing Dalton the photo.

"That's Andy's kid; what the hell is her picture doing here?"

"You tell me, the tape said 'they hope you like the picture' thoughts?"

"Plenty, and none of them good. But now I think of it. Yeah, I remember how close I came once. A secret I've kept; I came closer to getting her than I told Andy. Only I didn't know to who she belonged. We tagged onto a traffic stop after a passer-by called in a black van on the M25, parked on a slip road. I saw somebody with a struggling child in the back. By the time traffic stopped, the child was asleep, and they looked like an ordinary family. I didn't know until I reached the carnage at Andy's house,"

"You weren't to know, so this bastard is taunting you,"

"Kicking shit in my face as he does. To think I buried that memory,"

"How were you grabbed? Did you get a look at them?" Dalton handed me the bag, looking at the photo with regret.

"The last I remember, I was heading to the car when I felt a painful jab at the back of my neck out of nowhere. Within seconds, I was dropping to the floor. All I saw on the way down was a mask in the window reflection,"

"Of what?" My only question was whether he'd been drugged: was the puppeteer working alone? They'd already made it clear they weren't a part of the 'devil's circle.'

"A fucking wolf,"

"I, erm... How sure were you sure that it was a mask?"

"Too cartoon-like; whoever is wearing it knows many secrets. In particular, the shit you're just finding out," If Dalton's right, then the game is taking another twist because who would know what Skip has been hiding?

"Any idea what's in the bag?" the light-headedness was gone, but the nervous sweat was raining on me hard.

"No, I woke up where you saved me from. I shit you not; never have I been so scared of dying," the tremor in Dalton's voice, albeit partly because of the gag, was genuine; Dalton was genuinely scared. I couldn't help but check for a piss patch on his trouser leg.

"Don't blame you; my morning hasn't been much better. I got shot twice. The upside is, I bloody survived; I fear the puppeteer of all this was watching slipped me a tape to start the games,"

"What the hell? How are you so calm, let alone still standing? We must drink the bar dry once this is over."

"Don't be fooled. I'm still digesting; it's a little thick to chug down. Wait... You said three of us, me, you and Skip. I assume if you got caught, then so did he. So, who's the third game?" I'd caused Dalton to go silent; the cogs turned slowly while he put together a plausible guess list. In my head, there's Charlie, Kelcher and unknown risk Mathew. Only Charlie was the closest, even if the alarm bells were ringing about him.

"Fuck knows, Charlie?"

I reached into the bag, only to feel that familiar confusion; I'd hit something sharp. Not wanting to risk losing more blood, I emptied the contents onto the floor. It looked more like the makings of a bad Halloween costume. One that got my brain swirling was a copy of Freddy Kruger's glove from the nightmare on Elm Street film. Unlike a costume, the blades looked very real.

Next up, a pair of red goggles; they looked narrowed tactical, maybe adapted military. I noticed a switch on the side that I couldn't resist touching. With a quick flick and the goggles glowed red, I stopped dead, taking a step back. Separately, I wouldn't have batted much of an eyelid, but together was all so different.

'Eye for an Eye, tooth for a tooth, is the big bad wolf ready for the truth.' The writing painted on the skipper's wall sprang to mind. Why was it in the same place as twenty-five years ago? I thought more about the run-in as I pulled outside the house. It wasn't another wolf or shapeshifter; someone was wearing gear to make it look that way. The person was covered in darkness with red eyes; the fingers looked long, possibly claws.

Wait... Lewis, the slices through his throat, looks slashed by claws. It's hard to notice if the wearer isn't looking for it; the finger grooves and knuckle plate had dried blood residue. Instead, it was done by Freddy's glove. I peered closer at the blades; Dalton was bug-eyed and curious, leaning closer too; his overnight panic, sweat and dirt wreaked as it gushed past my cheek.

They'd been cleaned, but not well enough. Thin, but there's enough to tell me they'd been used to cut, I was hoping the deeds were limited to the pig, but deep down, I knew better. Dead Chris told me to trust my gut, and that's been screaming all sorts of warning signals lately.

'How do you like the truth? To know how close you've been—lucky number seventeen, eh? Unlucky for some. You probably think this was a little easy, waiting for the other shoe to drop. To watch your lives go up in flames. With knowledge of things you won't be able to do anything about—speaking of flames — you have roughly ten seconds before you're trapped again. The fun has only begun; I've spent a lifetime waiting and planning for the right time.'

"What pile of horse shit are we mixed up with here?"

Dalton grimaced a valid question; I didn't know. I'd been pointed in one direction and a world waiting to be brought down, only to not listen to Dalton, 'the closer you look, the less you see,' and get blindsided.

"Honestly, I didn't see this coming, but I feel everything was created for this. Chris's death is a consequence of a planned misdirect,"

"Well, this bastard wants to drag skeletons out into the open. We need to nail his balls to the wall before that happens."

"To do that, we need to play his game; two moves left. The question is, how many has he thought,"

"Erm, we're about to find out. Look," Dalton pointed to a sudden burst of flames far left corner. Low and by a bundle of straw, we were in the middle of a ready-made bomb fire, waiting to go, which is what we should do, leaving.

'TikTok best get a move on. 'Av, a look in the old skyrocket, me old.' To coin a phrase from cockney's dictionary.'

"That cheeky bastard,"

"There'll be time for that. Let's get outside first." The flames were building, and so was the smoke; I grabbed Dalton and the bag's contents, dragging them through the cage and the doors to the open and fresh air. Until I saw the lovely white family home fully on fire. How was he pulling this off?

'Hurry, they're playing your song,'

Another speaker interrupted; I didn't care to look where from, only that I could hear sirens in the distance. It sounded like local water fairies, meaning fellow blues wouldn't be far behind. The fire in the barn could be one solution for me: my blood. The heat should melt the plastic, ripping through everything inside.

Having the glove and the goggles may be helpful for forensics, but also it would compromise continuity. I could say the same for many I work with; if the last couple of days has shown me anything other than how fucked up my life is. There is a bed of corruption needing routing out.

Warren Whitlock has integrated himself; another hell could be on its way if we survive this. We jumped in the car, chucking the sum of this steaming pile on the back seat. A knife glove, red-eye goggles and a mystery box I can't open. That's not to mention the gun in my waistband.

"Shit, skyrocket; what's it mean, Dalton?"

"Crap, pocket,"

Dalton pats around himself, frantically feeling for his inside pocket while I casually but quickly pull away. After the old girl had some much-needed rest, she was about to be put through her paces on to Game two, wherever that is.

"It's a fucking tape," I ejected the last one from the tape deck in anticipation.

"That's been the pattern so far,"

"We need to keep all of this for when we catch the jumped-up son of a bitch,"

'Click,'

'*Congratulations, Georgie. I'm sure you're a little rattled and worse for wear. Yet, what you gave up is nothing compared to those around you—the losses they've taken. Do you think they'd make the same choices if they had a do-over? You can't truly understand someone until you've walked a mile in their shoes. By the end, you'll know. For now, let's play fetch. -*

TikTok.'-Your following location is the old Bryant and may factory, Fairfield Rd, Bow. You have one hour and thirty minutes, allowing for the tragedy that is the M25 traffic. Little wolf and the house made of sticks; — in this case, making sticks. I figured you'd enjoy the irony. Perhaps in ways, you've yet to realise.

The wheels spun, mud rumbling beneath; I stared ahead, catching the streaks of dried blood on my arm, wondering when I would return to reality. All were correct and accounted for one, two, three, four, and five.

CHAPTER 38

'1.30 pm Fairfield Rd,'

I'd been left to dwell on my thoughts. My mentor, in waiting, slept the entire journey, which, for me, was dangerous. So much so I was on the edge of being sick. Riddled with anger towards the puppeteer bastard that's turned everything on its head.

Yet also sadness for him; behind the games and cryptic comments, there's a message riddled with pain, and he is hellbent on inflicting some. By now, I would've hoped to get a better insight and size them up like most suspects. Yet, I feel he's not like most. There were a few minutes to spare.

The skies were greying, and the road had died to an occasional flow of cars coming and going. We stopped across the street from looming ten feet high walls—charcoal brown with a slimy trail off from low gutter pipes. The entrance couldn't be missed; I faced two extra-large blue metal gates. Not the railing type; these were solid sheets, with a smaller, normal door to the bottom left.

We sat a moment; I didn't have the heart to wake Dalton after being blindfolded, gagged, and nearly beheaded. Yeah, they shot me, which I will digest at some point. When that is, I don't know; life has been a dysfunctional and unusual whirlwind. Everything outside looked normal; even the number eight bus was chugging its way past without a care.

Knowing that even if we survive this task, there's one more to go didn't fill me with joy. I couldn't determine the end game if the puppeteer gets us in check or if we can pull it off and save the following two. What happens, then? I was missing something, and not for the first time.

"Urgggghhhhh, we there yet?" Dalton stirred; I would love to say no, but it wasn't to be.

"Yep, I guess there's no time like the present," I cut the engine and scramble my way out, met by a wall of smog.

"So, any ideas?" Dalton's tired face looked clueless, contrasting to when he interviewed me.

"Dalton, I was about to ask you the same thing,"

"So, this is it?"

"Yeah, apparently so,"

"No, this is where your foster mother worked when you entered her world." There was another connection to me. All the talk of lifetime planning could be true; if that's the case, our luck was about to go from bad to worse.

"Whoever this arsehole is must know a lot about me and all of us. I don't remember how old I was when I went to Mother."

"That's no surprise; it was a traumatic start. As for the 'whoever', I'm stumped; Andy told me about the bug at your place. There's no telling how long that's been going on. Perhaps we should assume that if this guy has planned as well as he thinks, then the listening could've been on all of us for some time."

"Or at least long enough to hear anything of use. I don't know about you, but I feel so violated. My flat, my car. Integrated into my life,"

I shook my head in disgust, trying to throw the horrible thought away. No point hanging around; we only had a few minutes left and still had to find the game in what looked like a large factory. Crossing the road once the coast was clear, the blue gates were far more daunting up close. They looked seamless until I saw the crack around the edge of the smaller door.

"I guess that's our way in."

Dalton noticed it, too. I reached out tentatively, still a little shaky from earlier. We hadn't the time to stop for anything, so I was a little weak. My finger catches the cold metal to prise it open. A grating squeak came first, and the hinged sheet was four feet high by two to three feet wide. Heavier than I expected. Sure enough, we were in the right place.

On the inside of the door was another smiley face, dripping red. I didn't need to breathe deeply; the sweet iron had become familiar. Human blood, having drained a pint of my own, those precious moments stuck with me. Hanging from the inside handle is another grey tape recorder.

"Do we go in? You've already done this, so I bow to your experience, me' old mucka," Dalton had an unfamiliar depth look on his face. I could relate. Everything about this has me that way.

"Experience? They call it sink or swim. Yeah, we go in before time runs out. So far, they've made it seem like they're watching. How that's possible, I don't know." Grabbing the recorder, we edged our way through with a bus roaring past behind us, having to bend, exposing my head in first.

The inside looked like a small town that time had forgotten, with decaying architecture and steam drifting from large silver funnels hanging out of walls. An ornamental fountain of a winged lady holding a jug and vines wrapping themselves around tight. The place is daunting, stepping through to a large grey yard, much like a school playground, only more morbid.

This one had to be 300 feet by 200 feet across the factory entrance. Six floors high and made of orange-red bricks, each line had twenty large windows across. We could be watched by any of them; the rest of the grounds were vast, with other smaller outbuildings and gardens.

I closed my eyes, letting the air hit me, feeling the eerie, smog-laden breeze brush over my face. My ears pricked up, hearing faint whispers being carried with each swirl. 'Help us, help us is all I can hear, women's voices and lots of them. I open my eyes, forced to hold a breath for a second, finding where some of those whispers belonged. In the distance, I see several grey women of various shapes and sizes drifting aimlessly through walls.

This was great planning based on the puppeteer knowing a lot about me, or he got lucky by choosing a place that's haunted and bound to throw me off. Lucky for Dalton, he hasn't seen anything yet. This may be a needle in a spooky haystack, bigger than the previous game. The place was closed and has been for some time. All the parking bays were empty, with no sign of life. All set to play the tape when the tannoy booms out.

'Welcome, welcome, one and all. Who's the worst wolf of them all? The question is, can you make the sticks fall? Huff and puff, blow them in. Did you know... lying is a sin? Welcome, Georgie; how do you like the ambience so far? I think it has an air of death. I'm sure you're dying to get on. baboom,' that clears that up; he knew about the dead, me and what I can see.

"What the hell? Was this how the other one started? Are there dead people or something? His last remark was bloody strange." Dalton's face was priceless, gormless without the answers for once.

"Not as poetic, but similar. The puppeteer is getting a kick out of it, though. As for what was said, it's probably best you don't know." The puppeteer was too comfortable with his voice. Made me dread what we might find in the game or who we had to save.

'Click,'

'Dear old Georgie, are you ready to play? Two moves, and it will all be over... for now. The only question is, will you like how it ends? But before we get ahead, we must earn the next truths. On the main factory floor, a place familiar to someone close, you will find a giant VAT of white phosphorus, courtesy of those good old match stick girls. This task has two elements of danger; as you will see, victim number two is dangling ten feet above, ready to go head first. If you fail, they will submerge and experience everything those poor girls multiplied a thousand times. That boiler suit can only protect so much. While that's happening, the room temperature increases until it reaches eighty-six degrees Fahrenheit. Your victim will be burnt alive-

-When I say a lot of planning went into this, it's no joke. Now it's on you to save them before it's too late. The second the two of you enter the front door, the timer starts; you have ten minutes to find a ten-digit code that will shut the VAT lid and save your victim.

As each minute passes, the temperature rises a degree. Now, I appreciate you're going to feel a little queasy after the last exertion, but I'm afraid you'll have to pull on your big boy pants because needs must. -

-The number from the first game is the first clue to what room you will find in the beginning quest. Complete it and get a number to the next room. That number also becomes a digit in the code. Now here's the bit I could fuck with your minds. Will the numbers be sequential? If I say no, there are thousands of possibilities. So, for you, I've kept it simple out of the goodness of my cold heart. Fail, and the fire wins; forty rooms on a floor should be easy enough for someone of your ability. Good luck... Oh, remember the first room is from the first game,'

We were stunned to silence; for that to happen to Dalton takes some doing. With his life experience and length of service, he would've seen and heard a lot of bad stuff. This left him speechless. I was still a little weak and not prepared to sprint between floors. We had ten minutes, and the first one was room seventeen, on the first floor.

"Is he fucking serious? There are six flipping floors," Dalton finally spoke, raking his shaky hands down a tired face.

"We need to get moving,"

Shoving the heavy door open, I hear a loud click, and another green digital timer is immediately in front. We had walked onto the factory floor, racing green painted concrete under our feet. At two o'clock, there is a huge rusty grey VAT. Hanging helplessly above is someone covered in a large nylon sack. All I can see is a pair of black boots with a rope tied and knotted around the ankles.

That rope is sophisticated and rigged to a pulley system behind the timer. The body is squirming and swinging around; the room felt warm already. Through the middle are conveyer belts and tables with trays. It looks like it has been a while since anyone last used it. Arrows painted in faded white directed through a walkway.

Grabbing Dalton's arm, I dragged him through until we came to a dark brown door leading to the staircase. There wasn't time to think or talk;

we had to hurry; ten minutes would cut it fine. The paint was flaking off the stairway walls in strips, leaving me to believe no one would come here soon. I could still hear those whispers as we moved, throwing me off a little.

On the first floor, soiled carpet walkways left and right, broken ceiling tiles, and lights barely hung in place, but I could see green arrowed signs pointing to other walkways. We had to go right; if my senses were treating me well, it was the fourth door on the left. It had to be ten rooms to the left, divided on either side and the same to the right.

It could take an age, then I thought, 'someone of my abilities,' that's what the voice said. I wonder if scent could guide me; I've already come across bloodied arrows and smiley faces. Breathing deeply, I pick up on the usual sweet iron, but not much. The more I breathed in, the more I picked up another aroma, a little bloody but different.

"Dalton, fourth room along there, we best be careful. I'm picking up on something," pointed ahead, barely making out some numbering seventeen.

We moved forward, careful we were in the unknown; the game seemed well thought out; I had to assume there were traps if we deviated. Keeping my sniffing going, I tried to see if there was anything else. My ears only picked up two heartbeats, mine and Dalton's. Both were accelerating the closer we got. The scenario reminded me of a burglary call two months ago; police got called to attend a townhouse on Ocean Drive. Number twelve, I believe it was.

The caller says the suspect was still on the scene; a torch is seen dancing around in the upstairs bedroom. The back window was the entry point, with the whole window stripped out. I nearly fell climbing through, but I had to approach how Dalton and I were now. Careful to keep quiet, not knowing what we're looking for. I caught the guy red-handed, holding expensive handbags. This time, my hand was poised on the cool office door, listening but not hearing anything. In fact, if we were being watched, I couldn't see how.

'Bingo Georgie. But TikTok,'

Right on cue with my thoughts, the voice comes, confusing me further. The door swings open, leaving me a little underwhelmed; I'm not sure what I was expecting, but I saw a stranded table in the middle of the room. On that table were a typed A4 note, a small wooden box and the blood I'd picked up on—another smiley face. It had to be a camera somewhere close.

"Is this it?" Dalton hung back; I could hear the trembles in his throat.

"Afraid so; the question is, how does the puppeteer know?"

I stood in front of the table, haunted by the bloody face. The other smell was coming from the box, torn, which to do first; apprehensive about both.

"The box, get it out of the way; we don't have time, as you say," Dalton gave me the prompt I needed.

My hand shook now; the box was only two inches by two inches square and of a similar thickness—dark brown wood. Untying the string, the box lifted a little; it was light. What could it be? The lid slid up with ease; the smell came stronger; dragging it free, I found something I wasn't expecting. Nestled neatly on a pile of matchsticks, much to my horror, was an eyeball. Blood smeared around the shiny white sclera with the optic nerve neatly wrapped around it. The Iris was green and brown.

The urge to be sick came at me fast; This puppeteer bastard is sick. 'Eye for an Eye, tooth for a tooth,' the writing on Skip's wall came to mind. It can't have belonged to Lewis; Skip would have noticed a missing eye; who's, was it?

"This keeps getting better; put it in this for after. In case forensics can get anything," Dalton handed me an evidence bag from his inside pocket. Normally I would question why, but it's coming in handy now. Not wanting to look at it any longer, I jam the lid back on before shoving the box in the bag and moving on to the riddle.

The paper was a crisp white with typewriter lettering, with no smudges.

'Hello Georgie, I told you Eye for an Eye, and it's only the beginning. I'm sure that delicate stomach of yours is doing somersaults about now. Fighting the urge to spray the table, I doubt it's gotten better over the years. The first quest is easy... remember to keep the numbers in mind.'

'If there are three apples and you take away two, how many apples do you have?'

Is he bloody kidding? How could it only be the beginning? There's only one game left; again, the talk is of familiarity, making me wonder if there was anyone I knew and had forgotten in the past. I am coming up blank.

"That's straightforward, isn't it? Three apples. You take away two that leaves one. The answer is one, right?" Dalton made sense as if it was simple maths.

"Can't be that easy. There are three apples, and 'you' take away two apples. How many apples do 'you' have? It's what you have once you take them... the answer is bloody two." It had to be that one is obvious; the riddle plays on words; it had to be how many I had once taken them.

"Flipping hell. That's right. Let's get to room two," the whispers continued to rattle my ears while my brain was being consumed, searching for anyone that may know me well enough and be crazy enough to pull off something like this.

CHAPTER 39

Dalton took his turn to drag me away, skipping me across the floor. We had to turn right out of the room, the far end door on the right. We had eight minutes and twenty-nine seconds left and no time for second-guessing what was on the other side of the door.

It flew open to a view of surreal emptiness. Bordering spooky, I couldn't see a note or anything apart from more soiled carpet, plain flaking walls, and what looked like a storage cupboard door. The word 'storage' on it was a dead giveaway.

'Welcome to your second quest, as I'm sure you're baffled, feeling like crap and wondering how this genius of a control freak is making all this work. Knowing your thoughts, Georgie, it's 'bastard instead of genius'. Anyway, now the room may look empty; that's merely a matter of perspective. As the cockney chancer would say, 'the closer you look, the less you see' am I right, Michael? So, for this task, you will need some of your main senses to get going. -

'-Particularly, you, Georgie, 'why Grandma, what big eyes you have. All the better to see you with, my dear.' There's a little clue for you to get those tired mice running around those wheels again. Time to get those hands dirty, Michael; what's a little blood between friends? TikTok,'

True to form, there's nothing simple about our situation. The 'bastard' is enjoying taunting us, able to watch us, yet we're none the wiser. He talks about using senses and, in particular, for me. All I could assume is when he mentions 'Grandma and eyes' that I'm the big bad wolf. Something he keeps calling me, but how does that help?

"Cheeky twat, you know what he means, sunshine? Big bad wolf must put his skills to good use. I don't know much of this wolf nonsense, but think about how you can see differently while I try the cupboard."

"Yeah, he loves dangling us on a string; we have to be quick,"

Dalton dashed the door while I took a deep breath, focussing on what I could see; just like at the house in Surrey, I could see things I normally wouldn't. My body heated, the knotting in my stomach pulling at muscles. Only this felt easier and less painful—a small win under the circumstances. I got to take what I could get at the minute. It wasn't long before glowing appeared, far more controlled and almost normal, apart from standout messes that I didn't dare try to guess what they were.

My sense of smell heightened, too, picking up on stale urine to account for some stains. That sickly feeling swam around inside; I was looking at the aftermath of an uncleaned brothel or similar, owing to the copious body fluids. Then I saw it, smeared across the wall to my left, another smiley and an arrow pointing to the floor. Meanwhile, Dalton is yanking on the cupboard handle for all it's worth.

The arrow smeared down to the carpet edge; I wasn't going to like the next part. I'm getting my hands dirty; judging by this place, I'll need an antibacterial bath if we survive all of this. Bending down, I hear the usual knee popping, nearly getting knocked out by the vibrant stench the closer I am to the floor. My claws were out; I caught Dalton starting, showing an expression that wasn't fear. More cheerful confidence. Perhaps because we're on the same side.

The carpet feels damp and icky; Dalton edges closer. The claws catch the edge, prying it up with ease. I must've pulled it towards us a good three to four inches before I saw the beginning of some letters. The more I saw, the sicker I felt; the puppeteer knew a lot, but that's what I had to repeat aloud for Dalton.

'In the early hours of Friday 17th April 1959, the Kidnap of a young boy took place,'

The first couple of lines from the missing newspaper clipping. I could clutch at straws, assuming this person had the article and wrote straight from that, confirming my thoughts that the folder had been stolen. Or that they're good at research and found a twenty-eight-year-old copy. The smart money is on the former.

"How do they know about that, and how to connect it to you?" Dalton hovered near my shoulder, not knowing what I was looking at; I could smell his sweaty aftershave, welcomed for once instead of enduring the carpet aroma. There was another arrow at the end; I had to carry on pulling up the dirty floor covering.

"I have absolutely no idea. Apart from this person knows too much,"

"We need to catch them; maybe they'll have an accident in the Thames,"

"Why the Thames?"

"Well, having this all come out won't be good for any of us. I lied to cover up Matthews's murder because it was too hard to explain and stop Andrew from getting pinched. The job thought he'd killed his family after catching Mrs having an affair,"

"Lying is a sin-"

"-steady on there, buddy. People in glass houses shouldn't throw-"

"-No, not you. Sorry for interrupting, but that was written on the downstairs main door. We must assume this puppeteer bastard knows everything. So far, it had nothing to do with the families Chris was looking into."

"Ah, right, I get you. I stand by my 'Thames' comment,"

Dalton was right to worry; I tried not to show it, but I was scared senseless by how much this person knew, considering I've not long found out myself. Much to my stomach's disgust, I continued peeling back the layer of filth, smothering our quest. Quite poignant, considering that's all I've been doing the last couple of days.

'He was aged two years. The family home in Denby way was broken into while the household was asleep.'

The next few lines were more of the same article, only staggered. A foot away from the left corner of the wall was where the writing started. This lot was three feet closer to the middle and had moved three feet towards the centre of the room. We were directed to a point in the room; under the carpet were solid tiles, maybe metal and plastic. All liftable, making me think the next numbers could be underneath.

I continued to pull back, weary of time, with six minutes and twelve seconds left. Dalton kept checking his watch, putting me on edge; a watched pot never boils,'. The temp downstairs had already risen nearly four degrees.

'It's unknown what the main intention was, only that it appears the boy was all that was missing. The family are distraught and unable to comment,'

The final three lines took us three feet from the windowed front wall and three feet down from the previous lines. Another arrow is pointing down; sweat dripped off my forehead, landing amongst the dirty grey tiling. I stood up to step back when I heard clicking from beneath my feet. I froze, staring at Dalton; his expression in return meant he heard it, too; he was worried.

Dalton's gurning face stayed in one place while his pupils darted around faster than a druggie on ecstasy. A low whirring came from nearby; I was caught in two minds. Stay put in case it was a pressure plate for an explosive. Or make a dart for the door and pray.

"We need to move away now; this bastard isn't playing fair," Dalton reaches out to grab my arm, making a valid point. Why put us through this only to blow us up?

We were down to four minutes and forty-five seconds and were still none the wiser. I'm facing Dalton and our exit; he's facing me when his face turns wide-eyed. Dalton points over my shoulder as I hear a click and a low creaking. I could feel a faint fanning of air towards my neck.

"The fucking door is opening; I couldn't get that to budge for love or money," Dalton cranked out his throat, looking confused.

I turned in time as the door rested fully open, and out slid a six-foot monstrosity—an effigy made from matchsticks, thousands of them. It wouldn't have looked so bad if it weren't for the blood. Smelling strong, human, but not fresh, snail trails oozed from any gap it could find. At first, I couldn't understand its purpose, but then I saw the eye holes.

One socket had a human eye, green-brown, the same as the one in the box we had from the last quest. Hard to tell, but I suspected there was a human body underneath. Owing to the blood and missing eye, my money was on them being dead, if I'm right. There was no movement; the figure was strapped upright to a pole. Some underneath showed through, but all I could see were bin liners.

'Well, Georgie, what do you think of our friend here? He's a bit stiff, not the kind of starting a conversation... Jokes aside, I'm sure you're wondering about the blood, maybe even getting hungry. I wouldn't if I were you; they've been dead a couple of days. Don't worry; nobody you knew, they got a little nosey. -

-Now, the important part. Time to get stuck in the guts of your task. 'Beauty is in the beholder's eye,' and find the last clue of this room. As I'm sure, you've been doing so far, instead of thinking the message was to haunt you. TikTok'

I hadn't thought about how the writing could be clues; I figured the lines were a guide. The problem is, I didn't know what to do next.

"Fuck, any ideas, matey boy? Maybe we need the eye?"

Dalton looked stumped, but it made me think. What if we had to replace the missing eye? It had to be enough so we didn't run out of time. I will try anything to get the job done. I slid the box free, whipping off the lid; my stomach churned. Was I about to touch an eyeball? It felt squidgy, gelatinous, and slippery.

I gagged a little while Dalton hid his face. I thought a man of his seasoning would've been made of sterner stuff. Then again, what did I really know about him? Other than a cockney accent with a penchant for secrets and helping Skip.

The eyeball slotted in easily across the rough stick; the harder I pushed to ensure it held in place, I heard a click. Then nothing, about to rethink the next move, when a sudden splattering lands across the floor. Looking like a bucket of organs had been emptied at the figure's base—all human, heart, liver, kidneys, bladder and intestines. 'Stuck into the guts of the task' is what the voice said. The clue was amongst the bloody mess.

One problem, the sight and smell, was driving me crazy, but the other part of me was. I could feel my pulse quickening; my claws slid forward. Dalton's heart jumped; his foot stepped back.

"Sorry, Dalton, I can't do this one. It's driving me nuts, and I don't know what will happen if it takes control,"

"Yeah, I was thinking the same; any idea what we're looking for?"

"My guess is a number,"

"In guts?"

"Wait... try the intestines first. Bound to something solid, undissolvable,"

"Oh, lucky me,"

Dalton was open with his disgust but bent to the task anyway; time wasn't on our side. His hands hovered near the bloody carnage, tentatively pinching at the stomach entrails. Glistening, marble-like red brings back horror images of Chris's exposed brain. Then I got to thinking about what the voice said a moment ago, 'find the last clue of this room. As I'm sure you've been doing so far, instead of thinking the message was to haunt you,' The message is more than a blast from the past; I was supposed to see them as clues.

Dalton was wrist-deep in blood and guts; I needed to figure out what I'd missed. There was one carpet to pull back, but that would be too in the face. I'd found eight lines sounding plausible. So far, the first room was number seventeen; the second gave number two, leading to where we are now. '17.2' gives three digits, or '17.02.'the lines would make '1728.' It wasn't the case; that would leave us six numbers short and low on time.

'The closer you look, the less you see,' I had to take a step back and look at the bigger picture. Dalton was struggling; the hunger eased by moving further from the blood. Only a little. We had one message, three sections, and eight lines. Wait... three feet from the first lines to the second, three feet from second to third. In three pieces, a total number of nine.

The puppeteer wouldn't have made it easy; one... nine. '17.02.19' Had me thinking it was a date for this part of the code, anyway. Meaning Dalton needed two numbers from that mess, leaving two more. Only if I'm right. Or the actual date on the article message, '17.04.1959.' Eight digits out of ten. I couldn't discount that either; my head was spinning, but we were dangerously close to failing.

"Ewwww, you bloody well owe me one after this, buddy. I think I've got something,"

Dalton stood up, holding at least four feet of intestines extended while the rest puddled on the floor. One hand smothered in crimson juices gripped the tip while the other drained down like the smoothing out of a cord. The more Dalton squeezed, the splurges of blood-covered crap pooled across the floor.

"What does it feel like?"

"Fucking horrible," Dalton looked as though he was going to puke.

"No, I mean what you're feeling,"

"Well, roughly two centimetres; there's a few of them," It keeps getting weirder.

Sure enough, Dalton was right; the next pile flowed on the floor. Scattered amongst the mess were tiny pebbles or similar. The urge to savour blood was getting stronger, but I had to find the numbers fast. I dropped to my knees and began sifting, claws circling through the blood, pinching a piece.

"They're teeth, 'eye for an eye, tooth for a tooth,' That message on Skip's wall had more meaning than I could've imagined.

"What's that?"

"There was a message on skipper's wall, eye for an eye, tooth for a tooth. Either way, we must hurry." I had a handful, blood smell riding me hard, swirling them around in my palm.

"Shit, this one has an engraving. A number two,"

"That sums all of this up, one big number two,"

Moving the pieces around in my hand, I found one, too, a number six. I'm curious if it's engraving or if they had burnt the number in, but it's there. We now had '17, 02 or 2,1926; it looks like a date, but what's important about '1926'?

Ding, ding, ding, we have a winner, or should I say, winners. So far, you should have eight digits. Your final room is the last two digits; the question is, which way around? I could toy with you and let you chase your tail, but I want you to survive this game to make it to the grand finale. Nine months of preparation after years of planning deserve an ending. -

You need to go high, and the last numbers you need represent an age. Call it a time of innocence, or at least it should've been. You don't have long and will require a final sprint, but the next quest is easy. TikTok,'

"Sixty-two, we have to go to room number 62," the end was near, but his words didn't fill me with joy. This may be a game, but it's not one geared for us to win.

"Come on then, what about the stick, man?"

"We don't have time; once this is all over, then we can put in some calls," A final look at the blood oozing, I wondered who might be under there. Hoping it wasn't someone I was close to. Any death is terrible, but being someone I know is worse.

CHAPTER 40

'Room 62: Two minutes, ten seconds left,'

Dalton was breathing heavily and chugging up his lungs; the hallway door nearly came off its hinge as we burst through. With my face planted against the thin corridor wall, it may have only been one floor up, but the panic was hitting us hard.

The door swung open, and I nearly lunged to pull it shut again; things just took another turn for the morbid. The space had been blacked out for extra eerie, faced with three ghostly women who looked to be in their late twenties about fifteen years ago, judging by the clothing. They looked sickly if there could be such a thing for the dead, but their faces were deformed, swollen and missing half their jaws.

They were merely the appetiser, hovering near a dirty old coffin on a table, causing a thick, musky, rancid stench. This coffin had been robbed fresh out of the ground, caked in a sludgy clay-like mud; varying colours of fluids rained down from cracks and corners onto clear plastic sheeting underneath the table. The original colour was a dark brown-red mahogany type. The sick bastard had dug up someone's grave.

To desecrate someone's resting place like this is awful, proving to me the lengths they will go. It must have been between ten and twenty years since being committed to the ground. Dalton's face had turned a shade of stale milk; the coffin was relevant to one of us, but I couldn't think of who it could be for me. Unless my birth parents were dead, this belonged to one of them.

"Is this for real? Never in my life have I experienced games like this." Dalton was slowly recovering. Still, the face had me thinking he'd blow his guts any minute.

"We don't have long, as creepy and downright bloody disgusting as this is. I think the number will be" Dalton's jaw nearly hit the floor; he didn't want this, and neither did I, but lives were at stake.

'Glad to see you've made it; it's a quick one; you could say it's visiting a loved one—only not one of yours. No, this is far more personal, opening some old wounds but a necessary evil. You're calling me a 'sick fuck' or a 'sadistic bastard'; I'm just a man that's shedding light on a tragic past. -

-The kind that's involved coverups and lies. Too many have got on with life without a care in the world. You're about to see a hint of what got left behind. The collateral damage was caused by people who thought they could play God. Creating a pet, they could train as a weapon. Instead, all that happened was a trail of devastation, and that pet became a dirty secret blending with the real world. Now, I will burn it all down until everyone understands what it's like to lose it all. While bringing the ugly truth into the light.

-

-Your task is to open that earthly bed and retrieve a captured memory. Within that, you will find the digits you seek. Then it will be a sprint to the finish. I suggest you remember those numbers, assuming you make it. TikTok'

There was no time to waste moving closer; the stench was awful, making me feel sick. Gripping the old brass side handle, I felt a slimy dampness that had my palm slipping a little. Dalton stood and watched; the wood creaked and yawned. Time spent trapped six feet under had taken its toll on the casket.

A gap started forming, releasing an even greater, sickly smell. Death like I've not smelt before; this was trapped, pent-up decomposing. I didn't want to push further, but we had no choice. One big shove and the lid flew open; the stench hit my face like a brick wall. I dropped to my knees in disgust, feeling like I was about to pass out. My body went limp, fleeting, with bitterness swimming around in my mouth. Fighting against everything that screamed at me not to, I pulled myself up; what I saw belonged in a horror movie.

A dark, scarily charred skeleton, the head had been separated from the body, resting on a dirty white pillow. I could make out the jagged edges across the gristle of the throat. Counting the stray hairs still dug into the scalp, eleven wiry-looking strands. My eyes widened, having an out-of-body experience. Was I seeing this? Judging by the size, it was an adult male in his late thirties or early forties when he died, but who?

Scanning the bony frame, sure enough, between the two skeletal hands was an A5 size picture in a wooden frame. I yanked it free, nearly bringing my fingers with it to the sound of spooky clicking. The face was obscured, and the picture was old. Flipping it over, the faded brown back had blue-inked writing, 'To Dad, love you always, Ethan, ten years.'

I could be pissing in the wind again, but our puppeteer's name could be Ethan, and this was his father. He feels the need to drag us through the crap for whatever reason. What else fits? The body looks like the result of a murder or a nasty suicide, which didn't seem likely. The wound... jagged, torn through the throat, had been ripped in two, taking the head off. Wait... 'Heads on the floor, bodies positioned in a circle.' Could it be?

"Dalton, you've heard Skip's story. The one in the basement?"

"Yeah, of course; why?"

"I think this is one of the bodies; it looks old enough, and I suspect we're being toyed with by a family survivor,"

"For real? Shit. We need to get out of here before it's too late. I have a bad,"

We had '17021962 and 10.' I slammed the lid shut, and we sprinted out of the room. Fifty-two seconds remained, and the temp was almost at its peak, causing the phosphorus to combust. My blood boiled with a single-minded thought. Get to the VAT as quick as possible. Leaping from the top step of each flight, I cleared one after the other without stopping or buckling of knees. I'd reached the ground floor in seconds, leaving Dalton behind.

I was faster, stronger and able to make up ground and time; I felt good, using the other part of me, adrenaline coursing through my veins. The room was hot; steam drifted through the air; our victim was hanging inches from their doom. They were flipping and thrashing around like a fish out of water; it would be close.

I reached the right side of the VAT, feeling a boiling barrier between myself and the metal surface. There's a black digital display with a white keypad; the screen flashes green words 'Enter Code two'. Then another shoe dropped, 'Code Two.' There were two panels; we had to divide the code, and Dalton wasn't near yet.

'TikTok Georgie, you didn't think this was a solo task, did you? Why do you think I allowed you to save a companion first? Dear Georgie, you've been behind several moves and always will be. The codes must be inputted together,'

Dalton reached the bottom, looking leggy; he had to hurry; sixteen seconds remained, and we were on the verge of failing, costing someone their life. Loud clops from Dalton's expensive shoes thundered across the floor, nearly crashing into the metal siding, spraying exhausted saliva as drool trailed from his bottom lip.

'10, 9, 8...' A countdown voice roared out, making me jump in surprise, different from what we'd heard.

"Quick, Dalton, on your keypad, try 17021,"

'7, 6, 5...'

"I'm doing 96210." my heart thumped through my head, drenched in sweat; I didn't think we would make it.

'4, 3, 2, 1. Beep, beep, beep.'

I slumped to the floor, too scared to look, too tired to move and too numb to rationalise everything we'd gone through. I still had no idea who the puppeteer was other than a possible first name. If he has been several moves ahead, what's coming could be hell.

'Bang, bang, bang,'

A loud thumping on metal breaks my self-pitying; I peer around to see Dalton sitting down, looking equally defeated. The noise wasn't coming from him; he hunched over, leaning against tired old knees. A dishevelled mess, exactly how I felt.

"You hear that?" I woke him up. Dalton's head tilts up.

"I think it's coming from up there,"

Pushing myself from the dirty green floor, I'm hearing it clearer, focussing my ears on the thumps and feet stamping on metal. Dalton and I step away from the VAT, both looking up. We had made it; the second victim stood on the lid, stamping impatiently. A penny for their thoughts, close to death, knowing it's out of their hands, surviving at the last second. It came quick, I was shot, and it went black.

There's a ladder mounted to the front; Dalton didn't look up for it, so I am the good sport. I began climbing; I could guess who it was by its size. It's Skip, feet planted on the crack where the lid came together. Oh, so close. The sack came apart easy enough; gaffer tape braces the ankles. Sure enough, he was gagged and in a boiler suit; he seemed a little unsteady on his feet, possibly drugged.

'Wow, wow, wow. Isn't this exciting, Georgie? Are you having fun yet? Christ, I was on the edge of my seat, will he? Won't he? Those unique skills of yours came in handy in the end, didn't they? Now you can have a little mother's meeting and see if there's any way of catching up. Oh, how many have you seen so far? I knew at least three died in that last room.'

CHAPTER 41

The gag flew off with wads of spit; Skip was beetroot red, sweat dripping down his face. The back of the boiler suit had another series of numbers: '230552.' The way this quest has gone, it had to be a date, but what's the purpose?

Skip was busy stripping down the terrifying reminder to reveal his uniform; he had to of been snatched end of his shift last night. He was in half-blues when he came home to find that pig mess. Shaking loose the last of the rags, I noticed another recorder swinging around his neck. Surely our next truth.

"Took your blooming time, lad." He may be tired and pissed off from being near death, but he still has a sense of humour, projecting a brief smile.

"Yeah, sorry about that; I got caught up reading the news," How the puppeteer knew that article would apply to me; has me confused. Taking the folder is one thing; understanding it is another unless Skip's place had been bugged, too.

"Looks like we have another one of those truth things," Dalton pointed to Skip's chest while Skip looked to be trying to remember how he got into this mess.

"Skip, where were you snatched from? Remember, anything?" Skip grabbed at the recorder, bringing it into the light. I could see a red smiley face on the front.

"Well, I was busy catching your blooming scent out the window, which I'm none too pleased about, by the way. But you saw the board, which I will explain later. I assume you came back to mine for some reason, saw someone leaving and the place insecure. You went inside looking and found the room but heard me and thought it best to leave. -

Pissed off with the mess downstairs. I needed a drink after having my home violated; I poured a double, must've barely made it halfway through and felt dizzy; my eyes blurred, and it went blank. The next thing I knew, I was hanging by my legs, feeling the blood rush to my head, and I still couldn't see. Now, do you care to blooming tell me what's going on?"

He must have been drugged, but how would the puppeteer know what Skip drinks? He would need to know him well and where it's kept. That cupboard had older bottles; he wouldn't dust off another for only him to self-pity. Was Skip being watched? That would be the rational thought; the trouble is that not much of what's happened has a sensible explanation. More to the point, whoever moved him would need to be strong.

"Well, we are wrapped in a sick game with at least one more life at stake; the puppeteer of it all rigged us from the very bloody start. He somehow got Chris to chase that investigation. Flushing out those families, I assume he had Chris killed by fake 'Lewis', having disposed of the real one and made everything point to me. He has been leading me around by the frickin' nose ever since. On a side note, I found my so-called family home address in your room. Something that important. When you told me that story, you should've told me you knew exactly where it was. -

-You're right about one point; I encountered someone outside; they had red eyes like in my dreams. I took the bait and went to that home, looking for answers. It seems they set me up. I ran into two thugs who shot me twice, and I should be dead, but, for better or worse, I'm not... There is so much more to this and the people they're from; honestly, it scares me. All of this does. -

-I woke up covered in blood, and the thugs butchered me. I found a tape in my pocket and started a game where I had to save Dalton on some farm. This guy knows everything about us and the past you've told me so far. As you can see on this recorder, he signs everything off with an annoying smiley face. There's one more game to go; I think he has Charlie,"

I purposely left out that I found a pendant and a weird stone; I need to know the truth once and for all. It didn't stop me from taking a quick look at my hand to count the fingers, hoping I was dreaming. Then when I saw five, I checked the wrist. Twenty-two seconds, this time, before the symbol disappeared.

"Lad, I don't know the exact address; I hadn't the chance to go that far. There's been too much going on."

I didn't respond; I couldn't; if he didn't know, then the paper had been altered by someone else. Another element of this game that's been manipulated. The puppeteer, Ethan, wasn't joking about their claim to be several moves ahead. Right now, I'm holding off checkmate; I feel he already knows what I'll do next—starting with the next truth.

'Click,'

'Georgie, if you hear this, you've earned the right to know some more truths. The first one is a bonus just for you. In fact, your bodyguard too. I'll let you in on a little secret; you're not going mad. Those blackouts you've been having aren't real. They were some of my early moves. You have your weekly Wednesday milk delivery to thank, a thin gauge needle delivering low doses of ketamine, not too much, just enough to make you doubt. Access to everything else has been easy. You didn't even notice what was in front of you, and you're not going to see it coming. None of you will. -

-The tests began years ago on a fat boy there. I'm sure he woke with strange headaches and dizziness, thinking he was hungover; that was the practice until I got the right setup. Georgie, you woke in your car and couldn't remember how I saw you on a park bench? The first doses caused sleepwalking. I can't account for the blood along the way. The bonus for me was your dreams; they're very much real, made more potent by the drugs. Told you, planning. I've listened, watched and lingered until the right time. The rest of what's

happening to you isn't down to me. That's all on you and what you are. What both of you are, soon Georgie, you'll be able to do much more. -

-All because of people wanting a weapon; the beauty of it is that nobody realised what they already had. I learned that if you want to win the game, it's all about strategy and control, a game of chess; the latter was born from mistakes. Trust this when I tell you it will not be repeated. One can never be too careful when dealing with things such as yourselves. I'm not what you call an imposing man, so I make up for it with intellect and a willingness to listen, playing the long game, even playing the fool. -

-Cockney was right; when you look closely, focus on what you want to see. You miss what's happening, like five years ago, oblivious to life. I'm sure you'll get all bent out of shape, but here's another truth. Do you remember the taxi to the hospital? It was a navy-blue Cortina estate; I believe it had a white oval ' label on the back. The driver who so gallantly didn't hang around? That was little old me, poor old Helen and the baby. I'll let you fester on the 'is she or isn't she. How sure are you about what they buried? That's a problem for another time-

-For your next task, the little piggy and the house made of bricks. Can you huff, puff, and be brave enough to enter where it all began? It may not be far away, but you may wish to be elsewhere by the end. The three of you are on converging paths that have intertwined for years and, for one cause—keeping secrets. Like the one cockney has held, how close he came to the fat boy's daughter. Imagine all those birthdays and Christmases missed. But you weren't to know, right? Just bad timing, I guess. The mass hysteria to come is all on you, the kind people lose their heads over. The journey takes ten minutes; once you leave this building, you will have nine minutes to get there, any longer, and the fun starts without you,'

Neither of us spoke; I was busy reeling by the 'Taxi truth.' the bastard started way back then; did he kill them? The 'is she isn't she's confused me; I buried what was supposed to be a baby; they both died, maybe even killed. Now I feel the urge to claw my brain out and forget everything. If that was possible, Skip's face had turned redder, thinking over the revelation. We have been on a wild goose chase while the puppeteer rigged the game. What's the point of continuing where it feels like we're fighting a losing battle?

"Is there any point?" I broke the silence, snapping Skip and Dalton to their senses.

"To be honest, lad, I have no blooming idea. So, Michael, what the hell? What did he mean?"

"Before you jump the gun, it's nothing as bad as it sounds; I tagged on the back of a suspicious traffic call before I caught up in the chaos at your house that night. I had no idea, and they looked like a family. I didn't even register it until a while later; by then, you were far too deep in the pain, and nothing I could add would help. Another reason I took the risk of the deep cover, for you," Dalton looked sad, brushing a slight tear. Skip mellowed; he could understand where Dalton was coming from, even if it was painful.

"Right, let's finish this and nail the shit-stirring bastard. We've come this far, or shall I say, you have, Georgie. Let's finish the next task, escape, regroup and go again."

"Exactly, sunshine, we might lose the battle, but the war is far from over. The blue army is far greater than this shite can throw at us; we need to find who we can trust. We may have been blindsided, but what Chris dug up is real with many corrupt officers. So, pull up your big boy pants, and let's go,"

Dalton was right; we can pick the bones out of the mess once we've saved the life from the next task. I fear we will never be the same in whatever shape we are in.

CHAPTER 42

Our conversation and that recording left a sour taste in my mouth; I couldn't help twitching as we walked past the ghosts; the dripping blood and pool of guts in room two clung to my nose hairs. Dalton and Skip could be grateful they don't see these grey things.

I'm missing my content obliviousness, happily catching glimpses of Helen, believing I saw a memory. Thanks to the last recording, the cab driver that injects their passenger, I'm in limbo. What psychopath does that to a pregnant woman, anyway?

At first, Chris's appearance was a novelty, but what we were leaving behind belonged to a movie. I can only hope I'm not going to see the dead all the time; it will make life more disturbing than it already is and far more confusing to those watching. Felt like a persecuting curse.

Shuffling out of the building, a swirl of cooler air meets us, whistling through my leaky shirt with grey clouds edging overhead; it's going to piss down any minute now. No sooner had we stepped out the door than I heard a loud click as if the power had switched off. Skip limped across the road, staring into the distance; he knew where we had to go, which terrified him. I thought he'd become fresh milk white after the blood had finally drained back to his feet.

The metal slammed together, and Dalton jumped; the bags under his eyes drooped like deflated tyres; we were all feeling the strain. Skip was deeply agonising over what was to come, wrestling with a carnival of demons from the past. While the three of us wallowed in our respective relief to have survived, the world was none the wiser. Fairfield road was a calm daydream.

Especially compared with what's coming. I'm staring at a pigeon ten feet to my left, blissfully pounding away at a slice of rotten bread, doing what it can to survive. I picture my head in the bread's place; the pigeon's beak is a hammer thumping the information into my brain. Too much to try cramming in; it's been one revelation after the other without being able to stop and think.

We had been warned that everything would come full circle; I don't think any of us thought it would be so soon—Skip's aura hung like a noose around his neck, and him a condemned man on death row. Edgy and abrupt, he snatches the keys out of my hand. Riling me up a little, insisting on driving, claiming to know a quicker route, and leaving Dalton and me staring at each other.

The old girl had been treated rough enough; now Skip was going to manhandle her in ways she didn't deserve. My hunch is Skip's agonising over Dalton's secret; I know I have been; the question is, can he forgive?

Would he let the daughter's revelation be water drifting under the bridge? After all, the cockney prince wasn't to know; there were many moving parts by the sounds, and the stars didn't align that night. Meanwhile, Dalton was occupied, checking on me, making little glances as we walked, perhaps doing some reflecting of his own.

I struggled; my mind spun like a blender churning around my memories. Everything I thought I knew could be bullshit or yet another misdirection to throw me off. Even second-guessing what we put in the ground five years ago. This guy had us in the crosshairs; I want to know why.

The searing heat as the bullets tore into me. Feeling the holes in my shirt, nothing but slight bruising remains; surviving a gunshot is fine; I can't say I'm in a rush to experience that again. Only to wake in pools of blood that weren't mine; the thought of it and the massacre still bothers me; how could one person control everything the way he is? How does he get everything to run like clockwork?

My stomach swirled, the claws sliding back and forth without control. Painless, without me trying to do it. The other side of me was revelling in my chaotic emotions while I sat in the back, feeling like a foreigner in my car, seeing the world from another view. Swerving a sharp left caused everything we've gathered to slide towards me—our nightmare collection, the box, goggles, bladed glove, the gun and a couple of recorders.

One flipped on its side, slightly sticking its butt in the air, causing me to notice small ink splodges. Looking closer, I saw remnants of an old label; it must have got damaged by water and ripped off—leaving behind ground in ink residue. Normally I wouldn't care, but I could see part of an address, 'Ac-DC used electronics, 296 Bethnal Green road,'.

The bulb flashed above my head as the welcomed distraction swung into action. I grabbed the other one to compare identical recorders, make, model, and everything. The same label remnants too.

If the puppeteer used a shop in Bethnal Green, they might have closed circuit television. Then came the downturn; who else said they were living in that area, 'Charlie'. It had to be a coincidence; our tormentor knows us all well and did this based on how my mind works to get me thinking in that direction. They've both said it, though, Skip and Dalton.

Is Charlie behind all of this or connected somehow? We may have our first proper lead or another misdirection. One that's best shared with the group later. To think how close I came to him. If I'd had the courage of my conviction, I would've reacted quicker and sooner, chasing him over that fence. Maybe none of this would be happening.

Skip planted the pedal to the floor, throwing me across the back seat with every turn; in the mirror, I saw his eyes narrow. The thoughts going through his head caused his demeanour to change suddenly, becoming focused, almost aggressive. His hands gripped the wheel tight, and then they came. One by one, on both hands, the claws slid free. Skip was pissed; I rechecked the mirror; his eyes glowed. They're different to what I expected, pitch black with a bumblebee Yellow, glowing Iris.

"Skip, your eyes, they're different."

"Yep, lad, vision improves too, makes up for age, senses ramp up, among other things,"

"But yellow?" Confused because I got the sense that mine was red.

"I know yours goes red. Once we get a grip on this, the colours are a hierarchy; from research over the years, that colour makes you an Alpha. We are the makings of a pack, and I'm a Beta. But there's something else: we have kept some secrets. You're more than we've figured out. To put it blooming mildly, you're more a demon wolf,"

"What the hell?" the hits keep coming; I can see why that wouldn't be the first thing I'm told. Even the wolf part has been a stretch; wouldn't I have known or remembered something? How could I be a demon wolf and not know it?

"There's a lot to get your head around; you went wild and killed small animals as a kid. So, that guy you saw in the paper that you queried, he is what I told the story about. He could make that part of us dormant until the next 'blood moon.' after your thirtieth birthday. It was a gamble that I prayed to God worked, and the age sounds odd, but I wanted to give you a fraction of a normal life before the shit hit the fan; we didn't know it would pay off. That's why you see the dead, unlike what I told you. You can see and talk to them. At least you did as a kid; that's what you kept drawing, and now Chris,"

I don't know why he told me now; perhaps because of where we're going, he figured it would be best to say some more. He meant well, even if it still didn't feel real yet. Did I understand it? No, not really and hopefully, there will be plenty of time to come to terms with everything in the end.

"Did I do anything bad? As a child? Charlie gave me the impression I had," I thought back to his words, 'it was funny until.'

"Well, there were plenty of difficulties; as I said, you drew everything, mostly to explain how you felt. Then one full moon, you were at your peak; I'd managed some resemblance of control, but you were unhinged. Attacked Hannah, and she fell down the stairs trying to get away from you, breaking her fibula and tibia clean through. I locked you in a cupboard until the moon passed,"

How did I not remember any of this, especially hurting my mother? Dormancy of what we are is one thing, but no memory is another.

"W...w... why can't I remember?"

"We got lucky; once you felt normal, your mind couldn't handle what's happened. Repressed your memories, not wanting to have them." Skip's words made me dread what would come out if I remembered again. It would be best if they stayed repressed. Does that explain my nightmares?

I could feel the car slowing down; the side-to-side shuffling had become less frantic. We rumbled forward with hardly any traffic; in the distance and slightly uphill, there seemed to be a dead end. Looking out the window, the road was lined with red brick maisonettes left and right before passing a pub on the corner.

A large cul-de-sac turns into something completely different, with borders of tall trees and a pathway veering up to the right. The closer we drew, the more I saw it was boarded off, unlike the Surrey place, shielded by wood. All except a gravelled driveway swinging around to the right.

Skip ground to a halt. Squelching beneath the wheels and sliding onto some grass before slumping his head against the wheel. The boarding continued to the left of us; it had to be ten feet high, blue and white. I couldn't see what was behind, only that the pathway ran to the back and a low fence.

Dalton and I stepped out first; I picked up a hint of dirty water in the air. Nerves were creeping in slowly, and not like the first two tasks. This felt different, something strangely familiar, but I couldn't understand why. Small fractured images flashed through my mind as I looked around me. It's night-time; there are flashing blue lights and smoke, and lots of it, wrapping and smothering anything in its path. That is exactly how Skip described it in his story. Glimpses, but feeling so real.

Skip hauled himself free from the car; we had thirty seconds left. I'm looking and not seeing a way in—only a large grey stone twenty feet into the board line. More curious was it looked out of place. A calm deep breath, seeking past the dirty water, the dog poo fifty feet behind us tucked in a bush and Skip's dripping fear. He was bathing in it, looking shaken as he walked toward us.

Beyond that, I smelled blood; we were in the right place; the game had begun. I had to trust whatever I was going to be, let it happen and regain control, something the puppeteer was fond of saying at the warehouse. The red glow came; looking over the rock, I noticed grooves: a small square shape, five inches by five inches. The stone was at least part fake.

"Quickly, check the stone," Dalton darted to it, feeling around but looking at me with a confused expression.

"What do you see, matey?" Ignoring him, I move to tap around, still using the glow. I felt about the texture changed; it's cold metal. I tapped away until a press caused it to spring open. A keypad, much the same as the one on the VAT.

"That's what I was seeing; the only problem is we need a code" I could see the cogs spinning in their respective heads.

"Wait, back the truck up. What was on the back of that bloody suit Andrew had on?" the hamsters in Dalton's wheel were working overtime.

"You might be onto something. '230552',"

"Hey, Lad, you sure it's not a trap? I'm sensing something funky here, apart from the blood,"

"It's all we have,"

Tapping in the code and hoping for the best. Silence, nothing but distant engines throttling about their daily business. Until I caught a heartbeat other than ours, I first thought it was two, but with ours competing for who could go the quickest, it became hard to tell. Skips was in the lead, screaming for help.

That leaves me worrying about where the puppeteer could be; the last task felt like he was there watching or good at rigging cameras and other equipment. Skip had drifted further down the path, looking to the boarding; his head looked gone. Lost in his thoughts, he knew this place well; how?

"We should leave this be, Lad; chalk this up to a journey too far. Some sacrifices are for the greater." Skip's voice shook with fear; being held captive had done more harm than I thought. Unless there was another problem I was missing.

"Andy, are you kidding me? We're already here; we can't let this bastard get away with toying with us. He's killed at least two." Dalton had a little fire back; his heart raced, but he was up for it, at least.

CHAPTER 43

They were the devil and angel on my shoulders, one saying go for it, the other telling me it's not worth it. Me in the middle, questioning how it had come to this.

Was my Helen alive? What did I see in her coffin? He had to be playing with my emotions to put me off guard. There's no way someone comes back from the dead. That's what I would've been saying had I not survived or heard Mathew was alive, at least according to his passport.

Our way in was a ten by five feet concealed entrance to go with a hidden entry system. The display turned green; the code worked, and a panel sprung forward. My hackles jumped, a sixth sense feeling; what's behind that panel is far more off than we can imagine. It felt like death, different and a lot.

"We have to." I moved forward, pulling the panel open.

Cut off from the world, how the place in Surrey was. There used to be grass where I stood. The space in front of the house had died. I look to see another ghost, a young bloke in his mid-twenties with short-cropped hair and clothing that had the look of a sixties disco, drifting back and forth over the brown grass. He seemed troubled; I could hear his whispered voice, heightened anxiety repeating the same phrase.

'I need to tell someone; this isn't right; this place is bad,'

Dalton caught me staring into space, knowing better than to think it was nothing. He moved to my side, placing a firm, reassuring hand on my shoulder. How Skip sometimes does before the nightmare starts.

"What you have seen, matey?" he spoke quietly, hesitancy trailing at the end. I could understand why; we all knew we were on a hiding to nothing.

"Depends. Is seeing another ghost ok?"

"Another?"

"Afraid so. If you only knew what I saw at the other place,"

"Should've guessed that was the case; saw that blank expression a few times,"

Chalking it up to another blip along our journey. Ignoring the ghost, moving closer to the looming broken home, decayed foliage bordered the dirty White House, burnt-out low window to the left, glass blown out with boards inside.

Musty dampness whipped past my face, haunting a place I wouldn't want to be in at night. Skip nudged beside me, looking over my shoulder to the right. I saw a dirty, dark wooden hatch with weeds wrapping around the edges. His face had turned Casper, flitting between it and the house; up ahead is a crumbling black door set a top five steps; Skip kept fixed on the wooden hatch; I wasn't ready for that yet.

Sometimes the simple route is the best. That hatch no doubt led to nowhere nice and can wait. I was busy eyeballing the round brass door handle. Swinging helplessly from it was another recorder, undoubtedly another of 'Ac-DC used electronics' accessories.

'Home sweet home, for some at least.'

Another loudspeaker, the voice was coming from my low left; all I see are rotting bushes, weeds and a bundle of rubbish. Breathing in, I soaked up the earlier stench, shuffling sideways, learning from past mistakes like the puppeteer said he had. Understanding that nothing is ever as it seems.

There's another smell, at least three days old, surrounded by buzzing flies, scrounging to whet their appetite. Decomposing flesh is what I've found; it's buried beneath the inconspicuous bundle—the unbearable stench of another dead body being carried on the autumn breeze.

Dalton found the recorder, clumsily ascending the few steps to retrieve it. Whether I liked it or not, my body was moving towards it and playing back the opening message. I look at him and wonder where this ranks in his tenure, especially considering his affiliation to the 'devil's circle,'. Did I have his full support, or did he run to them as soon as we were done? I want to think he wouldn't, but as the minutes tick by, there's a feeling in my waters; there'll be another twist, and we won't see it coming.

Using my foot, I trample down the jungle of stinging nettles, sifting between the weeds and crusty bushes that were merely ornamental. Drawing back the rubbish curtain reveals a pair of black, worn patrol boots. Size ten, carrying at least three years of mileage on the tread.

They're Police issued. Dried mud crammed within the grooves wasn't from anything near here. It's too dry; our path is mostly stoned until the dead grass. All squared away, evened off by meeting dry concrete afterwards, trimming it down from a park or a muddy alleyway like the one I escaped from at the back of Skip's house.

"Skip, you need to come here," I called, pulling him from staring at the hatch.

A black tarp laid across, flopped down like an inconvenience, not even wrapped. The puppeteer wanted us to find this. Otherwise, he wouldn't have the speaker wrapped in a bush. Light brown surround with a dark brown mesh front. I kicked a bit freer, revealing muddied trousers, also dry.

Drag marks ran three-quarters from the ankles. The attacker wasn't as strong, so they chose to be sneaky. Whoever this was had been subdued in a surprise attack and then dragged away.

"Oh, blooming hell, another one?" Looking dejected, Skip's hands raked down his face. He had had enough, and I couldn't blame him. I'm only surprised he wasn't using his senses; maybe he didn't want to know too much too soon.

"Afraid so; I think it's a job uniform. If we're going by the mud, been dead for at least three days," Skip bulldozed forward, frowning in thought with half an idea.

"Penny for them?"

"You don't want these thoughts, lad, but I reckon it's Harkes; that's who I think," It could tie in with not seeing him the other day.

The tarp flies off; sure enough, Skip was right. He's still in full uniform. Three days. His body is swollen with foamy blood oozing from his nose. His left hand had cuts and was grazed with smears of dried mud when the arm dropped limply. Harke's head rested to the left, revealing blunt force trauma to the rear lower quarter of his skull. No ripped throat like 'Lewis'.

Harke's attacker was shorter than him; at five foot ten, Harkes was shorter than me, assailing five feet eight at the most. An upward blow would be too awkward, a chance to miss or only graze off the edge. Taller, the impact comes down on top; no, this was like the one who pointed the gun at my head. Harkes must've been looking into something, and the suspect finds him. Smashing him on the head, spur of the moment. Whereas Lewis was planned.

'Oh, Georgie, don't worry yourself about the poor little piggy, not yet. He's merely a loose end. The real fun is behind the doors,'

'Georgina, since when do you listen? Step back and see more. Oh, what's with the dead hangout? The last place was bad, but this is crawling with them,' Chris appeared to my left, making me take a step back; the comment on the other dead didn't fill me with joy. Although I could feel it in the air.

While Skip was busy being chewed to pieces inside, staring at the sky, looking lost. I saw Harke's was dumped; in a weird running pose, angles on his side. Scanning down his body was almost a bust until I caught a tiny detail. Barely noticeable because his right hand was clenched. Within the mottled crease was a triangle-shaped tip of paper. Roughly two to three millimetres, poking out the bottom. A last valiant effort to keep hold of something that could be useful.

"Skip, his hand, grab that paper, quick," Skip snapped to it; Dalton handed me the recorder. I first checked the bottom—the same ink remnant address.

"It's a parking slip, Eton square Bethnal Green, dated the 18th at eleven thirteen. On the day of the crime scene,"

Dalton produced another small evidence bag; how the guy remembers things like that are beyond me; perhaps he can teach me a thing or two after all. Skip slipped it into the bag, looking bemused towards Dalton, who nodded yes.

Without arguing why, Skip placed it into his pocket, seemingly not seeing the relevance yet. But if that adds to the electronics shop, it could be another clue, and there's nothing we can do about it yet. The claws slid forward without control; I wasn't even feeling anything. No pain, nothing. At first, I thought it was a reaction until I noticed Skip's hands; it was happening to him too.

Then came the piercing noise; I dropped to my knees amongst the straw-like roughage, feeling my brain bleeding out of my ears. Skip was the same; it was excruciating, but Dalton remained unaffected, staring at us as if we were losing the plot. It lasted a few minutes, coming from the speaker. The puppeteer was trying to get our attention and distract us. It worked.

'Click,'

Well, here we are, home sweet home. By now, you've found our nosey friend. Constable Harkes thought he was smart. All he did was interfere by trying to jump on somebody else's bandwagon. He would be a problem, trying to follow a wild goose. Look where it's got him. How are the ears? Who'd thought a dog whistle could do so much? Sit, roll over, and play dead. The last one I really like.-

-Now, your final game is all about nostalgia and moments that brought us to where we are. You could say responsible for the men we are today. This time, there are no dead bodies in caskets; all I ask of you is a trip down memory lane before the fun starts. As

the saying goes, a chain is only as strong as its weakest link, even in the dark. Time to see just how fragile.'

I couldn't help but suspect this task wouldn't be easy. The words 'memory lane' caused a loud 'oh fuck,' to escape Skip's mouth. Dalton had turned his back to us, looking in the distance. We could see the top of the wooden panelled surroundings on the steps. Dalton squinted his eyes, trying to focus; his attention had been grabbed. I couldn't see what he did; it doesn't mean I shouldn't be concerned.

"Dalton, are you ok?"

"I don't know; I have a weird feeling; years of experience tell me when I have eyes focussed on the back of my head. We're being watched. Five hundred yards down, I've just seen three cars rotate, changing parking positions. That only happens on surveillance to confuse people on the lookout. Even with a brief flash in the windscreen, I had it pegged as a glint of sunshine. Now, matey, I'm not so sure,"

"I looked but couldn't tell, unnerving all the same,"

There's a loud click, followed by grating hinges, and the door yawns open, letting a roar of horror. Cooped up blood and charring.

CHAPTER 44

'Horror basement Canton House,'

There was no light that I could feel, one hand grating across the flaking wall while the other gripped the wooden bannister, thinking over my nightmares. Every creaking yawn of timber played out like before I woke to find Chris.

Only I wasn't barefooted, and I had company. My ears home in on the whistling wind, listening for heartbeats, hoping to hear more than ours. Skip and Dalton were flying, but someone was faint down there.

Dalton sparked a lighter; the little yellow flame flickered as we went, brushing across some strange symbols. Like the box in my car, I think back to Skip's story, Latin. We may not have been able to see too much going down, but I knew we neared the bottom. The smell was stronger.

Call it nerves, flight or fight, a sense of impending doom. Whatever way it dressed up, I was being hit with a giddiness that had turned my legs to jelly, hoping they wouldn't escape from under me as we hit the stone, dusty floor. Like in my dream, my feet kick through the dirt, sending a shower through the air.

"Oh my God, that's fucking vile. Can you smell that? Butchers' meat gone rotten," Dalton croaked out between yacking up his throat, with sickly saliva dribbling down his chin.

"Welcome to hell,"

"What, Skip?"

"That Latin as we came down, it's welcome to blooming hell,"

All I could see was a looming, flickering silhouette cast by the lighter. The space felt larger than I imagined. I stood in the same spot, spinning around in a daze, letting the smouldering circle my lungs until the goose pimple chill from my nightmare came true. Hearing a speaker. Heavy iron chains pounded against the concrete, sending a metallic clang rippling through the air. Once... Twice... Three times... It was the ghost of my Christmas past.

'How does it feel, Georgie? Is anything coming back to you yet? I can always shed some light on you. Let you revel in the horror before the fun begins,' the puppeteer echoes around us, adding to my trepidation.

I step back, reaching for the bannister; burnt blood swirls through my lungs, and drool pooled around my gums, feeling the lust build up. Loud clicking rocks around us before a dim light flickers on. We all gasp, staring in horror; Skip stumbles backwards, falling into a craftsman's bench with a vice. Pinched within that was a bony hand, rotten, more bone than anything else. I look around to see blood sprayed chaotically throughout, enveloping the thick dust and grime.

There are four adult-sized bodies beheaded in kneeling positions. Hands and feet are bound in chains, with the remains of thick tape melted across the mouth; they couldn't move or call for help, even if they wanted to.

They're more than decomposed, burnt—masking the clothing. The puppeteer had the bodies placed around a circle, an old etching that had been touched up to look new. There are two triangles, one upright, the other flipped. Devil worship. That is exactly how Skip saw it twenty-five years ago.

My stomach rumbled with the lure of blood I couldn't escape and the want to spew its contents amongst the dirt. The bodies were fresh, only a few days old, remains of ordinary torched clothing. My eyes were glued to the depravity, trying to understand where this game was going.

All we have so far is dead, Harkes, and these unfortunate souls caught up in the chaos. I'd stared so hard that all I could see were the heads on the floor; everything else became a blur.

The jagged edges of the protruding charcoaled flesh ended short of the throaty gristle and neck cartilage. Each flailing was a different length and width, not made by a knife, axe, or any other symmetrical blade, at least not in the beginning. No, they made these look like claw marks again. The same that had been done to Lewis, using a bladed glove. Was it the same one in my car, or was there another murder weapon waiting to be found?

My pulse pounds in my temple, throbbing in my ears; I'm lost in darkness, different from what we came down to. My arms feel heavy, dragged down limply, feeling the tightness around my wrists. I look down to see thick, chained clamps.

Only my arms aren't my own; they're smaller, burnt red-black skin, bubbling and breaking. A pair of bolt cutters break the chains; I'm lifted into the air like a rag doll before being covered in a sheet. I'm being carried; there's a haunting red glow in the corner coming my way. It's a nightmare, and I have nowhere to go.

"You ok, Georgie lad?"

"Huh. Y... yeah, I think so,"

Skip calls to me; my eyes clear, and I'm back staring at the stranded heads, sockets exposed with eyes popping. I could barely see strands of hair on any of them. One, two, three, four and five. No extra fingers this time; I wasn't dreaming. Not now, anyway. But I'd seen myself being carried away, breaking from darkness; it felt more than a horrible dream, more a memory but so real. Nightmarish real. The way my arms looked and smelt, it's the same rancid I'm picking up on now.

'Surely you remember now seeing my little masterpiece. Volunteers recreating what happened, showing you how my parents, my sister and my grandmother died. How you were lucky to survive. The rest you'll get if you complete the game,'

So, that's the motive driving this bastard to do what he has— murdering innocent people to make a point and push us around. I could feel the venom in his words thumping around. The chains rattled again on the far-right side, still in the shadows. I strain to look; all I see are dirty brown pillars made of solid wood that's weathered over time—other Latin symbols carved into each one, with a little difference.

"Skip, any ideas?" pointing to the nearest to us. Much like the strangeness of the box, a few resembled letters from the alphabet, only with extra squiggly lines.

"Well, it's old Latin, I think. I'm not that smart, lad. Daemon, esto subjecto voluntati meae. Demon, submit yourself unto my bidding. Something like that,"

The puppeteer's family didn't mess around looking to summon demons. Not so long ago, I would've laughed that off as nonsense. Now, anything is fair game. The next pillar, ten feet to my right, had a similar.

"What about this?"

"Ad ligandum eos pariter eos coram me. To likewise bind them before me. That's the gist; when the stupid sods delved into this shit, they created sigils. They wanted to trap whatever they summoned and use it. But remember, I told you about that big bloke at the hospital? He's something like that."

Another bump in the road: the newspaper clipping, a bedtime story from Skip and a tall tale from Charlie that he gave him in the box. If we weren't in unchartered territory, we are now, and my hackles are rumbling to attention. Dalton had moved to a row of wooden shelving, mould smothering the sides; his curiosity and screwed-up face piqued my interest. The longer we lingered, the more we saw; I ticked off a mental checklist, comparing the things I'd been told.

With Dalton examining the shelves, I could see another horrifying detail. Jars, row after row of wide, dusty glass three-quarters full, sickly body parts swimming in a dirty green liquid. Some are limbs from babies, including a head, only different. Small fangs and two lumps on the forehead, beginning horns. That is just how I was told. All truly disgusting; we needed to finish this and get the hell on the road to shutting depraved bastards like this down.

Dalton went to move; his leg wobbled beneath him, his once immaculate posh shoes scraping through the dirt. The day had taken its toll, and we were nowhere near done. I could feel the tension in his bones as I pulled him to his feet; his arm shuddered within my grip, hearing a sudden rumble of a fluorescent light as it stuttered on. Not bright, but enough to know where our game was. The back of my eyes began to slowly warm, blood vessels boiling with a throbbing in the sockets; I wanted to rip them out, stop their need to bleed.

Little piggy three, dressed in a boiler suit, suspended horizontally, thick silver chains clamped to the limbs and pulled tight. There's another chain wrapped around the head like a noose—the same for the abdomen. Each one feeds two cogs in different basement parts; power cables run to a big junction box on the wall—low and behold, another keypad. Besides that, the annoyingly familiar red smiley face, large, dripping down. More blood.

"Is this bastard for real? That looks bloody medieval. How the hell do we solve this one? More to the point, do we agree that this twisted wanker isn't working alone? How else would he do all of this?"

Dalton was traumatised, and Skip was not much better, but he made a good point. Psychologically, he's steps ahead and well organised, already professing that he's not physical, so who is doing all the heavy lifting? Maybe that's the burnt bodies; he uses them and then kills them.

CHAPTER 45

Being around all this death. The smells drifting out of the nightmare are giving my body a mind of its own again. Claws were sliding free; I could feel my jaw tightening, changing with the fangs coming; I needed to get a grip. I look at the keypad again.

Upstairs, we got the number twelve; the rest must be around us. The cogs juddered a little, shaking the chains as they pulled tighter. Piggy three let out a pain-riddled squeal, bringing my neck hairs on end; they're going be ripped apart if we don't end this. Each major cog turned clockwise, clunking away, connected to a spindle with a round track underneath that cranked the chains tight.

'Surprise! Bet you were pissing your pants hearing the chains. How do you like it? Do I at least get points for originality? Silly horror films are all the same these days, run, scream, stab, die. Rinse and repeat. I wanted this to be a little different; nostalgia meets hope meets a twist. Now, the question is, can you save a little piggy and earn yourself the ultimate truth? I only hope the ending is to your liking. Around this 'basement of horrors', as someone once put it, there will be four numbers, a simple six-digit code. A date of somebody's birth. But who? That's all pinned on you. Four minutes is all you have. TikTok'

Neither of us spoke; Skip began looking around the craft table, and Dalton moved towards the stranded victim, checking over and under the body suit, looking for numbers. I stayed by the jars playing over the message; they made me gag. Every rattle from the struggling chains made me shudder, twisting my neck. There had to be something out of place; we were looking for the impossible.

All I saw were the countless times these people experimented, torturing kids and when it failed. Break them apart and start again. I'm looking at a jar with a sticky label on the front, holding an arm no older than three or four, yet no one cared. Even after the crime scene in 1962, it's all left in place. Thick dust, as if none had been touched.

Corruption is all I keep coming back to; going on for years, and nothing has changed. No wonder Skip bounced around a while after that, trying to find somewhere he could fit it in. Only for Chris to inadvertently open old wounds. Prompted to by 'C', if it had been Charlie, surely Skip would've known about it. We were down to three minutes, and still no joy; I was missing something obvious like it's felt all along.

'Remember Georgie, the closer you look,'

Chris pops up behind me; my heart nearly leapt into my mouth. His timing was terrible, but he had a point. I was two feet away, soaking up the savagery and limiting the view. I took three strides back, feet clumsily crashing into old gardening equipment. We all jumped; Skip looked like he wanted to kill me for the mini heart attack.

There are six rows at least eight feet long, each holding twenty jars with small labels. My first thought was the number six for the rows or zero six if I were thinking back to the previous game. Dalton was coming up blank, fingers trailing over markings in another pillar, claw marks. Would the puppeteer follow the same pattern with limited time?

I almost disregarded the jars to move on when I saw the third row down, eight jars across, facing the other way. Thick grit squidges under my fingertips; the jar was cold, the green fluid sloshing around as I carefully twisted the glass. Up close, breathing in the nauseating ripeness had me feeling a little lightheaded. The label came into view, thirty-eight and another smiley face.

Seeing that each time was getting to me, taunting me. We had twelve and thirty-eight, a little under two minutes left. I heard every clank, rattle and painful scream in surround sound. Little piggy three was being stretched apart. Cartilage is clicking, and muscles are tearing little by little.

"Either of you got anything?"

"Other than a bad back, and the urge to be sick, fuck all," Dalton was pacing in circles, fingers tearing into his hair.

"Knout all lad, I'm about had enough of this; we're short on time and me on patience," Skip was looking at the wall above the bench; I hadn't noticed it before, but on the wall, a crusty dark red. There's another symbol, the one Chris drew on the post-it note. Another element of the story is coming true.

The swirling body and fork through the head were hypnotising; looking at each drip, I zoned out a little, but my ears didn't. Upstairs, I heard footsteps, not inside the house or even within the boarded grounds. I heard six pairs of feet moving slowly. It could be a group walking, but they seemed to get closer. Another clank and crunch brought my mind back; time was tight, and all we had were four digits.

"Ere, when you two are done fawning over some fucked up symbol. It's not like I don't see that every day or anything. Could I borrow your eyes for a minute, Andy?

Dalton was over by a pillar six feet from the shelves; he was retracing his fingers. Going over the symbols, I saw earlier. Skip had already told us what they meant.

"What you doing, Dalton? We're wasting time; we know what they are,"

"Steady on, me 'old mucka. We know the first part, but that's old. The carvings are dirtier and more settled. Below that is fresh; messier, the wood hasn't had time to soak in the moisture from the leaky pipe above. Carved within a week or two," Dalton was right; the other symbols had ageing and scorch marks in the wood; this part was still breathing.

"Ah right, let's have a butchers then," Skip bulldozed forward; my eyes flitted between them and the chains.

"Can you read it? If not, we can't waste time,"

"Hold your blooming horses. Yes, I can read it; you might be glad I did. 'J' 'U' 'N' 'E' it's the month of June. Wait a goddam minute. What numbers do we have?"

"Twelve and thirty-eight," Skip's eyebrows raised to meet the frown lines.

"He said, somebody's birth, pinned to you, date of birth 12.06.1938. That's when my Angela was born; her skin is upstairs pinned in that frame." A tear trickled down his cheek; the sick puppeteer loved this far too much, tearing Skip apart.

"Quick, we have twenty seconds left; try 120638," Dalton shimmied to the keypad, and the display lit up green again.

The chains churned; the cogs were speeding up. Every click made me cringe; I could feel each cutting close again. The keypad beeped with each digit; I stared at my watch, counting down, tensing up, bracing myself for the worst as another click bellows through. Five, four, three, two, one, the last digit was entered, the clicks stopped, and so did the cogs.

There was a unified sigh of relief; I chugged down burnt blood and roasted flesh. I look up to see the chains slacken; piggy 3 lowered within two feet of the floor. Dalton's hands were shaking, and a small river of sweat streamed from his sideburns.

'Oooh, another close shave, Georgie boy. Looks like you survived... or have you...? In fact, why don't I start with the truths? Twenty-five years ago, you killed my parents, so I made it my mission to make you pay and anyone that's helped you along the way. I saw you and the fat boy breaking from the darkness. My family was into all sorts of crazy shit, but they were my family all the same. Their experiment on you looked to be working. Still, they didn't foresee how violent you'd be or realise that you were already a shapeshifter. It was a full moon, so you were even stronger; I'd been staying at a cousin's house and was brought home in time to hear the screams. -

-My uncle and I crept into the basement in time to see you tear their heads off. They'd made the circle too close to the chains. You were going through a change and ripped

their throats out, making the heads roll. My uncle was connected to the same people they were and said all hell was about to break loose and things needed to be covered up. He tried burning their bodies to hide who they were; you were out of control, and he thought you wouldn't survive anyway, so he burnt you too. -

-The little wrinkle to the plan was the trapped demon, so we left the basement and set the house on fire, hoping the fire would cover everyone's tracks. You'd taken my family from me when I was only ten years old. We were seen escaping the scene via a canal boat, who'd thought boats make good getaway vehicles. No one suspected a thing, and it was too dark for the nosey neighbour to be a problem for us. With each year ticking by, I bounced around until I found the right place. I grew up learning, staying in the shadows, and gaining everything I needed to bring the house of cards crashing down. Not just you, by the way; I intend to ruin that fucking group who abandoned me because of my parents. Bring them into the light, bring all of you into the public eye and cause chaos. You, the werewolves, and the willing servant with you, the public, need to know monsters are real. While I watch you all burn. -

- More bodies will fall. I intend to make the streets bathed in blood, and the beauty of it is that nobody will know who's responsible. After all, who is Ethan Conrad? A name lost to a dysfunctional childcare system. A letter sent to the wrong address, or a series of banks, utilities and driver's licences registered to a flat in Sutton Quay. We shall see, but don't worry, you will hear from me again; a game isn't fun when only one person plays. And in this chess match, I've been moving ahead and always will be; the first lesson you need to learn is 'the reminder from the cockney twat, 'the closer you look, the less you see'. This game was to save a little piggy; I didn't say which. Check,'

Another loud click rattles our ears before a huge crash of metal flies down a separate set of stairs. A large cupboard dropped from the one place we still needed to check the hatch exit. It must've been hooked up to the underside of the still closed hatch doors in the darkness, or at least chucked through quickly, accounting for the footsteps.

The brown metal cabinet, at least five feet long, was sprawled across the concrete floor; everything went quiet. 'Crash' the doors pop open, revealing another body. Chains were strapped around the ankles, waist and wrists, with gaffer tape across the mouth; it's Charlie. His eyes are closed. I listen for a heartbeat; it's calm and unusual considering what happened.

CHAPTER 46

'Now for the twist.'

The puppeteer's voice rattles out, followed by a sudden loud clunk. Chains quickly ping in the air, the cogs spin out of control, and the helpless body is now head height; I can hear the pain, the bones cracking and breaking, and my toes curl each time.

Terrifying squeals rip through me, making my blood run cold. Dalton and Skip looked in a helpless daze, mouths hanging open. The wooden beams let out a worrying creak; the chains were fighting to either break or tear-free.

There was nothing we could do; Dalton grabbed a crowbar, jamming it into the latch on the beam, trying to bust it free. Skip, and I joined in, pulling on the chains. Even with our extra strength, it was feeling like a lost cause. There was a little give; two heavy-duty nuts bust free, just as I thought we could do it.

The cogs raced, and I heard loud crunching and gurgling from the body; they were choking on their blood. A thousand trees snapped in a forest, echoing all around. Bones cracked, and then...

I dropped to the floor, holding three chains attached to a dismembered right leg. The other passed Dalton's face, sending a glaze of blood across his cheek. Skip, and I pulled as hard as we could, and the bolts felt loose. The cogs spun too fast; the crank was too strong, and the body ripped apart as easily as tearing paper.

Skip had slumped against the workbench, spewing his guts; all I could see was blood, intestines and torn limbs. Charlie remained unconscious in the cupboard. Neither of us saw that coming; perhaps we should have. The little details were pointing to him. Not that I could imagine that, even after I'd been warned.

'Now for the twist.'

That's what the puppeteer said, and he wasn't wrong. The head came to rest in the corner, facing away; neither of us was ready to see, except I knew we had to know. See who the latest victim was, maybe even chalk a name off the suspect list. I still couldn't see myself killing the puppeteer's family, as he said, or remember.

Dalton was a mess; his suit was sprayed with blood, and he was leaning against a beam, still holding the crowbar. My hands finally let go of the chain, planting amongst the dirt and blood to push myself up. My movement caught some attention, waking the other two. Tentatively, I shuffled forward. Stepping over the torso and spilt bladder, the hood came free in the dismemberment. Seeing the hair close gave me an idea of who it was without touching the head. It's Kelcher.

"You hear that?" Skip was looking at the ceiling, wiping his mouth.

I'm listening close; the footsteps again, six pairs trying to creep. Their heartbeats were calm, giving an air of confidence. Two by the hatch, four had found their way inside. Strange, because the door had locked on me. Something was off, more than the surrounding carnage.

"Half a dozen; they're not rattled in the slightest." I moved in unison with theirs, edging towards the steps leading to the hallway.

Until my ears buzzed, Skip heard sirens in the distance, heading our way fast. None of them spoke; all three of us were looking in the same direction. My hackles ruffled; I was getting a bad feeling.

'This is the police; there's no way out; it will be easier if you give up now,'

That would explain the calmness; how would they know? If Harkes's body could linger for days without being called in, how would they suddenly know to come right after a body had been butchered?

"This could be great; get some help with this mess. Now, there are no games,"

"Dalton, we're covered in blood; this is Kelcher's body," he was clawing at the front of his suit as if that would clear the blood; Dalton was panicking.

The footsteps continued; two sets were coming down the stairs. All three of us backed away, distancing ourselves, ending near the cupboard. Charlie remained out cold.

"Georgie lad, put them away," Skip whispered, pointing at my hands. My claws were out, and I hadn't realised.

Two sets of uniformed trousers came into view, crawling; I could hear the faint squeals of their radios. They were genuine; in the official sense, were they corrupt?

Two young officers reached the bottom; neither looked ready for what they saw. Open-mouthed, caught in two minds. Move or don't. Another set of feet headed down, a dark grey pair of trousers; he wasn't uniform. In full view, he could almost pass as Dalton's younger brother by at least fifteen years. It must've been the way he dressed and the designer stubble. CID, for sure.

"Hey, this isn't what it looks like; we're police too. We've been sent on a wild goose chase involving some rather fucked up near-death games," Dalton spoke up; I guess he thought being in similar departments would find some common ground.

"We've been watching; we know exactly who you are. Someone tipped us off you'd be coming. Lo-and-behold, here you are." the guy was well-spoken and differed from Dalton in that respect, except he carried Dalton's earlier confidence. And bullshit bravado.

"There must be some confusion, lad; who is it? You think we are?" Skip piped up; I was too busy trying to keep my lust at bay with all the blood and gore around us.

"Detective Dalton, Sgt Morris and Officer Reynolds, or should I say, Ethan Conrad. From what I gather, there are at least two murders you're good for and the mess down."

"That's not us. We're being set up; we have proof,"

The guy didn't flinch; something was wrong, more than being blamed for murder; for me, that hasn't changed since this started. No, I'm missing more; the real Ethan or puppeteer claimed he's many moves ahead; it's like we're about to experience another one.

He smiled, itching the side of his face, soaking up our surroundings, looking like he attempted to count the body parts. Not even I was that brave. His eyes darted to Charlie in the cupboard, bound and still unconscious. My hackles were dancing; I could feel what was coming. Ethan Conrad had us in check; it may as well be checkmate.

"Take them," he rattled down his radio. The hatch doors flew open, and two officers came steaming down, followed by the two in front of us. A spare remained upstairs as a backup in case the shit hit the fan. It's too late for that. We didn't resist; there was no point.

I was the first one down, hitting the blood-covered floor hard. Skip, and Dalton followed; Skip struggled a little; his eyes glimmered yellow for a second until he reined himself in. Small intestines are inches from my face, and laughter echoes in the background as the officers are all but giving each other hi-fives.

I look around and see a frightened little boy riddled with pain trapped in chains, looking up at beheaded adults on fire with another stepping towards throwing out a flame. A sense of Déjà vu as my eyes flit between the charred remains in the circle, an arm hanging from a chain and then Charlie.

Had we all been guilty and too quick to look in his direction? He saved me from the diner, yet he lingered in Skip's life without me knowing?

Had he been doing it to learn? Find the skeletons in our closet. Or was he just my forgotten foster brother? He lays bound in the cupboard; nothing adapted for it to hook on, so it had to have been thrown down.

His hands are chained to the front, not the back; they're clean with no scratches or dirt. His clothes, too, no struggle marks or dribbles of blood from his head. Though light brown mud, on his black boots crammed within a crocodile tread, dried and shaved the same as Harkes. There's more to Charlie, and it could be too late.

With us lying where it all began, amongst pools of blood and body parts. A twitch, a rattle, chains scuff across the metal; I'm being hoisted up, dripping blood, in time to see a flickered smile creep on Charlie's face. Small, only the corner, enough to make me think.

This game had taken us to rock bottom, ugly truths laid bare. My life had come full circle; I felt broken with a sense of, 'was it worth it?'.

Thinking to myself that the man I grew up with. The one I called 'brother' isn't who I thought. Charlie is Ethan Conrad.

All I got to do next is prove it and clear our names.

The end... for now.

Printed in Great Britain
by Amazon

21123596R00180